I0673783

A Shadow of Black Water
- Abel Kane Book 1 -

by
John Wilson

Cover and Interior Design by Vinnie Corbo

VOLOSSAL
PUBLISHING

Published by Volossal Publishing
www.volossal.com

Copyright © 2024 John D. Wilson
ISBN 978-1-963359-11-4

For Margaret and my family

PROLOGUE

The morning after his uncle's welcome home party, seventeen-year-old Abel Kane came out of the front door with a piece of toast in his hand, heading to school. He was an average-sized boy with a not unpleasant face and dirty blond hair. He stopped on the porch, enjoying the cool Gulf breeze—the day was not yet insufferably hot—and inhaled the earthy scent of Bayou Lacombe. Realizing he wasn't alone, he turned to look at his uncle and cousin.

Uncle Deacon was sitting in a busted-out cane chair, nursing a real cup of coffee—not the watery prison coffee he'd been drinking yesterday up at Angola. Abel's cousin, René, was perched on the porch swing next to his daddy.

Deke Kane was a boss in the Dixie Mafia—a bunch of White trash thugs with judges and police in their pockets. He had gotten caught with stolen goods and sent up when Abel was eleven, leaving Abel, his sister, his cousin René, and Aunt Hennie to fend for themselves.

"Sit," he commanded, pointing to the decrepit rocker that Abel hated, the one that progressively jumped to the left every back-and-forth. Abel sat and looked at his uncle, still getting used to the fact that Abel wasn't the man of the house anymore now that his uncle was back. Little fingers of tension grabbed at his intestines, and he realized by their sudden presence how much lighter he had felt while Deacon was locked up.

Kane had come back from prison with more muscle and gristle and this morning was wearing a nice blazer that actually fit. The clothes he'd worn coming out of the prison gate had been too loose, given that they had been stuffed in a bag on some shelf in the prison while he'd been throwing weights around in the yard for six years. But he still took after Elvis with his pompadour and sideburns—the handsome Elvis, not the droopy, fat version.

Abel's uncle sat there, bleary eyed from the festivities the night before, the highlight of which was when he'd dragged his bony wife, Hennie, back into the house yelling, "I got some catchin' up to do!" His gathered crooks, cronies, and informants had laughed and cheered him on. It was hilarious because Henriette was normally so prim and proper.

Deacon set his cup down. "I was caught short when I went in and we coulda lost it all. I didn't have a chance to set y'all up. Hennie couldn't have made it without your help, Abel. I know she appreciated it—hell, we all appreciated it."

Abel thought to himself, *Right . . .* Aunt Hennie hadn't said thanks to him ever. It was like she was mad at him for helping. Maybe she was angry that he'd involved René. Was she upset that Deacon had depended on him instead of René? Or maybe she just considered his sister and him a burden ever since they had been dropped on her doorstep when their parents were killed.

After all these years, he still felt like an outsider. Like he was the moon, circling and watching the earth that was Deacon, Hennie, and René—a tight little family with a mother's love and a father's approval. The subtle ache that never went away constricted his heart.

"I helped, too. I did the Lake Charles run lots of times," René said to his daddy. He was a few months younger than Abel, handsome like his father with dyed blond hair and black roots showing in contrast to Abel's naturally blond hair. They'd practically grown up as brothers except Abel'd had to watch the golden child get the spotlight his whole life. And like every baby of the family, René was good at getting attention, especially from women, especially from his mother.

He continued his whining. "Abel couldn't have done it without me." Neither Deacon nor Abel responded.

"What are you going to do now?" asked Abel.

Deacon said, "I'm going to start making money. I've got catching up to do, but I've got to take care of something first. Abel, I'm going to need your help. I've got to set something right."

"I can help you, too, Daddy."

"Naw, René, you need to go to school. This is something I need Abel to do."

Some place inside Abel lit up.

"Let's go, Abel."

"I've got school."

"Skip it. I need you."

"But I've got a test."

"C'mon, school is bullshit, and you know it. We've got a job to do." Abel followed Deacon down the street until they reached a beat-up tan Chevy Cavalier that Abel had never seen before. "Git in, you're driving."

Deacon got in the passenger side, moving a can of orange spray paint that had been lying on the seat. Abel started up the car and nervously looked at Deacon.

"Don't worry. A friend of mine boosted this down in the city and drove it up here last night. No one's looking for it. Now head toward Slidell."

Slidell was the next town over from Lacombe, where they lived on the north side of Lake Pontchartrain. It was bigger than their town but that wasn't saying much. They drove down Fish Hatchery Road, away from the bayou, past live oaks draped with Spanish moss. They weren't stopped by Lacombe's only stoplight. When they entered Slidell, Deacon directed Abel into a residential area that contained small houses, most of them neglected. The street didn't have curbs, and each house had a big gulley in front, every driveway had a car or truck, and some houses had vehicles parked on the lawn, too. The odd drainage ditch had an egret standing on one leg or a night heron watching and waiting for a crawfish to make a move.

"Tuck in here. We're going to wait a bit and watch."

"Watch what?"

"See that shitty-looking white house up there?"

"They're all shitty looking."

"The one with the wannabe F-150, the crappy blue Ranger, that's Benny Mark's house up there. He was on one of my crews and got busted doing coke in a parking lot. He rolled on me. It's 'cuz'a him I got sent up. We're going to watch him and see where he goes."

"What are we going to do?" Abel's stomach started to roil.

"Y'all are my brother's kids—when your parents died, I took you in. Did I ask any questions then?"

"No, sir." Abel mulled over what Uncle Deacon had said and clamped his lips shut.

"Look."

Benny had come out the door of the broken-down white house followed by a woman and a daughter, a teenager somewhere around Abel's age, probably younger. Abel could tell, even from a distance, that the girl was pretty, petite with wavy black hair. The mother followed the girl around to the passenger side and reached out with a brown paper sack. The girl swung her backpack into the front seat, took the sack, and climbed in. The woman leaned in and kissed her, then went around, and Benny rolled down his window. She kissed him as well.

It was exactly the family that Abel often imagined for himself even though this mother had dark hair, and the memory of his own mother was that of a golden-haired angel.

"Isn't that sweet—motherfucker's a family man?" Deacon said. "The whole six years I was in prison that rat bastard's getting kissed every morning. I'm in a zoo with wild animals, smelling shit and piss, my own family growing up without me." Abel saw Deacon's expression and pressed his lips together tighter.

Benny pulled out. Abel started the car, but Deacon touched his arm. "Wait, let him get ahead a bit . . . Now. Just hang back; we know he's taking her to school."

They followed the Ranger until it pulled up to the high school. Abel tucked the car behind a line of parked cars. The girl stepped out with her backpack and started toward the school but stopped when Benny opened the door, stood up, and yelled something at her. She came back, and he handed her the lunch bag. Benny's daughter kissed him and then turned around and jogged back toward the group of kids in front of the entrance. Benny stooped back in, and his truck slid into traffic.

Abel waited a bit and followed. Slidell wasn't exactly New Orleans, so it was easy to keep Benny's truck in his sights. He took Highway 10 south and crossed the lake on the Twin Span, then took an off ramp after passing Bayou Sauvage. Benny navigated a few surface streets, then drove up to a large warehouse surrounded by a ten-foot fence with razor wire strung across the top. He paused at the gate. It rolled open with a grinding noise.

"I knew he was driving a truck but for a beer distributor? Son of a bitch's got a real job now," groused Deacon.

Benny drove up and parked near a row of giant garage doors. Deacon and Abel sat and waited. Time passed without much conversation, not that they ever had heart-to-hearts. Abel started getting anxious and couldn't stop himself from asking, "What are you going to do to Benny?"

"Nothing! I just want to talk to him. He put me in the jar, while he got to make money and be with his family for six years—he owes me!" Deacon said vehemently.

Abel looked at the clock on the dash, 9:05. He was amped up, which made the minutes drip by like molasses coming out of a cold bottle, but then he heard the big garage doors on the warehouse roll up with a drawn-out rattle and then a slam.

"OK, get ready," Deacon hissed.

As the first truck got to the exit, Deacon peered closely at the driver. "Not him." It drove through, and the second truck rumbled up to the gate. "Shit, that's not him, either." Deacon banged on the dashboard with the flat of his hand. "We saw him go in."

Abruptly, the third door started up, making a racket like heavy chains dragging and clicking against gears. "OK, OK, here we go. When he gets out, give him room, stay back." The beer truck came up to the gate. "Yeah, it's him," Deacon confirmed. "OK, wait, wait . . . a'write, ease out. Now hang back, but don't fuckin' lose him."

Abel shadowed the truck up onto 10, then up and over the High Rise bridge and then off onto the ramp, circling back, and taking Alvar south, skirting the edge of Desire. They passed the projects where the road turned into France Street, then into Poland, as they drove by the Musician's Village; the streets were familiar to Abel from his drug muling days. Benny signaled right, then turned on St. Claude. Abel took the turn, too.

"There's bars everywhere. He's gotta be stopping soon," said Deacon, and right on the heels of his statement, the truck slowed and double-parked in front of the Blue Cat Lounge. Abel wondered what the heck the name meant. "Pull ahead and park in front of the hydrant, and keep the fuckin' car running."

Benny had already jumped down out of the truck, disappeared behind it for a few moments, and then appeared on the sidewalk with a handcart loaded with a keg. He backed it up and over the curb onto the sidewalk, spun it around, and then pushed it up to the bar's door.

Meanwhile, Deacon had positioned himself outside Abel's door, the orange spray paint jutting out of his coat pocket, his ball cap tipped forward, and his back pressed against Abel's window.

Benny was pushing the empty hand truck back out of the lounge. There was a loud clatter; Benny loaded the hand truck, then he walked up the street side of the truck. Deacon started moving toward Benny. Abel wormed around on the seat and got up on his knees so he could see out the rear window. A car drove by, and Deacon paused, then reached under his jacket. Benny opened the truck door and jumped up, but Deke took three long, quick steps, and got his left shoulder inside the door. There was a shout. Then crack, the truck's windshield was painted with a smear of red. Then crack, crack, crack. The window glass was crazed but still in place. Deacon stepped back and slammed the door shut, then pocketed the gun. He grabbed the paint can and sprayed something on the door. He calmly walked back up the street with his head down and got back in the car.

Abel had already turned around in the seat, his hands jittery on the wheel. "Shit! Shit!" He was almost crying. All he could think about was Benny handing the lunch to his daughter. "You said you were going to talk . . ."

"Shut up! DRIVE!"

Abel launched the truck.

"SLOW DOWN! Yeah, if I told you I was going to kill him, you would have been a pussy. Everybody's chickenshit the first time. That rat needed his ticket punched, and I needed someone I could trust."

"You just walked down the street and did it—someone must'a seen you!" Despite his fear, the tiniest of embers glowed in Abel's heart.

"Maybe, but I had my head down. I sprayed a big *G* on the door. Everybody is goin' to think it's some G-Strip gang bullshit. Nobody is going to know what the fuck. Plus, I've got a buddy who owes me. He'll alibi me—we're good. Now shut your mouth and keep it shut; you just saw what happens if you don't. You're in this as deep as me."

CHAPTER

ONE

T he stolen SUV paused, and the guys rolled out. Then it moved down the street, sliding into an empty spot, the engine idling, Rabbit at the wheel. Abel looked up the street at the check cashing business and watched a Black guy with dreadlocks enter the facility. Another stocky, middle-aged man walked in on his heels. Abel was reassured. The information that Deke had provided seemed accurate—a lot of Mardi Gras workers doing cleanup and standing down the carnival, cashing their paychecks.

He was point, the rest of the crew behind him: René, Harm, and André. His crew had masks, and no way would they buzz the lock for his boys, so Abel was going in with a disguise: a dense, curly black wig and heavy nerd glasses. He'd go in first and hold the door.

Abel moved fast toward the door, René and the rest about five steps back, dropping their masks down over their faces. They each had the same mask—Day of the Dead skulls with black eye sockets. All the guys were wearing light Kevlar body armor vests under their shirts for protection, but that was it. The vests were light. They could move.

Abel paused at the door, heard the lock buzz, threw it open, and reached under his shirt almost in the same motion, drawing his Magnum. He jammed the pistol into the neck of the security guard as he was getting up out of his chair while the guard slapped at his holster, trying to get his own weapon out.

"Down, down, down," screamed Abel. René and Harm pushed in behind him. The guard went to the floor quick, and Abel moved into the room as René took over, shoving his own pistol into the folds of fat at the back of the guy's neck, pulling out the guard's pistol and tucking it into his waistband, then reaching into his pocket for zip tie cuffs.

Harm pointed a sawed-off twelve gauge at the ceiling and fired. Ceiling tiles turned to shreds and snowed down onto the patrons still standing in front of the counter. "EVERYBODY DOWN—DOWN, MOTHERFUCKERS, —FOUR MINUTES," yelled Harm.

The Black guy with the dreads was already down, pulling the stocky man down with him.

Harm leveled the shotgun at the customers on the floor. "DREADS, get flat and stay down." He aimed the gun at the stocky middle-aged man lying next to Dreadlocks. "YOU, OLD MAN, move away from Dreads—now, don't fuckin' move."

A little old lady, her neck bent and pushing forward like a turtle's, clutching a social security check, was still standing and looking at Harm through Coke bottle glasses. Harm moved up to her, pushed her down, and moved back from the three patrons on the floor. The lady was on the ground in a sprawl, her dress riding up on translucent support hose with purple veins showing through.

André had entered last, behind Harm. He'd gone straight to the counter and was already behind it, stepping around the two female clerks on the floor, one White, one Black.

"Boy, you goin' straight to hell! Didn't you mama take you to church?" said the large Black lady with a shiny, blonde wig, hanging long and straight.

"You don't know what you gettin' into, sonny," said the older, wrinkled White clerk with patchy, gray hair, looking up from the floor. Both women were cooler than the customers in front of the counter who looked to be scared shitless.

André continued to reach into the cash drawers, grabbing loose cash and banded stacks, knocking each pack against the counter and listening for the hollow sound of a dye pack before dropping it into his bag. "Shut up, Granny, and you'll be OK."

Harm and René had the lobby area in front of the counter covered. Abel took one of his uneven steps and half climbed, half vaulted over the counter to join André for the money grab. He bent down to the older White woman on the floor. "Who can open the safe?"

"What safe?" she asked.

"The one behind that door. The one that's going to get you killed if you don't tell me who can open it."

"THREE MINUTES," shouted Harm, the time pouring down the drain—fast.

"C'mon, Granny, you wanna see your grandkids again?" Abel cocked the Magnum and touched her ear with it. He was tempted to fire a shot by her ear. They both would be deaf if he fired the revolver in the closed-in space behind the counter, the old lady permanently.

"Don't shoot, please, don't shoot. My son opens the safe."

"He's back there?"

"Yes."

"He armed?"

"Yes. Don't hurt him. Don't hurt him." She was calm before, but now she was whimpering, presumably thinking of her son. "Don't hurt my baby."

"Get up." Abel hauled her up by the arm, the loose skin hanging from her upper arm bunching in his grip. He pulled her in front of him and yelled through the door, "I got your mama out here. Put down your gun." The door had a dead bolt that turned from the other side and a peephole. "Open up." Nothing happened. "Your mama going to get killed, son." Abel heard the dead bolt slap open. "She's in front of me, so put down your gun. Put it down. She's coming in first."

The door slowly opened into the back room. Abel pushed his hostage forward into the room and looked over her shoulder at the man. *Baby?* thought Abel, *He's gotta be forty-something.* The son had an exaggerated pear shape with narrow shoulders and a pot belly like he had literally swallowed a basketball. He was mostly bald with monk fringe and a few pathetic hairs arranged side to side. The office held a desk with a computer on it, a beat-up swivel chair with a greasy seat, and it stank of pizza, cheesy foot smell, and body odor. It was bad enough to make Abel gag. He swallowed twice to repress it. A squat floor safe took up the rest of the room. It looked old school and substantial. He pointed his revolver at the man. "Where's your gun?"

"Over there." The man nodded with his head in the direction of the corner of the room. A Glock was resting on the floor between the two walls. He took out a cloth handkerchief, yellowed and glued together in spots with mystery deposits. He wiped his domed head, pushing the comb-over strands every which way.

Abel kept his .357 pointing at the man. "Turn around." The man slowly revolved; Abel couldn't see another weapon. Abel edged over to the Glock and reached down, all the while watching the man, Abel's Magnum never leaving the man's face. He stood back up, jamming the Glock into his pants against his spine.

Abel twitched the gun toward the safe. "Open it."

"I can't. Only my boss can open it."

"Bullshit. You have to be able to move cash in and out all day. And anyways, your mama already told me you could open it." Abel stepped to the side, his gun still aimed at the clerk's head, and shoved the old lady back to André. "Take care of her."

"Wait, what are you going to do with her?" The son's voice went up in pitch.

Abel ignored his question. "Did you call it in?"

"No, not the police—our own security."

"How much time do we have?

"Ten minutes."

Abel figured the son was half lying. He probably didn't call the police, but their private security was imminent, not ten minutes. "How much time left?" he yelled out to Harm.

"TWO MINUTES," came Harm's shout. "You better get movin'."

Abel brought his attention back to the stinky son. "You don't want her hurt, then get down on your knees now, otherwise you aren't going to be her favorite son any longer. Crack that safe open now, or you'll be orphaned."

The back-office man spun the dial and linked up four numbers. His fingers kept slipping, and he must have misdialed because the safe didn't open when he pulled down on the handle.

"God damn it, wipe your hands on your snot rag, and run the numbers in careful. Do it right this time, or you're going to hear your mama killed, and then I'm going to do you."

The clerk tried again, sweat dripping off his chin, his hands shaking. Every now and then they would do a palsied jerk, like the dial had suddenly been connected to a live wire. Abel doubted this try was going to work. He was starting to sweat, too. More odor came wafting up—fear stench. The man yanked on the safe handle again, and this time it dropped to 5 o'clock, and he pulled open the door.

Inside the safe was money. Not payroll money. A shit ton of money. Looked like Uncle Deacon's intelligence was accurate. Deke had heard that this check shop was the last stop on a money laundering chain, the cash going into some offshore banks and the clean money coming out this end. Abel didn't quite understand the mechanics, but that pile of cash, sure as shit, was clean money to him. He wouldn't have to fence it off—the cash was one for one, one hundred percent profit. Hard not to just stop and stare. He mentally slapped himself, pushed aside the man, and started sweeping bundled cash into the short, wide-mouthed duffle hooked to his tactical belt.

"Are you in? We gotta go, man, c'mon, c'mon—ONE MINUTE!"

"I've got it, I'm out!" Abel pushed up off the safe, the bag of cash actually heavy and banging against his leg. He hustled out of the office, his left leg, damaged from the car crash that killed his parents, making him tick-tock back and forth. He slid over the counter, landing among the patrons still on the ground. André, René, and Harm were by the door already, Harm with the shotgun still pointed at the three customers on the floor, the zip-tied rent-a-cop jamming himself into the corner as tight as he could get. The boys started through the door, Harm turning and going out ahead of Abel.

"LOOK OUT!" Abel heard and turned back to the people on the floor. Dreadlocks, the Black patron on the floor, was on his knees swinging his arm down, and the stocky customer was bringing his arm up, a pistol in his hand. The collapsible combat baton in Dread's hand went snick-snick-snick, extending to full length just as it made contact with the older man's forearm. A sickening crack as the arm broke could be heard milliseconds before the gun fired. The gun skittered across the floor.

Ringing ears, a pause. "FUCK!" cursed Abel, stunned. He lifted his arm and looked, blood showing in his armpit. The dreadlocked customer leaped up off the floor and grabbed a handful of Abel's shirt and dragged him through the door and out onto the sidewalk, instantaneously transforming back into Abel's best friend, Tank. The dreadlocks were a simple disguise, and Tank being planted as a customer—insurance.

Rabbit had the SUV right there, the doors open, and the crew piled in with André in the front, René first into the back seat, launching himself up and over into the third seat, and Tank pushing Abel into the back seat like he was the president and Tank was Secret Service. Harm looked around in all directions, then bent his head and tucked himself in. The door slammed itself as Rabbit gunned it off the curb.

"Are you hurt bad?" Tank asked, concerned.

"Nope, through and through, just the edge of my pit. Missed the edge of the vest. God damn it, Tank, that was close. You saved my ass again," grunted Abel, biting off the words as his armpit started to burn.

"Yeah, third time. Pretty much guarantees I drink for free the rest of my life, don't you think?"

Harm checked his watch. "And TIME'S UP! Nailed it!"

Rabbit, the wheelman, was a pro. He shot around the corner, took another turn, and was out of sight of the check shop. Immediately, he eased off and became Mr. Mom, driving a bit less than the limit. They were at the exchange in a couple of minutes, switching into two anonymous stolen cars: André and his bag of cash into one with Harm, and Rabbit driving. They got moving.

Abel, Tank and René stayed back just the time it took Tank to pop the rear hatch on the SUV and grab a gallon of bleach in each hand. He started pouring the caustic liquid over all the surfaces of the getaway car they might have touched. René took the wheel of the second change car, and Abel slid into the back, lying on the seat. He unclipped the cash duffel, and it fell to the floor.

Tank jumped in. "OK, let's roll."

CHAPTER
———

TWO

René stopped in front of Abel and Callie's house and turned his head back to look at Abel who was still lying on the back seat. René's face filled with concern. "How're you doing?"

"OK—it's just a flesh wound." Abel tried to joke, but it was said through clenched teeth, his jaw muscles prominent, his attempt at a smile a grimace. His shirt was dark with blood, and the car seat was smeared red.

Tank, a lean twenty-something Black man with close-cropped hair, had jumped out as soon as René pulled up to the house and was already pounding on the door and yelling for Callie to open up. She had worked the night shift at the University Medical Center emergency room, a level one trauma center, so he was probably waking her up. He paused his knocking to hear if she was coming, didn't hear anything, and started hammering on the door again, alternating with ringing the doorbell. The curtain in the door's sidelight pulled aside, and Callie peered out, her strawberry blonde hair mussed from sleep.

She immediately opened the door—instantly an adult in charge—and asked, "What happened?"

"Abel got shot."

"What? Where? Is he dead?" Her face started to collapse.

He reached out and touched her shoulder. "No, no, we've got him. He's bleeding a lot, hit in the armpit."

She was already moving to the car. "Shit, there's a big artery right there. Why didn't you take him to the ER?"

"We couldn't. He wouldn't let us," said René over his shoulder, bending into the back seat as he tried to get Abel up and out.

"Get out of my way." Callie pulled René out of the doorway and leaned in. Her face registered relief at the sight—there was no regular spurting of an artery. "Oh, thank God, it looks like it missed the axillary artery." She looked Abel in the eyes, her apparent relief morphing into anger.

"God damn it, you're going to get yourself killed." And just as quickly her anger morphed back into concern. "How bad does it hurt?"

"Not too bad."

"Right, you're white as a ghost." She grabbed his good arm, and René reached in and started pulling on both of Abel's legs. Together, they slid him out till he was sitting on the edge of the seat, his feet resting on the running board. "Can you stand up?"

Abel put a foot down and eased his butt off the seat and started standing, placing the other foot down. Both Callie and René put their arms around him as he began to sway. They slowly walked him up to the front door, Tank anxiously moving around aimlessly in front of them, clearly unsure of what to do.

"Tank, go into the linen closet by the bedrooms and get me some towels. Get a bedsheet, too," Callie ordered. Tank took off.

"I'm OK. I don't need your help," mumbled Abel.

"René, we're taking him through the house and out into the backyard. I need to lay him out on the picnic table, in the sun, so I can see what's going on," said Callie.

René and Callie had Abel up the stairs and into the house when Tank met them with the linen. Callie grabbed the towel and lifted Abel's arm.

"Shit!" Abel yelped. "Take it easy."

Callie folded the towel into a pad and pressed it into the armpit area. "Clamp down, Abel. Tank, put that sheet on the picnic table out back." He ran ahead.

They walked Abel through the house, past the big wall of books in the living room, then through the kitchen, and out the backdoor to the table in the yard. All three of them eased him up and laid him out flat. Callie ran back into the house to get supplies. She volunteered at a homeless shelter once a week down in the city, so she had a stock of standard first aid supplies.

Back at the picnic table, she carefully straightened Abel's arm above his head, ignoring his pained grunts, and instructed René to hold it still. René's handsome movie star features twisted in sympathy, mirroring Abel's. She pulled away the towel. "Tank, we've got to get the vest off." He stepped in and helped René prop Abel up while Callie released the armor's buckles. The three of them jockeyed the vest off the good right arm, fed it underneath Abel, and then slid it up the left arm with Abel cursing nonstop. Callie took her scissors and cut away his shirt, finally getting a look at the wound.

Abel's armpit was swollen—like somehow a tennis ball had gotten under the skin—and scarlet, effused with blood and fluid. The entry wound was about the size of a pencil eraser head, hardly bleeding. She rolled Abel to his side and could see where all the blood was coming from. There was a ragged, oblong exit wound, the size of a quarter. "Ahhh, not too bad."

Abel was relieved. He knew that Callie would know—she saw a lot of gunshot wounds in the ER—since most of the shootings took place in the night, on her shift. The bad guys waited till after school or work to get into it. Since her hospital was a trauma center, most of the mayhem passed through its emergency room. "Keep him on his side, so I can get to the front and back. This isn't going to take long."

She set her supplies out on the picnic bench, then slipped on some blue nitrile gloves. "We don't have to do much, just want to make sure it doesn't get infected. This is going to sting and feel cold, but I'll be quick. Stay still." She picked up a bottle of polyhexanide from her row of supplies and squeezed it, a strong stream of antiseptic wash spraying the entrance wound. Abel jolted, the cold fluid uncomfortably running down his back. She slightly tipped him away from her so she could get to the exit wound. She carefully squeezed more antiseptic over the wound, washing away blood and debris, the fresh blood leaking and coloring the runoff. Callie repeated the washing again, making sure she covered everything twice. The second wash was almost clear as the bleeding had lessened.

She stood up, grabbed a package, tore it open, and removed a fresh pair of sterile scissors. "I don't have any lidocaine. This is going to hurt. Tank, help René hold Abel still. Abel, are you ready? Don't move, I've got to clip off a piece of loose flesh." She bent to make the cut but Abel stopped her.

"Wait." He took a deep breath, girding his loins.

Callie bent over and started snipping the largest of the loose flaps of skin and trimmed another questionable spot. Abel slightly jerked every time she cut. "Alright, done with that. I've got to dry the area and bandage it now." She ripped opened a packet of sterile gauze and blotted around the wounds, drying as best she could. She tore open a surgical drape and placed it over his side, protecting the area, while she found some wound gel in her supplies.

She took another stack of 4x4s and squeezed a generous blob of Prontosan Wound Gel in the center, removed the drape, and pressed the bandage onto the entrance wound. "Rip me a piece of tape." Tank handed it to her. "Another." She tried to avoid Abel's armpit hair but didn't have great success. It was going to hurt like a bitch when she changed the dressing tomorrow morning. She'd have to shave him before she put on the fresh bandage. She repeated the steps on the exit wound and then stepped back to survey her work.

Abel's well-formed face contorted; his straw blond hair was disheveled, and his already fair complexion paler still. "René, give me some Oxy," ordered Callie. René made a face like, "What are you talking about?" and she continued to look into his eyes. They shifted guiltily. Finally, René reached into his pocket and pulled out a little ziplock.

"How many do you want?" asked René, guarding his stash.

"All of them." She snatched the bag.

She turned to Abel and handed him two pills. "Chew these up and swallow 'em."

Abel didn't do drugs, not even weed. "No, I just need some ibuprofen."

Callie wasn't having it. "If you come to me instead of the ER, then you'd better do what I say, or this is the last time I patch you up—or your buddies. Plus, you're going to heal better if you're not hurting. So shut up and take them— and keep taking them."

She turned to Tank and René. "Hey, Abel needs some rest, how about you guys take off for a while?"

"Are we still meeting later?" asked Tank.

"Yeah, we have to go over things," said Abel.

"That's good because I have to go to work tonight, and you guys can keep an eye on him." She started bustling around, cleaning up her supplies. "Why don't you guys help him inside and put him on the couch?"

Tank and René maneuvered Abel off the picnic table and walked him up the back steps. They situated him on the couch, Abel carefully getting himself comfortable. "OK, I'll see you guys later—thanks." Abel's eyes were getting heavy as the Oxy started setting in.

Callie was getting ready to leave, making some noise here and there, and Abel started to move around on the couch. He finally sat up, making a sound like an old man getting up out of a chair, tenderly propping his arm in his lap by grabbing his wrist with his good working hand, handling the limb like it was a very precious piece of dead meat.

Callie pulled a chair close and sat. "Alright, what happened?"

"We hit a check place, got the cash, and just as I was leaving, one of the customers shot me. Luckily, we had Tank planted, playing possum as a customer, and he hit the guy's arm just as he was firing."

"Did you guys hurt anybody else?"

"No, and if that asshole had just stayed down, he would'na got hurt, either."

"Yeah, and if you hadn't robbed the place, he wouldn't have gotten hurt at all. How bad was he hurt?"

"I don't know, but Tank hit him pretty hard with his ASP—probably broke his arm."

"One of you is going to get killed, or you're going to kill someone. It's just a matter of time." Callie was getting worked up, her eyes starting to tear up. "Abel, you've got to stop. It sounds like if Tank hadn't hit the guy's arm, he would have killed you."

"Naw, I had on armor. It was just bad luck."

"You've got to quit this before something really bad happens."

"Maybe you're right, but what am I going to do? Work in Uncle Deke's junk shop? This is what I do. This is what got you through college."

"Don't use me as an excuse for what you're doing. You're hurting people. You're better than that. Find something else."

"We didn't hurt anybody. We scared the shit out of them a bit, but none of us were going to shoot anybody. We just did a little shock and awe. It was all acting."

"You *BROKE* a man's arm. You probably traumatized those people so bad they'll never get over it. I spend my nights trying to fix people, and you spend your days hurting people."

"Wait a second, this wasn't a regular business with good people trying to do right by their customers. This was a check casher, taking a huge cut, ripping off regular people who are so poor they can't even get a bank account. Plus, they had too much cash on hand. Deacon said they were a money laundering front, which is why we hit them in the first place."

"Uncle Deacon! Pffft. He's one of the biggest bullshit artists you know. You think he's looking out for you? He's just using you as usual. All you're doing is rationalizing away the wrong you are doing."

"Maybe. Anyway, what am I going to do? I don't have any other skill, and I'm good at this. What are my guys going to do? They didn't go to college; they can't go to work in some office . . . Hey, don't you have to go to work?"

"Yes, I have to go to work. And I have a good job, so why don't you let me support you like you supported us? You could take some time to learn new skills—you could do anything." Callie stood up and walked to the front door, looking at him as she was opening it, sadness clouding her features. "Abel, I know you are a good person inside. You could use your brains to do something worthwhile. I don't want to lose you; you're my only family."

Abel settled back into the corner of the couch, glad that Callie was gone. She meant the world to him, but her disapproval on top of his bullet wound was too much to take at the moment. He reached for the bag of painkillers and dry swallowed a couple. After a while, the Oxy started wrapping him up in its warm embrace.

THREE

Abel should still have been buzzing after the successful check casher robbery only a few hours before, but with his wound tended to and a load of Oxy on board, he had dozed off after Callie left the house. He was sitting on the couch, slouched with his chin on his chest, snoring off the drugs. He woke with a jerk, his heart rate accelerating, when the sound of the front door opening cut through his stupor.

"Hey, Abel, where y'at?" inquired André, coming in with the bag of bills from the check store cash drawers.

"A'write," mumbled Abel, still slightly dazed.

André was Tank's brother, the gentle giant of the crew, now all grown up. He was a bear of a man with a formidable square head. People were generally smart enough not to start anything with him, but if they did, he would try to deescalate. It wasn't that he wouldn't defend himself, it was just that he had a calm demeanor and preferred to rationally and fairly work issues out instead of immediately lashing out in anger.

The guys sometimes called him Rain because of the movie *Rain Man.* They teased him because even though he was the youngest, it seemed like he always knew the answer, no matter the question. He could calculate odds, do complex calculations, or remember some arcane fact from the countless nonfiction books he'd read. He could use a computer like it was a piano he'd practiced his whole life.

Abel's intelligence was different from André's. Abel didn't have the patience for computers. Abel was cunning. But he wasn't cunning because he was trying to put one over on someone. Instead, he understood people. Whereas Callie sensed people's pain, sadness, and joy and almost felt them herself, Abel could see people's ideas, motivations, and tendencies. He didn't have extrasensory perception. It was more like "a person like this, in this kind of a situation—might hit me in the face." Abel's insight could have come from a childhood where bad things came from every angle causing him to develop an early warning system, or maybe it was just his nature, but whatever the source, it gave him an edge and made him a good leader.

"How much did you get out of the cash drawers?" Abel asked.

"Around forty-two hundred." André shrugged. "Not the biggest haul."

"Don't worry, the safe was packed. I don't know what Tank did with the duffel. Check my bedroom—maybe under the bed. If it's not there, he's still got it."

André went off to look, and Abel eased back into the corner of the couch, still holding onto his arm like it was paralyzed and moving it around with his right hand as he tried to get comfortable. He closed his eyes but popped them open when he heard a ruckus. It was Rabbit and Tank coming in, carrying a couple of sacks. Rabbit was his usual self—agitated and antsy, making noise.

Rabbit held up his bags. "I brought food."

"There better be something besides salad," said Abel. This was in reference to an episode when they were kids, and it was why they still called him Rabbit. One time, they all went to McDonalds and loaded up on Quarter Pounders and Big Macs; Rabbit was the last to order, and he asked for a salad. With a group of teenage boys, the smallest of reasons can justify a boatload of good-natured abuse, and his random urge for some vegetables created a lifelong joke that by now wasn't even funny, it was just expected.

Rabbit being Rabbit, replied, "Nope, no salad. I know you guys won't eat it. I got tofu instead."

"Sheeyit," grumbled Tank. "André, what are you doing?" A muffled sound came from the bedroom down the hall. Tank went off to find André. In a minute, he was back, his brother on his heels, carrying the money bag. He spoke over his shoulder. "C'mon, Rabbit brought dinner. We're having tofu."

André looked crestfallen. "Wait—what?"
René showed up a minute later, and then Harm rolled through the door, looked around, and said, "Where's Callie?" This was followed by jeers from everybody.

"Give it up, Romeo."

"Callie was waiting and waiting for you, but you missed her, she just left."

"Yeah, a doctor from the hospital just came by and took her to dinner."

Harm had been nursing a crush on Callie since they were kids. But Callie was having none of it. She was kind, but she knew how hard Harmon was inside. He was a joker with the crew and loyal to a fault, but outsiders didn't have any real meaning to him. Where Callie instantly attached to people, Harm saw people as things or black boxes that were just part of the scenery. He had only ever really bonded with his mother and Abel and the guys. In fact, he still lived with his mother.

Whenever Harm entered the picture, the mood of the room slightly changed. Harm added an element of menace. It felt like you didn't know what was underneath, what he might do. He wasn't a large person, but he seemed big and came across as a country boy or even a hillbilly. His hands seemed too big for his body and were corded with muscles and tendons. He put other people on edge, but the guys didn't find him dangerous. They were used to him, and he was Rabbit's best friend.

Rabbit was unpacking the food and paper plates in the kitchen, and André, impatient to start eating, grabbed Tank, and they helped Abel up off the couch and over to the kitchen table. The rest of the crew took their seats, René putting a couple of slices of pizza on a plate in front of Abel and a helping of salad.

Abel smiled when he saw the greens. "At least it isn't tofu." He doubted that he was going to eat anything because the narcotic was making him nauseous. The rest of the crew piled pizza on their plates, except for Rabbit who took a generous helping of salad and then looked around, daring anybody to say something.

The guys were quiet for a bit, eating furiously, but Abel only took one small bite of pizza and leaned back in his chair. After a minute, he said, "André, what was the take?" André, his mouth still full, said, "71,200."

"What are the splits?" Abel leaned forward in the chair, poised to measure his performance. It made him feel good if his buddies did well. They had his back, and he felt like they needed to benefit.

"With Deacon's cut of twenty percent, no loss for cleaning, the rest of us are going to walk away with almost ninety-five hundred."

Rabbit gave a low whistle. René put his slice down. "Wow, that's the best we've done in a while."

"Yeah, but the cost was higher for us this time. Well, for me anyway." Abel grinned ruefully. "Look, we did a few things wrong this time. We didn't search the customers. I guess it makes sense that we assumed the old lady wasn't carrying, but the guy who shot me, we should have frisked him." Abel looked directly at Harmon. "Harm, you've got the front. Next time, you and René have to lock it down. Hell, even the old ladies—you never know when one of them is going to be packing these days. René, you've got Harm with the shotgun standing overwatch. Just zip tie everybody. 'K?"

"A'write."

"I got lucky. If Tank hadn't whacked him with the ASP, I would have been a goner. Makes me think." He sat up a little taller, his expression serious. "Warehouse jobs and trucks are one thing. If we're going to hit places with a lot of people like this, we got to tighten up. I don't want any of you guys hurt. It's not worth it for ten grand. And we had to hurt a citizen. Tank probably broke his arm. He was just a regular dude, probably cashing his dock check for food. Now he can't work. Callie gave me some serious shit for that." Despite his excuses to Callie, Abel's conscience was bothering him.

"You dripped blood on the floor, too. Now your DNA is probably evidence," said André.

Tank immediately responded. "That place was crooked. They probably cleaned the blood up and downplayed their losses. If they paid off the customers, maybe NOPD didn't even show up. And if they did, they aren't going to pull evidence for some piddling thing."

"They don't have my DNA on file anyway. I'll just have to be careful from now on."

"I didn't hear anything on the scanner the rest of the afternoon, and I was listening for a couple of hours. Maybe they kept it all in house," said Rabbit.

André cleared his throat. "Another thing . . . I don't think we can depend on a guy unlocking the secure door. It was pure luck that it was his mother behind the counter. If'n it was just some clerk out front that kinda guy wouldn't have opened up, unless she was his girlfriend and he was banging her."

"Well, when I scouted the place, the door was open. I didn't see that it was a secure door. I just didn't think," said Rabbit lamely.

"We shoulda gone in more than once before the job," added André. "If we knew it was a heavy door, we could have brought in our door kit."

"Yeah, the intel was weak." Abel sighed and screwed up his face in frustration. "Deacon's slipping."

René was quick to jump to his father's defense, his pale face getting blotchy. "It worked, didn't it? He was right on about the loaded safe. He knew we could handle it."

"Alright, alright. Anybody else got anything to say?" André asked, ever the peacekeeper.

"It felt like it took too long. I was lying on the floor, sweatin'." Abel knew Tank hated to criticize, and his voice was mild, but everyone listened.

"I was yelling the time, and we stayed on track," Harm said.

"When I was on the floor, there with nothing to do but count seconds. While André and Abel were dicking around trying to get through the door and then waiting for the guy to open up the safe, I expected either the police or his security to show up. It would have been a gunfight."

Both Rabbit and Abel spoke at once, Abel backing off. "We scouted the area first. No patrol cars and nothing on the scanner," Rabbit said. "We had five minutes easy, and we were working off a four-minute clock."

Tank interrupted Rabbit. "Maybe, but we didn't know they had their own security. We didn't know what they looked like. We didn't know how many."

Abel agreed. "If security showed up while we were in the back, it would have been mainly Harm and René covering the front, and there was an armed man behind them on the floor waiting to take his shot. The truth is, this could have gone way south."

"We coulda handled the security, right Harm?" René asked, still defensive.

"Hey, let's step back a bit. I've been thinking about things lately. And I don't mean this afternoon since I was shot." Abel shifted his left arm with his right to try to get it more comfortable. "René, don't take this the wrong way. Uncle Deacon took me in no questions asked, and I owe him. But we got to face it. He's gettin' on. The old Deacon would have known about the check shop's security team. He would have known how many. But shame on us, we took some shit for granted.

"The jobs are getting farther apart, and they feel like they are more desperate. We know 10K will probably carry each of us a couple of months. Maybe not that long. Harm's got his mama, and Tank and André have their mama. Callie and I have a house to pay for plus her school bills.

"I'm wondering whether we got to think about doing something different. Not saying we get jobs at Walmart, but I don't think we can live off piecework from Deacon. Maybe back in the day, but everything is connected now, there are cameras everywhere. The feebs have the banks locked down, and if we do too many warehouse jobs, NOPD is going to focus on us, and then we're done. A money laundering check cashing business is a blue moon."

"The risk benefit on home invasions is too low as well. Deacon's not as connected as he used to be. His network is drying up. They're getting old and decrepit," André added.

The whole group thought of themselves as a tight pro robbery crew. They'd had many successes, and this one was the first really close call where one of them got hurt. They were silent.

Harm stood up; his face unconcerned. "Well, what are we going to do instead?"

"Why can't we just keep doing the same as we're doing? The jobs are still coming regular, at least enough for us to pay the bills and have fun." This was from René.

"Look, I said I was thinking. I don't have any answers. I feel like we have to do something different, but I don't know what yet. This cash gives us a couple of months. Let me talk to Uncle Deacon next week when I'm feeling better. Maybe he's got some ideas. In the meantime, why don't you guys go out and celebrate; we hit it big today."

"You don't need to tell me twice!" René laughed and he, Rabbit, and Harm took off.

"Are you coming?" Tank asked.

"Naw, I'll stay here on the couch."

André said, "C'mon, brother, you've got to come. Just for a bit. Take a couple of pills and ride with Tank, and you two old codgers can go back home when you get tired. They got a band at The Flying Machine." He went to Abel's room and rooted around in his closet, finding a loose aqua fishing shirt. Tank and André helped Abel put it on his good arm and then slipped it over his wounded side.

Tank, André, and Abel drove to The Machine, Abel regretting his decision to go—every bounce of the car caused what felt like an explosion of flames to burst from his armpit. *If it hurt this bad getting shot just in the flesh of your underarm, what would a gut shot feel like?* he wondered.

They parked, and Tank had to help Abel get out as he was busy trying to keep his wounded arm from moving. They shuffled through the parking lot, the place busy since no one really had the time to go all the way into the city in the middle of the week.

The bar was packed inside, the music loud. Happy partiers kept banging into Abel, his face contorting with each impact.

"C'mon, let's get outside to the patio," Tank shouted into Abel's ear. He stepped slightly ahead of Abel, snowplowing the drunks and dancers around Abel. They made it to the patio and met up with the rest of the guys who had commandeered a table. They had already gotten a bucket of Abita Ambers. Rabbit handed an iced beer to Abel, while Tank reached for his own.

René had ordered a round of tequila. The waitress, who seemed just a bit older than the typical college students hustling for tuition, brought the shots and set them up in front of the guys, pausing to look at Abel's face. "Are you OK, honey?"

Abel gave a faint nod. She stepped back and surveyed the group, then brought her gaze back to Abel, her face expressing sympathy. She could see he was hurting.

René lifted his shot. "Brothers!" He hammered the tequila, and the rest followed suit. He turned to the waitress and said, "Another round!"

They sat and drank for a while, René getting more and more loose, talking loudly, occasionally saying something about the day, making innuendos about the score. The louder René talked the quieter Abel got. Finally, Tank told René to shut up about the job.

"Fine, you guys can keep sitting here. I came to have some fun." He got up and walked toward the area where people were dancing.

Rabbit stood up, too. "He's right. Harm, those girls over by the bar are eyeballin' you. They must be from the school for the blind. C'mon, I'll be your wingman."

André and Harm left like rats exiting a sinking ship, leaving Tank alone with Abel, a conflicted expression on Tank's face.

"Oh, for Christ's sake, go. I'm fine." Abel didn't feel like talking anyway. He really just wanted to go home and lie down. Tank didn't need any more encouragement; he was up and headed toward the people dancing. Abel carefully stood and moved to the other side of the table and sat, leaning his back against the table, his feet stretched out and pointed toward the gyrating crowd. It was always amusing watching his buddies crash and burn.

"Are you still alive?" The waitress, had come up from his blind side and sat down next to him.

"Yeah, but I'm running out of steam. The tequila on top of a couple of Oxys was stupid. I'm pretty hammered. I really just want to go home and sleep."

"Looks like your friends want to stay. Why don't you call your wife or girlfriend?"

Abel looked at her out of the corner of his eye. "Don't have either right now, so it looks like I'm going to have to wait till Tank embarrasses himself enough that he calls it quits out there."

"I could cut my shift short and drive you home. You look like shit—no offense."

"Naw, it's all good. I'll wait. Can you sit a bit and keep me company?"

"Yeah, until my boss sees me. What happened to you anyway?"

"I fell at work, and something punched a hole through my underarm."

"Ouch, construction?"

Abel grunted, neither a yes or no, a noncommittal look on his face. "What's your name?"

"Olivia Pascal."

"Are you married or attached?" Abel was acting casual, but inside something was trying to break through the booze and drug fog. She wasn't the hot girls that René always hit on, the kind that were usually dumb as a rock. No, she was cute and a little bit wild looking with black hair in a pixie, a pert nose, and the body of a dancer. He looked into her eyes, and he felt like he'd been punched in the chest.

"No, I'm divorced and happy about it. You never told me your name."

"Abel Kane." And then Abel waited for it...

Olivia got a grin on her face. "Niiiice, what was your mama thinking? She got a sense of humor, or is she a Baptist?"

"I think my daddy was a Cain, and she was hoping to counteract that." Abel didn't feel like telling her his parents were dead and getting into all that.

"I have to go. Here comes my boss." Olivia pulled a pen out of her bar apron and quickly wrote her phone number on Abel's good hand. Then, she was gone.

Abel felt her absence immediately, like the loud silence after an explosion. He brought his attention back to the dance floor and saw René dancing with a girl, pretty, at least from a distance. Whatever shortfalls René had in general, striking up relationships with beautiful women was not one of them. It was like he emitted some kind of chemical attractant, or more likely, it was just his looks. Like his daddy, he kind of took after Elvis, well... a dyed-blond Elvis with black roots, but whereas Deacon had the hard edge of a tough and was on the small side, René was tall and favored his mama slightly, his features a touch feminine, which created a countenance that was apparently irresistible. Abel continued to watch the inevitable, wondering what the girl was thinking, wondering whether she had an inkling of her short future with René.

René was thinking about the girl in front of him, too. She was hot. Just his type and all over him. She had grabbed him and pulled him out to the throng of dancers, and they had danced to five or six songs. He hadn't even got her name, and she was up close and rubbing on him, turning around and putting her hands in her hair and pressing her ass tight against him. He was totally aroused and put his hands on her waist, pulling her even closer. He yelled into her ear, "Let's go to my truck."

She turned around, put her hand halfway into his front pocket, and pulled him toward the exit. The gate slammed shut behind them, and René took the lead, directing her to the vehicle. Harm's truck was backed into a spot on the edge of the lot, tucked in among the trees. René guided her around to the back of the truck, shielded from the parking lot light.

She was laughing, more than tipsy, not making a whole lot of sense and tugging on his pants. She had gotten his pants down around his ankles, and René spun her around and leaned her up against the vehicle, both his hands running up her legs, lifting her skirt. She wasn't wearing any panties and had reached down with both hands, guiding him into her, beyond ready, one leg wrapped around his thigh. She drove her hips forward, and he thrust into her, one of his arms pressed against the tailgate to support them, the other around her, pushing against the small of her back. He smelled her perfume and their animal scent, and it was all over in one intense minute.

Breathing hard, he scanned the lot. He couldn't see anybody paying attention to their secluded corner. René leaned in and kissed her hard. "Ahhh, that was nice—let's go back. I'll get you another drink."

They walked back, slower this time, having to go back in through the front entrance. René walked her up to the main bar and yelled over the music for a vodka cran. He handed her the drink and took out his phone and went through the charade of taking her name and number. "Hey listen, I've got to get back to my crew. Are you going to be able to find your friends?" he asked abruptly.

"Sure, I'll find them. Are you going to call me?" she asked, looking downcast.

"Of course, we'll go get dinner down in the city." René made his escape, primarily feeling relief, and headed back to the patio, already searching for the rest of the guys. The girl was gone from his mind.

He went through the back door to the patio and saw Harm and André talking with a cluster of people just past the outdoor bar. In a blast from the past, he realized that one of the people was Henrí, his nemesis from elementary school, junior high, and high school. René had heard that Henrí was an enforcer for a loan shark down in the city—a perfect job for him.

He didn't understand why André and Harm were even talking to him. René was drunk enough that his normal self-preservation instinct was blunted, and he was still riding on the success of the day. He said, "Hey, Henrí, peed yourself lately?" in reference to a time in elementary school when Abel and René had been getting beat on by Henrí and Tank had piled on. Henrí had ended up pissing his pants in front of all the kids. "Still living with your mama?" This was an ironic jab given that René still lived at home, too.

In any normal human, a third-grade insult like that would probably just result in a "FUCK YOU!" in return, but René somehow forgot to consider Henrí's limited emotional development. Henrí drove off the line like a defensive tackle, collecting René in his arms, lifting him up, and throwing him onto the bartender's table that was covered with dirty glassware and spent bottles. Harm and André grabbed Henrí before he could do any more damage to René who was on the ground amid glass, bottles, and the broken table.

Abel saw the end of the action from a distance with René on the ground and André wrestling Henrí away, the bouncers coming. "Aw shit," he said out loud. He was ready to go anyway.

CHAPTER

FOUR

She sensed a man was standing over her bed in a room that was only a room because it was set off with stained sheets hanging from the ceiling. He reached down in the dim light and touched her.

"This bitch is dead."

"Qué?"

"La puta—mierde! She's dead."

Only she wasn't dead. She was in a cocoon, warm under the covers, the weight pressing down on her but somehow feeling like she was floating, all the pain gone. Her eyes felt like they were open, but the world wasn't there to see, just cottony black. She could tell it was Tattoo Face that was speaking, irritating her when the sounds pierced her bliss. The voice caused a door to open all the way down a black hall and light shone in. She wanted the door to close.

"What'chu want me to do, jefe?" asked the other man.

"Dump her."

The other man picked her up and put her over his shoulder, the other girls mumbling. One cried out. He carried her out to the car in the alley and threw her on the backseat. He drove for a while. All she could hear were the wheels humming on the road. Neon colors briefly flashed on her face. He turned at the next corner. The man paused the car, then the door by her head opened. He grabbed her under the arms and dragged her out. Her feet flopped onto the street when she cleared the seat. He shuffled backward, and she vaguely noticed her bare feet scuffing along the street. He stopped and let go. Her shoulder hit the curb, whiplashing her head against the concrete.

A bright flash illuminated her darkness. It faded away.

The emergency room was quiet, not really, but slow compared to the action during Mardi Gras. The after-dinner rush was over now, too, so if anybody showed up, it was going to be serious. Callie was able to take a breath. She'd already caught up on the paperwork for her discharges, so she took the opportunity to go room to room, a lithe young woman moving with agile purpose, checking supplies and restocking the gloves and linen. Anyone watching might think she was a beach volleyball player in her spare time. She had that look— California girl.

When she finished, Callie checked in with the attending physician, who urged her to take a break. He'd been a medical officer in Afghanistan, so his advice tended to reflect the homilies of a soldier.

"Sleep when you can. Eat when you can. Shit when you can," he advised with a brotherly air. "You never know what's going to happen."

She didn't need to do any of the three but got herself a coffee from the break room to help her get through the rest of the shift. Callie enjoyed it when it was chaos; that's why she was in emergency to begin with. When the action slowed down, the minute hand stopped moving.

She had just sat down with her cup when the triage nurse pinged her on her walkie-talkie.

"We have a fifties male with abdominal pain in room three. Can you handle it?"

"Sure," she fired back and set the coffee down.

She was in the room getting the IV started when the doctor stepped in and did a cursory exam. "Let's get some pain meds onboard and get a CAT scan to see what's going on, see if there's an obstruction or something else." He stepped out to enter the orders.

"I'll be back in just a minute with something that will make him more comfortable," Callie told the wife of the sick man.

She came back a little later and injected some morphine, getting an almost immediate response from the patient. He visibly relaxed making a soft "ahhh" noise, his eyes going to half-mast. "I'm going to come back in a bit as soon as we get the X-ray scheduled. He's going to have to drink some dye before the test. Can I get you anything before I go?"

The wife was less upset now that her husband was not thrashing around, so Callie went off to make another try at her coffee.

He'd had enough drinking for the night. The game on the crummy TV above the bar was long since over, and after the fifth double whiskey, he couldn't stand the place. The only thing the joint had going for it was that it was cheap, and people left him alone to drink. It was close enough that he didn't have to drive his crappy car very far to get back to his cruddy apartment.

He settled, putting the load on his credit card, with its ever-increasing minimum payment, and stumbled on his way out the door. *Get a grip,* he thought. He wasn't that looped. Out the door and under the neon, he walked down to the corner and turned, heading for his shit-mobile. Vague light from the flickering streetlight cast his distorted shadow forward on the sidewalk, the monster growing the farther he got from the lamp. It rippled oddly by the curb, making him feel like he *WAS* that drunk and was seeing things. But as he got closer, the ripple turned into a shape and the shape into a body.

Another loser like him, who couldn't even make it to his car, sleeping it off in the gutter. At least he hadn't fallen that low. As he got closer, he realized it wasn't a drunk like him; it was a tiny, barefoot girl, a black splotch pooling under her head, half on the curb and half in the street. It looked like she was dead, pale and still, but when he bent and touched her cheek, an eyelid twitched. He bolted upright and shambled back to the bar to get help.

Callie was back with the man who had come in complaining of abdominal pain when suddenly "Code Blue Emergency Room—Code Blue Emergency Room" blared out of the speaker mounted outside the room's door. That was the signal for a medical emergency like a cardiac or respiratory arrest.

Callie was on the crash team—she had to go. She turned to the aide. "Tape the tube to his nose." She headed out of the room at top speed. The EMTs were rushing a gurney down the hall with a girl on it. At the same time the doctor motored down the hall from the break room. All of them converged on the first empty trauma room.

The four of them lifted the girl off the stretcher. One of the EMTs immediately commenced bagging the teenage girl. The other EMT supported her head carefully.

"Possible drug overdose, blood pressure sixty over forty. She's stopped breathing, faint pulse," yelled the tech that was bagging the girl. "She was moving her hands and her feet some when we put her in the ambulance. Spine's probably OK."

"Has she been given naloxone yet?" asked the doctor.

"Yes."

The respiratory therapist who was on the crash team that night came in through the door.

"OD," Callie said with urgency. She was busy putting the pulse and oxygen sensor on the girl's finger. The girl's fingernails were blue, and she looked up at the girl's face, noticing her lips were bluish as well.

"Keep bagging her, her O_2 is crashing. Callie, get that IV jacked in."

Callie was already on it; the tourniquet was in place, a bag of saline hung. She was proficient at getting IVs started, but this poor girl's veins were beat up, and Callie couldn't find one on the back of her hand. She moved up her arm to the inside of the elbow, eventually managing to find a good vein. She jammed her thumb next to the vein, trapping the vein between her thumb and the needle and then slowly increased the pressure. The needle pierced the vein, the blood moving up the tube. She slipped the needle out, leaving the plastic cannula in place and connected it to the saline.

"We're hitting her again with Narcan." The doctor was setting up a syringe from the crash cart with another bolus of naloxone, the drug that was used to counteract the effects of an opioid overdose. He moved to the IV line and injected the naloxone into the port. He waited a few minutes. The oxygen sat was moving up due to the EMTs continued bagging. "Stop bagging for a sec—let's see if she's breathing on her own."

They all paused, staring at the girl, hoping to see her chest rise. The battered girl's abdomen spasmed, and she vomited yellow-green bile. Working in unison, one EMT supported her neck, the other immediately rolled her onto her side, wiping out her mouth with a gloved finger to clear any obstruction. He held her for a minute and then laid her flat. It appeared she wasn't going to throw up again. They watched intently. There was a slight rise, a long pause, another weak rise. The respiratory therapist had her eye on the monitor, the oxygen sat still low. She fixed an oxygen cannula around the girl's nose.

"OK, watch and see if the saturation improves. In the meantime, let's examine the rest of her and see what else is going on." The doctor squatted and looked at the contusion on her head. "That's going to need stitches." He stood, then bent over so he could look closer at her face, straightened and moved to her side and palpated her abdomen, his eyes staring off into space, trying to visualize her organs. "Looks like someone used her face as a punching bag," he mumbled to himself. The doctor checked the monitor. The blood pressure was up some. There was no obvious internal bleeding. He ran his hands over her arms and legs and didn't feel anything amiss. While he was examining her, Callie had cut her jeans off. One of the EMTs helped her gently slide them out from under the poor girl. The female EMT quickly covered her with a drape.

Finishing with the survey of the bones and joints, the doctor lifted the drape covering the girl's pelvis. He adjusted the light over the table and looked closer. "Aw shit," said the hardened army doctor with a hitch in his voice. "We're going to need a rape kit and more stitches."

He stepped back, removing his gloves and talking to the respiratory therapist. "Keep running oxygen. CAT scan of the head—possible concussion, antibiotics for possible STDs. I'll be back in a few minutes to stitch her up. If I can't get her into the ICU immediately, we'll keep her down here." He left to put in orders. The respiratory therapist stayed, watching the girl's breathing, watching the monitor, ready to step in and start bagging if necessary.

Callie left and went to check that the man with the intestinal distress was resting comfortably, and there were no new cases—a lull after the storm—so she took the opportunity to walk back to her desk to decompress. She took a sip of her coffee and grimaced. She dumped it in the trash and started wrapping up. Her shift was almost over.

Twelve hours later, Callie was back on her shift. She'd come a few minutes early, expressly to check on the traumatized girl. Callie had woken up from her day-sleep, and the whole time she was taking her shower and putting on her scrubs, she was wondering how the teenager was doing, worried that she hadn't made it.

She went straight to the ICU, hoping to find the girl still hanging on at least by a thread and was happily surprised to see that the assaulted teen was no longer on oxygen.

The ICU nurse came in. "They've upgraded her to serious. She's on the mend—at least, her body." The nurse's voice conveyed concern. "The doc stitched her up while she was out, and she has a concussion, but she's getting moved out of intensive care in the next hour."

Callie still had a few minutes before her shift and sat down next to the girl, peering at her face, curious how a youngish teen had ended up thrown to the curb like so much trash. She felt mad at the world and angry at a God who would let that happen. The girl twitched, moving slightly.

"You're OK, honey, you're safe go back to sleep."

The girl opened her eyes, a sudden look of fear distorting her whole face. Her mouth stretched open like she was trying to scream, but no sound came out. Callie jumped out of the chair and put her hand on the girl. "You're safe. It's alright. Don't be scared. I'm here. You're in the hospital." Callie stroked the frightened girl, her body taut under Callie's hand.

"Is he here? Is he here?"

"Who, honey?" asked Callie.

"The man. The man with letters on his face."

"No, sweetheart. No, it's just me. You're safe in the hospital." The girl's body relaxed just a bit. "What man, honey? Who did this to you? What letters?"

"The man. His face—*M*s and *S*s," she said in a horrified whisper.

Callie kept stroking the teen until she went back to sleep and then hustled down to start her shift. The first chance she got, she called back to the ICU and recounted what happened, asking the RN to get the doctor to order a counselor and maybe a dose of lorazepam to calm the girl.

CHAPTER

FIVE

The hour-long ride home after her shift at the hospital was Callie's time to decompress. At six in the morning, she was going counterflow back to their home in Lacombe on autopilot, and her mind wandered over her mental to-do list, taking side trips down her worries, foremost being her wounded brother. She was sure she had treated the injury properly and that no major structures were damaged, but with Abel refusing to go the ER, they were taking chances. She understood that it was an obvious shooting; it would be reported, and Abel didn't need that kind of exposure. But still, it was a bullet wound, you never knew. Why take the risk? Though she knew Abel wouldn't budge. He would never do anything that might put his friends at risk. She had let him sleep, drugged up, all the previous day, but now her concern caught up with her.

When she reached home, she skipped her morning routine and went straight to his bedroom. "Abel, wake up! I'm coming in." Callie gave him a second and then barged in.

Abel wasn't really woken up, lying flat, a prone Vitruvian Man except for his boxers. He popped one eye open. "Mmmmm arggh," he groaned, his face a mix of sleep and suffering. His whole body hurt, and his armpit throbbed in time with his heartbeat.

"Wake up, I've got to change the bandages. Or do you need me to help you to the bathroom first?"

"I've got it. The last thing I need is my sister helping me piss." Abel grabbed his bad arm with the good and then carefully dropped his legs to the floor and sat up, supporting his arm the whole way. Inarticulate sounds came from his chest unbidden.

He wasn't censoring his discomfort in front of Callie, but she knew that if one of his crew was watching, Abel would have been stoic. "Lie down when you're done peeing. I'll get my stuff."

She brought her supplies, set them down on the nightstand, and opened the blinds. The morning sun blazed into the room. She leaned over Abel and peeled back the dressing covering the entrance wound. The injury was so swollen, you could hardly tell it was an armpit. The skin pushed outward in a baseball-sized hump, the inside of his arm black and blue all the way down to his wrist. "The front looks good. No infection that I can see." She re-bandaged the front, glad that she had shaved off all his pit hair the previous day.

"OK, now the back." She helped him turn over, feeling his muscles tense under her hands. Callie gently peeled the tape loose and removed the stack of 4x4s covering the exit wound. The large open sore had stopped bleeding but was still raw and inflamed with redness extending out from the margins of the injury. Surprisingly, the back didn't look as bad as the front with all its edema and bruising. It was still oozing fluid but no blood, no pus. She bent close and sniffed—good, no stench. Her neck and shoulders relaxed; she had been tensed up, expecting the worst. Liberally coating the stack of 4x4s with wound gel, Callie patched up the damaged area with the fresh bandages, then taped them down securely.

"How're you feeling?"

"Like I got shot . . ."

"Haha, do you want some coffee? You've got to take your antibiotics. Do you feel like taking more Oxy?"

"Yeah, I'll have a cup, but I don't want the drugs. I've got to get over and talk to Deacon, and I don't want to be fuzzy."

Callie went to make coffee, and Abel scooted his butt back in the bed so that he could sit up against the headboard, closing his eyes while he waited.

"Wake up. Here's your coffee." Callie placed it on the nightstand near his good side, then dragged a chair over to the bed and sat. The window was behind her, casting her shadow over Abel. They were quiet for a minute, sipping their coffees.

"Thanks for helping me," Abel said, breaking the silence. "How are you doing? How's work?"

"I'm doing fine. The ER has been pretty slow since Mardi Gras. Although a couple of nights ago, we had a really upsetting situation."

"What happened?"

"This young girl, probably sixteen, but looked about twelve, came in on the edge of death, respiratory arrest, code blue, OD'd. The crash team worked her for about an hour, multiple loads of Narcan, bagging her the whole time, you know the drill."

"Did she make it?"

"Yes, she crawled back to life, her heart barely beating, her oxygen sat in the seventies. She had these horrific injuries. She'd been raped multiple times. Poor kid. I checked on her first thing my next shift, expecting to find out she didn't make it. She was still alive, and I sat with her a while.

"But listen to this. I was just sitting there watching her face. She was beat up, but she looked so peaceful. Then, her eyes opened. Her face transformed; it was like she woke up from one of those dreams where you've been screaming. She looked at me like she was seeing a monster.

"She started mumbling. I think she was talking about the man that did all that stuff to her. She said his face had letters—she wasn't that lucid; I think she meant tattoos. She kept saying *M*s and *S*s."

"You know what that sounds like?" Abel said. "MS-13."

"What's that?"

"It's a gang from California. LA, I think. Made up of guys from El Salvador. I don't know what the thirteen comes from, but the MS is Mara Salvatrucha."

"What would they be doing here?"

"I don't know, but I've heard they are into everything like drugs, prostitution, human trafficking, arms trade, and murder for hire. I guess they're like cockroaches, and they overran California, so now they're here."

Callie had a horrified look on her face.

"Yeah, and another thing I heard—they can't put MS tattoos on their face and neck unless they've killed people. If they've killed one person, they can put a little tear drop by their eye. They can only put the big Ms and Ss if they've killed something like five people."

"So that poor girl really did see a monster," Callie said with a slight waver in her voice.

"And MS-13 don't just kill people, they torture them and hack them apart with machetes or set them on fire and hang them from bridges so everybody gets the message that they are badasses." Abel paused and then said, "Maybe that little girl was lucky she was just overdosed."

"She was brutally raped multiple times so not so lucky. That was bad enough. She's just a kid. A lost child, alone."

"Where's her family?" Abel mused. "Do you think she's a runaway, or did they kidnap her?"

"I'm going to find out tonight, when I check on her." Callie leaned back in her chair; she felt tired. With the sun backlighting her blonde hair her head was surrounded by a glowing aura, but her eyes were in shadow.

"You know, if there is one girl caught up in this, there's likely to be more."

"When I start thinking about that, it makes me depressed." It was difficult to see Callie's face because of the bright light coming from the window, but her voice had a plaintive note. "Those gangbangers have sisters and mothers; how could they do that to innocent people? Why are there always more people willing to hurt folks than there are good people trying to help?"

"Callie, the world isn't that bad."

"Abel, you've always taken care of me, you're my family, but even you aren't on the right side. You have your crew and me under your tent. That's it. And you spend your days planning how to take other people's money. How different are you from this MS gang? You and your friends just hurt an innocent man. A man who was just trying to get his paycheck cashed after putting in a solid week of work supporting his family."

"You don't know that; he could have been a crook." Whenever Callie started picking on him, he got defensive. "Hey, what was I going to do? I was fourteen, Uncle Deacon was in prison, Hen was losing it, and Tank's family couldn't make ends meet after Antoine died. Selling hamburgers wasn't going to cut it."

"Yeah, maybe that was all you could do then, but our lives are different now. We're grown up, and we can make our own decisions. You're smart, and people look up to you. You could do anything. You could help so many people."

"Callie, I can't take care of every stray cat you bring home. I can't just stop and leave my crew hanging—they're my family, too. I didn't even graduate from high school. What am I going to do?" Abel's excuses sounded weak.

"You talk about taking care of your crew. What if it was Tank who got shot or even killed at the check store? What would André and Isabelle do then? She always said she saw a devil on your back, and she was right. She saw it and tried to protect you from it because she loves you. But Antoine dying killed a part of her, and she lost the strength to keep watching over you. Every time I see her, she's less. Seeing Tank and André on the wrong side of the line is breaking her apart bit by bit, and soon she'll be gone. Is that what you want?"

"Callie, OK, I get it. I'll think about what you said." Abel just wanted her to stop. He hated how it made him feel, not because she was nagging him but because he knew she was right.

"That's what you always say, and yet here we are, a hole blown through you. You could be a protector, a hero, a leader, with a thousand people under your tent. You always say that I remind you of our mama, that I'm just like her. Then don't you think that if I want you to stop, that is what she would have wanted you to do, too? Someday you're going to have to decide which side of the line you're going to live—or die—on," Callie said sadly.

CHAPTER

SIX

A bel stayed in bed for a while after Callie had gone to bed, thinking. Despite his pushback and excuses, he cared about what she thought of him. It hurt that she basically considered him to be in the same group of lowlifes as those gangbangers. He craved her respect, and for the life of him, he couldn't figure out how he had gotten to the point where he had lost that. It had happened gradually. When he was taking care of all of them, she had idolized him. Even now, he couldn't exactly place the time when her adoration had tipped over into disrespect, or worse, disgust.

The sun in the window beat on him while he lay, stewing. Finally, he made a conscious effort to shut down the voices in his head and sat fully upright. He jockeyed himself to the edge of the bed, sitting there a minute to let the dizziness subside, then stood up and took a pace, reaching out to the chair Callie had left by the side of the bed, steadying himself.

Flicking on the light in the bathroom, he went about his ministrations, thankful that the injury was on his left side. Still, it was difficult to do things, even putting toothpaste on his brush. He ended up squeezing some on the counter and scooped it up with his toothbrush. Gross, but not as bad as not brushing his teeth. He was glad that Callie wasn't watching. She would have freaked.

Once he'd finished, Abel grabbed the bag of cash he had reserved for Deacon from the check store score and then detoured through the kitchen on the way out to reload his coffee into a travel mug. He made his way to his F-150 and climbed in, each move causing a jolt like a hot wire being jammed into his armpit. He'd always imagined he had a high tolerance to pain, just like all the heroes in the movies, but Callie had explained that the armpit was rich with nerves, blood vessels, and lymph nodes, and with all the swelling, the whole area was inflamed and putting pressure on the nerves, amplifying the discomfort. Yeah, maybe there was an excuse, but he was still acting like a pussy.

On the way to Deacon's, Abel ran through the score, getting the details straight in his head. His uncle always wanted to know how the job went, probably because he was calculating how much risk he had that it would blow back on him. That, plus he seemed to enjoy telling him where Abel and his crew had gone wrong. But his uncle seemed to take pleasure in mentoring him, too. For some reason, if Deke complimented him on some aspect of a robbery, it felt good—made Abel proud—and he was at a loss to explain that, since disdain for Deacon was usually foremost in his mind.

Abel pulled the truck into Deke's warehouse lot and climbed out, trying to ignore the jabs of pain from his armpit. He dropped the travel mug next to the entrance and trapped the bag of cash next to his body with his bad arm, grimacing, and pulled open the door.

"Deke, I'm here."

Abel heard a faint, "C'mon back," and went on into the warehouse part of the junk shop.

Deacon was sitting at his desk cleaning his fingernails with a pocketknife. "You don't look too bad. I heard you were shot, hurt bad."

"Naw, it was just a flesh wound. Callie fixed it up—still swoll up like a baseball, can't hardly move my arm, but doesn't hurt much." Abel minimized like it was just par for the course, acting like it happened every day.

"Heard you boys got into some trouble over'n The Flying Machine. Slidell ain't your town, but it's close. You don't need to get a bad rep at home. You got to keep your crew in line."

This seriously irked Abel, considering it was René that had started the trouble, and he had been dealing with his loose cannon cousin's fallout since they were boys. Uncle Deacon expected Abel to keep the man's own son from screwing up. Abel didn't even bother to make excuses; he just swallowed his frustration in a bitter lump.

Deke shifted gears. "How's your sister?"

"She's still working nights, twelves. Her spring semester's about done, too. I don't know how she does it. Guess she got all the brains on this side of the family."

"She surely did. You ever going to get your GED?"

Abel ignored the gibe. "Last time I saw her, she was pretty worked up 'bout some teenage girl that showed up with an overdose at the ER. Looked like the poor kid was somehow being kept by the MS-13 down in the city, probably for the sex trade."

"Yeah, those bangers are into that. Fuckin' bottom-feeders. Someone needs to clean out that scum," Uncle Deacon said with a disgusted look on his face. "Dealing little girls—makes me sick. It ain't right. Anyway, don't you have something for me?"

Abel picked up the bag of cash and pushed it across the desk.

"How much?" his uncle asked. Deacon fell on the money, not waiting for an answer, as he pulled out the stacks, licking his finger and toting the bills up.

"Seventy-one large, your cut is over fourteen grand." There was silence for a minute as Deacon continued the count, not one to trust anyone, including his nephew. Then, he said, "I thought there would be more. I heard they were doing some serious money laundering. You sure that was all they had?"

"It's not like the place was huge. They only had the one safe. Plus, the guy didn't seem to be the biggest operator I've ever seen. Seemed like a loser. Hard to picture him in the middle of some big syndicate."

"Well, I heard they were moving hundreds of thousands."

"Did you hear the back office door was armored and locked from the inside? Did you hear they had private security?" Abel had an edge to his voice.

"Are you saying I set you on a bad job? You disrespecting me?" Deacon's hair-trigger temper lit up. He was quick to anger at the smell of an insult.

"No, we still got out with some serious cash—clean cash. Just wondering how reliable your source was."
Deacon backed off a bit. "He may not be as plugged in as I thought. Maybe I should have checked it, but the guy has always been solid. What did your crew think?"

"I'll be honest, Uncle Deacon, they're restless. The jobs are getting farther apart and are harder to do. Except for this score, the take has been getting smaller, too. They're worried about the risk versus the reward, André especially. There's talk about doing something different."

"Kids nowadays—want everything handed to them on a plate. There's always been risk. I've had to do my time. It's part of the business. This is just more of that millennial bullshit."

"My crew aren't kids. They're grown men, and they've been doing this with me since we were teenagers. Tank went with me on my first drug run. We're barely making the same money as a guy who's working legit without the risk of prison hanging over his head. Callie makes about the same as me." Abel's voice was rising. "If Tank hadn't diverted that shot, we wouldn't be having this conversation. I'd be dead."

"Well, what do you want to be doing instead?"

"We haven't got that far. I told them I would talk to you."

"OK, let's think about it," Deacon suggested. "Robbery, murder for hire, drugs, money laundering, fencing, loan sharking, stealing cars, illegal arms dealing, or extortion; take your pick.

"Not seeing you and your crew doing assassinations. Maybe Harm, but not the rest of you daisies. That goes for extortion and strong-arm stuff as well."

"Yeah, you're right," agreed Abel. He had long ago learned to ignore Deacon's slights, at least most of the time. "The gangs and cartels have the drugs wrapped up, so that's out."

"Or we could take your drug running from the old days into the big time," mused Deacon. "If you could figure out how to move huge amounts around the country, the cartels would be very interested in that. Although the downside for bungling that is serious time or your life."

"That's off the table. My drug muling days are over." Back when Deacon was in prison and Abel was just a teenager, he had moved drugs around Louisiana for the Dixie Mafia to make enough money to keep the family afloat. But those were desperate times; he had moved on.

"Lookee here, you basically have the money business: cleaning money or loan sharking. You've got the arms business. And then there's your forte, the robbery business, including: stealing cars, hijacking trucks, hitting warehouses, and the fencing pipeline. But you've got to forget the banks; the Feds have that closed down." As long as he wasn't blowing his top, Deacon had a very organized mind.

"If we go into laundering, street loans, or weapons, we're going to need a decent bank roll to start, which we don't have. That still takes us back to robbery. My crew is good at that. We just need bigger jobs—better targets. Can't you find us deals like that?"

"Here's the thing, Abel. I'm sixty-three. My network is getting worn out, people are retiring and dyin'. They're out of the loop. I'm ready to get out of the Life. This place and my business are dying, and everybody knows it. The police don't even bother coming by. All I really want to do is sit in my pirogue on the bayou. The business needs someone younger to rebuild it. I don't know, maybe I waited too long to pass it on."

"Why don't you give it to René and let him take over?"

"Number one, I ain't *giving it* to anyone. I said it was dying, not dead. I got to get something to set up my retirement. I'm not livin' hard in my remaining days. Number two, you and I both know René can't cut it. I love him, bless his heart, but he don't have it in 'im. It's always been you, Abel, right from the beginning. Why did you think I turned you out while I was in jail and made you start drug running?"

"A'write, what if it is me? So what does that mean for me now?"

"Maybe nothing right off, but over the next couple of years, I take you under my wing, hook you into my fencing network, all my connections and sources, and get 'em to trust you. Bring you with me when I set up all my other crews on jobs. When they're working for you, you'd get twenty percent of all the cash, the margin for fencing the goods, and your crew would keep one hundred percent of your own scores. Or they could all start their own crews and feed up to you."

It sounded sweet to Abel. "OK, what's the catch?"

"You've got to buy in. Either a big lump sum or a bigger cut of all the jobs your crew pulls over the next two years."

"What kind of cash are you talking about?"

"Half a mil, at least."

"There's no way I'm going to be able to do that with things the way they've been."

"Yeah, I get it. I'm going to have to get creative and find you bigger and better scores." Deacon was getting more animated as he saw the possibilities of his imagined old age. "Plus, bigger jobs mean more money in your crew's pockets. That'll keep them happy."

"Well, it all sounds great, but five hundred grand is a big number. How are we going to find jobs that pay out like that?" Abel wanted to believe but still wasn't buying it.

"Like I said, we get creative. Maybe you guys start hitting drug houses. Maybe you do some work over'n Houston. That's what your daddy was doing when he got killed. He had a network of meth labs and was tied in with some Texas biker gangs. He had big ideas.

"When you was talking earlier about that MS-13, that got me thinking. I heard some talk about them bein' deep in the illegal arms business, running guns and ammo and explosives out of the port that are brought in containers, then passing it on to skinheads."

"White supremacists dealing with guys from El Salvador?" Abel was doubtful. That sounded like bullshit. He was not sure that his uncle was still plugged in enough that his intel was accurate.

"Yeah, can you believe it? You could hijack either end of one of those deals, and we'd be talking some serious money."

"If we start taking on that gang, that really ups the danger, given what I've heard." Abel wondered whether his crew would be willing to join the big leagues, if getting involved with MS-13 was part of it.

"Yeah, they're heavy duty. I've heard some crazy shit. Check this out. To get into the gang, you've got to be 'jumped in.' That means everybody in the gang gets to beat the new member for thirteen seconds. They punch and kick the guy, all at the same time, and if he lives, he gets in. If one of their members does something wrong, just something the leader doesn't like, they 'yellow light' him. They stab him and dump him in front of a hospital. If somebody in the gang does something worse, like rat, the head guy gives the 'luz verde,' the 'green light,' and then some banger murders the guy. They don't just kill the guy. They torture him first. They hack him apart with a machete, or stuff him in a stack of tires, douse him with gas, and burn him alive—just for the fun of it."

"Good sales job, Uncle Deacon, I'm in," Abel said sarcastically, easing himself up and out of the chair. "Let me start running this by the guys, at least the part about bigger jobs. And by the way? You're the one that needs to break the news to René that you want me to take over, not him. He's going to be pissed."

"René does what I tell him. When he thinks about it, he'll know it's for the best. And I'll start sniffing around MS-13's business and any other opportunities I can find."

CHAPTER

SEVEN

A bel had spent the week after meeting with Deacon lying about the house, pondering his future. He'd worked all the paths and circumstances that he could come up with and had convinced himself that eventually taking over his uncle's business was probably the best option for improving his crew's situation. A good portion of the deliberation was centered on how he was going to explain expanding his criminal efforts to Callie, knowing that, while his crew would be on board, Callie was going to forcefully push back against the decision. He knew she was going to be disappointed in him, but his choices were limited. He just didn't see how he was going to get his crew into a business that would work for all of them. They were good at robbery; they just needed to get better. That was their future.

One thing he was sure of though was that if he did decide to take his crew up the ladder, they couldn't completely depend on Deacon in the future. They would have to develop the ability to find the kind of scores that had a big payoff and a low chance of sending them all to prison or getting them killed. Deacon was talking big, but Abel wasn't certain he had it in him anymore. If they could up their own game, develop their own network of information, even if his uncle failed to come through, his crew could make more than a living.

Once he'd solidified his strategy about the future, Abel began to get increasingly bored with the healing process. Toward the end of the week, his imagination was straying to Olivia. She had written her number on his hand, and he had transferred it to a scrap of paper, but he couldn't find it now, and the phone number on his hand was just a smear. Somehow, he had lost it, which was frustrating because he hadn't even left the house. He'd have to go back to The Flying Machine and track her down.

It was highly likely that since it was Friday, she was going to be working at The Machine, so he impatiently waited around home, bouncing from one thing to another, till it was late. He hoped to catch her at the end of her shift, assuming that she was working. Around midnight, he headed over to Slidell and The Machine, hoping that she would be there.

Since it was the start of the weekend, the place was hopping, the lot full, and drunks spilled out of the doors, yelling to each other over the loud music. He pushed his way through the throng of people blocking the door, greasing his way with the occasional "excuse me." A purple-haired waitress crossed his path, and Abel reached out, not quite grabbing her elbow, his hand grazing her bare arm. He leaned in. "Is Olivia working tonight?"

"What?" the waitress yelled back.

Abel moved closer, practically yelling in her ear, "Is Olivia here? Is she working?"

"Yeah, out back—she's working the patio."

"Thanks!" Abel said over his shoulder, already moving.

The patio was twenty decibels quieter. It had speakers all over, but it wasn't hemmed in by walls, so the sound was tolerable. Abel was relieved. He wasn't exactly the smoothest operator with women, and he didn't want to have to scream at Olivia to be heard on top of that. His eyes were casting around the patio when someone grabbed his shoulder from behind. He turned.

"Hey, you never called me," said Olivia, pretending to be mad.

"I lost your number and came back tonight to track you down."

"Likely story," she said with a grin.

"No, really, I wrote it down, then lost the paper," Abel said feebly.

"How's your arm?"

"It's better, thanks."

Olivia was holding a bucket of beers, and they seemed to be getting heavy. "I've got to drop these over there—I'll be back."

"Wait, do you want to go get breakfast after you get off?" *Wow, slick,* Abel thought. He couldn't even hold off till she got back and work it into the conversation.

"Sure! I get off at two." And with a smile, she turned and headed off to unload the beers.

Abel was pumped, and he headed to the bar to grab an Abita Purple Haze to kill time. Leaning on the bar, he watched Olivia serve customers for the next hour. She had an easy way with people, spending time talking to everybody at the table, teasing people, and the guys flirted with her, stuffing her tip jar with bills. Every time she came back to the bar to get a new load of drinks, she came up with a new comment to tease Abel. Eventually, Abel heard last call and impatiently waited for her to finish up. She took her time, making sure that all her customers were satisfied.

She breezed back and told him to meet her out front, that she had to clean herself up first. So he joined the revelers making an exodus and stopped outside the front door to chat with one of the bouncers. He'd gone to high school with the guy. They joked about René getting into it with Henrí the last time they were in.

The bouncer laughed. "Yeah, those two are never going to stop. They'll be at the old folk's home fighting over the red beans and rice."

Olivia came out, magically transformed from a waitress to a girl ready for a date. Abel felt the heart punch again.

"Do you want me to drive, you being hurt and all?" she asked.

"Yes, that's nice of you." Abel liked the idea of her driving. He could look at her the whole trip.

"The only thing open around here is the waffle place by the highway—that OK?"

"Sure, you're driving. You pick." *Jeez,* Abel thought. He definitely needed to study René's technique. He sounded like a doofus.

Olivia walked Abel to her car, which felt weird and kind of backward, but at least she didn't try to open his door for him. He climbed into her well-worn tan sedan, a child's seat strapped in the back. A vague sour odor, like ancient spilled milk, permeated the vehicle. A crack in the windshield snaked all the way across, faint tendrils forming a starburst on the window directly in front of Abel. On the short trip to the waffle joint, it was quiet. Both taking stock.

As it was after 2 am, they had no problem finding a seat. They picked a booth as far from the few patrons as they could, unconsciously trying to make a little privacy for themselves. Still, they couldn't avoid hearing an old bent man with a frizzle of gray hair arguing with the haggard night waitress.

"Bacon? I can't chew this bacon; I don't have any teeth!" he complained.

Olivia looked at Abel with a faint smile. "Well, thankfully, you still have all yours."

"Yeah, I've got that going for me." He paused and switched gears. "So what's your story? I saw that child seat; do you have a kid?"

"Yes, a sweet little guy. He's almost three," Olivia said with her head down. She looked up into Abel's eyes. "You wanna hear all this?"

"Sure, it's more interesting than my life." Abel returned her gaze.

The waitress walked up to their booth, interrupting their conversation and irritating Abel. He wasn't that interested in eating, but Olivia was. She ordered enough for two people.

The waitress finished writing down the order and started yelling it to the short-order cook while she was walking toward the counter. Olivia watched her back, listening to the cryptic order shorthand. Olivia turned her gaze back to Abel. "Ok, my dad died when I was a teenager."

"I'm sorry," Abel said sincerely. "My dad died, too—both my parents died when I was like five."

"Wow, that must have been tough. That's pretty young. Do you remember them much?"

"I just have kind of a sense of them. What happened after your dad passed?"

"Life got hard. My mama had to work more. We had to move into an even smaller house than we had. I ended up going to community college instead of LSU."

"Delgado?"

"Yeah, it was OK. Basically, it felt like another two years of high school, the same kids. I got an associates in business, which really is kind of useless unless I go back to college and get a four-year degree. So, after that, I started at The Machine. The tips were decent, and I was saving for school, then I met a guy. Cliché—skip college, meet a townie, get pregnant, and get married, like half the girls in my class."

"You did better than I did. I didn't even make it to community college," Abel confessed. "What happened with the marriage?

"We just married too young—not the worst guy on the planet. Tommy wanted to be a mechanic, and he was working at the Ford dealership doing tire work mostly. His fingers and hands were always crusted with black shit. The truth is, he really didn't want to get married but tried to do the right thing. After the baby, we gradually stopped doing things together. He wanted to hang out with his friends. Get drunk. Play video games. I was trying to make it work: taking care of the baby, working part-time, cleaning up after him, shopping, cooking, and I got tired and frustrated. I realized I didn't like him much. I'm sure I was mean. He did a lot of weed, some Oxy, no meth—thank God—and drank more. He wasn't the nicest guy when he was loaded. He never hit me, but he pushed me around. He didn't have the patience for a toddler, and when he started yelling at Owen and getting rough that was the last straw for me. I went straight to a lawyer and filed. Tommy didn't even fight it. He just left. He hasn't seen Owen since the divorce went final."

"Does Owen miss him?"

"No—we moved back in with my mama, and she dotes on him. Between the two of us, we can afford the house, and she doesn't have to work very much. She watches Owen while I work, and in the morning, when I'm sleeping. She works at a Starbucks, mainly for insurance. What's your history?"

"When Callie and I were really young, we were in a car crash in Houston. My parents died instantly. My sister didn't have a scratch on her, but my leg was broken badly, and it's still an inch short to this day. If I try to run, I almost go in circles." Abel gave a short laugh. "After that, my aunt and uncle took us in over'n Lacombe.

"We had some money trouble too when I was in high school. I had to work some extra jobs and help support the family. Couldn't do school at the same time and I quit before I graduated—I don't even have my GED, but I'm going to get that one of these days," added Abel.

"I can tell you're smart. It would be easy for you. Don't you want to go to college?" Olivia had an incredulous look on her face; she seemed unable to imagine anyone not wanting to go to college.

"I think about it every now and then. I'm not sure what I would even take—probably business, something about money and finance maybe. But in the meantime, my crew and I work for my uncle."

"Your crew?"

"My friends—my cousin, René, my best friend, Tank, his brother, and a couple other guys, Harmon and Rabbit."

"Ok, I've got to ask—Rabbit? Is he fast?"

"No, he just eats a lot of vegetables." Abel chuckled.

"What do you do for your uncle?"

"We work in his pawnshop and warehouse, shipping and receiving—that kind of thing." It wasn't like Abel could outright tell someone he barely knew that he and his crew were pro robbers. And it was sort of true. They did a prodigious amount of receiving—of stolen goods. Still, it felt bad having to shade the truth like that—really just outright lying.

"Do you have other brothers and sisters?"

"I've got my cousin, René, and my friends who are like brothers. Especially Tank—his real name is Thomas—and his brother, André. I spent most of my childhood in their house. Their family practically raised me. Tank's mama, Isabelle, gave me lovin' like my mama would have done, if she hadn't been killed in the wreck. Tank's daddy is dead, too. It's weird we all have that in common."

The tired waitress came back to their table with their plates and set them down. Olivia attacked her plate immediately. Abel just poked at the limp waffle with his knife. He peeled open the industrial lubricant packet someone had the audacity to call butter and halfheartedly spread it over the waffle. They ate in silence for a few minutes, Abel not wanting to interrupt Olivia—she was obviously starved.

Olivia straightened up and leaned back away from the table. "Man, I was hungry!"

"Yeah, I was afraid to get my hand near your food," Abel kidded.

"Haha, very funny. All I've had today was a cup of coffee."

Abel grinned. "How do you have the energy to take care of a kid and work at a bar all night? Do you even have any time for yourself?"

"Are you asking whether I'll have time to go out with you again?" Olivia said, and she smiled.

"Well, that too, but do you get to do anything fun?"

"Taking care of my little guy is fun, and it feels like that's my reason for living. But I do other things, too. I read tons of books."

"No kidding? Me, too!" He rarely bumped into anyone who actually liked to read. He even had a library card—in fact, it was his second card because he had literally worn out the first.

They traded their favorite books back and forth, Abel telling her about a book he loved from his elementary school days called *My Side of the Mountain*. The book was about a boy who ran away from home and went to live off the land by himself. He and Tank had acted out all the different survival techniques they'd found in the book in the woods around the bayou. They'd go camping and made shelters, started fires, cooked potatoes in the coals, hunted with homemade bows and arrows, fished and set traps. They were holy terrors in the forest.

"Now that we are all grown up, we still do that shit," continued Abel. "We've even got an airboat and 4x4s. We tear it up, hunt feral hogs with spears, set up deadfalls and pit traps. It's like we never grew up."

A phone made a buzzing sound, interrupting Abel's bayou adventures, and Olivia pulled it out of her purse. "My mom's checking on me. We'd better go. I've got to get up early to take care of Owen."

Abel went up to the counter and quickly took care of the check, and they hustled out to Olivia's car. They chattered back and forth about the details of their lives, comfortable with each other. It didn't feel like a first date. Olivia pulled into the bar's parking lot, and Abel directed her to his vehicle. He walked around to her side, and Olivia rolled down her window. Abel leaned in and kissed her with Olivia responding and putting her hand on the back of his neck, pulling him into her soft lips. They broke apart after a moment, and Abel straightened up. "I'll call you tomorrow—is that OK?"

"Sure! But how are you going to do that? Didn't you lose my number?" asked Olivia.

"Jeez, what an idiot I am," Abel said and then pulled out his phone and typed in her contact details as she dictated them to him.

"Call me before I start my shift, like five-ish." She gave a little wave and rolled her window up. Abel stepped back and watched her drive off, already missing her—man, he had it bad...

EIGHT

C allie made sure she arrived at the hospital early. After her discussion with Abel, the abused teenager was on her mind, and she wanted to check on her. She didn't know exactly how just yet, but she intended to help the teen.

The girl had been moved, but the charge nurse was familiar with the case and directed Callie to the girl's new room, two floors up. She took the elevator and got out on a surgical recovery floor where one of the floor nurses showed Callie to the girl's room. This time, the teen was sitting up in bed watching TV. She looked much better than the last time Callie had seen her. "Hi, I'm Callie, one of the nurses who worked on you when you came in the other night. Do you want some company?"

The girl reached for the remote and flicked off the television, instantly erasing the grating sound of a laugh track. "Sure, that TV show really sucks."

Callie moved around the bed and pulled a chair closer. The girl adjusted her position so that she was facing her. The teen was blonde like Callie, though the girl's hair was almost a white blonde, her eyebrows barely visible they were so fair. She had a light complexion. Callie couldn't tell if that was because she'd been sick and traumatized or if that was her natural coloring. She was petite with an air of fragility, but even beat up like she was, you could see that she was pretty.

"What's your name?" Callie asked.

"Katie," she replied.

"How old are you?"

"Sixteen."

"You were really in a bad way. You almost died—did they tell you?"

"Yeah, they said I was lucky." Katie paused, her eyes tearing up.

"That must have been terrible. It sounded like you were being held by awful people. When I saw you the other day, you were still frightened. I felt so bad for you."

"I still feel scared."

"Do you mind talking to me?" asked Callie.

"No."

"Well, you're safe now, and we'll take care of you. Are you from New Orleans?" Callie intended to get the whole story from the girl, so she could help her.

"No, I'm from Minnesota."

"Where are your parents?"

"Back there," she said with a shrug. It was obvious that Katie didn't care, or at least it seemed she didn't care. "I ran away."

"Wow, you're a long way from home. How'd you make it all the way here?" Callie asked, amazed.

"We took a bus. My friend Anna and I decided to run away. Her old boyfriend moved to Austin, so we decided to go there. I wanted to go to a warm place, so that was fine with me. I thought it was going to be difficult to get a bus ticket without a parent, so we got fake IDs from a kid at school. It turns out we didn't even need them. I had a job at a burger place, and I had some money hidden away, plus

I'd been taking money a little bit at a time from my mom's purse. Anna had some money in a savings account."

"Why did you want to run away?" Callie couldn't imagine anyone wanting to leave their real parents.

"My stepdad was coming to my room and forcing me to do stuff. I couldn't stop him when I was younger, but when I got old enough, I'd put up a fuss. He still wouldn't stop, and I kept telling my mom. She was mad at me, like it was my fault. She kept saying I was a slut and that I was the problem and slapping me and shit. I think my mom wanted me to leave—I hate her."

Her story made Callie's heart ache. In her imagination, a mother was the ultimate protector. Even though she missed out on having that kind of a relationship with her own mother, she knew that a child was supposed to have a protector. If Uncle Deacon had done anything like that to her, Abel would have killed him—of that, she was certain with every ounce of her being. "What happened in Austin?"

"It was fun—at first. It was like a vacation. In fact, it was probably the first real vacation I've ever been on. My mom never had any money to go anywhere, it was always something we were gonna do. Anna and I stayed at a cheap hotel, ate fast food, and went to bars and danced practically all night. She tracked down her old boyfriend and thought she was going to get back together with him—in her dreams. He already had a new girlfriend. He didn't want anything to do with Anna. Then, her money ran out. I didn't have much cash to begin with. It stopped being fun and started just being shitty."

"I'll bet. How did you live without money?" Callie was intrigued and was hanging on her every word.

"How did you eat? Where did you stay?" prompted Callie.

"We found a shelter for women, and we started begging on the street. But that was hard, too, because it's like every corner had a guy or a couple of people that acted like that was their territory, and they would try to run you off. That was scary. Some of those people were fucked up and crazy mean. And when we would go back to the shelter, some religious person was always all do-good and shit and interrogating you, acting like they were better'n you. Then at night some nasty dyke would be on you. It was as bad as my stepfather. You had to be pushin' them off, like you couldn't really sleep deep. You were always just on the edge."

"I can't even imagine that. How awful. You've been through so much."

"Anna and I started fighting and bitching at each other. She had made up this whole thing where she came to Austin and surprised her old boyfriend, and he was so impressed or something with her that he falls back in love and then it was all—*they live happily ever after.*"

"Yeah, when that didn't happen, I bet she was shattered."

"When she found out he was with some beautiful rich Southern girl or some shit, she lost it and just wanted to go back home. That was all good for her. Her father wasn't trying to have sex with her every night. The only reason she ran away was 'cuz she had this whole thing built up with her boyfriend. We fought about that for a while, then she just gave up and left. I don't even know if she made it back."

"I can find out for you, if you want," Callie offered.

"Yeah, that'd be nice. I mean, it's not like I hate her for leaving. She's still my friend, and I want her to be OK. I shoulda stopped her from coming in the first place, except I was too chickenshit to run away by myself."

"What was it like after Anna left?"

"I got super lonely. I was on a corner begging, and a group of other people showed up. They were Travelers, you know, like gypsies. The girls were complete bitches, and they forced me to go to another corner, but one of the boys followed and started talking to me. He was older, like maybe twenty, and made the other girls stop being such assholes—although they still sucked; they were never nice to me.

"They had all these ways to get money. Mickey was all proud and shit and said they were grifters, whatever that means. I hung out with them some because they were better'n nothing, and they would share their food. They lived in this trailer park and would let me crash there, although, basically the only one who would talk to me was Mickey.

"When I told him I wanted to go to Miami Beach, he was all over it. Those weren't even his people. His group of Travelers were in Mississippi, and he wanted to go back there. So we left and hitched along I-10."

"I didn't even think people hitched rides anymore," said Callie.

"When we were trying to get a ride, we'd hang out at a gas station just before the ramp, and I'd hold up a piece of cardboard with the next big city's name written on it. You know—Houston or New Orleans. I'd look all defenseless and innocent and shit. It was easy to get a ride. We didn't even have to sleep rough. We made it all the way to New Orleans in a day.

"There was this hotel down in the French Quarter that greased up these poles that were holding up their balcony so stupid guys wouldn't try to climb up them when things got wild during Mardi Gras. A big crowd of tourists were milling around watching these guys trying to climb up anyway and slipping down. Everybody was laughing at these idiots making fools of themselves.

"You must be used to that crazy stuff," Katie said.

"I haven't gone to Mardi Gras for a while. I'm always working in the ER. The hospitals are crazy busy during it." Callie missed it. They all used to go and party—her girlfriends, Abel and his friends. René, of course, would be working the girls in the crowd trying to get them to flash their boobs. He would buy these high-grade beads for cheap after the previous year's Mardi Gras was over and save them for the next year. He'd flirt with the girls, tease them, and flaunt his beads. All the girls in the crowd would fight over them. He was such a sleaze, but he was hilarious.

"Mickey and I hung out, got drinks, and walked around all day just watching the weird people and looking, like all the rest of the tourists—I've never seen anything like it. Later, he scored some molly, and we got high. It felt so good, like I loved everybody in the crowd. Whenever anybody said something to me, I completely understood what they meant, not the words exactly, but what was behind the words, what was inside the person. I don't know how long that went on. It all became a blur, then it was night, and we were walking around. I kind of remember we were in this alley, and he was holding me and we were kissing. The next thing I knew, I woke up, and it felt really late. Mickey was gone. I couldn't figure out where I was, and I walked all around trying to find him—maybe he woke up and walked off and then couldn't find the alley again or something. I looked around and went down another really dark street between these two old buildings."

"Didn't anybody tell you not to leave the main streets?" Callie asked, aghast. Every year, people got robbed or murdered down some dark, lonely street in the Quarter during the festival.

"No, it felt safe. All the people were just having fun. I checked out the street and went to the end, and Mickey wasn't there, so I turned around and walked back to the main street, but before I reached it, two guys appeared.

"At first, I was scared, but they were really nice. They were dressed like frat bros, although they kind of had an accent. They were just kids like me, and they asked me whether I needed help. I told them about trying to find Mickey, and they offered to help me look for him. We tried for a while but couldn't find him, so one of the kids said he had a car and that we could go get some more of his friends to help. I was frantic by then—that sounded like a good idea.

"I followed them to their car. It seemed kinda far, and I was so tired. Then, it was just about fifteen minutes in the car to their house, which was this skanky dive. Somehow, they seemed like they would be living in a nicer place—"

"Oh, Katie . . ." interjected Callie. She could see where this was going.

"We went inside, and there were all these guys—gangbangers. It smelled like weed on top of BO on top of a clogged toilet that had just sat there for a week. Most of the men were in wifebeaters with tattoos all over their arms and shoulders. There were some girls, but they looked as nasty as the men, and they were hanging all over the guys.

"When we walked in, they all cheered. You know how your stomach feels when you do something wrong, and you know you're going to get punished? I knew I was in trouble. I could feel it."

"Oh my God." Callie's mouth was hanging open.

"This guy with these big letters tattooed on his face came up to me. He had a capital *M* on one cheek and then an *S* on his other cheek. His neck had *'MS-13'* tattooed around it. He grabbed my arm and said something like, 'C'mon, puta.' I didn't want to go and tried to hold onto one of the boys that brought me, but he just pushed me and said, 'Go on, bitch,' then he laughed.

"The man dragged me into this bedroom in the back and pushed me into a kitchen chair that was just sitting there, like in the middle of the room. He straddled me, and I was pushing him away, but then he pulled out this big knife and told me to stop moving or he would cut me. He had my hair in his hand and was pushing the knife into my scalp—I could feel it digging in. He's like, 'Calm down, puta, I'm not going to hurt you. I'm going to make you feel so good. Open your eyes, open your eyes.' Then he squirted eye drops into both my eyes. It burned. He got off me and took a handful of my hair and threw me on the bed. The bed had these horrible sheets, and he kept pushing my face down into them; they smelled like old piss."

Callie was beside herself; she'd seen and heard terrible things in the ER, but this was the worst. The way Katie was telling it, Callie felt like it was happening to her.

"I could hardly breathe, and then he rolled me over. He kept picking the knife up and pressing it against my throat, then yanking on my pants, then pressing on my neck with the knife, and then pulling on my pants. Then, he ripped my panties off."

"Katie, you don't have to tell me anymore. I'm so sorry." Callie regretted asking her what had happened. She didn't know whether reliving it was helping or hurting her.

"No, I've got to tell someone."

"Then, keep going."

"He was really rough, and he hurt me. It's hard to remember though, it was getting blurry, and I was dizzy. The eye drops must have had something in them. The next thing I remember is two of those gang girls picking me up off the floor and getting me back on the bed. Tattoo Face was gone. I was really limp and floppy. I was kinda going in and out, and the girls were muttering. I felt a sharp jab in my arm, and then it just felt like warm, syrupy melted wax was spreading over me."

"It sounds like they were shooting you up with heroin." It was everywhere. Most of the ODs coming into the ER were smack. The victim thought that they were taking their regular dose, but for some reason the load was extra hot, usually because of some mistake when it was cut, but every now and then, it was spiked with fentanyl.

"When I woke up, I was in this big room with lots of other girls, maybe ten or twelve. Each of us kinda had our own little room. They hung these plastic shower curtains between us—on one side of my room it had pictures of fish on it. I would stare at it and pretend I was a mermaid swimming with the fishes."

"How long were you there?" asked Callie.

"I don't know. A week? A month? It felt like a long time." Katie's eyes stared off into space.

Callie did some calculations in her head. "You were there about three weeks. I don't know how you stood it for so long."

"It felt like a nightmare. I'd go in and out. I'd wake up a bit, and a guy was on top of me. I felt there, but not there, like I was just standing there watching. I remember getting up to pee and walking by these other girls just lying there in their little rooms—gross men coming and going."

"Besides the gang girls, were there other people watching over you?"

"Mostly Tattoo Face. He was like the guy who ran the place. I remember a couple of other men who showed up. I think one was his boss. He ordered Tattoo Face around. The boss guy almost looked like a regular person, but he talked like all of the rest of them."

"How did you escape?"

"I don't remember."

"Oh Katie, I'm so sorry all that happened. I'm glad you made it, and I promise you I'll help you, but I've got to go do my shift. Can I get you anything before I go?"

"No, they'll be coming in to give me something soon. They're bringing me down from all that skag, and it makes me sleepy."

Callie got up and headed to the door but stopped and looked back at Katie. "I'll come by and check on you when I get a break. Get some rest."

CHAPTER

NINE

Growing up in Uncle Deacon's house, they had very few big sit-down meals. Aunt Hen loved her house and decorating it, but she wasn't that interested in slaving away in the kitchen. The food was uninspired, the conversation was superficial with rarely any laughter, and when they were older, they just ate when they were hungry. It was Callie and Abel by themselves, sometimes with René.

Tank's house was different; their Sunday dinners were how meals were meant to be. Tank's mama, Isabelle, knew what it was like for Abel and Callie, and consequently, Sunday dinner became an important fixture. Even after Antoine died, Belle kept it up, making sure that her extended family didn't come apart.

Sometimes Abel and Callie went to church with Isabelle, Tank, and André. Other times, they just showed up right after church. Isabelle expected Callie and Abel to help with the meal as much as she counted on her sons to do their part. They made the meal, then sat down and ate it as a family. They talked about the events of the week and what was happening in the world and in Lacombe. It was never rushed, and they stayed at the table talking long after dessert. After, they'd all pitch in and clean up. It rarely took long. They would meander out into the backyard. Sit in the double swing. Maybe walk down to the dock or sit in the chairs around the firepit, staring off into the bayou, continuing the conversations from dinner with the hum of cicadas in the background. When it was finally time to go, Isabelle would force dishes and packages of food on them to take back home.

About every couple of months, Isabelle had her sons invite the rest of Abel's crew to Sunday dinner. Tank had been reminding the guys all week long that it was that time again. The boys were always bugging Tank or André, wondering when the next dinner invite was going to happen, hoping to shorten the wait.

When Sunday came, Abel and Callie showed first. Callie pushed Abel to be timely. She could see that Isabelle was slowing down and wanted to get there to help her. She loved spending time with Tank's mama; it was the closest relationship she had besides Abel, and she hated to think of Belle starting the cooking without her.

They paused on the front porch, with its haint blue ceiling, and took a moment to take in Isabelle's carefully potted violets, which were flowering, then walked through the front door and went straight to the kitchen, the center of life in the Chevals' home. Reminiscent of a farmhouse, the room had green cabinets and a board ceiling painted white that was held up by sturdy beams. Of course, Isabelle had already started and was halfway through peeling the yams. Callie gave Abel a glare. "I told you we were gonna be late."

"Don't you worry, honey, I put the roast in before church. There's only a few things left to do." Isabelle gave Callie a sweet smile that took over her whole face. She stopped working on the yams and turned to Abel. "Oh, cher, what have you done to yourself?"

"I just hurt my arm doing something for Uncle Deacon. It's a lot better, see?" Abel lifted his arm up and moved it around, putting on a good face.

"Now, you stop that foolin' around. I can see the pain coming out of you. You go sit down in that chair and keep us company while Callie and I finish up."

Abel sat down, looking at Isabelle and taking stock. For the longest time, she had looked the same, in the way that some women never seem to age. Her coffee complected face was locked in a gentle beauty. She was a woman with kind eyes of indeterminate years. But it was as Callie had said the other day: that had suddenly changed. Underneath Isabelle's joy at seeing them, she was subtly diminished. Her face held a certain sadness. Almost like it was poised in the act of falling. After her husband, Antoine, died when his shrimp boat caught on fire, she was strong, caring for her boys and Abel and Callie. But something was different. It could be that age was catching up, and her energy was finally depleted. Or the realization that Thomas and André were grown men, eventually leaving to start their own families. But a part of Abel wondered whether it was his fault, like Callie had said—pulling her sons into the Life, taking them away from the righteous path that Belle had set them on.

As if she could read his mind, Isabelle came over, her hands dusty with flour, and took his face in both her hands. "Now, why are you fretting? I can feel it all the way over there. Don't you worry. Everything is going to be all right. I can see it. Let me and Callie finish up in here, and you go find where Thomas and André have gotten to. Tell 'em to bring the sun tea."

Abel went out looking for the brothers and eventually found them out front talking to Rabbit, Harm, and René. The first thing out of Harmon's mouth was, "Is Callie here yet?"

They all laughed. "Dude, give it a rest. She doesn't like you that way!" Rabbit chimed in.

"Yeah, I hate to break it to you—for the hundredth time. You're in the friend zone," added André.

"Wrong! Someday she's going to realize I'm the perfect guy for her."

Tank and Abel exchanged grins. Tank rolled his eyes. Abel didn't have the heart to tell Harm it was never going to happen. "Hey, let's go in. Isabelle is asking for the tea."

"Wait, I got Callie some flowers. Let me get 'em." Harm jogged back to the truck.

"Aw jeez," groaned Rabbit.

The guys all went inside, and André set the tea on the dining room table. The room was comforting with its dark wooden floors with rag rugs, a white board ceiling like the kitchen, and one red brick wall. Tank and his brother started setting the dining room table, a large plank affair that could easily sit ten. Isabelle liked to make the dinners an event, so they knew to use her good china.

While they were working on ensuring the table was perfect, the rest of the crew were impatiently pacing around and chitchatting to pass the time. It was getting on into the afternoon, so they were famished.

Tank went into the kitchen to see if he could help dinner along. Isabelle instructed him to take out the roast, slice it, and arrange it on the serving platter. She had the pie in the oven, and it would finish while they were eating dinner. Callie and Belle started moving the dishes out to the dining room, while Tank followed with the meat. The women made another trip, then Tank's mama announced it was time to sit down.

The guys made a rush to the chairs, hungrily staring at the meal: rolled pork roast stuffed with a homemade chow-chow of cayenne peppers, garlic, and bacon, baby lima beans cooked with andouille, candied yams, Belle's special macaroni and double cheese with pimento, and a lime shrimp and corn salad to lighten things up. The pecan pie and ice cream were arriving later. The boys were itching to eat, but they all knew to wait until Belle said the blessing.

Isabelle Cheval was a respected hoodoo root doctor and was called upon to conjure frequently by folks in the community. Regularly, she was asked to perform rituals, put together mojo bags, or sooth someone's troubles. Too many times, Abel had seen Belle foretell some event, but he couldn't figure out whether it was magic or just empathy and insight. At the same time, she was a staunch member of the church and had no trouble commingling those two disparate ideas.

She settled back into her seat and reached out and took the hands of Callie and André. André grabbed Abel's hand and so on around the table, ending with Harm reverently grasping Callie's hand as he had engineered it so that he was sitting next to her.

Isabelle cleared her throat. "I give thanks to you, Lord, with all my heart; I will tell of all your wonderful deeds. I will be glad and rejoice in you; I will sing the praises of your name, O Most High. Your blessings upon me are more than I deserve. I thank you today, for as I look around at my life, my children, and my friends, there is so much to be thankful for. Thank you for those rough places in my life, for even they have turned out to be blessings in disguise. You have taken my dark days, my lonely nights, and turned them into light. As long as I have breath, I will praise you.

"Thank you today for this bounteous meal of which we are about to partake. Prepare us for what is coming. Guide and shelter us through the looming storm. You will protect us in the coming dark. For you truly are the blessing in our being.

"Amen," they echoed.

Abel heard the foreboding note at the end of her prayer, sat up straighter, and responded, "Thank you, Lord, for this opportunity for our friends and family to gather and celebrate our lives. We are grateful that we are all healthy and strong. Whatever difficulties we may encounter, we will face together, gathering strength from each other. We will overcome, thanks be to God. Amen."

André reached for the pork, took his helping, and passed it along. The next few minutes were spent handing round plates and dishes. Then dinner passed in a flurry of teasing and happy conversation, everyone eating more than necessary. Isabelle took the time to try to catch up on each person's life. "Harmon, how is your mother?"

"She's doing well. She's got me helping her with the spring cleaning, of course. I've finished all the windows this week. The nagging has just about ended, and I can go back to my normal life." He laughed.

"Have you had time to make any more knives?" Abel asked.

"I'm working on a big bowie knife. I'm putting on scales made from the antlers of that fourteen-point buck I got last fall."

"Can I stop by after we eat and check it out?" asked Rabbit.

"Sure."

Rabbit was a part-time mechanic and could appreciate the steps involved with knife making. He looked like a mechanic, too. Wiry and twitchy, there was usually a cigarette glued between his knuckles, and his fingernails displayed crescents of black grease.

Belle moved on to Rabbit. "Charles, how is your daddy's garage? Are you still helping out?" Isabelle never used their nicknames.

"Yep, my dad lost one of his mechanics, so I've been almost working full-time for the past few weeks."

Tank asked, "How's that Chevelle coming?"

"How's your little sister?" Callie interrupted. She knew she'd better divert Rabbit, or they'd be in for a lengthy discussion on nuts and bolts and zeros to sixties.

"Oh, she's doing awesome. She's coming up to spring break. I think she's going to get straight A's. She's in tenth grade now, you know?" he replied in rapid fire.

They all knew. Rabbit's parents' youngest was a surprise, happening later in their lives. The whole family spoiled her rotten, but she was actually sweet. Rabbit loved on her and was practically another parent to her.

"I heard you guys got into some trouble at The Machine the other day," Callie said, keeping the conversation rolling.

"That was René," André said. "With Henrí. What's the deal with that anyway? You know he's crazy."

"I don't know. He never liked me and was always picking on me. I came up on you guys talking to him, and it flipped me out. He gave me the eyeball, and I made a preemptive strike."

André corrected him. "More like, he made the first move."

"Just leave him be. Your dad even hassled me about it," Abel said.

Callie agreed with him. "Yeah, everybody knows he's a psycho—don't mess with him. I'd rather hear your stories of picking up girls than ones where you're getting punched in the head by Henrí. Speaking of which, did you meet anyone nice that night?" She preferred romantic comedies—just like René's dating life. He was movie star handsome and flirty, so he always had lots of funny stories.

"Oh, I met a nice girl, and we danced and stuff," responded René.

"Yeah . . . and stuff." Rabbit laughed.

"I've got her number. Maybe I'll take her to dinner."

André jumped on that. "Or not."

René always got a little irritated when they ganged up on him. "Well, at least I'm getting some action. It's better than watching you losers. Rabbit, you didn't even dance with anybody. All you did was talk to people all night long."

Callie moved on with her romance progress checks. "What's going on with you, Tank? Have you met anyone new?"

"He's got the hots for a girl at church," André gleefully answered for Tank, always acting the little brother.

"Yeah, her name's Kisha. She's in the choir," Tank replied laconically.

"All this time, I thought you were going because you liked the sermons," joked Isabelle. "How did I miss that? What about you, Abel? When are you going to get interested in some nice young girl? Isn't it about time you started settling down?" The boys' love lives were one of her and Callie's favorite topics.

"Well, now that you ask, I did go out with a girl the other night."

"What?" exclaimed Callie. "When were you going to tell me?"

"With who?" Tank asked, as amazed as Callie. Abel hadn't mentioned a thing. "When did you have time to do that?"

"It's an imaginary girl. He's been taking too many of the pain pills," said Rabbit.

"Do you guys remember our waitress the other night— at The Machine?"

"Wow, that girl? When did you ask her? I didn't see anything."

"I remember! She was hot," was René's assessment.

"I went over to The Machine and asked her out to breakfast after her shift. She's divorced and has a little boy named Owen."

"Well, do you like her?" Callie demanded.

"Yeah, we talked for like two hours." Abel's expression was a little bit moony. "We're going out again."

"I'm not done with you yet, Abel." Callie mock scolded him. "I'm going to get every detail out of you tonight."

Isabelle laughed. "And then I'm going to get it all from her tomorrow."

"Hey, is that pie ready yet?" broke in André, trying to change the subject before his mama and Callie started in on him.

"Wait! Why doesn't anybody ever ask me about my love life?" complained Rabbit.

"What love life?" said Harm. "When was the last time you had a date?"

"Dude, that hurts . . . coming from you."

Isabelle, her curiosity piqued, asked, "What's going on with you, Charles?"

"I'm engaged."

There was dead silence at the table, then everybody started talking at once. Finally, they calmed down enough to get the story. "It's my second cousin, Crystal. I saw her at our big family reunion a couple of years ago, and she was all grown up. We've been texting and calling each other since."

"Dude, why didn't you tell me?" asked Harm, his feelings obviously hurt.

"I don't know. We were just talking for a long time, and then somewhere, it turned into something different. I don't even know when, gradual like."

André had a funny look on his face. "Isn't that like incest or something? I thought you weren't allowed to marry your cousin."

"Jeez." Rabbit groaned. "Second cousins. Perfectly legal. We checked."

Years of these Sunday dinners and nothing interesting in their romantic lives, then in one dinner Abel, Tank, and Rabbit pop up with women—and Rabbit getting married! "When's the wedding?"

"This summer. We're gonna move into the apartment over my dad's shop."

The table erupted again in a flurry of discussion. They chattered happily back and forth, blindsided by the news. Rabbit had flown under the radar; they never saw it coming. Isabelle got the pie and ice cream, while Callie pumped Rabbit for more details. They talked, happy for Rabbit, and ate till they couldn't any longer. Finally, they slowed down, and Isabelle suggested they move out to the yard.

"Mama, you go out and sit. We'll clean up," Tank said. "It'll take us ten minutes. You go out and sit with Abel. He's no good with his hurt arm anyway."

Belle and Abel went out to the back, but neither were ready to sit, so they continued on down to the dock. Tank's pirogue was loosely tied to the pier, gently rocking in the breeze, and every now and then knocking up against an old tire fixed to the side of the dock. Isabelle broke the silence. "What's troubling you, cher? You think I don't know what you and my boys been doing all these years? You don't think I can't tell you're hurt worse than some trip and fall helping your uncle?"

"You never said anything."

"What am I going to say to three grown men? I taught you all right from wrong a long time ago. You all have good hearts—I know it. You had to do what you had to do when your uncle went away."

"Maybe Thomas and André would have done something different if I hadn't got them mixed up in my business."

"From the day Thomas laid eyes on you, he was going to do what you were doing. You two were tied at the hip. I couldn't even stop him the first time you two ran off. And André was going to do what his big brother did. It was lucky I could hold him off till he got out of school. Y'all were a package tied up with a bow. No. There was no stopping it.

"When I look at you, I see evil around you, like spilled paint dripping down the air you walk through. But when I look in you, I feel the good down deep, and I feel the steel. God's got a purpose for you, and he's been preparing you. He's put you in the forge and been pounding on you with his hammer and hardening you in the cool water. All your friends and family have been tempering you, softening you just enough so that you won't shatter when put to the test."

"You're making me out to be some hero."

"No, you are a regular person. But every now and then, one of those regular people get called on. And God does his homework, gettin' 'em ready to fight Satan. I don't know what's coming, but I can sense it. I can smell it like meat on the turn.

"My boys, all my boys, are good. I know it, or they wouldn't be allowed in my house. I've got faith in our Lord Jesus; we live the good news. Jesus sat with us at dinner. But his Father now is Old Testament angry and preparing his righteous soldiers. The battle—"

"Hey, what are y'all so serious about?" yelled André, cutting off Isabelle and leaving Abel standing there with an open mouth.

Abel and Isabelle walked back down the dock to meet up with everybody. Abel's expression was distant, his mind caught up in worry about Isabelle. Callie was right—something was going on with Belle. She was always quietly and unshakably faithful in a web of the church, nature, and her hoodoo rites and rituals. But he'd never heard her go on like that. Ever. He was going to have to talk with Callie and Tank. Maybe there was something wrong with her. Maybe she was depressed.

Tank interrupted his thoughts. "Hey, it's getting chilly out. Let's go light up the pit and sit for a while."

They all meandered over to the firepit, taking seats in the odd collection of chairs while Tank and André puttered around getting the fire lit. Callie sat down on the double swing hanging from some ancient beams, her favorite spot. Harm ran to sit next to her like it was the last seat in musical chairs. She sighed, her mouth settling into a slight smile.

The conversation resumed from dinner, a little bit quieter for some reason and a touch more serious. Harm asked Callie how the ER was going. They broke off after a while, Isabelle forcing them all back through the kitchen so she could provide them with leftovers while insisting that the food would go bad before she and the boys ate it all. No one turned down her offers, and Tank and André sadly watched the delicious remnants from dinner go out the front door.

CHAPTER

TEN

O n the short drive back to their house, Callie brought up Isabelle's blessing before dinner. "What was the deal with her prayer? It got dark. Then you answered her blessing with one of your own that sounded like you knew what she was referring to."

"I was just trying to say that if she was worried about the future, then don't, because we are all in this together. Maybe it was also a little bit of me trying to reassure myself. I'm uncertain about the future, too, I guess."

"What were you guys talking about on the dock?"

"She was actually trying to make me feel better. She said she could tell I was in turmoil or something like that. She even brought up that she knew what Tank and I have been doing all these years and that it was OK. But then she got scary. She started rambling about Jesus and the devil and some big battle against evil that's coming." He paused for a moment. "I'm really worried about her."

"Maybe we should get Tank and André and sit down with her and talk—see what's going on. Kind of like an intervention," Callie said.

"That's exactly what I was thinking." His thoughts shifted to Callie. She had seemed distracted after dinner. He wasn't just worried about Belle. "Callie, what's going on?"

They had arrived at home but were still in the truck, not ready to get out with all the loose threads unresolved. Callie sat quietly for a minute and then replied, "I think I'm upset because Katie reminds me of me. Like she didn't have a lot of security growing up and had to fend for herself. We didn't exactly have parents loving on us, and she didn't, either. I had you at least, watching over me, but she didn't have anybody. Even her mom didn't have her back."

"Well, you guys saved her life. You helped her. There is a limit to how much you can do and how much you can do for the people coming through the ER. You can't fix all their problems. If you can't compartmentalize this stuff, it's going to eat you up."

"I know that. This situation is different though. And Katie is going to be OK—she's pretty tough. The social worker got her into a shelter for battered women for the time being, and they're going to get her set up in a foster home."

"Why don't they send her back to her family?"

"Are you kidding? Her stepdad was abusing her, and her mom wasn't doing anything about it. Katie told me there was no way she was going back. The social worker even called her mama, and the bitch said that it was better that Katie was gone. Can you believe that?"

"Man, that's cold." He had trouble picturing a real mother doing that to her kid, at least the mothers in his imagination.

"They are going to place her with a family that works with older kids."

"That sounds good. Then you can walk away and stop worrying about her."

"No—I told her I would help her and check on her, and she could call me and stuff, like I was her big sister. You could help her, too."

Truthfully, Abel wasn't really feeling it. But here they were, still talking about the girl, and he cared that Callie cared. "Yeah—sure, I'll help out."

"And I wish you could do something about those MS-13 guys. Kidnapping and raping basically children. It makes my heart hurt. They still have those other girls captive, and it doesn't look like the police have a clue."

"Yeah, it pisses me off, too. I'll think about it."

Seemingly mollified, Callie finally got out of the car. Abel slid out but not before grabbing the bag of leftovers that Callie forgot to take. There was no way he was leaving those behind.

Abel was sitting across from Deacon at the junk shop. He could have talked with Deke on the phone, but his uncle was paranoid and would never impart any info. If he did manage to get Deke on the phone, he would usually talk in some obscure code that would force you to track him down and have him explain it. Usually, the best you could do was to get him to agree to meet someplace, and even then, he would reply vaguely. "I'll meet you at the restaurant later on." You just had to know he meant Red's Fish Camp, his favorite place.

Abel skipped the appetizers and went right to the meat. "So did you come up with a decent score for us?"

"Well, I did find more information about MS-13 and that gun deal I was talking about. My info was wrong—I knew it didn't make sense. Turns out that MS-13 is buying guns from the Aryans, not the other way around. They basically put in a big order, and the AB is getting it together. My source figures about two to three weeks till the deal goes down." Deke leaned back with a satisfied look on his face.

"How sure are you that it's solid?" asked Abel, still skeptical after Deke's weak check shop intel.

"This came straight from the Brotherhood, a guy I met in the joint. He's AB, but we got tight. We took the same business classes, and we did homework together—I shit you not. We still get a beer and talk now and then."

"Hmmm." It seemed plausible to Abel. Up at Angola, things were different. A White guy didn't have to be a member of the Aryan Nation to be safe. There were enough guys floating around from the Dixie Mafia, even the present-day, watered-down version, that there was a familiar faction that Deke could join. The Dixie felons were just as vicious as the AB. They were a smaller, tighter group, and they had a who-you-know, not a what-you-believe-in policy. Joining in with the prison Dixie Mafia group wasn't a life sentence like committing to the Aryans, plus Deacon knew many of them before he went in. In Angola, the AB and the Dixie Mob were aligned, a special relationship like the US and England. And it wasn't like they were that different to begin with. The Mob was just about as racist as the Aryans, especially the old-school Dixie thugs.

"My guy said that the transaction is big, real big. He thinks these New Orleans MS are positioning themselves to be the middleman between the AB and all the Mexican and Black gangs that the skins refuse to deal with directly. From here, they can move the guns to all the MS cliques around the country. There was some talk that they were also trading with the Mexican mafia and maybe the cartels, too. Apparently, the MS made some kind of pact or deal with the Mexican mafia way back when. It was called the Southern Pact or the Sureño Alliance or some shit.

"Also—check this out. He said the MS clique was trying to get a minigun, that motorized machine gun used on military helicopters. You know, the one the door gunner uses? It just tears shit up. Apparently, the gun goes for more than a quarter mil. Real hard to get. Only two companies in the US make them, and the government makes sure nobody can get them because they can cause massive casualties. Turns out, the AB has a line on a guy that is making them in his shop, dark net, black market stuff. Costs fourteen thousand to make, but the Aryans can turn them around for big bucks. The cartel wants them to fight back against the Mexican government."

"Holy shit!" said Abel, thinking about the upside.

"So that's the deal. My buddy is going to give me a heads up when its close. I'm not sure he's gonna be able to deliver the location, so your crew is going to have to start watching the AB close and try to figure out where they keep the guns and then catch them when they start moving.

"Those bastards are running a gun range out in the country. Makes sense, doesn't it? I've got the address written down here somewhere, and I'll give it to you before you leave."

That wasn't all that Abel needed. "What about the MS-13? What do you have on them?"

"Not much. They hang out at this bar near the Ninth Ward called El Luz Loco. That's The Crazy Light to you, since you didn't finish high school. Who the fuck knows what that means? Anyway, I don't know much else. You're going to have to put your whole crew on tracking them down. You probably have three weeks before you hit 'em."

"Oh, and Abel? Just hit the MS before the deal goes down and take their cash. Stay away from the guns and the AB or I'm dead."

Callie had convinced Abel to go with her while she visited Katie at her new foster home. Abel didn't really mind—after all Callie's talk, he was interested to see what the girl was like. Callie and Abel met the foster parents, and they seemed like decent people.

Katie showed them around the house and her bedroom, the place in a bit of disarray, but in a happy way, then dragged them outside to her new favorite place, a tree swing. The backyard had a mature live oak that was perfect for the wooden swing. Katie climbed into it, and Abel dragged over a lawn chair for Callie and found one for himself so they could sit and chat with Katie while she swung gently back and forth.

Callie was worried that Katie would be shy around Abel, but that wasn't the case at all. She took to Abel immediately, and soon they were chattering away like best friends. At first, they were just talking about her new situation, but then Katie moved the conversation toward her time in captivity.

"Did Callie tell you about what happened to me?" she asked Abel.

"Yes, she told me most of what happened. It was terrible, and I'm glad you got out. Do you remember anything about when those guys took you to that house? Like something you saw?"

"I told this to the police, but I don't think they even wrote it down. After those two guys found their car, and we were driving for a while, I saw a street sign that said 'Galvez', then we passed these big train tracks. Like twenty tracks right in a row with box cars all lined up and shit."

"What else?" asked Abel.

"We did a few turns, and then we ended up at that house."

"Do you remember which way you turned after the train tracks?"

"I'm not sure. The area looked kinda poor and beat up."

Abel had hoped for some better information. This was pretty vague. No wonder the police didn't bother with it. "What was the color of the house?"

"I couldn't tell 'cuz it was dark. We had to walk up some stairs to a porch to get in the door. I don't remember anything else."

"What about the other place where they kept you? Do you recall how you got there?"

"No, I just woke up there, then I remember these dreams of men on top of me, and then I woke up in the hospital. There was one time I was more awake. This guy was slapping me, and he turned me around and was choking me from behind, and then he did it that way. I looked up, and Tattoo Face was standing there watching."

Katie had spoken nonchalantly, but Abel was doing a slow burn inside. Seeing Katie at sixteen was reminding him of Callie as a teenager. Deep in his head, he was conflating the two.

Callie spoke. "I don't remember you telling me that before."

"One of the girls tried to talk to me, but Tattoo Face punched her. She's still there," lamented Katie, her face screwed up, close to tears.

We'll see about that, Abel said to himself. It was different hearing it directly from her.

Katie's foster parents came out and politely suggested that it was time for dinner. They invited Callie and Abel to dinner, but Callie understood that they needed space to attend to Katie, so she graciously declined before Abel had a chance to take them up on the offer.

On the drive home, Callie once again asked Abel if he and his crew could do something about the other girls still held captive.

Abel had been ruminating on that since hearing Katie tell the story. "Yeah, I'm going to try. Those pieces of shit make me sick. I've already been talking to Deacon, trying to get some street information about them. He gave me a good lead."

"For once, he's doing something good for someone else," Callie grouched.

"Well, not exactly," Abel said, leaving it at that.

CHAPTER

ELEVEN

T he crew was on Abel's back porch drinking beers from a cooler. The perfume of the bayou washed over them, filling their nostrils with the scent of grass, fish, and a tinge of sulfur. An outsider would have turned up their nose, but to the boys, it smelled like home. Looking toward the bayou, a shadow of black water could be seen through the trees.

They had come over to Abel's house after dinner, and the sun had yet to go down, so the mosquitos weren't bothering them too much. The guys had been catching up, bullshitting around. André ran both hands through his hair, fluffing out his Afro, then spoke up. "Abel, did you get a chance to talk to Deacon?" The rest of the guys went quiet.

"Yeah, I had a good discussion with him. I busted his chops a bit about his intel. He got kinda pissed—you know Deacon. And after he calmed down, I told him we were all getting uncomfortable with the current state of affairs, um, the fact that the jobs weren't paying as much and we weren't getting enough work."

"I doubt he took that any better," interjected Tank, a skeptical expression on his lean face.

"No, actually, he handled that OK. I explained we almost were at the point that we couldn't make ends meet and like, what was the point? We're facing prison time if something goes wrong and barely making more than a regular dude working the docks. He did say some shit about us being spoiled millennials, but I threw it back at him.

"Eventually, we started talking about all the different things we could do, but in the end, we were right back at what we do best—robbery."

"How does that help us? Same old shit," grumped André. "We gotta up the take and drop the risk."

"Yeah, and that's when it got interesting," Abel said. "René, did your daddy talk to you yet?"

"You mean about the business? Yeah."

Abel had known his cousin since they were little, and he could hear the bitter note in his voice. He used to sound whiny when his feelings were hurt by Deacon. Now, he just sounded resigned. "Well, Deke started talking about retiring. Said he was getting old, and the business needed younger management, meaning we take it over." *No need to get into Deacon not handing his business over to René,* Abel thought.

"Just like that? We run all his crews and fencing and shit?" Rabbit said excitedly, dollar signs in his eyes.

"Haha, not so fast. There would have to be a transition period. Plus, we got to pay him off."

"How long, and how much?" Tank asked, beating his brother to the punch.

"Deke thinks the transition period would take about two years, and we gotta get him like 500K on top of his usual or feed him a bigger cut along the way."

"Knowing my dad, he'll probably want a pension on top of all that—bleeding us forever—till he's dead," said René, frustration distorting his handsome features. He wasn't immune from criticizing his daddy, but it bugged him if someone else did it.

André, leaning back in his chair and pulling on his bushy natural hair, said, "How does Deacon think we are going to come up with half a mil to buy him out, given the shit scores he's been delivering?"

Abel continued to recount his discussion. "Deke promised to up his game. He was getting pumped about quitting and said he was gonna find us bigger and better scores. To be honest, guys, I'm not sure he's got what it takes or the connections to get us higher paying gigs anymore. I think we have to start finding our own work. He did say he would hook me up with all his sources and with the people on his pad. Over the next two years, he committed to tying me into his crews and bringing me up to speed on the fencing side of the business.

"He thought each of you guys could start your own crews if you wanted and expand that way. I'm not sure how y'all see the future, but I don't want to break up the crew. I trust you guys with my life. I say we stay tight. We either build or recruit more stand-alone crews. Eventually, we start taking his twenty-percent cut off the other crews and keeping one hundred percent of what we get out of our own scores, plus of course, the margin on the fencing operation. Do any of you want to run your own crews?" asked Abel.

There was a chorus of nos.

"We all know Deacon can be a bullshitter. Has he come back to you with any potential work?" Rabbit asked, picking at his grease-encrusted fingernails and speaking without thinking about René's feelings.

"A'write, so check it. Deacon's prison buddy in the Aryan Brotherhood clued him in on an arms deal going down with the MS-13."

"The AB are buying guns from spics?" Rabbit sounded skeptical.

"No, the other way around. Apparently, they're buying guns to arm their cliques all over the country, or they're fronting for the cartels, not sure which, but it makes sense. It's supposed to be a huge deal. Deke's informant is saying that there is a minigun in the deal. That alone is 250K plus.

"He insisted that this is the type of score he's gonna bring us in the future and that we ought to do this job. He suggested we hit them before they buy the guns, while they're still sitting on the cash. And coincidently, these are the same guys Callie just told me about."

"How does she know about these guys before we do?" asked Tank. Abel related the horrific details about Katie and how upset Callie was. He described Tattoo Face and what his ink represented.

Surprisingly, Harm was the first one to speak. "I'm in. Let's take those motherfuckers." The rest of the guys knew he probably didn't care about the girl, but Callie was upset about the MS assholes, so Harm was onboard. The fact that he even spoke said he was all in.

"Aren't those MS guys crazy psychos? Like, cut-off-your-head types?" Tank was all for big scores but also weighing the risks. Listening to his brother, André, who was always harping about risk versus reward had rubbed off.

"Yeah, but if we hit the other side and take the guns from the skinheads, we'll need a truck and the time to load the guns. We'll have to fence them and take the loss. Plus, who would you rather have after you, the AB or Central American shitheads that are fish out of water here in New Orleans?" replied Abel.

"He wasn't saying do the AB over the MS-13. He was saying don't do any of this insanity," clarified André.

"Well, just be glad I'm not saying we hit the meet and take both ends," Abel joked. "Look, I'm not going to force you guys to do this. I'm just thinking that this is the kind of deal we need to get ourselves set for the future. It'll go a long way toward buying out Deacon. Plus, it's the kind of target that you don't feel bad about ripping off. It's like we're doing something good and killing two birds with one stone. We can cripple these asswipes and find out where they've got those girls and get them loose, too."

"You know, I want that big money but also want those pieces of shit gone," Rabbit said vehemently. "That little girl coulda been my sister. That's sick."

René hadn't weighed in yet. Usually, his cousin was in as soon as he heard the dollar potential. Abel looked him in the eye. "What do you think, René?"

"The money is right. Let's put these assholes out of business."

Abel turned to André; he was the hold out since Tank would do whatever the group decided. "André, yeah, this is really dangerous. We just have to identify all the shit that can go wrong and then figure out how to deal with it. That's what you're good at. Let's do the work, scout 'em out, and build a plan, and if y'all don't think we've got it covered, then we'll pull the plug."

André thought it over for a minute. "OK, that makes sense. That's too much money not to at least try to get it."

"Yeah," said Tank, closing and opening his hands and splaying out his long fingers a couple of times, "I agree with my brother."

Abel stood up and went to the cooler and tried to open it with his bad arm without thinking. He grimaced. The damn thing was getting better, but the wrong move sometimes shot a pain down his arm and up into his neck. He continued, forcing himself to open the lid. He grabbed another beer and popped the top off with the opener screwed to the railing of the deck.

"That's it, then. I heard that we all are good with eventually taking over Deke's business." He handed the beer to Tank and reached in and grabbed another for himself. "Agreed?"

Tank nodded, and André said, "Agreed." Harm and Rabbit raised their beers.

"Sounds good, Cuz," replied René with a neutral tone that was slightly less than enthusiastic.

Abel kept going. "André, you are going to find us more scores. Good jobs. High money, low risk. Ones that aren't going to get us shot. Do you think you can handle that?"

André patted his 'fro, making sure it was perfect, then looked at each guy, ending with Abel. "Yeah, I think I can. I've already got some ideas."

"OK, that's what I figured. Now, let's talk about the short term." Abel noticed that Rabbit had killed his Abita. He walked over to the cooler and pulled out another, popped the top, and turned and handed it to him. "Next, we're going to take those MS sons of bitches. Send 'em back to Cali, broke-back motherfuckers.

"We are going to hit 'em in front of the deal, so the AB doesn't get too pissed—we can't let them make the connection to us. We can't have both of them after us. No way we can handle that. Deacon thinks we got three weeks to put this together, but we don't know for sure.

"Harm, you and Rabbit are going to find out where the skinheads have the guns. Deacon told me where the Aryans hang out—they have a gun range out in the sticks. You'll be watching them, trying to figure out who's in charge, where they have the weapons stashed. We need a heads up for when the deal is about to go down.

"Maybe you can go over there and do some shooting. Hell, you two resemble AB to begin with. It should be easy. We sure as shit can't have Tank and André hanging out round there." Abel laughed.

"What about me?" asked René.

"Oh, I got a special job for you. Right up your alley. Your daddy found out the name of the bar down in the city where the MS bangers drink. You're going to hang out there and get the skinny on them. You know, do the shit you always do. Dance with some of their women, talk to some of the soldiers. Be discrete, just get background. You love that shit." René grinned.

"What about the rest of us?" asked Tank.

"You, me, and André are going to hang out outside the bar and track these bastards back to their nest. I got some landmarks from that girl Katie. These fuckers have a house somewhere in the Florida area, you know—Ninth Ward, east of the train yard. I checked it out with Google Earth, André—you should be proud of me."

"So, while René is in the bar dancing, we hang out outside watching? How do we know when an MS-13 punk comes out? They could be anybody," André asked.

Abel had had a head start thinking it through. "Right, but René is inside trying to identify guys with MS-13 tattoos. Especially that piece of shit, Tattoo Face. Whenever one of those guys with MS-13 ink leaves, René is going to text me. Then, one of us is going to follow him. We'll all have our own trucks. If they don't go up toward the Florida area, then we break off and come back to the bar. We'll be in constant communication on our phones—in a three-way call all night."

"That'll work," said Tank.

"We have two to three weeks to figure out where they're located and who the head dudes are. Map out all their sites—figure out where the girls are. Learn as much as we can so we can stay ahead of 'em. We want to know who the leaders are, what's the hierarchy, what are they driving—all that shit. Maybe they got some drug houses, too. If they do, we can hit those as well."

"If we figure out where the girls are being held, are we going to tell the police?" André asked.

"Naw, we gotta wait till after we hit 'em. If the police get on them, that might stop the gun deal, then we can't get their cash," said Rabbit. "Obviously . . ."

"Right, but if we decide that we can't hit 'em for the money before the deal with the AB, then we drop a dime on them with NOPD and have them swoop in and free the girls," said Abel. He wasn't going to walk away without doing something about the girls no matter what happened.

Hearing Katie describe her ordeal had made too deep of an impression. "I think that's it. Are you guys up for this?"

There was a round of assent.

"Yeah," said Harm, "that's enough talking. Let's get hammered."

CHAPTER

TWELVE

R abbit and Harm were excited about their mission to get the lowdown on the AB. While the MS-13 was new to them, the Universal Aryan Brotherhood was not. The UAB was familiar to people on the other side of the law in the South, because in truth, they were primarily criminals. The public saw them as racists with a white supremacist agenda, but the reality was that they were a for-profit business, driven by greed like any other organized crime organization.

The "Brand" or AB was a ruthless group with the motto "Blood in—Blood out," meaning a person had to kill or maim to become a member, and the only way out was to be killed yourself. Rabbit and Harm should have been intimidated by that, but they'd grown up with a few guys who were now AB, and most of them were dumber than rocks and were pussies when they were kids. So they figured they could hang around them without drawing attention to themselves and weren't that worried. Hell, they actually were prime candidates to be AB, since they both resembled redneck peckerwoods, even though they weren't believers in the AB's bullshit.

They were sitting with André at his computer getting some background on the gun range the Aryans were operating out in the country. According to Deke, it was the base of their operations in the area. André had pulled up a Google Earth image of the compound, north of Covington.

"The range is along this dirt road, off of 437. Probably the signs will say 'North Lee Road,'" André said. He pointed to a thin brown line penetrating a large green area on the screen. "Look how much wild area they have behind the range—no problem for stray rifle rounds."

Rabbit bent over André's shoulder to look closer. "Good, there's only one way in to the place."

"Zoom in," ordered Harm. "I want to see the layout of the compound."

André moved the mouse and scrolled the wheel, diving the image into the gun range. The screen went blurry and then crystallized. They could see a parking lot fronting a building on the right side of the road and a cleared area on the left, which was obviously the outdoor rifle range. Behind the first building on the right side was another parking lot with a bigger structure that appeared to be a warehouse or garage of some sort.

"André, did you find out anything else on these guys?" asked Harm.

"I found their business license and saw some online reviews, but I don't think that's helpful. Oh, and the range allows walk-ons. You don't have to be a member or anything." He laughed abruptly. "One of the reviews said that the clerk at the range was argumentative—so he's probably your typical skinhead asshole. Harm, you and he will be best buds—maybe you should let Rabbit do all the talking."

They all laughed.

"So what's the plan, Harm?" asked Rabbit.

"Let's go back to my house and pick up my AR15 and Glock, then run over to your place and get your Sig.

We can go up after lunch, scout the place out, and see if they'll let us shoot. You can suck up to the clerk and make friends," Harm said, chuckling.

Almost at the range, Harm and Rabbit were finalizing the details. "Basically, we're just trying to figure out if the Nazis have the guns—right?" asked Rabbit.

"We need to know in advance that the skins have the guns ready because that means the MS-13 probably has the money in place for the deal."

They reached the entrance road and turned. The parking lot showed up on the right, and they pulled in and parked. "This place looks legit, all cleaned up and painted and shit. I expected nothing less of the Nazis," said Rabbit, snidely.

They got out and removed their guns from the black toolbox spanning the bed of Harm's truck underneath his rear window. "Listen, I'm going to hang back, and you do all the talking to the clerk. Tell him we want to take turns shooting on the long range with the AR. I'm going to act like a stupid redneck."

"Shouldn't be hard," said Rabbit.

"Fuck you," shot back Harm.

They went into the range office, which doubled as a gun store. There were pistols and rifles displayed on the walls and a glass counter that had scopes and various other weapon accessories. A shelf unit in the center of the lobby had stacks of ammo of various calibers. The clerk behind the counter did look like a neo-Nazi. He had a scowl on his face, the edge of a tattoo peeking above the collar of his polo shirt, and a shiny head. But contrary to the review on the internet, his face broke into a big grin when he saw them. "What can I do for you gentlemen?"

Rabbit replied, "We were wondering whether we could get on the rifle range and shoot my buddy's AR." He smiled just like the clerk. "We've got a little bet going—see who's better out past three-hundred yards. He beats me up close but doesn't think I can kick his ass on the long shot. Man, you guys have a nice place here. How long you been open? I bet you love working here. You can shoot all the time."

Jeez, thought Harm, *he's going to ask him out in a minute.*

"Oh, about three years. My bet is on your friend. He's got that killer look in his eyes."

"Aw man, another nonbeliever." Rabbit sighed. "We're going to need some targets and forty rounds of two-twenty-three for the AR. Do you have any eighteen by twenty-four Splatterburst targets? Those are cool."

"OK, two outdoor range fees, two boxes of two-twenty-three, and a pack of big Splatterburst—that's going to be $145.97 plus tax."

Rabbit turned to Harm. "Your turn to pay. I paid for lunch."

"Lunch was fourteen dollars, asshole," Harm said, but he reached into his pocket and pulled out a roll of twenties.

After handing Harm his change, the clerk said, "OK, walk down the dirt road—the long range is on the left. You should find the range officer sitting on his ass, smoking. He's a former jarhead drill instructor, and if you screw around, he'll run you off the range. Steiner does NOT have a sense of humor."

They walked out and stopped by the truck to pick up some binoculars. Harm's AR had a scope, but this would give the other guy eyes on the target, facilitating immediate results. It was a short walk to the range where they met Steiner who had a hand-rolled cigarette drooping from his lip. Steiner tossed the butt, picking fragments of tobacco off his tongue, and gave them the range rules. The shooting area was roughly enclosed by a fence, and the range officer closed the gate behind Harm and Rabbit, then flipped over a sign that indicated that the course was in use. He went back to his seat and tipped it back to lean against the wall. "A'write, boys, go set your targets."

The guys walked down range and clipped their paper targets on a couple of plywood target frames, each marked with a spray-painted three. "OK, I'm going to kick your ass first and make a good show for the Marine, and then we'll tell the guy we're going to go shoot our pistols. You know—give you a second chance. We'll take the long way around and check out that barn," said Harm.

"Yeah, with this guy in the chair and the clerk up front, looks like we can walk all over this place, and neither'll have a clue."

They got back to the shooting station and set up the AR15 on the bench rest. Harm took the first turn. He made five shots to get calibrated and shot ten more times, the splatter targets lighting up greenish-yellow blotches wherever the bullet hit, several in the ten-ring. Rabbit was ribbing Harm constantly, hoping to throw him off his aim, but Harmon was unshakable.

Rabbit took his turn. Harm laughed every time Rabbit completely missed the whole target. Afterward, they walked down to the targets, and Harm said, "I'll let my target speak for itself."

"Yeah, well, next time, we're racing our dirt bikes. We'll see how you do then," Rabbit replied lamely.

They went back to the shooting station and picked up their gear, the boys kidding each other. "Yeah, you may have me with the rifle, but I'm going to get you on the pistol range next," said Rabbit, making sure the range officer overheard. He walked over to the Marine and shook his hand. "Thank you, sir. I bet you could nail the ten-ring every time," he said unctuously.

"Yup," was the laconic reply, then he spit onto the floor just to the right of Rabbit's foot.

Harm and Rabbit let themselves out of the gate and walked across the road to the parking lot in front of the warehouse building that resembled a metal barn. The range officer was out of view, the rear wall of the shooting station blocking his sight. "That ole bastard almost spit on my foot," Rabbit complained.

"Man, this place is dead. I thought it was a hotbed of Nazis," observed Harm.

"They probably all have jobs during the day, you know making pretzels or some shit. This place only needs about two people to run it," said Rabbit, his head on a swivel, making sure nobody was watching them. "Maybe they only come here for meetings and such." The parking lot was empty except for a beaten-down box truck with some washed-out lettering on the side. Rabbit could just make out the word *Produce*.

They peered into the gloom of the metal barn, the big double doors wide open. There was an empty space in front of the doors, big enough to park the box truck. In the back was a rough wall, unpainted, just the gray of drywall. There were two doors inset, one with an oblong window adjacent, the other with *MEN* stenciled on it—it looked like an office and bathroom.

The building seemed empty on first look with no obvious crates of weapons. Harm took a couple of steps into the structure so he could see into the dark corners next to the main doors.

"Holy shit!" he exclaimed. The minigun was sitting on a tripod right out in the open in the corner, not even covered up.

Rabbit had followed Harm into the warehouse. "Wow, these guys didn't even hide it. They either are massively overconfident or just stupid. That's all we need to see— let's go!"

They stepped back out of the structure, the change from the dim building to the bright light blinding them.

"Hey! What the fuck are you doing?"

Rabbit jumped. "Shit!" He turned to see a beefy man, who had just come around the side of the warehouse, dragging a blue tarp.

Guess they're not stupid, Harm thought. *We just got lucky; this dude was in the process of covering up the gun.*

The man wasn't a skinhead. He had a full shock of straight black hair, a bowl cut, probably done by his dear old Nazi daddy. But for certain—full-blooded AB. He had a big, black *'1-2'* tattooed right over his Adam's apple and the word *'Aryan'* inked down his right forearm and *'Brotherhood'* marked down his left. Rabbit figured all the guy needed was a pencil thin mustache, and he would look like Moe from The Three Stooges and Hitler got together and made a baby. Instead of the mustache though, he had a cluster of pimples erupting above his lip, ripe and ready to burst. Rabbit started to babble. "We were just over at the outdoor range. My friend and I had a shooting match. He won. Man, that old sergeant over there sure is a piece of work—"

Harm interrupted. "Now I'm going to kick his ass on the pistol range—thought this was the place."

The man eyed them suspiciously. "The indoor range is in the back of the main office. How could you miss that?"

Rabbit had calmed down. "I don't think anybody was shooting up there. I guess we didn't notice. We were busy buying ammo and targets and getting directions from the clerk."

"Get on up there. This is private property back here—members only," ordered the man in the tone taken by all assholes engorged by a speck of power.

"Sorry, sir." *Maybe this was the clerk that the internet review was referencing, the argumentative one,* thought Harm. They headed toward the office, the dickhead standing in front of the warehouse and watching them the whole way.

They spent another half hour on the indoor range, and on the way out, Harm noticed a neatly dressed man talking to the friendly clerk. As he and Rabbit got closer, Harm could hear him giving what sounded like instructions. It was only a snippet, but it was something about closing early and getting ready. It wasn't like they could stop and listen exactly, but he strained to hear more. The man saw their interest and abruptly stopped talking. He walked around to the back of the counter and popped the cash register open. He drew out an indeterminate amount of cash and stared at Harm. "Y'all come back now," he said. It didn't really sound like an invitation.

At the truck, Harm stood in the bed while Rabbit handed up the weapons. He pulled the leftover ammo boxes from one of his cargo pockets and tossed them up to his buddy. "Man, got a little chilly there at the end. Do you think that was one of the AB bosses?"

"Dude—keep it down!" Harm hissed. He wished that Rabbit had a little closer rein on his mouth. "We can talk on the way back."

Rabbit contritely hung his head and climbed up into the cab, looking slightly embarrassed. He knew he had a motormouth. They peeled out of the lot. Harm said, "Yeah, I think that fucker was leadership. He sure acted it, not like that a-hole at the barn."

Rabbit, seeming relieved that Harm wasn't going to give him shit about his big mouth, replied, "Yeah. Pretty good scouting mission though. We got lucky seeing the minigun like that."

"Yeah, unbelievable timing. That Nazi turd was going to cover it with that tarp, looks like. So we confirmed the deal, and obviously it's close, but I didn't see any other weapons or ammo stacked up. I think we have some time to get our act together. We should come back after hours and sit on the place. Maybe we can catch them trucking in some guns."

"Right, camo up and hide in the woods by the main road. Watch what goes in and out the dirt road," agreed Rabbit. "You should bring your night scope, too."

"Good idea. It'll be like we're at the deer stand," Harm said with a smile. "Hey, call Abel and give 'em the update."

THIRTEEN

A bel was working under the assumption that they had some time before the gun deal went down, but when Rabbit called him and gave him the heads up that the minigun was already in place at the AB stronghold, he realized they'd better get moving, that the deal was imminent. Rabbit and Harm were going back to camp out on the gun range, watching to see whether vehicles showed up after hours. They figured that was when the guns were going to move in or out.

He got on the phone and told René to get his act together and alerted Tank and his brother to meet up at his house. They were going to convoy down to the El Luz Loco, the bar where Deacon had told them that the MS-13 frequented. Abel hoped that they could nail down the MS-13 house, the one real link they had to those bastards.

Tank, André, and Abel were going to go down to New Orleans an hour earlier than René and scout out the whole Florida Development Area where they were pretty sure the MS-13 was located based on Katie's clues. Abel wanted to make sure they were going to be able to navigate the area while following the MS-13 targets.

He heard a double honk; it sounded like Tank had showed up. He went to take a piss and then got a six-pack of water bottles from the pantry for the stakeout. Tank banged open the door, saying, "We're here. Let's go. We should have got started earlier. I was hoping to check out Florida while it was still light."

"I just heard from Harm and Rabbit—I thought we had time. We don't. The Nazis already have the minigun. We gotta pinpoint the MS dudes fast."

"You think the deal is going down like tomorrow? That soon?"

"No, not that quick. Rabbit said the rest of the weapons weren't there. We're still counting on Deke's info. The deal is a minigun plus other weapons. If that's not the case, then were gonna miss the boat."

Tank and Abel went out the door. André was leaning against his old Ford Bronco parked next to Tank's truck, a black Dodge Hemi. "Do you guys have your phones and chargers?" Abel asked.

André answered. "Yep, we're set. I also brought my DSLR, too, set up with the long lens. Maybe I can get some pictures."

"Awesome," replied Abel. "You and Tank should take the first two Maras that René marks. I'll hang back and make sure René doesn't get in a jam. If one of you isn't back in time, I'll follow the next MS guy out the door."

Tank added, "Follow me down to the train yards. We'll post up there and jump into one truck, then drive around the area. OK?"

"I figure we need to get back to The Crazy Light around nine-thirty or ten. None of those assholes are gonna leave sooner than that. It's not like it's a school night," added Abel.

They drove down separately, Abel finally able to steer his truck without a constant jab of pain every time he moved the wheel.

Periodically checking in with each other on their phones, they loosely coordinated and finally parked on a side street off Galvez, just past the tracks. Abel and Tank locked up their trucks and jumped into André's Bronco, Tank calling shotgun and Abel not arguing, given that it was his brother's car.

They started at the railroad and drove up and down over a ten-block span, then systematically did the same on the cross streets. They'd all been through the Florida Development Area before but never had paid much attention. For some reason, maybe because it was adjacent to the train yard, they had a preconceived notion that it was some kind of ghetto. It wasn't quite like that. There were some well-kept houses that were painted vibrant colors, recent-year vehicles parked on the streets, and several nicely tended yards. At least, that was what they could make out in the near dark. Hurricane Katrina had forced positive change. It was only every now and then that there were a few houses clustered together that looked like possible gangbanger hangouts. The most likely candidates were near the tracks.

They had gotten slightly hypnotized by staring at house after house, and finally Abel broke the spell. "Hey, I think that's enough. We've got to get to the bar. René is getting there at nine-thirty." André drove back to where they had all parked, and Tank and Abel shifted to their own vehicles. André led the way to The Crazy Light with Abel and Tank tight behind him.

Abel called René to find out his ETA at the bar and found out he was already there. "I don't know, Abel, this place is dead." René paused, and Abel heard a cough in the background. "There are only a few people in here. A couple of old dudes, a handful of construction workers, one Hispanic couple that looks like husband and wife."

"What's the place like?"

"It's a bar. Smells like beer and piss. It's fairly big though. Maybe it gets hopping on the weekend."

Abel agreed. "Yeah, or the MS are night owls and are going to show up late. Just stay put and nurse your beer. We'll be outside in a few minutes, and we'll watch for a while. I'll call you."

In the end, it was a bust. René got a buzz on, the boys outside got numb asses, and no likely Mara Salvatrucha candidates made an appearance. At 1 am, Abel got on the phone and told René to pack it up. He walked over to Tank's car and motioned to roll down the window. "We're done."

"Guess the bangers went to bed early. We'll come back tomorrow night," replied Tank.

Abel caught André's attention and waved his hand in the air as if to say, "Time to go."

Tank had already pulled away from the curb, so André got the message regardless of Abel's cryptic hand signals.

The crew was posted up outside the bar again the next night. It was Friday, so they figured that this was their best chance to catch some MS-13 members at the bar. If they didn't show up, then Deacon's tip was bad—wouldn't be the first time. But if it didn't pan out, then they were back to square one. René had already gone in and called out that the bar was getting crowded. That boded well.

Abel's phone rang. He saw that André was calling and picked up. "Abel, check that group coming down the street—they're moving like bangers."

He laughed. "Yeah, I see what you mean." The men in the group were all kind of walking with a similar gait. Hard to describe, but it telegraphed *I'm a badass.* There were two girls in the group as well, and when they approached the door to El Luz Loco, Abel could see that they looked hard and were heavily made up.

Two minutes later, his phone rang again. It was René this time. "OK, they're here. Tattooed up the ass, definitely bangers. I'm going to get closer to see if I see any MS-13 ink."

"Be careful," cautioned Abel. "There're more bangers coming down the street. This is it. Be patient and just watch. Text me if anything happens."

He immediately conferenced Tank and André. "René just reported that there are bangers. He's gonna get close and check 'em out. I think tonight's the night. We hang until they start coming back out."

Tank eagerly added, "I'll take the first one."

"André, you get next. I'll post up here and make sure that René doesn't get himself in trouble. As soon as you nail down where they are going, circle back here."

They all plugged in their phones to keep them charged and kept the three-way conversation going. They spent the time making funny comments about each person entering the bar, but eventually the conversation dwindled, each man lost in his own thoughts.

While Abel and the brothers were sitting in boredom, René was walking around in a maelstrom. El Luz Loco was packed to the walls with revelers. Friday night was the night. Maybe it went all weekend, but the place was a cacophony of yelling people, flying insults, and laughter on top of an already loud band crammed into a corner. Women and men were grinding on each other to the music, no footwork involved. There were old and young, Cajun, Creole, and definitely MS-13. He caught sight of maybe twenty inked soldiers, most wearing wifebeaters or colored tank tops, the better to show off the tats running up and down their arms and on top of their shoulders. There were only a handful of men with Mara Salvatrucha tattoos on their necks or cheeks. René was on the lookout for Tattoo Face but still hadn't seen the bastard with the big *M* and *S* marked on his cheeks.

He was going to have to station himself by the door and watch them as they were leaving. He had already decided to keep it simple and notify Abel only when the fewer older Maras with the most tattoos left.

One thing he had noticed was a couple of men that seemed to be dressed for business. They didn't have any ink, but they seemed to be getting respect from the younger gang members. Maybe the older man of the two was the leader. Each guy in the clique managed to check in with the older man, and sometimes the boss put a hand around the back of their neck in a brotherly manner—sometimes it was a fist bump. Every now and then, he leaned in and whispered into the underling's ear, although with the sound level in the joint, it was probably more like a shout. The minion would smile or laugh out loud and walk away like he had been sprinkled with holy water.

The behavior of the gang women was different—it was more like a competition. Each was vying for attention. They were dressed provocatively, wearing tight, knit shirts with deep necklines and jeans that were painted on their bodies. They weren't exactly pushing each other away from the two men, instead, it was like they were only allowed a certain amount of time to rub up against them, and then the time was up.

One girl in particular caught René's eye. She never seemed to orbit the older man, the boss; instead, she placed herself close to the younger one. This man looked to be the older man's lieutenant, occasionally bringing him a drink, sometimes yelling in his ear, or pushing away a woman or man whose time was up for some indecipherable reason. The leader's face was animated, going from celebration to frustration to anger based on whatever he heard. Occasionally, he barked out a short laugh, loud enough that René heard it from across the room.

The second in command was different. His face was still. His eyes were dead. He made René uneasy. René didn't want to admit to himself that it was fear.

The girl had something that René couldn't quite put his finger on. A certain menace. She was exotic. And dangerous, like the man she was circling—René couldn't look away. He mentally snapped awake, telling himself to get a grip. He moved his gaze back to the lieutenant. The man was looking directly at him. Their eyes locked just for a moment, and then René glanced away. Shit! He had to be careful; he was supposed to go unnoticed.

If he got caught, or let one of the MS-13 leaders slip out the door without giving Abel the heads up, the crew wouldn't let him live it down. They always gave him the little chores to do, like he was the least of them, as if he couldn't handle the complicated stuff. This time, they'd put him in the heart of it. He wasn't going to fuck up.

Abel's eyelids were drooping. The surveillance had reached the point where nothing had changed for a while, and he was having trouble staying awake. He literally slapped himself with both hands and was about to call out to Tank on the open connection when his phone chirped. René had sent a text: "Tattoo Face is coming out."

"Tank! The banger with the tattooed face is coming out." Abel heard the sound of Tank's after-market cherry bomb exhaust system quietly roar. "Shit, keep it down. He's gonna hear you."

Tank replied apologetically, "Sorry. I'll go light on the peddle and hang back. He won't notice."

Tattoo Face sauntered out The Light's door, walking like he was two feet wider than how everybody else on the planet saw him, and headed to the lot. Tank was staged and ready to move toward the Florida Development Area. He watched the man get into a dark-colored Camaro. The muscle car eased out of the parking lot, but instead of turning up the street toward Florida, he went the other direction. "Abel! I have to turn around."

"Yeah, I see. But look, his right taillight is crooked. You got time; you won't lose him." Abel rolled down his window and leaned out, craning his head to the left. "I can still see him—we're good."

Tank said, "I see him. I've got him." In the distance, he caught the car turning left, waited a beat till the Camaro was out of sight, then hammered the accelerator, his exhausts burbling to a throaty roar.

Jesus, thought Abel, *it'll be a miracle if Tattoo Face doesn't notice.*

Tank dropped off the pedal, the growl subsiding. He coasted up to the turn, went left, and was suddenly close enough to the Chevy to have to go into stealth mode. He stayed off the gas, putting some distance between them.

The pair went west and south, staying on surface streets. Tank kept the Camaro in his sights, which was easy because of the slanted taillight. Suddenly, Tattoo's brake lights flashed, Tank's truck started closing the gap, and Tank took the pressure off the pedal. The Camaro turned right into the side street, Tank coasting up to the junction. He looked down the street and saw Tattoo Face almost immediately turn into a parking lot on the right. He had been giving Abel and André the blow by blow of the chase, but now he said, "I've got the motherfucker!"

André spoke up. "Thomas! Don't do anything stupid—be careful."

"Don't worry, bro," Tank said, responding to the concern in André's voice. He took the turn but continued down the street past the building where the Camaro had parked. He went down a couple of blocks, parked, and shut off his engine. "OK, I'm going dark. I'll call you back in a few minutes."

"Wait," hissed Abel. "Wait a few minutes. Let him go inside. You got him; he's not going anywhere. Take your time."

Tank sat back and willed himself to relax and loosen up. "What's going on there? Has René texted you anymore?"

"No. I guess they call this place The Crazy Light for a reason. People are still going in, hardly anyone coming out."

"Hey, I've waited long enough. I'm going. I'll be a ghost." He hung up and set the phone on silent, then eased his door open, slid out, and moved to the other side of the street. It was a desolate industrialized area with no one walking around. The dark and decrepit commercial buildings had plenty of cover. Tank kept to the blackest shadows and worked his way back till he stopped right across from the spot Tattoo Face had pulled in to.

The lot sat next to a small building. It had a front door set deep into an alcove flanked by a big window that was covered with newspapers on the inside. Tank couldn't see in—the papers blocked the view but emitted an orange glow, as they were lit from within. The parking lot had three or four vehicles spaced out. He moved a little way till he could see the side of the building. There was another door flush to the sidewall. He had put a pin on his phone's GPS map but wanted to confirm the location. He trusted technology less than André, so he walked the rest of the way to the corner and committed the street signs to memory.

Returning, he posted up across from the building, peeking around the edge of a conveniently situated dumpster. It had been monotonous waiting in front of El Luz Loco. Not anymore—he could feel his heart banging against his ribs.

There was a screeching noise, and light spilled out onto the parking lot. Tank's heart rate went right back to max. A man's voice spoke, his words not quite understandable, and the side door slammed shut. Tank watched him walk to a car—not the Camaro, thank God. He wouldn't be able to get back to his truck if Tattoo Face was on the move again.

He moved completely behind the trash container and pulled out his phone and texted Abel to see if he wanted him to camp out or return to the bar. Abel responded that André was already on the move following another set of MS-13 pukes, so Tank needed to get back to the bar.

He reversed back up the street to his Hemi, skulking in the nooks and crannies. When he drove off, he had that exhilarating feeling that he had got away with something.

He called to report in. Abel picked up on the heels of the first ring. "I'm on the road. André is tailing the head honchos." He took a breath. "I decided to follow a batch of regular bangers. René said they were all tatted up—definitely MS-13. I want to see where the troops are headed."

"Are they convoyed up?"

"No, they're all crammed into a piece-of-shit Caprice. Their heads are lined up in the rear window like a row of melons."

"What do you want me to do?" asked Tank.

"Stay put and babysit René. Make sure he gets out OK. You don't need to follow anybody else unless we strike out."

"I'm going to patch in my brother, then I'll hang and monitor you two." Tank fumbled around with his phone, managing to dial André with his thumb. "Dude, I'm heading back to The Loco. I've got a three-way going with Abel. He's following a pack of lower echelon motherfuckers."

"'K. Did you figure out where Tattoo Face was going?"

"Yeah, he went to a building between the Seventh and Ninth Ward. It's not the place Katie described. It's not the gang hangout. Maybe it's the place where they have all the girls stashed. What's your status?" Tank asked.

"I'm behind these guys dressed like MBAs. I would have never followed them, but René texted that they were the head dudes."

"Are they headed to that area of houses by the railroad?" Tank asked.

"No, I thought for sure that was where they were going, but then they just blew right by it. We are in an area with nicer houses."

"In Florida?"

"Yep. Well, maybe just outside it—wait, they just stopped. They're just sitting there. I hope I'm not made," André said, concern in his voice. "No—good. One of the guys is getting out of the passenger side and walking up to the door. The car is driving off now. A'ight, I'm on the move again."

"Did you get this guy's address?" Tank reminded André.

"Dude—give me a break. I pinned it, and I took a picture of his house. And I know what street I'm on."

Abel broke into the conversation. "Hey—my pack of dipshits are headed your way, André. We're on Galvez."

"Yeah, and my guy is headed back toward the rail yard," said André. He was silent for a few moments, then said, "Yeah, now he's slowing down."

"André, you're not too close, are you?" asked his brother.

"No, but it doesn't matter. He probably thinks I'm another MS member. It's a giant house party. There are cars parked everywhere. He pulled over, and I drove right past. Didn't even look at him. I checked out the house. It looks like the place the girl described. It's a dive. All lit up though and cockroaches, I mean bangers, all over the place."

Abel spoke up. "Yeah, my car full of melon heads is turning a few streets after the tracks. André, can you remember the house?"

"Yep," André responded immediately.

"Then I'm not even going to follow. We're done. I'm going to turn around, and I'll wait for you to pop out on Galvez, then we'll head back to the bar, drag René out, and head home," Abel said, sounding both relieved and pumped at the same time.

Meanwhile, back at El Luz Loco, René was congratulating himself on doing his part. Once that scary fucker had left with the big boss, he'd relaxed. The mission now rested on the other guys. He went up to the bar to get a refill and was leaning in, waving a twenty and trying to get the bartender's attention, when he felt someone press against him and heard, "Oye! Luis, get this hombre a drink."

René turned and realized it was the woman he'd been watching before. "Thanks! What can I get you?"

"Vodka cran," she answered.

Luis was standing in front of them, eyes on the girl. René reached out his hand with the twenty. "A vodka cran and an Abita Amber—keep the change." They stood there for a minute waiting on the drinks. Luis handed the chica her drink. She reached for it, her hand catching his forearm, and sliding down to the drink.

The girl turned and frankly appraised René up close. "You're kinda far from home, aren't you?" She took a sip. "C'mon, gringo, let's dance." She put her hand under his shirt and grabbed René's belt buckle, then pulled him toward the dance floor, René barely having time to grab his beer off the bar. The floor was still packed with people, forcing them together, the girl pressing up tight, moving with the music. She held her drink with one hand, her other hand had slid around and was tucked under his belt at the small of his back, drawing him into her.

René danced until his shirt was glued to his back with sweat, the girl willing, telegraphing her interest with little touches and tugs. Finally, he dragged her off the floor, and they made their way back to the bar, René taking advantage of her connection to the bartender again. They took their drinks as far as they could get from the band, to a half wall blocking some of the sound and offering a bit of privacy.

"What are you doing here?" she asked.

"A friend suggested it. He said there were a lot of women." René shrugged. "Not that many actually but a few really pretty ones, like you."

She gave a slight smile at the compliment. "So where are you from? You don't sound like a tourist."

"Lacombe," he answered. "I usually hang out at a bar in Slidell called The Flying Machine." He shifted the conversation back to her. "All these people look like they're from the same group. Do you know all these people?"

"We're all from the neighborhood, kind of like the same club."

"What's with all the ink? What does MS mean? Almost every guy has those letters."

"It just means the club started in El Salvador."

"Club? You mean gang?"

"Maybe that's what you call it here. It's really just a social club."

"How many people are members?" René continued to pry, not really noticing her picking up on his interest.

"Oh, maybe fifteen or twenty," she minimized.

René knew that was bullshit. He saw more in the bar right now. "I saw you hanging with that guy that looked like a business owner. He a member of your club, too?"

"No, he's part owner of the bar."

"He your boyfriend?"

She laughed. "Retaco? He doesn't have girlfriends."

"Retaco? You mean like the Mexican food?"

"No, estúpido, it means 'shorty.'" She put on a serious face. "And don't call him that to his face. He won't like that."

"Seemed like you and he were close," teased René. He felt his phone vibrate against his leg.

"Why do you care, muchacho?" she said, again with a vague smile. "I work with him sometimes."

"Maybe I'd like to see you again," said René, being René. "What's your name?"

"Mi amigas call me Lúcido." The corners of her lips tipped up slightly, one sharp canine exposed, making a little dent in her lower lip. "It's my street name, a nickname. It means a thinker, you know—smart. But it's a joke. Everybody really means smarty pants. Like I'm too smart for my own good."

"I can see that," said René, negging her. His phone vibrated again, and he pulled it out of his pocket. It was a text from Abel telling him it was time to leave. "Hey look, I have to go, my friends want me to meet them. Are you here every weekend?"

"Aw, it was just getting fun. You never told me your name."

René paused, then said, "Abel—Abel Kane." He didn't know why he said it but felt a little jolt of glee.

"Maybe I see you next week, Mr. Abel." She ran her hand down his arm and squeezed his hand.

He leaned in and whispered into her ear, "I hope I do," then straightened up and turned toward the door, looking over his shoulder at her one more time.

She stood there till he reached the door, then walked to the end of the bar and opened the door to the rear of the building. Lúcido slipped through the doorway, ran through the kitchen, and exited El Luz Loco through the back door. Moving silently around the building, she stopped and leaned against the front corner in the shadows and saw René, or Abel as she knew him, walking down the street.

Lúcido watched him stop at a truck and talk to the driver, then walk to another truck and do the same. Down the street, a car door opened, and a huge Black man got out and moved up the street to meet Abel. The two of them bumped fists, then crossed the street to the parking lot. The trucks simultaneously started, one with a loud roar, and pulled into the street one after the other. When she looked back to where Abel had been, he was gone. The large man shambled back to his SUV. Lúcido continued to watch until the vehicle slowly drove off.

CHAPTER

FOURTEEN

R abbit was sitting on the Nazis at the gun range and had called Abel in the morning with nothing new to report. He hadn't seen anything going in and out, and Harm was on the way to switch with him. The call had woken Abel, and he had continued to lie in bed after hanging up, thinking. The previous night, the rest of the guys agreed that they would each take one of the MS-13 locations and get a feel for how they operated, how they moved—see if they could start to put together all the people in the organization.

They knew they didn't have enough men to blanket the locations 24-7, so Tank was going to cover the hangout, André was shading the leader's house, and René had the Tattoo Face location between Seventh and Ninth Ward. Abel got Saturday evening off but was going to roll in after midnight and cover while André and Tank broke off to catch some sleep and attend church with their mama in the morning. René was going to help Abel as long as he could, then head home to sleep. They all figured that Sunday morning was going to be sleepy-time for the gangbangers anyway. Abel and René would nap during the day, and they would start up late in the afternoon with a different guy rotating in later in the night.

Abel dropped his legs over the side of the bed, sat up, and reached for his phone. He dialed Olivia, hoping it wasn't too early.

"Where y'at, cher?" she asked, all awake and cheerful.

"I'm great. I hope I didn't call too early."

"No, Owen wakes me up the second it gets light, all ready to play."

"I've got a free night and remembered you were off too and was wondering if you wanted to do something this evening."

"Sure, I can get my mom to watch Owen. What did you have in mind?" she asked.

"Well, it's kind of a surprise."

"Hmmm, that sounds intriguing, Mr. Mystery Man." Olivia laughed.

"Wear comfortable clothes," advised Abel. "Maybe bring a sweater, too."

"Wow, an outside date. You're not taking me hunting, are you? This better be a real date, if I'm giving up a Saturday night," she kidded.

"Oh, I think you'll like this—I hope you will anyway . . . I'll pick you up around six, OK?"

"'K, see you then." She waited a beat for Abel to say his goodbye, and then she disconnected.

"Alright!" Abel said out loud and jumped out of bed. He had a lot to do—better get moving! Now he felt all bright eyed too, just the way Olivia sounded.

Abel rang the doorbell exactly at six, hoping it didn't look like he was too anxious to see Olivia. On second thought, he decided he didn't care how cool he looked. He hadn't seen her in several days; he missed her already. Olivia's mother came to the door, carrying Owen on her hip. Abel could see Olivia in her mother's face—an older, sadder, more tired version but still attractive. The toddler also resembled her—he had Olivia's eyes, dark curly hair, and a serious face.

Abel introduced himself. "Hi, I'm Abel. Is Olivia ready?"

"Olivia—your friend is here," the mother called over her shoulder. She looked back at Abel balefully and didn't introduce herself, making the silence somewhat awkward.

The little boy stared at Abel curiously. Abel looked right back at him and said, "Hi, Owen, do you like cars?" He grinned at the little guy. "I like trucks." He motioned with his head to his truck parked on the street. "Hey, cher, do you know what I have in my pocket?" Owen shook his head, his lips pressed shut, his eyes opening wider. Abel rooted around in his pocket and pulled out a little metal truck that he had bought earlier in the day and handed it to Owen. "See? Just like mine." Owen's face lit up around the eyes with just the faintest hint of a smile on his lips. He held the truck up and compared it to Abel's truck in the street.

"What do you say Owen?" prompted Olivia's mother automatically.

Olivia bustled up at that exact moment. "Did you meet Abel, Mama?" Her mother nodded. Olivia looked toward Abel. "I'll be back before midnight, right?"

"Yes, definitely," reassured Abel, knowing he had to join the surveillance on the MS later that night.

She came out the door, and they walked down the yard to Abel's truck. As soon as they were moving, Olivia asked, "So what are we doing?" She didn't know Abel well enough yet to guess.

"I thought we'd go back to my house, watch the sunset, then I'll cook us dinner."

"Wow, cook dinner?" She laughed. "You're swinging for the fences."

"Yeah, too much—right? But I figured, all I had to do was beat that waffle place from the other night. I think I can manage that."

"And I get to see your house?" Olivia turned in her seat so she was facing him a little more directly. "I can tell a lot about a guy from his house," she declared with a big grin and arched eyebrows.

"Hey, don't forget I live with my sister. She won't be there tonight, but I live in her house, not the other way around." He continued, "I mean she's the decorator, but I take care of my stuff and help keep it clean."

"Well, if you at least pick up your own junk, you got that going for you."

Eventually, they turned off Fish Hatchery Road and navigated the long driveway through the woods that ended at Abel's front yard. As Olivia got out of the truck, the cool, wet smell of the bayou hit them, and Abel came around the truck, grabbed her hand, and ushered her up the steps and in through the front door. She stopped just inside the door, checking it out. She looked first at the big bookcase along the wall and immediately went up to it and began pulling out books randomly. "Don't you think that you can tell a lot about a person by the books that they read? Are all these yours?"

"Probably about three-quarters. Callie hasn't been reading that much lately because she's been studying for her master's."

Olivia stopped scanning the bookshelves and continued examining the room. The living room didn't have very much furniture: a comfortable couch, a large screen TV mounted on a wall, a couple of craftsman-style chairs. "Your sister decorated this room? This seems more like a man picked all this stuff out."

"Callie did this for me. She has the third bedroom all laid out with things the way she likes it. She does all her studying there."

They moved through the house, Olivia commenting on specific items she liked. She complimented Abel on his room, how neat it was. "You cleaned this up today, didn't you?" she teased. "You know I'm checking your bathroom later."

Abel laughed. "Go ahead! But you're right, I did clean it this afternoon." He dragged her out of his room. "Let's go outside. We're going to go out on the bayou in my pirogue—watch the sun go down."

Olivia picked on him again. "What did you do? Read a book on the ten romantic things to do on a date?" She punched him on the arm to show she wasn't serious. Abel flinched. "Oh, I'm so sorry! I completely forgot about your arm."

Abel laughed, playing it down by saying, "It's almost healed." He guided her through the rest of the house, finishing the tour, then led her out the back door and down to the bayou. They walked to the end of the dock and stepped into the boat, Olivia taking the front seat. Abel had paddles for it, but he had equipped it with a little electric trolling motor that was very quiet. He turned it on, and they whirred away from the dock.

"We're going to my special spot; the bayou opens up, and you can see the sun go down. Maybe if we're quiet, we'll see a doe come down and drink. It's too early in the spring to see a fawn—that's my favorite thing."

They slid silently through the bayou, absorbing the stillness, the air cool, only a few insects buzzing. Abel stopped the boat in an open area, the trees backing away like the opening doors of a church, the water surrounded by an uneven boundary of reeds, and here and there tufts of tall grass formed little islands. Through a trick of light, the clouds above were mirrored on the black water, obscuring everything below.

"This is so beautiful," Olivia whispered in awe.

"I know. This is the best time to be out here, too. Every time I come here, I say I'm going to come every night, but then I forget. And every time I come; I'm amazed all over again."

They sat there until the sun yielded to the night. Abel lit up the tiny motor and gently turned the boat around, navigating the dark tunnels under the trees, occasionally passing a home on the bayou banks, far back and on stilts, orange lights in the windows beckoning.

The boat coasted up to his pier, then Abel tied off tight against the bumpers hanging down. They clambered up onto the dock and headed over to Abel's firepit. He'd prepared the firewood earlier in the afternoon, a box shape of logs with kindling and a waxed cardboard fire starter all set up.

"Can I start the fire?" asked Olivia. "My daddy always used to let me do that."

"Sure." Abel handed her a long lighter, took out his phone and turned on the flashlight, and shone it on the fire starter. "See that wick? Light that."

In moments, the fire was burning enough that Abel knew it wasn't going to putter out, and he stood back up. "C'mon, let's get the food ready." He led her back to the dock, flicked on a dim light that hung over his fish cleaning station, and got down on his knees at the far end opposite from the pirogue. He grunted, lifting a slat trap onto the dock.

Olivia watched over his shoulder as he opened the trap, seeing three nice-sized catfish flopping back and forth, the catfish cheese bait sending up a serious stink.

"You really know how to wine and dine a girl," Olivia said.

"I can skip all this and take you out to a restaurant if you want," he said, his feelings a little hurt.

"No, I was serious. I absolutely love this. My daddy and I used to do this all the time." She put her hand on his shoulder and looked in his eyes. "Thank you. What can I do to help?"

"I'll clean these but could you go up to the house and get the rest of the stuff?" He thought for a second, making an inventory. "There's a bottle of wine, an opener, and glasses set out in the kitchen. And then there's a tray with stuff on it—bring that, too."

"Got it," Olivia said, and she headed up to the kitchen.

"Oh, and get the skewers of marinated vegetables in the fridge—and the tartar sauce," yelled Abel to her back.

He quickly cleaned the fish, ending up with six plump filets on a plate, and set them by the fire. Then, he ran up to the kitchen to get the remaining odds and ends he needed to make the campfire dinner. Olivia had set all the supplies she found in the kitchen on the picnic table by the firepit, and Abel placed a container of cornmeal mixed with his secret mix of blackening herbs and spices next to them. *Kinda like the Cajun version of the Colonel,* he thought.

Olivia watched Abel efficiently cook the meal, looking somewhat amazed. The fire had settled into a bed of coals, and he put a Dutch oven on one side of the fire and adjusted the embers around it. He dumped in some batter and some fruit, replaced the black pot's lid, and heaped some coals on top. Then, he moved around to the other side of the fire and placed the skewers of vegetables on a grill he had propped over the heat, first spraying some oil on the grate, causing a burst of flame. A cast-iron skillet was nestled into the fire in the last open space. The final touch was to place a foil-covered loaf of bread on the rocks abutting the pit. Abel plopped a chunk of bacon fat into the skillet and watched it melt.

He handed Olivia an oven mitt. "Can you turn the veggies while I cook the fish?"

They cooked side by side, Abel coating the fish heavily with the seasoning, pan-frying two filets at a time. By the time the fish was done, Olivia had grilled the veggies perfectly with just the right amount of charred, crispy edges.

Abel dragged the picnic table a little closer to the fire, and he and Olivia set out the food. She sat down while he pulled the cork and poured the wine. They sat next to each other, companionably eating and chatting, feeling the warmth of the fire while watching the bats flit here and there over the bayou.

After they ate, Abel shook out a blanket on the grass and they laid down together, on their backs, shoulders and hips touching. They were quiet for a few minutes, and then Olivia snuggled a little closer to Abel, capturing some warmth—it was getting chilly.

"Maybe if we watch a while, we'll see a falling star," said Abel.

They stared up at the night sky, scanning for a meteor, seeing more clearly as their eyes further acclimated to the blackness. "Man, I love this," sighed Olivia.

Abel couldn't see her face but knew it was lit up—he could hear it in her voice. They lay there for another half an hour until Abel got tired of a rock poking him in his back, and he figured she was probably really chilled but just too polite to break the spell he had cast.

"Hey, let's go up to the house. I can make some coffee or we can have a nightcap."

"Perfect timing. I was just about turned into an icicle." She pushed off Abel onto her knees and stood up, giving Abel her hand and helping him up. She kept his hand, pulling slightly, and led him up to the house. Abel reached around her to get the kitchen door. He reached to flick on the light, but she stopped him, encircling him with her arms, both standing just inside the door. Abel bent down and kissed her with barely a touch at first, then she rose on her tiptoes, joining, and he gently pressed in, feeling the softness of her lips. They shuffled backward into the kitchen, then broke apart, this time Abel catching her hand and leading her to his bedroom.

FIFTEEN

After taking Olivia home a little before midnight, Abel drove down to the stakeout. He took advantage of the time on the road to get a download from each crew member. Rabbit was taking the late shift on the Aryan Brotherhood and had reported that "it was all quiet on the western front." No unusual truck traffic at the range, at least when he and Harm were watching. Hopefully that meant the crew still had time to get their act together on the MS.

René was hiding across the street from the Tattoo Face house and had seen nothing major, just the occasional john being serviced.

At the gang house in the Florida Development Area, there was a lot of coming and going and some noise but none of the key gang leaders had shown according to Tank.

André was watching the El Luz Loco, which was going strong with groups of people in and out, similar to the previous night.

Abel decided to go straight to the El Luz Loco. He figured that was where the leaders would be parked, just like the previous night. He was getting the feeling that that was their headquarters, the place where they could meet with all the soldiers and probably profit from them at the same time. He wondered if there was an office in the building as well. René hadn't noticed one specifically but had commented on a door on the back wall next to the bar.

He tracked down André's SUV and moved up the street to an open space that still allowed a view of The Crazy Light's entrance. He popped out of his truck and walked back to the SUV, opened the passenger door, and leaned in. "Anything new since your last report?"

"No, but I feel like maybe it's slowing down a bit. Maybe people will start leaving."

Abel stood back up and looked at the front of the bar for a minute, then leaned back down. "I don't know, these guys seem like they party all night. In any case, why don't you take off and get some rest."

"Are you going to hang here all night?" André asked, concerned, knowing that he was going to be mostly by himself.

"Yeah, I had a nap; I'm good to go," Abel reassured him. "I'm going to have René stake out the sex trafficking spot a little longer, then send him home, too. I'll spend most of the time here and see if I can get a line on the number two dude—Shorty."

André responded, "His Lexus is in the lot. I never saw him go into the bar though."

"Call me when you finish with church tomorrow, and I'll bring you up to speed." Abel slammed the SUV's door and returned to his truck. The instant he pulled the door shut his phone rang. It was Tank beating him to the punch, calling from the gang house stakeout.

"There's a lot of action here, but nothing important as far as I can tell, kinda like a party, people going back and forth to their cars, bangers standing on the porch smoking, a few couples making out," Tank said, his voice tired. "I'm beat, I'm heading out—is that OK with you?"

"Yeah, I already sent your brother home. Take off and we'll sync up tomorrow after lunch." Abel hung up and then sat with one eye on The Loco, the wheels turning in his head. They knew where the leader lived. They nailed the location of the house where the girls were kept, and they had scouted out the bar. The one thing they didn't know was where Shorty lived. Hell, maybe he slept at the bar. Right now, he was the biggest loose end.

Abel started the truck and circled the block, eventually coming back down the street again, this time looking for a better location that allowed him to keep his eye on Shorty's Lexus. He found a dead-end street a short distance away that had a good sight line into the parking lot. He circled the cul-de-sac and parked with the nose of his truck aimed at the lot, then settled in for a wait, letting his mind wander back to his date with Olivia, his face relaxing, the knot between his eyebrows smoothing out.

While Abel was reliving his evening with Olivia, René was staring across the street at the Tattoo Face location. He was situated behind a dumpster with a good view of the building's parking lot. The neighborhood was made up of collapsing commercial buildings with broken windows and the stench of decay. It felt like the area was abandoned. Hurricane Katrina had killed it.

He saw headlights, his heart beating faster as a box truck pulled into the lot. Up till then, there had been sporadic traffic, mostly cars and pickup trucks, usually the worse for wear—beaters and wrecks. This was different. It looked more like a delivery truck ready to drop off or take on a load.

The driver got out of the truck, walked over to the building, and pounded on the door. He walked back to the rear of the truck, monkeyed around for a bit, and then René heard and saw him open the cargo door like a garage door. René shifted his position so he could get a better view of the rear of the vehicle. The lot itself had no lights, but some illumination from the streetlight allowed him to see some details.

The screeching noise of the building's side door opening disturbed the night, and Tattoo Face came out, his disfigured face apparent even from across the street. He moved to the rear of the truck with the driver, and gave an unintelligible order.

René watched the driver climb up into the box truck and saw two bodies being pushed out of the cargo area. Tattoo Face pulled the first body out—it looked like a girl with long hair. She was alive but shaky on her feet, the gangbanger supporting her. He walked her back to the building and through the open side door. In a minute, he came back out and moved again to the rear of the delivery truck. The driver pushed the second body, and Tattoo Face pulled it out— another girl. But this one couldn't stand and flopped to the ground. René couldn't be sure, but it appeared that the girl was naked.

Tattoo Face kneeled down next to the girl, and René could hear him from across the street repeatedly saying something to her. He watched him slap the girl's face sharply a few times in succession. Tattoo Face got up on one knee, then stood the rest of the way, and the two men bent down and picked up the girl and shuffled into the building with their load.

He continued to watch, wondering what was going to happen next. Five minutes went by, and then the two men came out and walked to the end of the truck. They faced each other, and René could hear the mumble of conversation. Suddenly, Tattoo Face slapped the driver. His arm moved like a striking snake. First it was down by his side, and then it whipped, hitting the driver, the cracking sound echoing between the buildings. Tattoo Face forced the man up against the truck, his left forearm pressing against the driver's neck, not quite shouting, but the tone sounded more and more angry. René figured the driver had raped or hurt the girl and then delivered the damaged goods.

Rapt, he watched Tattoo Face reach behind to his back pocket, a flash of light glinting off a blade. The banger made violent punching motions to the driver's belly. He stepped away. The driver crumpled.

Tattoo Face looked down at the body, wiped the blade against his pants, then brought his hands together like in prayer, folding the knife. Pocketing the weapon, he bent down and grabbed the feet of the driver, then leaned backward, dragging the body behind the truck and out of sight.

He walked to the street edge of the lot, turned his head left and right, peering up and down the road, then just stood there gazing across the street. René felt like the banger was staring right at him. He stood completely still, just his eye peering around the edge of the dumpster. He didn't blink. Tattoo Face reached into his pocket and a moment later a flame flared. René didn't budge. The smell of the cigarette floated on the night air.

The man reached into his pants again, brought his hand up, and then the glow of a phone screen lit his face, casting harsh shadows, his eyes appearing as black pockets in a skull.

They both stood in place, René watching the monster, until it turned on its heel and went back inside, screeching the door closed.

René immediately dialed Abel. "Holy shit!" he hissed. "I just saw Tattoo Face kill a guy."

"What? Tell me what happened!" René related the sequence of events to Abel.

"It's definitely the house where the girls are." Abel paused a beat. "No way are they gonna leave a dead body in their parking lot. Watch who comes, and whatever you do, make sure you follow that truck. We gotta find out where they keep that. If they have another location, we need to know where it is."

"Gotcha, Cuz." They disconnected.

Nothing was happening across the street yet, so René took a minute to drop deeper into the shadows, unzipped his pants, and relieved himself against a wall.

He moved to the dumpster so he could continue spying but then started to think. If he was going to follow the truck, he needed to be in his car ready to go. He'd lose them if he had to run back and get in and start it up. He headed back, keeping to the shadows, moving from one black pool to the next. Quietly, he opened the door of the beater that he had borrowed from Rabbit's dad, glad that he hadn't driven his own Jag, as he was sure it would have been noticed in this neighborhood.

Creeping slowly, he nosed down the street, parking the anonymous vehicle just short of the lot. René slunk down in the seat, his eyes barely clearing the steering wheel but still able to see the box truck. He settled in for a long wait, but shortly, a generic sedan pulled into the lot and parked next to the delivery truck.

Two MS soldiers, one wearing an undershirt and long shorts hanging past his knees, and the other in jeans and a nondescript T-shirt, got out and walked around the truck. Just like two workmen picking up a roll of carpet, they picked up the stabbed driver and swung him by his wrists and ankles up into the truck. The body's legs were hung up on the deck of the truck, and one of the soldiers gave the body an extra push to get it completely inside. The banger with the long shorts clambered up into the truck so he could reach the strap attached to the bottom of the truck door. He pulled down at the same time as he jumped off the truck, the door slamming closed. The crash echoed through the neighborhood.

The man in the shorts went around the truck, and René heard it start up. The other man climbed back into the car they came in. The delivery vehicle motored out of the lot slowly, closely followed by the sedan. René sat up in the seat and started his car, not moving till the two vehicles ahead of him got some distance. He waited till they were out of sight, flicked on his lights, and then eased after them.

They weren't going in any direction that he expected, so he hung close to them, eventually following them to a hospital. What the fuck? He watched them stop, open the truck, look around furtively, drag the body out of the truck, and plop it right in the street in front of the ER entrance. They jumped back in their vehicles and sped off, the whole thing taking about twenty seconds. He was baffled—there were better places to dump a corpse.

René continued to shadow them, eventually getting near the El Luz Loco, so he called Abel, who picked up on the first ring. "Hey, I think they're taking the truck back to The Loco. Are you still there?"

"No—Shorty left with the head dude. I'm behind them. Make sure you track the truck till it's parked. Then you can head home and catch some Z's."

"Wait, I didn't even tell you the crazy thing that just happened," added René. "They stopped at a hospital on the way to the bar and dumped the dead guy in front. Can you believe that shit?"

Abel exclaimed, "You know what that was? A *yellow light!* Deacon told me about it. See, if they kill a guy outside their gang, they have to get permission, and the murder is called a *green light* or getting the *green light*. But, if some member of their own gang screws up, they beat up the guy and stab him a few times and then dump him at a hospital—give him a chance to live, I guess."

"They sound like psychos," said René.

"Look, when the truck is parked, take off and get some sleep. I'm going to put this Shorty prick to bed."

Abel focused on Shorty's Lexus ahead of him. It looked like he was going to do the same thing as the night before—take the head guy home and tuck him in. Last time, they broke off the surveillance once he went back to the gang house. Tonight, Abel was going to follow him to the bitter end.

Shorty pulled up to the MS-13 leader's home and stayed parked in front of his house until El Presidente walked up the drive and through the front door. He accelerated away the second the door shut, repeating the pattern from the previous night and ending up at the gang house by the tracks. Abel idled a short distance away, tucked in behind another parked car, and watched Shorty briskly walk up to the banger party house and disappear inside.

He had his eye on the door, watching intently, waiting for Shorty to exit, then BANG. His heart punched through his chest. A random gang member had walked up from behind, slapped the side of the truck, and continued on, a girl hanging on his arm. Abel could hear them both laughing.

Motherfuckers, thought Abel, relieved that they hadn't stopped and hassled him. He scanned the gang house again and saw that Shorty was already out the door, heading to his vehicle. He had something in his hand—maybe a sack of some sort, it was hard to tell. He drove off again, and Abel discretely followed.

After about fifteen minutes, they arrived at El Luz Loco again. Shorty parked in the lot and went inside, and Abel took the opportunity to get situated back in his favorite cul-de-sac. Once again in wait mode, his eyes were fixed on the Lexus. It was quiet, and the lot was less full. Fewer people were walking out of the bar. Abel struggled to keep his eyes open. His head kept tipping forward, and then he would jerk upright. He slapped his face with both hands.

He got out of the truck and walked around the cul-de-sac, keeping his eye on the parking lot, then meandered back to his vehicle and rested his arms on the bed cover, watching Shorty's Lexus from behind his truck. He had imagined that staking out a location might be kind of interesting, but it was actually boring. That thought was interrupted by Shorty showing up in his field of view, heading down the sidewalk, his short legs moving at a fast clip, another bag in his hand. Abel figured it was The Loco's receipts for the night.

He followed him again. This time the gangbanger lieutenant drove around the neighborhood for only a few minutes before pulling up in front of a neat shotgun house. The windows were dark and manicured shrubs stood guard. Abel watched him carry a bag in each hand into the house. A window lit up, a yellowish glow cast onto the front yard, then it went out. Abel sat for a half hour watching nothing happen. He didn't have the nods anymore but was bone tired. He started his truck and headed home, intending to get a few hours of sleep in his own bed before setting his alarm and getting back in place before 8 am. Abel doubted that this guy was an early riser, but you never knew.

Seven am came early. Abel had three hours of sleep, but it felt worse than none. He probably should have just parked somewhere in the city and slept in his truck. He'd crashed in his clothes, so he dumped himself out of bed, hit the bathroom, then hit the road, his eyes gritty from lack of sleep. He autopiloted down to Shorty's house and discretely eased to the side of the road several houses away. He shut off his engine and settled in, sure that the banger wouldn't budge till noon or later.

A half hour later he was regretting not stopping for a large coffee on the trip down and sat there weighing coffee or no-coffee? But at 8:40 he was glad he didn't cave in to his impulses because the man popped out his front door and hurried to his vehicle. They were off—again.

Number Two went directly back to the head honcho's house in the Florida neighborhood and pulled into the drive. Abel watched as the top man walked out of the house in a dark suit and a bright white shirt open at the neck, his outfit finished off by black sunglasses. Nice clothes but an ugly, coarse face, his paunch barely disguised by the jacket. A woman who could possibly be beautiful, certainly from afar, paraded behind him, ushering two little boys ahead of her. Each boy was dressed in a dark suit, miniature copies of their father.

The Lexus retraced some of its journey and eventually pulled up to a Catholic church near the French Quarter. The family debarked and filed through the church's entrance arches. Abel pondered that for a minute—the head of the most vicious gang in New Orleans heading into church, Sunday morning, as pretty as you please.

When church let out, Shorty dropped off the family and went home. So did Abel.

CHAPTER
_____

SIXTEEN

T he crew, minus Rabbit and Harm, regrouped Sunday night before sundown on Abel's back porch for a strategy session. André had spent the afternoon mining various websites, searching for traces of the MS leadership. He had addresses for Shorty and the head dude and followed the bread crumbs through publicly accessible real estate databases, people search sites, sex offender registries, and public records.

The name of the leader was Alejandro Alverez, aged forty-one, married to Maria, with two boys Miguel and Benicio. When he was younger, Alejandro had spent minor jail time in Texas and in California for assault and a minor drug charge respectively. The guys were surprised that he had so little jail exposure. They expected a gang leader working his way up the ranks would have been nailed for various crimes along the way. Abel said, "He probably uses Shorty to do all the dirty work."

"He's smart. That's why he's the leader," added Tank, "He keeps himself away from the law."

Shorty's real name was Hector Garcia, and he was a few years younger than the boss at thirty-seven. André found a criminal history of violence with many charges. Garcia had jail time, but it looked like many of the charges never made it to a guilty verdict. "Yeah, he disappeared the witnesses," observed René.

"Oh, and another thing I found," said André, "Garcia owns the El Luz Loco. That agrees with what René heard from the banger chick, Lúcido"

"Makes sense," Abel added. "Shorty, or I guess Garcia, hangs there, and I saw him take a bag of money home from the bar last night."

Abel summarized. "OK, so we know where these guys live, where they hang, and who they really are. Plus, Garcia's the bagman. I say we—I mean me, Tank, and André—go down and dog Garcia tonight. He's the guy that does everything important. The gun deal is going to be his job." Abel nodded at René. "It's your turn to take the night off, since you went long last night."

They saddled up in each of their vehicles and traipsed back down to the city, linked up by a three-way conference call. They eventually found Garcia at The Crazy Light. They followed him on his rounds, watching him drop off the leader, get a package from the place with the kidnapped girls, and even go into the port. He came out of the NOLA Container Terminal with a bag in his hand, then he went back to his house. "Probably had to take a shit," chuckled Tank.

"Yeah, and drop off the money," added André.

Garcia was only home momentarily, then he was back on the road. The next stop was the gang house. Shorty walked up to the door, and a soldier came out and met him. The man's hair was long and slicked back into a ponytail. They moved away from the house and had a short, intense conversation. It almost looked like an argument.

"What do you think they're fighting about?" wondered André out loud. Garcia turned on his heel, got in his Lexus, and left.

They chased him all the way back to his house again. "Do you think he's done for the night?" asked Tank.

"I don't know. Let's make sure he isn't just taking another crap," answered Abel.

They watched from their parked vehicles, eyes glued on Garcia's house. The home lights cycled on and off, and the neighborhood was dead quiet. Abel started to say, "He's in bed—" when a car came down the street. It parked near the edge of Garcia's yard. A man got out and looked toward Shorty's house. "Hey, isn't that the guy he was arguing with back at the party house?" asked Tank.

"Sure looks like it," André weighed in.

The soldier walked up to the front door, knocked, then reached into his pocket for a key apparently, because he could be seen unlocking the door. The house lights stayed dark. The guys waited and watched outside. Nothing happened. They waited some more. Still nothing. Abel finally broke the silence. "I think our guy likes boys."

"Yeah, sure looks that way—interesting," said André. "Gangs freaking hate gays, especially Mex and Salvadorans. Super prejudiced . . ."

"I wonder if he keeps it a secret or whether he has so much power, he can do whatever he wants?" mused Abel. "Anyway, looks like he's in for the duration. Let's go home."

The three of them stayed in their phone conference on the return trip. They all agreed that at some point in the near future the MS-13 guys were going to roll to a meet with the Nazis, carrying a pile of cash. Abel started the discussion on how to make the grab. "Look we either hit 'em on the road, or we hit their bank."

André jumped on him. "If we wait till they convoy up with a bunch of soldiers in multiple vehicles, it's going to be a mess, an all-out assault, and we don't have enough guys in our crew to do that. The only way the road hit works is if it's an isolated car with the money."

"What about hitting Alverez's house and kidnapping the two boys and ransoming them for the money?" suggested Tank.

"Wow, sounds like you're channeling Harm." His brother laughed. "Pretty cold, dude."

"Yeah," agreed Abel. He knew Tank was just throwing stuff against the wall to see what would stick. "We're not snatching the kids."

"It all hinges on the bank. We just got to find it and quick," André said.

"The bank is tied to Garcia. We'll just smother him. All of us on 'em. Use different vehicles—keep our distance." Abel readjusted his position on the truck seat, then cleared his throat. "We've already seen that Garcia is handling cash. What else could be in those bags that he's picking up? We've just got to figure out where he's stashing it. Bank's got to be either in Alverez's house, Garcia's place, The Loco, or Tattoo Face's place."

"My money is on Garcia's humble abode," voted André.

"We could creep the place and prove it," said his brother.

Abel immediately quashed that. "No, we don't want to tip our hand. Right now, they have no clue that we're on 'em. The four of us will give ole Shorty a surveillance enema over the next few days and nail down the bank."

Over the next week, there was a least one of the boys tracking Garcia's every move. Someone woke up with him. Another guy put him to bed. It was obvious he was the real leader of the gang, in terms of the day-to-day operation—he was everywhere.

They caught him at the gang house walking out with a flimsy plastic grocery store bag wrapped around an obvious stack of cash. There must have been a meeting at the gang house because the neighborhood by the tracks was packed with vehicles, and there was a big contingent of inked bangers coming and going.

André had been busy researching Mara Salvatrucha, and he explained the structure of the gang to the crew, how all the MS members were required to attend regular meetings called maras where they had to pay taxes or dues, just like they were the garden club or some shit. If a member missed a meeting, or didn't cough up his taxes, he might get yellow-lighted.

They witnessed a beating behind El Luz, next to a stinking green dumpster where Garcia watched a man getting attacked by three soldiers who were taking turns. First, one guy punched the victim until he was tired, and then the second guy tagged in. The third banger repeatedly struck the victim with a broom handle whenever the other two took a rest. When the man had finally collapsed on the ground, Garcia stepped in and kicked him twice in the belly, then once to the head. They walked away and left him sprawled on the ground.

Garcia made his rounds, checking in on the kidnapped girls' building, sometimes leaving with a bag of cash. He would circle through the port, like he was making collections or maybe even payoffs. Often, he carried a briefcase like he was a legit businessman, now and then a simple paper bag. Occasionally, he would enter a restaurant or bar in the port neighborhood. Abel shadowed him into a bar once, pretending to be a patron. Garcia was discretely handed a packet of cash by the bartender—so they were in the protection racket, too.

When he finished at The Loco at night, he left with his briefcase or a grocery bag. Then he would drop off the leader and then go home himself. Abel and Tank figured he was probably handing a bundle of cash to Alverez during the drive, or Alverez was taking his share while he was at The Loco, but at the very end of the night, bags of money were going in to Garcia's house, and they never saw him enter any real commercial bank.

The final convincing piece of evidence placing the bank at Garcia's house was delivered by FedEx. André was taking the morning shift and observed the truck show up and the driver dash to Garcia's door, repeatedly ringing the bell. Garcia came to the door and signed for a package a little bigger than a shoebox.

It was well known that organized crime moved money by FedEx and UPS, so Abel and André figured that must be the cartel money for the minigun—$250,000 in 10K stacks would easily fit in the delivered box. Maybe it was wishful thinking, and they were jumping to conclusions, but it wasn't Garcia buying beauty supplies from Amazon.

Staking out the AB at the gun range was getting old, and both Harm and Rabbit were thoroughly tired of it. One of them had the dayshift, then the other showed up at sundown. Noticing the real action happened after hours, they both stayed through the evening.

The day shift was boring. There was just the occasional shooter. The day watcher napped on and off while the other guy got real sleep at home. The place heated up after 8 pm when groups of cars arrived. So Rabbit and Harm took to sneaking the place as soon as it was dark.

They had found a place to hide their cars about a half mile away and would skulk to the range through the woods, using a handheld GPS navigator to make sure they didn't get lost. Rabbit insisted they didn't need the navigator, being country boys and all, but Harm prevailed, saying the last thing they needed was to get confused in the woods and end up being mosquito bait all night long.

They would come in to the range from the east, scout the site for a while, nailing down where all the AB players were, then post up in the trees by the parking lot in front of the big metal barn where they had seen the minigun.

Some nights were as dull as the day watch. Others seemed to be scheduled meeting nights where a multitude of AB would show up and have some kind of camp revival meeting in the warehouse. One night, there was someone giving a haranguing speech, interspersed with shouting, the words unintelligible but the cadence reminding Rabbit of some old Nazi film clips he'd seen.

This time they were locked down in the woods as usual but in a slightly different position; it gave them a better sight line into the barn. They had snooped the place, and only a few Aryans were lurking around, and they figured they were in for another quiet night when two pickup trucks grumbled into the lot each with a tarp covered load.

"Holy shit! This is it," hissed Rabbit.

"Shss!"

Two men came jogging down the road from the direction of the office as the truck drivers exited their vehicles. The four men congregated near the tailgate of one of the trucks, and they stood there for a while in quiet conversation. Harm and Rabbit could hear the shape of the words, interspersed with periodic laughter.

Three of the men had lit up, and the ember of one cigarette could be seen wildly moving around, punctuating the cadence of the conversation.

"Fuck! Are they going to stand there all night?" complained Rabbit.

"Jesus, Rabbit—shut it!" whispered Harm.

The men eventually broke apart and removed the tarps, neatly folding them up, working in pairs like they were folding bedsheets. Then two by two, they started unloading crates and could be seen stacking them neatly inside the warehouse.

"Fucking Nazis," said Rabbit. "Look how precise they're stacking that shit. That's the guns for sure."

"Rabbit! Shut the fuck up!"

"Look who's talking now."

"Aw—" Harm started to say something but was interrupted by a minivan pulling into the lot next to the trucks.

"Hey, looks like Mrs. Hitler and her two little brownshirts are here with some strudel for daddy," said Rabbit.

Rabbit was way off. A beefy man stepped out and opened the sliding door of the old Dodge minivan, reached in, and stepped back as two dogs jumped out of the van, each on a leash.

"Fuck!" said Harm. "German shepherds of course."

Rabbit whispered, "We should go."

"Wait, don't move."

The dog handler guided the dogs over to the men and barked out a command. The dogs sniffed the men and then sat. There were a few words exchanged, then the handler started leading the dogs around the lot, working the fringes.

"I think he's just training the dogs," Harm muttered.

"We need to git," urged Rabbit.

"OK."

They slowly backed away from the lot as the dogs were getting nearer. Harm could feel the breeze at his back blowing toward the German shepherds, and it was impossible to be completely quiet. They continued inching away from the lot, the forest closing in around them.

Suddenly, BARK BARK BARK BARK. Rabbit jumped and started running.

"Hey! I hear something," shouted the handler. "There's something out there!"

Harm heard the other men start yelling and some thrashing noises behind him. He took off after Rabbit, thinking, *I better not lose him. He's got the GPS.* But Rabbit was hurtling through the woods, making so much noise that he was impossible to miss.

The Aryans were close, the barking and shouting felt right behind him, and he reached down and pulled out his

Glock, thinking, *Shoot the dogs first.* He ran as hard as he could, the branches whipping his face, taking great gulping gasps of air, pulling closer to Rabbit.

He reached Rabbit, grabbed his shoulder, and Rabbit flailed his arm back at him. "It's me! Stop!" They stopped. The dogs were kicking up a ruckus, one of them baying for blood. "Quick, check the GPS," demanded Harm.

Rabbit checked the navigator. "It's that way!" He took off. "C'mon—the dogs will find us."

Harm stayed tight, but each branch Rabbit pushed out of the way returned to smack his face. He ran with one hand up, the Glock in the other.

They reached their vehicles, the whole time feeling like the Nazis were just on the verge of catching them. "Goddamn, I'm glad they didn't let the dogs off the leash—we woulda been goners," gasped Rabbit. "We better call Abel!" They jumped in their vehicles and screamed on to the highway.

CHAPTER
_____

SEVENTEEN

R abbit's call woke up Abel, who'd fallen asleep just
before midnight. It was on. The arms were in place
at the Aryan Brotherhood's shooting range—that
was a fact. The crew was almost one hundred percent
sure that Garcia had the money in place. They knew he
was stashing some cash at his place; they'd seen it going
in and hadn't seen it going out. The FedEx delivery was
almost certainly the cartel minigun money. Abel and his
guys couldn't wait till it was ironclad, or the deal would go
down, and they would miss their chance at the score. They
had to hit them—now.

The next night, Abel and Tank were staged up the street
from Garcia's house. The MS-13 lieutenant was at The
Loco, and René, Rabbit, and André were in stolen cars
surrounding The Crazy Light, poised to take off after
Garcia if he came out and drove off. The plan was for Abel
and Tank to break into the bank at Garcia's place while the

rest of the guys were hanging on Garcia at the bar. If he moved, the guys could stop him.

If the house was a bust, the crew on Garcia would pinch him and see if he had the cash in his Lexus. If the money wasn't with him, they would force him at gunpoint to tell them where it was. Garcia was the key, and they were going to press him from all directions.

Abel called André. "We're going in—if he moves, lock him up!"

"Good luck, we got this end covered," said André.

Abel hung up and nodded at Tank who accelerated down the street and backed into Garcia's driveway. They exited the anonymous white Ford Econoline van, Abel opening the double rear doors and Tank dragging out the custom scissor jack they'd built to tear apart the house's back doorjamb. Abel grabbed the electric drill fitted with a socket, and they hustled around the house to the kitchen door.

Abel tried the door to see if they got lucky. Nope—locked. Tank lifted the jack in place, and Abel fitted the drill socket over the scissor jack's bolt and spun it till the jack was lodged firmly in place above the doorknob. Abel spun it down, the jack pushing the jambs apart, and the doorframe quietly expanded till the kitchen door swung open of its own accord. They were in.

They drew their guns and pulled down their balaclavas, then bent down and entered the house underneath the jack. They cleared the house room by room as a matter of course, not expecting anybody. Garcia had already left.

When they entered the bedroom, a person sat up in the bed. Abel almost had a heart attack.

"What?" the man said.

"Don't fucking move," Tank shouted, his gun in the man's face.

"Jesus!" Abel exclaimed. "It's his fucking boyfriend."

"Don't hurt me," the man whined. His words were distorted and slow.

"He's stoned," said Abel.

Tank jammed the gun in Garcia's boyfriend's ear. "Roll over!" Abel zip-tied the guy's wrist's together, then moved down, stripping the bed linens back, and zip-tied the man's ankles together, then to the footboard. The MS-13 soldier was wearing white socks and nothing else. Abel pulled off one of the socks and stuffed it in the man's mouth. "Don't move! Don't yell, and we won't kill you," Tank growled into the man's ear.

Next, they returned to the kitchen door, removed the jack, and threw it into the back of the van. The guys each grabbed a bag of demolition tools. Abel took a long crowbar in his free hand, and Tank picked up a heavy-duty Halligan, a fireman's tool used to rip apart houses, then they reentered Garcia's house.

They started searching for the money. The day-to-day cash pickups were somewhere in the house, and they figured Garcia had hidden the cartel quarter mil in a special place. But maybe he was stupid and complacent, and they would find it all in a drawer in the kitchen.

They zoomed through the house, checking all the obvious places first: freezer, under the bed, the top shelf in the closet. The quick pass netted them a cash box that was literally just sitting on a desk next to a bill counter in one of the spare bedrooms. It had a flimsy lock, which Tank defeated with a screwdriver, and was stuffed with loose bills. They didn't bother to count it, just dumped its contents into the black canvas duffle they brought.

Abel and Tank hadn't seen a conspicuous hidey hole for the cartel money, so they each took a room and started tearing them apart piece by piece. They moved furniture, ripped open mattresses, threw everything out of the cabinets, and searched for false bottoms in drawers. It wasn't a big house, but it still took an hour.

There was not much left to examine but the attic. They hadn't looked there in the first pass because the access panel was in the hall ceiling, and it required a ladder. Abel had noticed a ladder conveniently leaning in one of the rooms, but neither he nor Tank voiced the obvious question: Why did Garcia need a ladder?

Abel dragged the stepladder under the attic hatch, climbed the rungs, and pushed the plywood board covering the opening up and into the attic. He peeked into the dark space and brought up his flashlight, expecting to see boxes and the usual detritus, but saw a mostly empty space occupied by a water heater, an HVAC unit, and a bucket of wallboard mud with some painting supplies sitting on a board spanning two ceiling joists.

He climbed the rest of the way into the attic, balancing himself on two joists, and flashed his light around the space. Nothing. Frustrated, he carefully worked himself over to the water heater, stepping from joist to joist, and found it warm to the touch. The dry air in the attic was musty, and he could smell an underlying odor of rodents. He tiptoed gingerly across the joists, waving his arms to keep from falling, making his way to the furnace.

Tank's head poked up through the hatch. "Find anything?"

"Nope, place is empty," said Abel, disappointed.

"Nothing behind the HVAC?"

"I'm looking," said Abel, carefully standing on a two-inch-wide joist and aiming his light behind the air conditioner. He started to lose his balance and struck the boxy air handler at the end of the unit with his flashlight. A dull thud echoed through the attic.

"Wait," exclaimed Tank. "Do that again."

Abel rapped the large galvanized box that had several flexible air ducts emanating from it like tentacles. Thud. Thud. He shone the light beam on each of the ducts one at a time. "Lookee here . . ." The click of his switchblade opening sounded in the attic, then Abel cut into the largest air duct close to the air handler box. He tore it away and shone the light into the orifice. Inside was a black plastic bag. Abel pulled it through the opening. "That boy was getting clever on us."

"Yeah, who would have thought to check inside a working air conditioner?" marveled Tank, as he climbed down the ladder.

Abel followed him with the bulky garbage bag. As soon as his feet hit the floor, he ripped the bag open. It was filled with bricks of money, mostly banded stacks of hundreds but some roughly packed units of smaller bills. The whole bag went into the black duffle.

"Are we done?" asked Tank.

"Yeah," responded Abel. But something was bugging him, like a sneeze that wouldn't come. He reviewed what they had found. They had the arms deal cash and some assorted small bills from the money box. "Where's all the pickup money, like from the bars and the girls' house and shit?"

"There was a roll of shrink-wrap and a money counter in that bedroom," said Tank. He gestured toward the room. "They were counting and wrapping money. You're right—there's gotta be more cash here somewhere."

Abel's mind squeezed out the thought that was tickling his brain. "What the fuck is Garcia doing with home repair shit in the attic? Who needs wallboard mud and paint, unless they are messing with the walls?"

"The cash is in the walls!" Tank said excitedly.

"Get the tools out to the van while I check," ordered Abel, picking up the Halligan and brandishing his flashlight. He ran from wall to wall shining the light sideways. The harsh light raked the wall and highlighted any defects on the surface. Every rough spot got a whack and a pull from the Halligan, ripping out a big chunk of wallboard.

He circled the living room and moved into the kitchen. He examined each wall, then headed to the bedrooms but stopped and returned to the kitchen and dragged the refrigerator out of its alcove. He put his cheek against the dusty wall and shone the light. An obvious seam leaped out at him. "I found it!" he yelled.

"Motherfucker!" screamed Tank. "This asshole has a phone! He called Garcia. We have to get the fuck out of here."

"Wait!" Abel yelled, then speed-dialed André, who picked up on the first ring.

"What?" asked André.

"We're burned. We need a minute. You gotta stop Garcia."

"A'ight! He just dropped off Alverez a few minutes ago, and now he's driving like a maniac. He may be scrambling soldiers from The Loco. Get the fuck outta there!" He hung up.

Abel turned to Tank. "Get everything out, but leave the duffle. Get the van running. Call Harm and warn him!" Tank took off and Abel swung the Halligan against the wall behind the fridge and ripped a long piece of dry wall out.

It was like finding a dripping honeycomb in the walls: cash was shrink-wrapped and stacked up to eye level between the studs. He dropped the Halligan and started shifting bundles from the wall to the take-out duffle. His internal alarm was going off—*get the fuck out—get the fuck out—get . . .*

Abel had only shifted half the money, but the duffle was full, and his nerves were stretched tight. He grabbed it and ran to the van.

René, Rabbit, and André had followed Garcia when he left the El Luz Loco to ferry the leader, Alverez, back to his home. The MS-13 leaders had left earlier than usual, and the boys tracked them in a loose box around their Lexus. Garcia had unloaded the boss and headed back toward the bar and his own house but had suddenly put the hammer down, his vehicle shooting down the road, just before André had gotten the panic call from Abel.

André switched back to his three-way with René and Rabbit on his phone. "Heads up, the job's blown—Garcia knows. We've got to stop him and give Abel time."

"Are we going to pinch him?" asked Rabbit.

"Yeah. Let me get in position behind him and when you see me there, move in for the stop. René—float and get ready to pick us up. Put on your helmets!"

André pulled the strap tight on his own helmet, reached into his pocket, and took out a mouthguard, then inserted it between his teeth. He pressed the gas and maneuvered himself about a hundred feet back from Garcia's Lexus. Just as he hit his follow spot, Rabbit's stolen Dodge Charger screamed by him on the left, passed him, then barely passed Garcia. The moment Rabbit cleared the Lexus, he edged in front and slammed on his brakes. Garcia hit his brakes, too, in a panic stop, his tires screeching. They collided and Garcia's airbags blew. André feathered his brakes and hit the Lexus from behind, not getting an airbag in the face because Rabbit had previously disconnected it. André's car was pinning the Lexus against Rabbit's Charger. Everybody's brakes were stomped to the floor, antilock mechanisms ratcheting, smoke and stink boiling off the skidding tires.

The three cars ground to a halt and Rabbit and André jumped out of their cars, diving into René's getaway vehicle as it paused by the locked up cars. André took one last look at Garcia's trapped Lexus, the airbag partially deflated and Garcia's head leaning forward, his dark suit covered with white powder.

The side door of the building blasted open, banging against the side of the building, and Tattoo Face ran out the door headed for his car.

"Hold it, motherfucker!" screamed Harm.

Tattoo Face abruptly stopped and turned around to face Harm, who was wearing a black balaclava and holding a shotgun on him. "What the fuck, puto?"

"Get down on your knees!"

Tattoo Face stood there, looking at Harm. Dead eyes locked with dead eyes. "You don't know what you're getting into."

"Shut the fuck up!" Harm stepped in with the shotgun. "DOWN!"

Inked face defiant, he reluctantly sank to his knees. "You better kill me, canche! I'll find you, and I'll kill you. It'll be slow, chelón."

Harm circled the kneeling Tattoo Face. "Put your hands on the ground in front of you." Harm stopped behind him. He darted in and struck him in the head with the butt of the shotgun. Tattoo face fell forward, his arms and legs flailing. "No, I'll be killing YOU, when it suits ME—motherfucker!"

He stepped in and rapped the prostrate man on the head with the butt of the shotgun harder, then bent over the still man, lifted his shirt, and removed the pistol that was stuck down his pants. He quickly searched the gang member, pocketing his wallet and a heavy switchblade. Harm looked around and then ran down the street.

EIGHTEEN

The crew rendezvoused back at Abel's house, crashing in the living room. They all sat down, but then one or the other would stand up and mill around, jittery, their adrenaline still jacked. Shots of bourbon were passed around, more like medical intervention than celebration. The alcohol burned.

"How did the stop on Garcia go?" asked Abel.

"Intense. I did this sweet cut in on his Lexus—worked perfect—then, André hammered his butt. Garcia ended up looking like a ghost after his airbag blew," rattled off Rabbit.

"Any problems? Did they see your faces?" he prodded.

André tagged on. "No, we had helmets on. It's all good."

"I had it on with Tattoo Face..." Harm casually added.

"Wait! What?" Abel asked, incredulous.

"Yeah, he came scrambling out the house right after Tank gave me the heads up. I held the shotty on him, and he threatened to kill me, so I gave him a little pop on the head with the shotgun stock."

"You know in the movies, when the bad guy threatens that he's gonna kill you, you say, 'I believe you,' then you shoot 'em," said Rabbit.

"Well, I thought about it but figured Callie wouldn't like it, plus I didn't want to fire the shotgun and be seen or heard."

"Good thinking," Abel said. "Robbing them is one thing. Killing one of 'em changes the game."

"Yeah," said Tank, a worried look on his face. "But those guys are gonna be stirred up regardless."

"Especially since not only did we take the gun money but we also ripped into Garcia's private stash. I didn't have time to get it all, but I took like two-thirds of it," Abel said, not hiding the glee on his face.

"How did Garcia get tipped that you were ripping off his bank?" asked André, pacing around the room and running his hands thru his 'fro, trying to put it all together.

"Well, first off, the place wasn't empty. Garcia's lover was there, asleep, in the bed. We tied him up and shit and zipped him to the bed, but we didn't search the bed," admitted Tank.

"Yeah, he had a phone in there somewhere," Abel added in a frustrated tone. "We were in a hurry. It was my fault—it's my job to stop and think."

"This is the second time in a row that we got beat for not searching the people thoroughly," said André, somewhat accusingly.

Tank had Abel's back. "In our defense, bro, he was naked except for socks. And he was stoned out of his gourd."

"Nah," Abel said. "One time, we can make excuses, but this is twice. André's right. We have to secure and search the people. I don't know. The first time, I almost got killed. Now this time, we all had to react. It put us all in danger. And to top it off, because I had to hurry, I left like 200K still in the walls. I could kick myself. That would have almost paid off Deke," Abel said, his eyebrows pinched in, mentally beating himself up.

"Every job has a fuck up in it. That's life. We learn. We adapt. We stick together, and we tough it out. Motherfuckers—this was a win!" exclaimed Tank.

Abel laughed, instantly in a better mood. "Yeah, that's right—motherfuckers!" He had a big grin. "Speaking of the win—André, what was the take?"

"Seven-hundred forty-thousand and some change —motherfuckers!"

"Wheee haw!" shouted Rabbit. "MOTHERFUCKER!"

They all laughed their asses off, then René killed the mood. "How much are we giving my dad?" There followed a lengthy argument, swinging from paying him off the full half mil and getting Deke's business out right to just giving him his usual twenty percent. André, the voice of reason, guided them to settle in the middle at 250K, figuring if they paid Deke off completely, he wouldn't have any incentive to find them better scores. They each would net about 81K, which would be their best payday yet.

They moved to the kitchen and piled the money up on the table. Abel brought in the bill counter and vacuum packer, which they used to squeeze the stacks of cash into neat plastic wrapped blocks. The crew plodded through the job of counting and splitting the take, their energy ebbing. Each guy divvied up his money in portions, ready cash and stash. Then they vacuum packed the stacks they were taking to their safety deposit boxes. René packed Deacon's 250K into three bricks.

When they finished, Abel told them he would drop off Deke's share, then he admonished them. "Take your money to the bank first thing. Remember how easy it was to take it from those MS assholes." He paused, then another giant smile lit up his face. "And I'll see you tonight at The Machine. I'm buying—MOTHERFUCKERS!"

They had partied all night at The Machine, getting the celebration mayhem out of their systems. René, in rare form, did lines of shots and then escaped to the dance floor, moving from one girl to another. It was the middle of the week and not as packed as normal, but that didn't stop him. He was in a field with the occasional wildflower, and he was a bee going from bloom to blossom. With two trips to the parking lot already, he was going for a personal best.

The rest of the guys sat on the sidelines watching, trying to outdo each other with acidic commentary. Tank and Abel had developing relationships, and Rabbit was almost happily married. Harm was always dreaming of Callie, and the crew knew not to tease him too much. But André didn't have a reason to be sitting out, and the boys, of course, let him have it. Every time a likely candidate for him walked by, they joked and jeered.

André was running his hands through his hair over and over, getting progressively more and more embarrassed and irritated until Tank noticed that they'd about pushed his brother to the limit and backed them all off. As soon as they stopped, André jumped up and went to the far side of the patio, like an embarrassed dog.

It was late, and Rabbit used that as an excuse to take off home. Harm joined him, leaving Tank and Abel alone. Olivia came by to check on Abel, to see if he was going before her shift ended, whispering in his ear an invitation to come to her house when her shift was over. Abel put his arm around her waist and pulled her close and told her he would wait. She backed away with a big smile and a little wave.

The two men sat there not speaking, just listening to the DJ spinning tracks. Abel slid over closer to Tank so he didn't have to shout to be heard. "How are things going with Kisha? You haven't said much about her."

"Good," said Tank.

"Man, you got to tell me more than that. Do you like her? Is it serious?" probed Abel.

Tank shifted, like he was in the hot seat, clearly uncomfortable. "Yeah, it's serious for me. Not sure how serious she is."

"Does she call you and text you without you doing it first?" asked Abel, like he was an expert.

"Sure," answered Tank.

"How many times have you gone out?"

"Maybe seven times, but three of them have been church functions."

"Have you done it yet?"

"Jeez, Abel!"

"Look, man, I'm just trying to figure out how real it is. You're my best friend. I'm practically your brother. We gotta talk about this shit." He laughed. "I guarantee, your mama and Callie are—they're probably planning your wedding already."

"Sheeyit," sighed Tank.

Abel's face took on an earnest expression. "Have you told her what you do for a living?"

"Nope. How the hell do I tell a girl from the church I'm a robber?"

"Yeah, I know. Olivia's got a real job and a kid. Maybe it's just being a waitress, but it's stand-up work, and she doesn't have to lie to Owen. I don't have any idea how to start that conversation." Abel was worried.

Tank looked Abel in the eye. "When you started talking about doing something different—Callie getting on your case, all that? I started thinking maybe we should try going legit. Give this shit up."

Abel said, "It's on my mind, big time. I just keep going around in circles. I've been thinking that if we get some big scores, we're all set up and have a buffer. We can try going straight. But give René his dad's business? That'll work for a while, maybe, but then he'll run it into the ground. If that happens, what do Harm and Rabbit do? I just don't want to let anyone down."

"Abel, what do *you* want, man? If you're good, we'll be good," assured Tank, putting his hand on Abel's shoulder. "You, me, and André? C'mon, man, we can do anything."

"Yeah, maybe." His tone was uncertain, his features noncommittal. "Definitely something to think about. In the meantime, we need some bank."

"So we gut it out in the short term. But look, man, deep down, you know we got to do something different. All this shit is going to catch up to us. I've got your back, you know that. But the world's changing." Tank and Abel got up, Tank wrapping Abel in a bear hug. "We can do this together, brother. Now I gotta go collect André before he blows up the myth that all Black men can dance."

Abel walked up to the bar where Olivia was chatting with the bartender. Her shift wasn't officially over, but it was a slow weekday night. She bumped up against Abel. "Let's go to my house," she said, already heading out of The Machine.

"Sure," responded Abel to her back, laughing to himself and doing a quick two-step to catch up, then grabbing her hand.

He walked with her to her car, then ran back to his truck in his uneven gait, hitting the remote before he got there, opening the door, and swinging himself up into the seat. Olivia was already on the move, and he gunned his vehicle to get close behind her.

They were at her house in a few minutes, and at the front door, Olivia tried to get inside quietly, dropping her keys and picking them up, giggling. She opened the door and pulled Abel into the foyer, her finger at her lips.

They tiptoed down the hall to Olivia's bedroom. Abel stepped in behind her, and she reached around him and pulled the door shut with a silent snick and turned the little lock on the knob. Abel started pulling off his clothes, dropping them in a pile at his feet, Olivia only slightly behind him, adding to the pile.

In bed, Abel was on her, Olivia's arms wrapped around him, pulling him tight, saying, "Shhh, shhh, shhh . . ."

Afterward, they lay there in the dark, their hips touching, and Olivia nestled in Abel's arm. The moonlight coming through the window frosted their features. "This is something, Olivia—isn't it?" whispered Abel.

"Yes. This feels real to me. It makes me feel like I'm something besides Owen's mama. I don't want it to stop."

"Me neither."

"Call me Liv. Everyone else calls me Olivia."

"OK, Liv." Abel smiled in the dark.

She snuggled closer. "Besides Owen being born, this is about the best I've felt since my daddy died."

"What happened with your dad? Do you mind telling me?"

"No, it was a long time ago. He drove a beer truck, and someone shot him on his route. The police said it was gang related—some random gang initiation thing because his truck was tagged, but my mom said that was bullshit. I could never get her to explain why."

"Jesus, that's terrible," said Abel. One part of his mind was with Olivia in the present, the other part was in the past with Deacon. The bottom dropped out of his stomach, and a wave of sickness washed over him. "Where did this happen?"

"Down in the city, in 2007."

Abel asked, "What was your daddy's name?"

"Benjamin Marks."

Despair welled up and darkness crashed down on Abel's mind.

NINETEEN

lverez was beyond irate. He was pacing back and forth in the small office in the back of El Luz Loco while Diego Gomez, his tattooed face set in a worried frown, watched. It was three steps and turn, three steps and turn, then suddenly Alverez whirled and glared at Gomez. "Where is that puto?"

"Uh, you mean Garcia?" Diego's nose and forehead were raw and abraded from bouncing off the pavement when Harm had struck the back of his head with the shotgun stock. "He told me he would be right in."

"Go get that cabrón now!"

Gomez dashed out and returned almost immediately with Garcia. "Sit down!" commanded the boss.

This was barely possible, as it was a small room to begin with, mostly occupied by a desk and a filing cabinet. The cramped quarters increased the tension. Garcia and Gomez crammed themselves into the two chairs across the desk from Alverez, overlapping each other like two fat men flying next to each other in coach. Alverez stared at them. "What the fuck happened?"

Garcia delivered the bad news stoically. "We were hit. Somehow, they knew where the bank was. They were on me, too. They crashed into me, in my car. They had people on Diego and stopped him so he couldn't come to help."

"One of you assholes made a mistake. Either on purpose or through stupidity. One of you fuckers is working against me."

"They didn't take any of the cash at the whorehouse," said Gomez.

Garcia set his cold eyes on him. "You knew the bank was at my place." He continued to stare. "You think 'cuz they didn't hit the whorehouse and take your money that puts you above suspicion? It makes you look more guilty!" He turned in his chair, his face inches from Diego's. "Why aren't you dead? You have the stink of a traitor."

Gomez scrambled to defend himself. "That chele almost killed me. He was there waiting for me."

"What about Ramón? The thieves didn't kill him, either. How much does he know? Did you tell him something over the pillow, Hector?" asked Alverez accusingly. "Who else did you tell about the money at your house?"

"I questioned Ramón first. He knows the same as everybody—that I'm the bagman." The cold look on Garcia's face got colder. "And he knows what I would do to anybody that crosses me—so does everybody else." He locked his dead eyes on Alverez. "I'm surprised at you, Alejandro. You disappoint me." Garcia's expression took on a strange intensity "All these years and you still don't know me. Remember what you've seen, what I did to my own father?"

"Sí, sí, I'm upset. Lo siento," said Alverez, backing down.

Garcia said, "This is something different. They were pros. They had it all sewed up. It wasn't internal, and it wasn't a gang thing. Somebody got wind of our business. The deal got leaked, and these assholes must have watched us and figured it all out or else they were just lucky. If that is what happened, they will curse their luck. The three of us knew about it. The cartel—the Tamaulipas. The Brotherhood knew. Maybe it was the AB, maybe they are playing both sides of the deal. They walk away with our money and our guns."

"How much did the bastards get?"

Garcia cleared his throat, then answered, "All of it. The cartel two-fifty for the minigun, the money we set aside for our weapons, and the whole bank in the walls—another four hundred grand. All told, 900K."

"Then we are dead," said Alverez, slumping back in his chair. "The cartel will send their Sicarios and the AB will declare war—it's their country; they have the numbers."

"I don't think it's time to panic just yet," Garcia said. "What about all the money you've been taking? You've taken cream off all our businesses. Where's that?"

"I've got a family. I've used that to support them. Neither of you have dependents."

"You've spent it all?" asked Garcia, incredulous.

"No, I have about two hundred and fifty grand set aside. It's my sons' legacy," he lied. That money was his due. He'd be damned if he was going to spend any of that to save Garcia's or Gomez's miserable sociopathic asses.

"OK, we can at least cover the minigun. We can split the AB deal into two parts—do the minigun first and collect the cartel's second 100K payment on that when we deliver the weapon. We then use that to make up for our half of the gun deal."

"We'll still be 150K short," said Gomez, stating the obvious but demonstrating that he could at least do math. Garcia looked at him, silencing him and putting him in his place. Embarrassed, Gomez shut his mouth, looking mutinous.

Gomez's interruption served to remind Alverez of Diego's money. "How much is in the walls at the whorehouse now?"

Gomez, hoping that the money would be overlooked, grudgingly admitted, "About fifty-five thousand."

They're lying, of course, Alverez thought. But none of them were going to give up their personal stashes. He estimated that pooled together they all had enough to cover this debacle and walk away with their lives and probably even profit. But he didn't trust that he would get all his own money back even if they fixed the deal, so it would be a bad investment. And further, pushing either of these two pendejos to go deeper into their pockets would probably result in negative consequences. Gomez was impulsive and unbalanced, but Garcia would plan something slow and clever—he might not see it coming. "That still leaves us 100K short. We're going to have to track these assholes down."

Alverez continued, "And if it turns out that it was the AB fucking us over—well, that is a different problem."

"But how are we going to find these people?" Gomez blurted out.

"Lúcido mentioned to me that some gringo came into The Loco and was asking questions. I noticed the chele but didn't think anything about it. Maybe we can follow that thread," said Garcia.

"Sí, use her to bait the gringo and see what she can find out," said Alverez, referring to the MS-13's classic approach of using their gang chicas to get to their enemies. "I'm going to talk to the Aryans and see if I can sniff out a betrayal."

Garcia turned to Diego. "Put your best soldiers around Alverez's house. I want it covered with two guys night and day. Put more around my house.

"Sí, jefe."

"I like what you've done with the place, cuñado!" said Lúcido as she gazed on the havoc that was Garcia's house. Everything was on the floor, stuffing from the furniture gathered in bunches, and pieces of the wall were strewn about.

"Alverez is hot. He can't figure out who hit us and how they knew where the money was," said Garcia.

"Tell me about the gringo," Hector said to his sister-in-law.

"He acts like a big shot. He knows he is muy guapo and expects every woman to swoon over him. I'm sure they do. The gringo has something, even I felt it. Maybe like they say, he has the pheromones, you know, like the smell that attracts women."

"OK, that is good. Can we find him?"

"Yes, I think I can find him. He told me his name, and he told me where he goes to drink."

"Was he playing you, or is he just estúpido?" asked Hector.

"No, he is clueless. He can't imagine a woman being as smart as him," Lúcido said derisively. "He told me his name was Abel Kane."

"Was he by himself—a lone wolf?"

Lúcido recounted how she had snuck out of the building and watched him leave. "I saw him talk to several people waiting in their vehicles outside the bar. He also spoke with a giant man in the street. A Black man."

"Hmmm," mused Garcia. "When I got hit, I was still dizzy, but I remember a large man running to the getaway car." His eyes took on a faraway look, like he was trying to picture something in his head. "Gigante?"

"Sí! Immenso!" Lúcido exclaimed. "A bear!"

"Ahhh, maybe we will get to make that oso dance." Garcia chuckled.

Lúcido shivered. She knew what he was referring to. Garcia would hang his enemies by their hands and then burn their bare feet with a torch, the blue flame searing their flesh and the victim's feet would flail a macabre jig.

Garcia said, "I want you to go to this man's favorite place—where he is comfortable. Play him like a fish. Make him think he is doing all the work, but make him want you. Do whatever it takes, but find out where he lives."

Lúcido snorted. "You're giving me instructions on how to work a man?" She was amused. "I think I can handle that myself."

He stared back at her, his face gone cold. "I must know where he lives, and then I will take it from there."

"Sí, Hector, I'll track him home."

She knew Garcia had protected her up to this point. And she knew she had eaten the crumbs that fell off his table, and maybe she had taken advantage of the fact that the only person he had ever cared about was his brother, but she knew her connection to him was tenuous. If she did not deliver Abel Kane, she had a bleak future. But maybe if she worked this right, she could dine on more than scraps.

CHAPTER

———

TWENTY

L úcido wasn't stupid and could use a computer to gather intelligence with the best of them. She wasn't called Lúcido for nothing. Before she drove up to Slidell, she had tried to track down Abel Kane's particulars. The problem was his gringo name had many variations. There were actually more hits than she expected, and she couldn't specifically nail him down to a single location.

Rather than staking out multiple locations, she went with plan B—putting on her hottest minidress. In the mirror, the red dress popped against her black curly hair, it went low on top and high up her legs, accentuating her curves. That hound dog wouldn't have a chance. He had made a point about his favorite bar, The Flying Machine, so she'd go and wait for him to show up. Thursday night was like the new Friday night nowadays, so she'd hang out and watch for him and have some fun with these country boys. She would keep showing up till he did.

The trip up to Slidell went by quickly. Lúcido spent the time thinking about how she would play it, how to work the conversation. Her survival depended on manipulating men; you could say she had a degree in it. In her world, the men had the money and the power, and you had to work it out of them. You shook the tree, and the money fell out of it. This pendejo was no different; he was the path to her next paycheck.

She found The Flying Machine, giving the place a once-over as she passed it and pulled into the parking lot. She snorted. The chele had made it sound like his place was something special, but it was just another dive—no better than The Loco, although bigger.

Lúcido stepped out of her vehicle and adjusted her mini—pulling it down over her ass and smoothing it in place. She looked at her reflection in the tinted window and pushed against the sides of her breasts and tugged down at the waist of the dress, making sure her cleavage was shown off to maximum effect. After checking her makeup one last time, she ran her hands through her hair, fluffing it out.

The parking lot was rough, more cobbles than pavement, so she took her time navigating the expanse in her vintage four-inch-heel Candies. Lúcido made it to the door without breaking an ankle, and she hoped the dance floor was at least flat or else that part of the plan wasn't going to work. Her shoes were killer to look at but were going to crimp her dancing. The bouncer saw her and gaped, then pulled the door open for her. Lúcido laughed to herself, thinking, *OK—looks like I picked the right outfit.*

The Machine was packed, even more than The Loco on a good night. Most of the girls were wearing tight jeans; very few were dressed like she was. Bueno, this dog would want to score with the hottest girl there. She could take her looks, add on the attitude, and she would be number one.

She worked her way through the front of the bar, scanning the patrons, not seeing this Abel puto. As she made her way to the back of the bar, she realized that there was another area outside. She passed through the doorway, the music transitioning to EDM on the patio. The outside dance floor was hit with lights, flashing at a seizure-inducing rate, that did not seem to bother the crowd of dancers.

She looked around at the outdoor club—a big bar, a packed dance floor surrounded by tables, and the whole space enclosed by a tall wooden fence. Across the back wall was a stage with a DJ, but it was big enough to hold a band. There were steps leading up to the stage that was almost six feet off the ground. Lúcido made her way to the steps and climbed halfway up. This gave her a good view into the dance floor. Carefully she scanned the floor, systematically working her way across the bar, reaching the far end on the right, and ratcheting her head back to the left like a typewriter before starting the next pass.

There he was! Right in the middle of the dance floor. He really was a party boy. She expected this was going to take a few days, but there was the puto—a real perro de caza. She was surprised that he wasn't humping the girl's leg. She had to admit though, he was something. He went from girl to girl, almost all of them upgrading from their current partner to this pendejo guapo. This was going to be easy.

Lúcido took a bead on him and went down the stairs and walked to the edge of the milling dancers. She slipped through the gyrating people until she had the chelón in her sights, took a deep breath, and stepped in front of his current partner. Lúcido's sheer presence pushed the local girl deeper into the crowd, no longer part of the scene. She looked up at him, leaned in, and half yelled into his ear, "Señor Abel, why you don't come to The Loco anymore?"

René had a stunned look on his face, then he looked her up and down, and it turned to a smile. "Lúcido! You found me!"

"Sí, I wanted to see how the other half lives..." She tucked her fingers behind his belt buckle and pulled him a little closer. "Are you going to dance with me?" Her body was moving sinuously.

René stepped in, following her body with his. They danced, moving with abandon. They had danced at The Crazy Light, but this was beyond that. Lúcido's body was like liquid, covering him, touching him here and there, teasing him, exciting a hunger. They were covered in sweat.

Lúcido worked him to the edge of the dance floor, then pulled his head down and spoke close to his ear, "Take me someplace private, rápidamente!"

"C'mon!" He grabbed her hand, practically running to the bathrooms built along one wall of the patio. He pushed open the door of the men's room and looked into the small bathroom. Empty! René pulled her in, and turned the flimsy lock on the knob.

He wrapped his arms around her, his right hand sliding down her back. Her head tilted back, and he bent in to kiss her. She pressed into him with her hips, and René's hand cupped her ass, pulling her in tighter. He pushed her up against the sink, and she wiggled around in his arms so they both were facing the patchy mirror in the dim light. She bent over the sink, putting her forearms down, and her dress rode up. René dropped his pants, beyond ready, and entered her. Their eyes locked in the mirror, and René moved against Lúcido. She answered with her body. He pulled her hips tight to him, watching her face in the mirror, until he saw her face change, and then he finished.

They stayed coupled, panting. René took a step back with a gasp. Lúcido stood up and turned to look at him. "I think you should buy a girl a drink..."

René guided her to the farthest table from the DJ he could find, a crummy spot right next to the back entrance to the kitchen, but the decibel level there was the lowest on the patio. They might be able to talk without shouting. Normally, he would have been trying to brush her off, but he was intrigued. He wondered if it had something to do with the job, but he'd looked into her eyes when they were having sex, and he saw something there—lust or maybe danger. She was so different from his usual type. It wasn't her looks so much as her personality and attitude, a mixture of smarts, sensuality, and nastiness. And she looked at him like she wanted him. He felt a connection.

He had buttonholed the waitress, ordering the drinks before they sat down, and she came over with their cocktails. René pulled out a huge roll of bills, a stack of hundies wrapped around his chump change. He handed her a twenty and a ten, massively overtipping.

"Wow, you're nice," remarked Lúcido. "I wouldn't mind being your waitress," she said with a smirk. "You must be really successful. What do you do for a living?"

"I have an import business with a group of guys I grew up with. We bring in a lot of goods from Mexico and South America and then distribute it around the Gulf. We made a big deal this week, so I'm out celebrating," bragged René, stretching back in his seat with his arms resting on the chairbacks on each side of him.

He made it sound like he was moving drugs, a big drug kingpin, but Lúcido didn't bite.

"Why aren't you celebrating with your business associates?"

"We did already, but I wasn't ready to stop partying. I wanted more me time, you know?"

"Yes," agreed Lúcido. And she really did—guys like this pendejo? It was all *me time*. She got back to business. "So, Abel, do you live here in Slidell, too?"

René paused for a moment. "Naw, I live over in Lacombe. Where do you live?"

"I live near The Luz Loco."

"How long have you lived there?"

"About five years. I moved there from El Salvador with my husband."

René started to say, "Your hus—" but Lúcido interrupted.

"He died just after we moved here. I got stranded. The rest of my family is back in El Salvador."

"Do you have a job?"

"Yes, I used to be a waitress at The Loco, but now I run the place. Make the liquor orders, hire people, that kind of thing."

"I can see you running the place. You're smart. You could probably start your own place and get rich. Maybe I could help you get started. I have some money to invest."

"Hmmm, that's interesting." Lúcido gave Abel her best wide-eyed look. "You should come back down to The Loco—we can talk. Let's exchange numbers." She'd gotten all the information that she thought she could pump out of him without making him suspicious, and it was time to withdraw. "It's getting late, muchacho—I should head back down to the city. I have to get some sleep; I work long hours over the weekend."

"I'll walk you to your car."

René walked her through the door in the patio enclosure that went straight to the parking lot, and she guided him to her vehicle. He put his arms around her and kissed her. She broke away and said, "Are you leaving, too?"

"No, I'm going to go back inside and say goodbye to some of my friends, then I'm going to leave."

"OK, Señor Abel, I'm at The Loco almost every night till closing—come see me." She got in her car, gave him a little wave, and then bent down like she was looking in her purse.

René turned back to the bar. Lúcido waited a minute to make sure that he was going in again and then slowly drove out of the lot, looking for a good place to park. She situated herself with a sight line to the door off the patio and the entrance to the parking lot. She couldn't find a spot that let her see The Machine's front door unfortunately. She hoped that he would leave through the back door. He wasn't going to be hard to spot when he came out because of his bleached blond hair, but she might lose him when he went deep into the lot to get his own vehicle.

Meanwhile, René had gone back into the bar, not to say goodbye to friends but do some more dancing. He felt too good to leave just yet. He looked around and saw a pretty girl step off the floor and bend over and pick up her shoes. René casually stepped close to her and said, "What, you're tired already?"

She bit, of course, and René deployed his master flirtation moves. He dropped that he was a successful businessman, an investment banker who'd just won a big account and wanted to celebrate. He saw her dance, she was a good dancer, blah blah blah. René never got tired of the game. In no time, they were back on the floor.

Lúcido was getting irritated. *What is it with this pendejo? I wasn't enough for him—he's still in there partying?* Frustrated, but not willing to quit, she continued to watch The Flying Machine's parking lot. She waited another half hour, chain-smoking to pass the time. She was wondering whether she had missed him leave, when he suddenly popped out of the patio gate. She got out of her car and stood on the rocker panel under the door to give her some extra height. His head was visible as he passed through the lot. She watched him bend down, and soon his headlights could be seen moving toward the exit.

His car left the lot, the chelón babying his car over the little ramp down to the street. Of course, he was driving a sports car, some fancy foreign job—a Porsche or Jaguar. Just the car a person stuck on himself would drive.

When he hit the street, he peeled off toward the highway, and Lúcido was hard pressed to keep up in her little shit-box. They drove for a little while, heading toward Lacombe, and she followed, keeping enough distance that she figured she wouldn't register on his radar. Her gut told her that she didn't even need to worry because he was the overconfident, oblivious type, but she was careful anyway.

The sports car crossed a little bridge and then took a quick right on the road that was parallel to the bayou. The car traveled for a few minutes, then slowed down and carefully turned into the woods between the road and the water. It looked like they were on the outside of Lacombe just before it turned country. She waited a beat and then inched up to the spot where he'd turned. It was a driveway that disappeared into the forest going back in the general direction of the bayou. She couldn't see his vehicle, but she could see his lights bouncing off different trees in the distance.

Lúcido drove on and found a place to turn around. She passed the entrance again, but he never came back out. It must be his place, she decided, then headed home.

René stood on Abel's dock listening to the peepers making a racket. He walked to the picnic table and sat down and lit another smoke, watching Abel's back door. He sat for a time, barely moving, no expression on his face, and after a while, he got up and left.

TWENTY-ONE

"He thinks he's God's gift to women, this Abel Kane puto." Lúcido was briefing Garcia and Alejandro Alverez. Gomez was lurking in the background as usual. "He was flashing a big roll and talking about a big business deal, hinting that he was a drug dealer. Had a showy car—foreign sports car, a Porsche or Jag, something like that. Estúpido led me directly to his house and gave me his phone number, practically begging me to call him."

"Was he suspicious, you just showing up like that?" Alverez asked.

"No, he thinks all women want him. He is like a little boy," she said derisively.

"Is this the pendejo who hit us?" probed Alejandro.

"We don't know for sure it's this guy, but he has a giant Black hombre in his group, and the team that hit me in the Lexus had a huge man, too. Maybe a coincidence, but my gut tells me it's them. The gringo shows up at El Loco, he has a giant associate, and he is flashing a huge roll of cash. It feels right," Garcia added.

Alverez was standing with his hands behind his back, and he tipped his head slightly to the side, his suit coat parting, showing off his protruding belly. "I talked to some of my contacts around the city. These Kanes are old-school Dixie Mafia." He paced around a few steps. "The head man, Deacon Kane, runs some robbery crews; he is one of the go-to fences in the Gulf, and they live up in Lacombe. It is said that this gigoló, Abel, is his nephew. So I agree with Hector, it feels like these are the assholes that hit our bank, but the old man doesn't have much juice anymore. This seems beyond him. Perhaps the young man wants to take over the business from his uncle."

"What are you thinking?" asked Garcia.

"I am thinking that we need to finish our deal with the Aryans. We need to get the minigun to the cartel people and collect the final 100K. Gomez will pull out the 50K in the whorehouse stash. You need to come up with another 100K so we can get the truckload of guns and ammo from the Nazis. I went into my personal savings—now it is your turn. You helped create this problem. It is on you to help fix it," said Alverez, glaring at Garcia.

"I disagree, Alejandro," replied Garcia. "I think we should go directly to war with the AB." He pointed his finger at Alverez in a jabbing motion. "We kill off their leadership—hurt them so bad they won't come after us. The 250K we gave them? We take it back. Take all of the arms we ordered, and we don't put out a dime for them. We take them for free and turn around and sell them. That almost makes us whole right there."

"It doesn't cover the loss, not even close. But I've learned—one thing at a time. It is like a real war between countries. One front at a time. You split your forces; you lose." Alverez had stopped walking around like an avuncular professor and was holding up his fingers, counting off. "One—we get the minigun to the cartel and take our payment so we don't have cartel sicarios up our asses. Two—we get square with the Aryans. Three—then, we go to war—we go after the Kanes and get all of our money back plus everything else they have. Understood?"

"Yes," answered Garcia. But he meant no.

The whorehouse had a smell that Garcia couldn't place, but it disgusted him. The women were out of it, lolling about in their disheveled beds—their nakedness barely covered by the stained and yellowed sheets. He preferred the drug trade or extortion or just about anything else. But this was where he could find Gomez and talk to him privately without Alverez hearing about it.

Gomez seemed at home in the stench and was blithely eating a sandwich, a dab of mayonnaise stuck to the corner of his mouth. Garcia had been talking to him for several minutes, but Diego was being stubborn.

"Alejandro said we lay off the Kanes until we unload the minigun and get through with the Nazis," Gomez said.

"Look, Diego, we just keep digging deeper in our own pockets, and by the time we go after this Abel Kane pendejo, he and all his crew will have spent all of our money. I know you have more than 50K stuffed in these walls. Do you think Alverez is going to let you keep that if he is down a quarter mil of his own and the bank is down for 900K?"

Gomez was vicious and stupid, but he understood the value of money, especially his money. "Well, what are you saying, Hector?"

"I've been saying it all along. We need to hit this Kane asshole now and get all the money back. Then, we hit the Aryans and take the guns. Then we're not only whole—we are up." Garcia didn't complete the thought and mention that they would also have to move out Alverez. That, he would save for later.

"How do we do this?" Gomez asked.

"Get one of your best soldados. The three of us hit Kane's house. Lúcido gave me the location. We take whatever money is there. And we torture that motherfucker till he tells us where the rest of it is."

"Then we kill them all?" asked Diego.

"Sí—we hang them from a bridge."

TWENTY-TWO

I t was a clear night, and when the wind shifted the smoke away from him, Abel could smell the bayou— an earthy mustiness of mown grass and tropical perfumes. He pulled the cooler a little closer to his chair and reached in and pulled out a fresh Abita. The night had turned chilly after the sun had gone down, so Tank had built a fire of live oak. The three of them were having a heart-to-heart around the fire. Abel reached into the Igloo and pulled out another cold one for André.

Abel's mind had attained a clarity since Olivia had dropped the bomb that she was Benny Marks' daughter. She was the girl that he'd seen Benny drive to school, the girl that he'd seen kiss her daddy, the girl whose father he had helped murder. Even without Olivia bringing it all back, it had been there, deep down—like a hidden infection his body had been trying to fight.

"André, I don't know how much Tank has told you about our conversation at The Machine, but he and I've been talking about the future." Abel leaned back in his chair and took a large swallow of beer and wiped his lips with the back of his hand. "You know, this has been fun and all, but I've realized that we're never going to be able to have lives with normal families if we stay on this path.

"These one-nighters with trailer chicks and half-assed relationships have allowed us to pretend things are all good because we don't have to tell them the truth. Tank has a decent woman now, a girl from the church. How is he going to tell her about the Life? And although it's a remote chance, maybe someday you'll find a girl, too."

"Fuck you, Abel," André said, but he laughed.

Abel laughed with him. "So this girl I've met—Olivia? She's Benny Marks' daughter and doesn't know that her daddy was in the Life." Tank and André had heard vague rumors but didn't know for sure that Deacon had killed Marks, and they definitely didn't know that Abel had been the driver. Abel could barely admit to it himself.

"Shit—small world," Tank exclaimed.

"And you know, your mama knows all about us, too. We've been thinking we're keeping a big secret and we're hotshot robbers? Isabelle knows all about it—maybe not the details, but she told me the other day." Abel took another big gulp of beer. "Basically, she told me that you guys were in because of me, and she's right. She just hasn't been facing us with it.

"I'm worried about her; she wasn't just talking about robbery. Belle was looking me in the eye and speaking about good, evil, the devil, and shit."

"Yeah, she's been going on and on about it at home," added Tank worriedly. "I should have told you, I guess, but I was hoping it would just go away.

"And as far as her saying you brought us into this? Both André and I made our own decisions. After our dad died, we needed money to live. Mama's lunch-lady paycheck wasn't cutting it. You had to do what you did—and we had to do what we did."

André added, "We're practically brothers. You helped our family when Daddy died, so don't feel bad about what Mama said."

"She wasn't blaming me; she was just stating facts—it helped me see things. I don't want to grow up and be Deacon Kane."

"What about taking over Deacon's operation?" asked André.

"I'm going to sit down with him and tell him I'm out, and the two of you are out. Is that right? Are you out?" Tank said adamantly, "If you're out, I'm out."

"Same!" agreed André. "The world has changed. We can do something different—at least, the three of us."

"René was pissed that Deke handed off to me, so here's his chance to take over." But Abel's face was conflicted. "I'm worried about Harm and Rabbit. Rabbit can help his dad at the garage, I guess, but what's Harm going to do?"

"He's going to help René. There's no way René can take over by himself," Tank answered.

André disagreed. "I don't think Harm cares what he does. I think he just wants to be with us. So he might want to quit, too."

"Yeah, I'm going to set up a meet to talk this over with everybody, but I wanted to make sure we were on the same page first."

"Have you thought what you're going to do next? Or what we all are going to do instead?" asked Tank.

"I'm going to graduate from high school—get my GED. I'm tired of being embarrassed about that. Even Deacon busted my chops about it the other day."

"Yeah, that'll take you about a month to do. You probably could take the test today and pass," said André. "I mean, after that. Between the three of us, we probably have close to six hundred grand to cover us while we start something."

Abel said, "I was thinking we could become private detectives."

Tank laughed. "You've been reading too many books."

"Wait, Tank, Abel's on to something," said André excitedly. "I've got massive computer skills, if I do say so myself. We know guns and cameras and surveillance. We can creep with the best of 'em. If we need to get into a building to find something out, we can do that easy."

"It would almost feel like what we do now. At least we wouldn't be sittin' behind a desk, adding up numbers," said Tank. "We could do security, too. Harm would be good with that, and Rabbit for that matter."

"Why don't you start checking that out, André? See what it takes to set something like that up. I bet we need some kind of state license. We already have carry permits, so we're good there. But you know, this was just my first idea. It seemed interesting, especially since I've read about a thousand detective books."

"I knew it!" Tank laughed. "You want to live your fantasy life."

"When are you going to talk to the others, Abel?" asked André.

"I'll call 'em, and we'll all meet here tomorrow evening and go through this with them. I'm kinda nervous about it. They were pretty excited about taking over Deke's business. I'm not looking forward to discussing this with Uncle Deacon, either."

"What time?" inquired Tank.

"Five. I'll get some food."

"Great," said André. "Tank and I are going hog hunting tomorrow after lunch. The pigs are taking over again. We've scouted out a wallow on the other side of the bayou, and we're gonna see if we can take a few—get some baby-backs. Do you want to come?"

"Naw, I can't—I'm doing something with Olivia. Definitely sounds fun though. Sorry I'm gonna miss it. What are you guys shooting?" asked Abel. Whenever you went up against feral hogs you needed some firepower, since they had thick skins and some of them were huge. You didn't want some half-wounded, crazed boar charging you.

"We're trying some new ammo—we got Hevishot and some Triball-II from Dixie Slugs," André replied.

"I had to put a wider choke on my gun to handle the slugs," said Tank. "My gun still had my turkey choke on it, and it was too tight. The Triball will stop a pig for sure, not sure about the Hevishot though."

"Well, one of you better make sure you have your .45—if that Hevi load doesn't work, you're going to have one angry hog coming at you," said Abel. "Anyway, I'll see you tomorrow."

TWENTY-THREE

Owen toddled down the dock, and Olivia chased him, yelling, "Wait! Wait for me!"

Abel grabbed Owen up in his arms, laughing. "Whoa—slow down, partner." He set Owen back down and strapped a tiny life preserver around him, tugging here and there to make sure it was snug. Owen was excited and practically dancing on the dock. His face was a giant smile. He was not the same little kid who had just stared into Abel's face the last time they'd met.

Abel held the pirogue steady while Liv climbed down into the front. When she was situated, he passed Owen to her, then stepped into the back of the boat. He sat and reached up and untied the last line. Then, he said, "Owen, do you want to help drive the boat? Come on back here."

Owen broke away from Olivia and clambered over the middle seat and up into Abel's lap. Abel started the little trolling motor, then took the toddler's hand in his and wrapped it around the steering arm. The motor whirred, and they glided away from the dock. An expression of utter joy radiated from the boy's face. It was mirrored on Olivia's.

Abel and Owen steered their way up the bayou, past the cathedral-like spot where he had taken Olivia the last time, to a point where the trees leaned over the water casting pools of shade. He stopped the pirogue. Owen looked up questioningly. Abel put his finger to his lips, then whispered, "We have to be quiet now or the fish will hear us." The boy pressed his lips together.

The boat drifted up against a snag and stopped moving. They were in the perfect spot in the shade where the sun struck the water just an arm's length away. Owen's eyes were locked on the waving grass in the water where little minnows were flitting back and forth.

Abel motioned to Liv, who handed him a cane pole that Abel had fixed up for Owen. He leaned his head down to the boy's ear, whispering about the pole, the bobber, and the VERY sharp hook. Abel had Owen reach under the seat and get the little box of bait. He opened it and showed him the worms crawling around in the loose mossy dirt. Owen reached in and poked at one with his stubby finger.

Olivia watched, rapt. The image sent her back to her own daddy when he would have her wrapped up in his arms, his hands guiding her hands to bait the hook. They would swing the pole over the side of the boat, the worm and the bobber plopping into the water. Then, she would sit back in her daddy's lap and watch the bobber, waiting for it to jig.

Owen was nestled up against Abel, holding the pole, his little hands swallowed up in Abel's. The boy and the pole were all gathered up in Abel's embrace. They had dropped the hook just in the sun and were jiggling the bait a little to catch the fishes' attention.

Something loosened up inside of Olivia, and she imagined the three of them doing this every weekend. She pictured Abel playing catch with Owen. Them going to little league games. The three of them moving into their own home. Cooking dinner and cleaning up together. *STOP!* She was moving way too fast. But seeing how Abel was with her son, and the way Owen was looking up at him, was pushing her down that slippery slope.

The bobber jerked underwater. Owen squealed, and Abel flicked the tip of the cane and set the hook. They carefully pulled the sunny out of the water and dropped it into the middle of the boat. It flopped around, violently sending itself into the air and back down again. Abel lifted the tip of the pole and swung the fish back and caught it. Owen touched it and jerked his hand back when the fish abruptly wiggled.

"That's a big fish for a little guy like you, Owen! But we're going to put him back so he can grow up to be a big daddy fish. OK?" Owen nodded, his eyes glued to the fish. Abel showed the boy how to gently remove the hook, and then Owen watched as Abel placed the small fish carefully back into the bayou. The fish lay on the surface for a moment, then suddenly flicked its tail and flashed off into the deep.

Owen tore himself away from Abel and climbed back over the seat to his mother. He excitedly told her the story as if she hadn't been there to see the whole thing. Olivia hugged him tight, her nose in his hair, the smell of worms and fish once again bringing back memories of her father.

Pushing away from the snag, Abel started the motor and swung the boat around. Owen continued chattering happily to his mother, but she was looking at Abel. He was watching them and seemed lost in thought. She said, "Where are you, Abel?"

"Ha! Sorry, I was thinking of the first time I caught a fish. Tank's daddy, Antoine, took me and Tank fishing. We both had cane poles like Owen's." He nodded toward the boy. "It seems like it was yesterday. I remember wishing that Antoine was my daddy, too."

Olivia choked up a bit and couldn't respond for a moment. Then she said, "I'm sorry you lost your father at such a young age."

"Aw, don't worry about it. I just had a memory is all." But Abel stayed lost in his thoughts until the side of the pirogue bumped into the dock. He stood and jumped up onto the dock, the line in his hand, and tied off the boat. "Well, we didn't get a fish to eat, but we can go get a Happy Meal instead!" Liv handed up Owen, and then Abel reached down and grabbed her hand and helped her up.

She caught Abel in her arms and hugged him. "Thank you so much," she said into his ear. "You were so great with Owen! I've never seen him this happy and excited." She kissed him and then pulled away saying, "This brought me so many good memories of fishing with my daddy."

As Abel turned to walk up the dock, Olivia saw his expression change. It looked sad, and she felt a tiny bit of anxiety in her belly.

TWENTY-FOUR

C allie was walking around the house, neatening up. Things were in a bit of a mess, and Abel wouldn't care whether his friends showed up to a messy house, but she would. After living with Aunt Hennie all those years, orderliness had been instilled in her, and she had outgrown her childhood tendency for disarray. Placing one of Abel's books back on the shelf, she heard the front door open and turned to see René entering. "Where y'at, cher?" she said, greeting René with a smile.

"Oh, I'm all good," he answered. "I'm kinda early."

"Yeah, by an hour—no problem, you can help me finish straightening up," she teased. Both of them laughed because everybody knew cleaning wasn't René's strong suit. He would look at a pile of moldering dishes next to the sink, and it would be like they were invisible. Yet, if a hair on his head was out of place, or his shirt had a spot on it, he would be all over it.

"Why don't you grab a beer and keep me company in here while I finish up?" Callie said, picking up another book from an end table and walking it back to the bookshelf. René came back in and settled into a spot on the couch, putting his feet up on the coffee table, and tipped back his beer. "So how is your love life going, Callie?" He was genuinely interested. René was one of those men that actually liked to talk to women. He understood them and could see their viewpoints. That was the real reason for his success with women.

"I'm on a break."

"Weren't you going with that male nurse from your job? Seemed like you two were serious."

"Yeah, I liked him a lot, but he was one of those guys that would never settle down. He had itchy feet. He was ready to go on to a new place and wanted me to go. You know—drop all my shit and follow him."

"Sounds like an asshole."

"No, he was a decent guy, but he was interested in different things and wanted to travel—wanted to surf in Australia, ski in the Alps, that kind of thing. Deep down, I knew he wasn't for me either, I guess. I wasn't that broken up when he left."

"Are you working on a new guy?"

"No, like I said, I'm on a break. I'm grinding through my master's, and I'm working all-nighters at the ER. I just don't have the time."

"Don't you get lonely?"

"How could I get lonely? I have Abel and all you guys—it's like I'm Wendy, and y'all are Peter Pan and the boys from Neverland." She chuckled.

"I get lonely sometimes," said René. "I met this girl; I mean, it's never going to be. Wrong place. Wrong time. Wrong girl. But I felt this connection, and I think she did, too."

Suddenly, the front door flew open and slammed against the wall with a crash. Three men rushed through. The first man had tattoos all over his face and was brandishing a machete in his left hand. Callie was already up and running toward the kitchen. She instantly knew the man, although she'd never seen him—Tattoo Face—

and it was the first time in her life that she'd ever felt absolute terror.

She made it to the back door, scrambling at the knob, but the man spun her around, clubbing her cheek with his fist. She felt white hot pain, and she was falling. Her head squarely struck the mouth of a heavy ceramic jug—an antique she had placed on the floor by the wall as a decoration. Her head bounced up and flopped back down. Her body lay prone and twitching on the floor, like she was having a seizure.

René was slower to react, wallowing in the sofa and trying to get up. Finally, he made it. He had nowhere to go. There was a man in the kitchen and two other men blocking the front door. The soldier made a move to grab him, and René weakly pushed his arm away, skittering backward till he bumped into another soft chair and fell into it.

Garcia pointed his pistol at René's face. "Don't move, pendejo!" He nodded at the banger standing by René. "Go get a kitchen chair."

The soldier set the chair up in the middle of the living room, and the two of them wrestled René out of the leather chair he had fallen into and over onto the wooden kitchen chair. The soldier ran out to the front porch, then ran back in with a small blue athletic bag.

Garcia kept the gun on René while the other man yanked his arms behind the chair and zip-tied his wrists with ties from the blue bag. He fished out a roll of duct tape and taped René's legs to the chair, then wrapped several turns around his body and the chair for good measure. René sat there limply without offering any resistance.

"Don't hurt me. I'll help you. What do you want?" he whined.

"Where's the money, puto?"

"What money?" asked René stupidly.

With a nod from Garcia, the soldier put a strip of tape over René's mouth. "Check the bedrooms!" commanded Garcia. He could already hear Gomez in the kitchen, ripping into cabinets.

Garcia flicked his blade open and tore into the couch cushions, then bending down like a weightlifter, he picked up the front of the couch, flipping it over in place. He dashed to the wall of books, sweeping the books off the shelves. One of the books flew across the room and smacked the side of René's head who issued a muffled grunt from behind the tape. Abel's reading chair received a violent slash. Finding nothing, the Mara lieutenant ran to help the soldier search the bedrooms.

After a fruitless search, the three of them met back in the living room. René had tried to get himself loose while they were occupied but had only managed to tip the chair over. Gomez set down the machete and righted the chair. "Nice try, chele."

Garcia leaned in and tugged at the tape over René's mouth but couldn't get a corner free. Frustrated, he flicked his switchblade open and sawed an opening between René's lips.

René screamed, and a little blood leaked down through the opening in the tape.

"So, Señor Abel Kane, where's the money?" asked Garcia. "We know your crew took it. We know about Deacon Kane, the fencing, and the robberies."

"I'm not Abel, you've made a mistake. My name is René."

"What's your full name?" probed Garcia.

"René Kane."

"Oh, I'm sure I don't have the wrong person. We've been watching you for a while. WHERE IS MY MONEY?" thundered Garcia.

"I only have my cut. It's in the bank."

With a nod from Garcia, Gomez slapped René, rocking his head.

"Please, I'll take you there. I'll get you the money."

"How many assholes are in your crew?"

"Six of us—it's not my crew, it's Abel's."

"How did you know to hit us? Who told you about the money?"

"Abel got a tip."

"Who told him? One of my people?"

"I don't think so. We don't know any MS-13 guys."

"How did you know to come to El Luz Loco? I saw you there with my own two eyes. Did one of my people tell you about the bar?"

"No, no. Abel knew somehow. He talked to some other gangbangers. They told him."

"Who told Kane that we had the money?"

"I don't know."

Gomez let loose another openhanded slap. René jerked around in his seat, trying to cower but was taped too tightly and could only slightly raise one shoulder and dip his head.

"Please stop," cried René.

"I can't stop," said Garcia. "I need to get all my money back. I need to know where it is. I need to learn about Señor Abel. I need to find out who the traitor is." Garcia dragged the tip of his knife lightly down René's face below his eye, drawing little red beads of blood to the surface. "Was it the Aryans? The AB—those Nazi bastards?"

"No, wait, yes. I heard something about a snitch. There was a guy, he was AB—he told my father."

Garcia folded his knife, placing it back in his pocket. "Qué? Your father? Deacon Kane?"

René pressed his lips together.

Garcia looked at Gomez with a smile and then back at René. "Don't stop talking now, little puta." There was a snick, and the knife was open in Garcia's hand again. His hand whipped forward, then stopped short but not before jabbing a half inch into René's chest.

"AHHH," screeched René. "Please don't kill me."

"Who is that puta in the kitchen?" continued Garcia. Nothing came out of René's mouth. "Is she your whore?" René remained silent. Gomez smacked him again. René's head snapped sideways.

"Where is Abel, Señor René?"

"He's coming. They're all coming!"

"What are the names of all these cabróns that are coming?" No answer. "When should we expect them?" No words were coming out of René's mouth. Just a humming noise, like he was forcing himself not to say words. "Where is your padre?" More humming, louder and more urgent.

"You have stopped telling me things, chelón! So I think we've reached my favorite part of our little meeting." Garcia bent over, reached into the goodie bag on the floor, and pulled out a small kitchen blowtorch, like one used to caramelize the top of a crème brûlée. Garcia's face had taken on a large, dreamy smile, and the corners of his eyes crinkled—the very picture of bonhomie. He clicked a tiny button on the side of the torch and a hissing blue flame shot out. "I think we can encourage you to continue our conversation."

The pirogue rounded a bend in the bayou, and Callie and Abel's house came into view. Pushing against the arm on the trolling motor that was purring softly, Tank steered the boat to Abel's pier. André was jammed into the tiny seat in front, since a field-dressed hog took up the middle seat. The men were covered head to toe in brown splotches from settling in the mud of the wallow, waiting for the feral pigs to make an appearance.

André tied off the front line, and Tank pulled the back end closer to the dock, when suddenly, a scream broke the stillness of the later afternoon.

"What was that?" Tank whispered.

"Did that come from Abel's?" asked André urgently.

"AHHHHHHH!"

André started to scramble onto the dock. "Wait!" his brother commanded. "Load your shotgun, God damn it." André sat back down and started feeding in Hevishot shells. Tank finished filling up his Remington and then pulled his .45 G21 out of the holster, popped the mag, eyeballed it to make sure it was full, and then reinserted it. "We'll go through the kitchen door—let's go!"

André asked, "Don't you want me to go around front?"

"No, we're both going in the back. I don't want to be shooting at you."

"GAAAAAAAAAA."

"Shit! Move it!" urged Tank in a strangled whisper-shout.

They ran up the side of the yard, then cut across to the back porch, Tank leading the way. Tiptoeing up the steps, they moved to flank the closed kitchen door. André carefully peered through the window into the kitchen, and he motioned to Tank to check the other window.

Tank couldn't see anybody standing, but he could see somebody on the floor. He wasn't sure, but he thought it was Callie. He waved to André to move over behind him, then slowly tried the kitchen doorknob. It turned. Not locked—*good*. He slowly pushed it open, and just as it was almost open enough, it squeaked—a loud squeak. *Fuck!* A shout came from the front room, and Tank could hear crashing steps coming. He slammed the door all the way open, took two steps in and moved to the side, bringing his shotgun up.

A gangbanger appeared in the doorway to the living room, moving at them with a pistol in his hand. Tank's eyes tracked the gun, and he fired a load of Triball. The banger's arm blew out to the side, and the soldier turned to his right from the force—immediately he was rotated left when André's shot caught his left flank, blowing off a chunk of meat and spraying the wall behind him red.

Tank heard the front door slam open and the sound of footsteps pounding on the floor. He ran past René, who was still in the chair, to the door, ready to go after them, but was stopped short by André's shout. "Callie's hurt bad!" He looked out and saw that the two men were already in their car, then turned back to help Abel's sister. He ran past the banger on the floor, a piece of his brain registering that the guy's arm was in the center of a pool of blood, attached only by a few shreds of flesh.

André was on his knees, his hulking body hanging over Callie, trying to find a pulse.

"Is she alive?" Tank asked in a choked up voice.

"Barely," André answered, trying to hold back his tears. "Help René."

Tank went over to René who was jerking around in the chair, making noises through the tape across his lips. He had four burn marks on his shirt, in a line to his waist, that looked like big black buttons.

Tank opened his knife and cut the zip ties holding his friend. He had to kneel on the floor to cut René's legs loose. René picked at the tape and peeled it off his face.

"Those assholes burned the fuck out of me!" he screamed. He came up out of the chair, lifting his shirt to see the damage and grimacing. "They came in the door too fast. I couldn't do anything."

Harm ran through the front door. "What happened? Who were those guys that pulled out of the drive? They tore off down the road."

"MS!" shouted André.

Harm saw that Callie was down and let out an unintelligible sound. He ran over and tried to push André out of the way, but Tank pulled him off and held him for a moment. Then Tank pulled out his phone and called Abel. Harm went over to the wounded Mara soldier and stood over him.

The man looked up at him, entreating Harm. "Help me..."

Harm reached around and brought his pistol out, then fired two shots into the bleeding banger's head.

"Fuck!" yelled Tank.

Abel rushed through the front door, dropping two sacks of food, and lifting his shirt to get at his gun. Tank bellowed, "Stop! Stop!"

André yelled, "Callie's hurt! We got to get her to a hospital."

Abel rushed over, seeing the blood and Callie's eyes closed. He had a terrified look on his face.

"She's alive—we got to get her help!" André screamed to break Abel out of his trance.

Abel snapped out of it. "André—get the ironing board." He flipped his keys to Tank. "Back up my truck, open the bed, and drop the gate." He looked at Harm. "Get this mess cleaned up. Call Rabbit—get bleach and shit."

Abel noticed René and gestured. "Get him fixed up, too."

"I want to go with her," said Harm.

"No! We got to get this place straight in case the police come. René needs help."

André came back with the ironing board, and he and Abel carefully moved Callie onto it, Abel cradling her neck the best he could. They lifted up the board and gently took her to the back of Abel's truck and slid the board onto the truck bed.

"André, Tank and I are taking her to the hospital. Go back and dump the body in the bayou and clean up the mess as best you can."

Abel went to the driver's window. "Tank, drive us to the fire station. They'll know what to do. Don't hit any bumps. I'll steady her in the back."

TWENTY-FIVE

A bel and Tank had beaten the ambulance to the hospital and were already out and waiting by the entrance. The vehicle rolled up, the whoop of the siren tailing off. The doors of the Lacombe Fire Department ambulance flew open. The rear EMT jumped out and turned back to disengage the gurney and started to slide it out. The driver hurried around to assist, and they pulled it out the rest of the way. They oriented it toward the emergency room doors, which glided open, and three members of the trauma team ran out and surrounded the stretcher, all five with their hands on the gurney or on Callie.

Abel tried to get in close but was blocked by the surrounding medical staff, nonetheless he tried to push in to see his sister. "Is she still alive?" Abel cried.

One of the nurses turned, pushing him away. "Sir, she's hanging on, but please back up and give us space. Someone will be with you in a minute." The gowned woman immediately returned her attention to Callie.

Tank put his arm around Abel and physically held him back as Abel fought him, trying to stay close to Callie.

"Bro, she's in good hands. UMC is the best hospital in the city. Calm. Be calm. That's how we help Callie now. We got her here as fast as it could be done. This is her place. They love her here. They'll be all over her." Abel's face was torn up, but he nodded acknowledgment at Tank.

The two men walked into the admitting area, Tank still gently restraining Abel. As soon as they entered, a counselor from the hospital rushed up. "Are you with Callie?"

"Yes," answered Tank. "This is Callie's brother, Abel Kane." A stunned look was painted on Abel's face, his mouth hanging half open.

"Sir, let's go into my office. It's just through these doors."

"No, I want to be with Callie!"

"I'm sorry, they've got Callie in the trauma suite, and there isn't room for more people. We were notified as the ambulance was leaving Lacombe, and they scrambled the best people we have. We can sit and wait in my office, and I'll get you her status as soon as we know something."

"Is she going to be OK? You've got to fix her," said Abel.

"Callie is tough, and she is going to get the absolute best care we have. Now, in a minute, another nurse is going to come in and get Callie's history. Do you think you can help us and tell us what happened?"

"We'll do our best," Tank said, and he reached out and squeezed Abel's arm tightly.

Callie's army doctor friend was leading the team in the trauma room. He'd had copious experience with traumatic brain injury in Afghanistan. He looked down at Callie and murmured, "Oh Callie. what have you done to yourself?" He looked around at his team and was reassured. They were working seamlessly together—the trauma room dance— hanging fluids and jacking in to the port the EMTs had established, setting up blood pressure, pulse, and oxygen sensors. A cardio tech had already cut off her shirt and was connecting the leads from the electrocardiograph.

The doc began his exam. She was unconscious, and he could see blood matted over her right ear. He peeled back one eyelid, noticing the pupil wasn't completely dilated. It reacted normally to his little pocket flashlight. He hesitated for the tiniest of a second, dreading examining the other eye, the eye connected to the side of the brain that had been injured. Pulling back that lid, he was relieved to see that it wasn't blown. He flashed the light at the pupil, and it responded to the beam, sluggishly, but still narrowing some. *Not too bad,* he thought.

He looked up at the monitors. Not great: blood pressure low, pulse low, oxygen low. "Callie! Callie! Can you hear me? Wake up! Talk to me!" Callie's eyelids twitched and half opened, her right hand opened and closed, but the fingertips on her left barely curled—a few incomprehensible sounds came from her mouth. "Callie, you're in the ER, you've hurt your head. We're going to fix you up. Can you open your eyes?" This time there was no response.

"Shit!" the doctor cursed. He did a cursory exam of Callie's whole body to make sure that there weren't any other obvious injuries, then asked, "Do you have a strip yet?" to the cardiologist who was in the corner fiddling with the ECG machine.

"Almost," the heart doc answered tersely.

The army doctor yelled out the door, "Get Bill in here!" The neurologist hustled in, the nurses and techs parting to let him get to the head of the bed. The military doctor stepped back to make room for the brain doctor who commenced a complete neurological examination. Brainstem reflexes were checked—gag, blinking, and other tests trying to pinpoint from the outside what was happening on the inside of Callie's head and attempting to determine where the damage was.

"When you yelled at her, did she open her eyes?" the neurologist asked the army doc.

"Yeah, when I first talked to her," he responded. "She also mumbled something."

"Ok, this is bad but not too bad," the neurologist said. "She's about a nine on the Glasgow Coma Scale," he added. "Not quite a coma. Her injury is moderate, at least given how she's presenting right now."

The two doctors went out into the hall and quietly conferred, then the neurologist walked off, leaving the army doc standing in the hall for a minute, thinking. He went back into the trauma room and barked out some orders. "Let's get her oxygen up a bit more, then roll her down to imaging and get a CAT of her head done." The cardiologist handed him the strip from the ECG machine. The battle-hardened doctor reviewed it quickly. "Do you see any big problems?" he asked the heart doctor.

"Mainly just the slow pulse."

The trauma leader said to the room in general, "OK, let me know when the images and the radiologist's report are back. Put her up in the ICU when she gets back from radiology."

After reviewing the scans and report from radiology, the trauma doctor made his way to the room where Abel and Tank were anxiously waiting and introduced himself. "Hi, I'm Frank Stoddard, the trauma doctor taking care of your sister."

"Is she going to be OK?" Abel frantically asked.

"We've got Callie stabilized and up in the intensive care unit. The imagery shows a skull fracture just above her right ear and a small lesion behind that site—between the skull and the surface of her brain."

"What's a lesion? Is she going to die?" cried Abel. Tank put his hand on top of Abel's.

"A lesion is a hematoma or contusion on the brain. Her brain got hurt. It's bleeding, and the blood is collecting in that spot. Callie is hurt bad, but you got her here quickly, and my team is very good. Right now, she's stable, and we just don't know whether she is going to get worse. So we're going to aggressively monitor her. She's not quite in a coma—her numbers are just short of that, and she responded to me some when I talked to her. That's a good sign. The problem is that the lesion can grow bigger and press on her brain, causing further damage."

"What can you do?" asked Tank.

"We don't have to do anything for the skull fracture at this time. If we don't have to take action because the brain is swelling, then it'll heal on its own. We could immediately insert a brain pressure monitor into her skull, and that would give us the best insight into her condition. We would be able to tell that her intracranial pressure is increasing. But her coma assessment is just on the edge, and there is a slight chance that we could cause more damage when we put that in, so I want to wait on it."

"Are you saying we do nothing? We just wait?" Abel wanted the hospital to do something to make Callie OK. His features were in motion, moving through anger, grief, and confusion, then settling in sadness.

"No, we're going to make sure that she isn't hurting and are giving her drugs that can mitigate some of the bad stuff that might happen. We're going to be watching her closely, looking for signs of swelling. She'll get another scan. If it looks like there is more bleeding and the lesion is growing, we'll insert the ICP monitor into her skull. Then if it continues to get worse, we'll take her to surgery and remove a flap of bone that will give the swelling a place to go."

"Why don't you put the pressure thing in now—so we can make sure it's not getting worse right now?" Abel needed action.

"Abel, I've dealt with hundreds of these kinds of injuries. We're not there yet. Both the neurologist and I think this is the best route. We don't want to take any chance of hurting Callie more if she is going to get better on her own. Rest assured, we're going to watch her like a hawk. If there are any signs she is getting worse, we are all prepped to take the next steps. The best thing you can do is sit next to her in the ICU. Talk to her. Encourage her."

The hospital counselor walked Tank and Abel up to Callie's ICU room, telling them how much the staff loved Callie and what an awesome person she was and on and on, but Abel was in a daze, and none of it registered. Tank moved a chair in the room closer to Callie, sat Abel down, and lifted Abel's hand and placed it on Callie's arm, then bent down and whispered into Abel's ear, "Remember, talk to her, encourage her—she can hear you."

Tank moved around the bed, bent down, and kissed Callie's forehead. "Callie, I love you. We're all here for you. We're praying for you."

TWENTY-SIX

T he waiting room was filled with Callie's friends and Abel's men. The vigil was quiet, with small groups of people clustered together and talking in hushed voices. Henriette and Deacon were sitting on an uncomfortable vinyl couch with René between them, an unreadable expression on Deacon's face. Abel had come down to the waiting room after Callie had been taken to radiology for a second CAT scan and was standing with the guys. René pushed himself up off the couch with a grimace and went to stand with the crew. Aunt Hen leaned over to Deacon and whispered to him with a confused and upset look. Deacon held up both hands, then dropped them and whispered back angrily.

Abel watched the exchange on the couch, then resumed talking with the guys. "Did the police show up at the house, André?"

"Nope. Kind of amazing. I guess we got lucky."

"Not that amazing. You're so far back from the road, it was inside, and with all those trees, nobody could pinpoint the shots probably," theorized Tank.

Abel thought, *One less thing to worry about,* then brought the guys up to speed on Callie's condition—that she was medicated, not moving, and it was just a waiting game now.

"Waiting for what?" asked André.

"They're mainly worried that the injury is going to keep bleeding or the brain is going to swell and cause more damage," he said. Abel looked at René. "How're you doing?"

"I'm OK. Rabbit brought me to the ER. We came up with a story that it was welding splatter—they didn't question it. They just put ointment on the burns, bandaged it, and gave me some pain pills."

"Good. I'm glad you weren't hurt worse than that. I want to hear what happened but later. I can't think right now." Abel looked into each of his friends' eyes but couldn't say anything.

He ended up focusing on Harm. Harm gazed back at him, a different person than the guy who was sobbing at the house—the Harm that stared back was lifeless and cold. Abel squeezed his shoulder, but Harm didn't respond.

Abel walked around from group to group, thanking them for coming. Everybody was so kind to him; he could hardly stand it. He needed a fragment of good news to give him hope, an antidote for the terrible guilt he felt for bringing this on Callie. Isabelle pulled him aside after he made the rounds. She embraced him and spoke in his ear. "I'm so sorry, cher—I see your pain all around you."

Abel choked back a sob, his body spasming with the effort. "She's hurt because of me."

Isabelle squeezed him tighter. "Yes, honey—maybe. But she wanted you to do something about those evil people. This is just the beginning; we're all going to be involved before it is over. I told you before—this was coming. There are currents underneath us, and they take us where they want us to go."

"We robbed them. What did I think was going to happen?"

"You wouldn't have heard of them if they hadn't harmed that poor young girl. I told you the storm was coming—you can't stop the weather. But it's not done. Now is the time you have to do what you were put here for; you have to be strong. It's good to be sad, but you have to take that and direct it. There's a scourge, a pestilence, and it has to be beaten back."

Abel felt another hand on his shoulder, and as he started to turn, Isabelle let him loose.

The trauma doctor was standing there, a serious expression on his face. "I just reviewed the radiologist's report from Callie's second scan, and she's gotten a little worse. The lesion has grown bigger."

"How big? Why can't you stop the bleeding?"

"It's not huge, but I'm concerned enough that I think we need to take the next step and insert a pressure monitor in her skull. If it stays this size, that's one thing, but if it continues to grow, then the injury might be worse than we thought, and there could be more swelling. The monitor will allow us to understand what's happening and then take action as necessary."

"What action? Is it dangerous to put in this monitor?" Abel asked, worriedly.

"If vital signs start getting worse, if that lesion grows, if the brain starts to swell, we might have to take her up to surgery and alleviate the pressure on her brain. We'll cross that bridge if we come to it. But just putting in the IVC, the intraventricular catheter—we do it all the time."

"How big of a chance is there that you will hurt her more?"

"Well, we definitely don't want to cause her more problems by just trying to understand how she is now. We're very careful, and we place the monitor in the safest location possible—we keep it away from important spots like the speech area. We need you to give permission before we do this though."

"OK, where are the papers I have to sign?" asked Abel.

René was standing with Harm. He was good company because René didn't want to talk or think and was just concentrating on trying to shut up the little voices in his head. A movement down the hall caught his eye. *What the fuck?*

"Harm! Garcia is standing right over there watching us."

The expression on Harm's face didn't flicker. He didn't twitch a muscle. "Don't look at him. Where is he in relation to me?" he asked, calmly.

"Directly behind you in the hallway. Just outside the waiting room."

"What's he wearing?"

"Some kind of bluish jacket. It's dark, but his shirt is light."

Harm clapped René on the back like they just had a rewarding conversation and nonchalantly edged over to another group closer to the hallway, keeping Garcia in his peripheral vision. Garcia started casually moving away.

Harm went from standing still to a sprint, pounding after Garcia, who was bolting down the hall. Garcia banged into the door to the stairs, pushed it open, and slammed it behind him. Harm made it to the door a half second later and drove it open, ready to jump down the stairs, but Garcia was standing just inside the door waiting for him, a knife arcing down. Harm reflexively stepped into Garcia instead of backing away and got an arm up. Their wrists smashed together. Garcia's right arm was moving like a snake, but Harm managed to catch his wrist. The gangbanger had his left arm around Harm's neck and was relentlessly forcing the knife down toward Harm's head. At the same time, he was pushing Harm against the door, pinning him in place and preventing the door from opening. Harm punched Garcia's torso. He couldn't manage any force. He reached into his pocket, pulling out his own switchblade. Tank was on the other side of the door, pounding and trying to get it open.

Garcia dropped his left arm, wrapping up Harm's knife arm. They struggled in a standoff, Garcia pushing down on his knife and Harm trying to twist his own blade up and into Garcia. They rolled around against the door, each one trying to gain the advantage, their knives getting close to drawing blood.

Suddenly, a group of nurses came down the stairs from above. Garcia abruptly drew back from Harm, surprising him, and he lost his grip on Garcia's wrist. Garcia's knife came flicking down, the tip catching Harm's forehead, slicing down and through his eyebrow. Blood gushed into his eye, partially blinding him as Garcia continued moving backward. Harm's knife gashed Garcia's side as they drew apart. Garcia turned and ran down the stairs.

The crowd of medical staff clustered around Harm who was yelling and pushing them away so he could chase after Garcia. But they were surrounding him, like sharks responding to the sight of blood.

Tank managed to get the door open, and he burst into the crowded stairwell. "He went down!" yelled Harm, and Tank blew by him, around the people, and down the stairs after Garcia.

"He was gone by the time I got down the stairs," Tank said to Harm. The crew was back together in the waiting room after Harm had returned from the ER with his eyebrow and forehead freshly stitched back together. He'd also endured an interview with the hospital security where he mostly professed ignorance about the attack.

"Can you believe that motherfucker had the balls to show up here?" said Rabbit vehemently.

"Smart though," said André. "Know your enemy. Now he's seen all our faces—probably took pictures—"

"They're fucking dead," said Harm. He broke from the group and sat on a bench off to the side, staring straight ahead with an implacable look on his face.

Tank caught his brother's eyes and raised his eyebrows, and after a moment he said, "We're going to have to take shifts and keep our eyes on Abel and Callie. If these assholes are gonna show up here, we have to watch out. Abel's head isn't on straight right now. We gotta prop him up.

"It's late. Why don't you guys go home and get some rest? I'll stay tonight. André, can you come first thing tomorrow and organize coverage?"

"Sure thing."

Tank walked over to Harm to tell him the plan, but Isabelle stepped in front of him and sat next to Harm. Tank made a U-turn.

"How you holding up, cher?" she asked Harm.

Harm gazed at Isabelle, his features softening. "They hurt Callie. It feels like they hurt my mama or something. I've got this big ball of rage right next to this terrible sadness—it feels like I'm being torn in two."

"Oh baby, we all feel that. Callie is gonna be OK, I'm certain. You need to stay in control and work with the other boys. Y'all need to work together—stay tight. Give Abel a day or so, then look to him. OK, cher?"

"Yeah," Harm answered grudgingly.

"In the meantime, I need some things. I need a few personal items from these evil men."

"Like what?"

"Hair or money they touched, a piece of their jewelry that they wore—maybe a ring or bracelet—that kind of thing."

"Does blood count? That guy's blood is on my knife. I caught him when we were fighting."

"That's better than hair," Isabelle said.

Harm pulled his knife out of his pocket and handed it to her. "I've got Tattoo Face's wallet, too. It has some pictures in it and some money. Do you want me to get you that?"

"Yes, honey, that'll work. I've got to go home and make Callie a gris-gris bag—help her heal."

"Why do you need their stuff?" asked Harm. "Does that go in the mojo bag?"

"No, it's for something else. It's time I did my part."

The bright light from the window woke Abel early the next morning. He'd fallen asleep in the chair by Callie's bed, and when he opened his eyes, the first thing he saw was Isabelle bending over Callie and kissing her forehead. She fussed with Callie's covers and reached into her pillowcase, then withdrew her hand.

Abel stretched his neck, rolling it around, trying to limber up the stiffness. "Hi, Belle, how is she?"

"She's sleeping comfortably, I think. She's close to the surface—not down deep like last night. I made a little something to help her. Has the doctor come in yet?" she asked.

"No. I don't want to miss him," said Abel.

"I'll go down to the cafeteria and bring up some breakfast. After the doctor comes, you go on home and get cleaned up. I can sit with her a spell."

"No, I don't want to go home. The nurse told me I can take a shower here. But please stay for a while, Belle. I think Callie knows you're here."

"I'll call André and have him bring you some fresh clothes."

TWENTY-SEVEN

T ank, André, and Rabbit had spent the last three days trying to erase the havoc that had occurred at Abel and Callie's house. André had executed a quick cleanup right after the attack, but any close inspection would have turned up bullet holes and bloodstains. Luckily, the law didn't make an appearance, the house being so deep in the woods.

Rabbit and the brothers had to do an extensive cleanup on the bloodstains. There was spatter on the walls which could be handled by painting, but there were two big pools—one on the living room floor where the MS-13 soldier had bled out from the partially blown-off arm and the kitchen where Callie's head struck the jug. The living room stain was worse, of course. The gangbanger had dumped pints of blood that had seeped into the cracks of the wooden floor and inundated a throw rug.

They removed all the furniture and doused the wooden floor with Clorox to denature the DNA, waiting outside till the vapors diminished. But the Clorox damaged the floor, making an obvious mark. Rabbit eventually had to rent a floor sander, then stain and varnish the floor. While the floor was torn up, he patched the bullet holes in the walls and painted.

Tank and André had an easier job of it in the kitchen. Callie's blood had discolored the grout. André consulted the internet and ended up using a toothbrush and some hydrogen peroxide. That didn't totally work, so he shifted to letting some Shout sit on it for a while, then hit it with OxyClean. Finally, it was clean, almost too clean, but they sure as shit weren't going to be able to do that to the rest of the kitchen to make it all match—they were going to have to live with it.

Deacon brought over one of Henriette's extra throw rugs, and then all they had to do was wait a few more days to make sure the varnished floor was completely cured. Once it was dry, they could move all the furniture back. André figured he would put all the books back on the shelves himself, since he was the only one of the guys who could alphabetize them properly.

They were standing in front of the house loading the big floor sanding machine onto Tank's truck when Abel came home. He'd been at the hospital for three days. Isabelle finally forced him to take a break and go home. She was sitting with Callie.

Harm rolled up in his truck with René, who was still sore and couldn't drive himself because every time he moved, his belly burns screamed. He gingerly crawled out of the truck while Harm popped the back door and gathered up three large sacks of takeout.

"How's Callie?" Tank asked.

Harm had spent almost the whole time at the hospital, too, tag-teaming with Abel, so he answered. "Her pressure is coming down finally, and she woke up a few times."

"Yeah, it was touch and go for a while," Abel added. "They were sure that they were going to have to take her into surgery and cut out a piece of her skull to make room for her brain swelling, but then she turned the corner. She's disoriented and not making much sense. The doctor said that would get better."

Abel always wondered whether Isabelle's root work did anything, whether there was something to her hoodoo, or whether it was just so much hand-waving. He thought about it like it was just a religious belief, not exactly hokum but in the same class as miracles people talked about— ones you never saw yourself.

There was no doubt that Callie got better quickly, but maybe she hadn't been hurt that bad to begin with. Still, the doctors had been pretty gloomy when she'd first come in. The army doctor had acted a little amazed that the pressure had only spiked for a brief period. He had confided that he'd seen many soldiers go south with the same level of injury.

So he was left where he always was—maybe he saw an effect from Belle's conjuring—and the truth was that over the years, there were many circumstances where a person got better from sickness. A lost item was found. Some neighborhood girl found her soulmate after she consulted Isabelle. Those could be coincidences, or what was going to happen anyway, but there was no doubt in his mind that Callie definitely started improving right after Isabelle had put the gris-gris in her pillowcase. It sure made him think.

Abel put aside his ruminations and scanned his buddies' faces. "I want to thank you all for helping us so much. I don't know what I would have done if you all weren't there for me," he said, his voice getting a little jerky.

"Shit, dude, we're basically your brothers—you'd do the same," said Rabbit emotionally, his heart always on his sleeve. "When my mom was sick, Callie took care of all of us at my house. I don't know how many meals she cooked. All of you were there for me."

"That's right, motherfuckers—we're in this together. Now let's go drink some beers and cut out all this emotional shit. It's making me tear up," said René.

They all went around back to the porch, each filing into the kitchen, grabbing beer and food, then finding their favorite seat on the deck. Abel noticed René moving tentatively and examined him closely, seeing the cut on his face, the swollen and blackened eyes, and said, "Tell me what happened."

"They came in too fast. Callie was already up and ran into the kitchen with that tattooed bastard chasing her. By the time I got up out of the chair, they were on me. I couldn't do anything, and they tied me to a kitchen chair."

"What did they say?" asked Abel.

"They seemed like they knew it was us that robbed them. They wanted to know where the money was."

"Did you tell them?" demanded Harm.

"I said my money was in the bank."

"You admitted that we robbed them?" asked André incredulously.

"They already knew," René said.

"So now they know about all of us?" asked Tank.

"No, they knew about Abel. They called me Abel. But I didn't tell them about any of you—no names, nothing. They burned me with a torch, but I didn't tell them anything. I'm sorry. I'm sorry that I said anything." René was almost in tears, oblivious of his conflicting words.

"Man, anybody would have talked if they were getting burned like that—don't feel bad, René," said Abel sympathetically.

"What I can't figure out is how they knew where you lived, Abel," said André. "I thought Callie owned this house."

"Yeah, I'm not on the deed."

"I might have made a mistake," said René. "One of those banger chicks from The Loco showed up at The Flying Machine."

"What the fuck?" exclaimed Harm. "And you didn't tell us?"

"An MS chick that you saw at The Loco just randomly shows up at The Machine after you scouted them at the bar and we robbed them?" asked André, not expecting an answer.

"We just danced; it was nothing," said René lamely. "Then she left."

"Then why are you saying it was a mistake?" asked Abel.

"After I left The Machine, I stopped at your house to talk about Deacon giving you the business, then I realized it was too late. Maybe she followed me."

"You think!" roared Harm. "You led them right to us—all of us! Callie's hurt because of you."

René shrunk into himself like a turtle. Abel went inward, too—thinking—part of his mind angry, the other part following the logic. If the girl showed up at The Machine, the MS already knew they had been robbed by his crew. The beauty of the heist was that they were coming completely out of left field. There was supposed to be no way the bangers could connect them.

Somehow, they had gotten blown, and it was only a matter of time till the Maras had tracked them down. René's fuck up might explain how they'd shown up at the house but not them knowing his name. What he couldn't figure out was how they connected him personally to the job. How did they find out his name? René was holding something back.

Harm interrupted Abel's train of thought. "What are we going to do about all this shit? We know where Alverez lives, and he's got a wife. I'm going to put her in the hospital, too."

"No," said Abel.

"I say we hit that motherfucker and his family and take them down from the top."

"No!" said Abel adamantly. "We aren't animals. We're going to take them down without hurting innocents, but first we're hitting their sex trafficking operation. We promised Callie we would do something about that, and it's time. We already cut into their bank, so let's start to squeeze their money supply. I gotta believe their asses are in a pinch between the cartel and the Aryans—"

"I'm going to kill that bitch," interrupted René vehemently. "She doesn't know that I know she's involved."

"How do you know that she's involved?" asked Abel.

"She's the only link," René answered.

How did she know to check out The Machine in the first place? wondered Abel to himself. He was thinking that either René really fucked up or something else was going on.

Tank spoke up. "These guys could hit us again at any time. Abel, you've got to stay at our house. The rest of you guys should think about getting your family out."

Abel had been quiet for a minute as he sipped his beer, then he said, "We'll hit the girls' house the day after tomorrow. But we've got to figure out what to do with the girls when we burn the place down." He nodded at André. "Figure something out—they've gotta be gone before the rest of the MS show up."

TWENTY-EIGHT

"Where are you going, cher? I thought you were going to stay in tonight and watch a movie with me," said Harm's mother.

Shit, Harm said to himself. He had tried to sneak out through the kitchen, but his mama had a sixth sense. He was a former Army Ranger, who had been dishonorably discharged for striking a senior officer but was still afraid of his own mother. Maybe afraid was too strong a word—he just hated disappointing her. When she was disappointed, she had a knack for making him feel guilty. "I'm sorry, Mama, I promised to help Rabbit put an engine into one of his rebuilds—that's a two-man job. How about tomorrow night? Wait, I'm busy tomorrow night—I can't do it then."

"You don't have time for me anymore."

Harm sighed. "The day after tomorrow, I promise. Why don't we go out and see a movie?"

"That would be nice," said his mother, grudgingly letting him off the hook.

Harm escaped while he had the chance, stopping in the garage to grab a long duffel he had stashed earlier. He threw it in the back of his truck and tore out of the driveway, cranked the wheel, and shifted into drive. It was a few minutes past sundown, and the sky was filled with orange and purple clouds in unusual rows behind him as he headed southeast into the dark, into the city.

He mulled the plan over in his head—not really a plan, more like a feeling of structured rage. If the Maras were going to hurt his world, he was going to fuck up theirs. Alverez thought he could walk around with a wife and kids while he hurt Callie, a complete innocent? No, he was going to find out what it felt like.

The Florida Development Area rolled out in front of him, and he crisscrossed it, making sure nothing was shaking. He cruised by the gang house, noticing it was quieter than some of the other times they'd scouted it, then he headed to Alverez's place. He figured Garcia and Alverez were at The Loco, holding court like usual at this time of night, but if that motherfucker was taking the night off from the bar, then that was just his bad luck. If he was there, Harm could fix things in one fell swoop.

He motored to Alverez's neighborhood, parked on a dark street a block away from Alverez's house, jumped out of the truck, and retrieved the duffel from the back. He geared up, a heavy knife in a sheath strapped to his right leg, a pistol stuck in his belt in the back below his kidney, a short shotgun slung over his shoulder loaded with Hevi-ball, and a three-foot section of braided picture frame wire with wooden handles in a loose pocket of his pants.

The area was filled with shadows. While most of the houses had some lights on, there were pockets of dark that Harm used to sneak his way to Alverez's house, a double lot rebuild from after the hurricane. He ended up at the next house over, hunkered down in a copse of shrubs, a lucky find as landscaping was not a priority in the Ninth Ward. He camped out, watching to see if there were any guards walking the property.

An hour went by with Harm seeing only two Mara soldiers randomly walking around Alverez's property.

Occasionally, they would meet and talk for a while, stopping for a smoke—at least one of the times obviously weed as the skunk smell wafted over the slight breeze between the houses. *All the better,* thought Harm.

Just seeing two soldiers outside didn't mean there were no guards inside, so once he disabled the outside guards, he was going to have to move fast and overwhelm the inside guards before they figured out they were under attack. He wasn't prone to analysis paralysis, so when one of the soldiers walked around to take his station on the other side of the house, Harm crept up on the nearside banger who had just thrown his butt on the ground and was instinctively grinding it out with his foot.

The soldier's back was to Harm, who looped the wire garotte over the soldier's head and yanked back with both handles. He had precrossed the handles so when he pulled his hands apart using his back muscles the loop tightened on the unfortunate man's neck, cutting down toward his carotids and clamping them closed at the same time as shutting off his airway, preventing any shouts from escaping. If Harm had any kindness, he would have released the stranglehold the second the man passed out and zip-tied him, but this was Harm—his heart was empty of everything but anger for those who hurt Callie.

The man had flopped to the ground, Harm manipulating the body as it fell to land on its front. He put his knee between the soldier's shoulder blades and continued pulling up on the handles, the wire cutting deeper into the soldier's neck. Suddenly, the banger's bowels released, filling the night with stench.

Harm climbed off the man and grabbed his hair, yanking his head back, so he could disengage the wire noose that was now covered with gore. He grabbed both handles in one hand and whipped the braided wire, slinging off the mess, then stuffed it in his pocket, making sure there were no loose ends to catch on anything.

Next was the man on the far side of the house. The moon had risen and bathed the front of the house with silver light, forcing Harm to sneak around the back of the house. He passed a deck with lawn furniture guarding a rear entrance. He dropped to his knees and scuttled past it till he reached the edge of the house, where he dropped the rest of the way down on his belly and peeked around the side. The soldier was standing by a young tree, facing the street, his face bathed in the blue light from his phone.

Dipshit, thought Harm. Since there was now no other person outside to hear a death gurgle, Harm pulled out his heavy tactical knife and tiptoed up to the distracted banger like he was playing tag or capture the flag. He thought he had the man cold, but somehow the guy heard or sensed something and whirled, forcing Harm to rush the last few steps.

He came in with his left hand high, causing the soldier to raise his arms to block Harm. The ruse allowed Harm to drive the knife in his right hand deep into the banger's belly. The man's hands were flailing and clawing at Harm's face, pulling the balaclava askew and covering his eyes, but Harm didn't really need to see, as his left arm wrapped around the guy's neck, pulling him into an embrace, and his right hand on the hilt of the knife went into the man's guts. He pressed down on the handle, levering the blade tip up and then drove it toward the guard's heart and lungs, pushing it left and right, wreaking maximum damage. Abruptly, the man's full weight was hanging on the knife, and Harm let him down slowly, the body pulling itself away from the blade in Harm's fist.

He backed away and retraced his steps to the rear deck keeping low on the off chance there were guards looking out. If they had cameras and video surveillance, he was already fucked, but he figured they would have come storming out while he was dispatching the outside men if they did.

He slithered onto the deck, got to the edge of the house, too close to be seen through the windows, and reached the back door. It was a heavy-duty metal door with a dead bolt. He slowly turned the knob, and it rotated. Harm thought he'd gotten lucky, but when he tried to push the door open, he could feel the dead bolt catch. *FUCK!*

He dropped back down onto the deck and crawled back to the lawn, cursing himself for not thinking to check the guards' pockets for keys. He hit the ground, stood, then ran around the house to the man he had just knifed. He rifled his pockets, then rolled him and checked his back pockets. *Fuck! Of course—nothing.* Abandoning all care, he sprinted around the house to the other body. He was wasting too much time.

He immediately noticed a chain hanging from the guy's belt leading into his back pocket. Harm pulled out his knife and cut the banger's belt and yanked out a cluster of keys. Relief flooded through him as he wheeled around and tore back to the rear door.

Harm stood next to the door, willing his heart to slow down. He grabbed his wrist with his left hand to dampen its shaking and carefully tried the keys one by one. Tiny metallic sounds clicked and scraped, and Harm hoped he wasn't alerting anyone inside. The third key he tried slipped in, and Harm held his breath while he turned it. He could feel the bolt sliding back, easy...quiet...SNAP! The spring in the mechanism took over, slamming the bolt open.

He dropped the keys and took up the shotty that was still hanging by the strap around his neck, his right hand holding it up, finger on the trigger. He stepped to the side and eased the door open, thoroughly expecting a blast from an alerted guard blowing through the doorway. Nobody! He entered and softly shut the door behind him.

So far, so good—maybe they only had external guards. He crept through the house and heard a TV blaring deeper inside. It wasn't that late—could be Alverez's sons watching. Or perhaps they were in bed already, and it was the wife. Harm figured Alverez himself was at The Loco doing his usual shit, but what if he was here, too? *All the better,* he mused.

He'd entered through a utility room with a washer and dryer and skulked through a kitchen filled with state-of-the-art appliances, stone counters, and a huge built-in refrigerator. Obviously, Alverez had money to throw around. The house was new, but it felt homey and comfortable. It felt more like the house of a successful business man or executive rather than the leader of the New Orleans MS-13 raping and murdering gang.

The sounds were closer. He peered through the kitchen doorway, an arched opening that led into a fancy living room, the kind of room that nobody actually lived in—it was just for show—and saw an open door on the far side with light spilling out into the dim living room. Even though he figured that the residents were either in the TV room or upstairs, Harm quickly cleared the remainder of the ground floor, including a large master bedroom with an en suite bathroom containing an exotic marble shower with two heads.

The bathroom brought home to Harm how far above his own station Alverez was. *Being the leader of a gang sure paid well,* he reflected. He shared a tiny bathroom with his mother containing a single sink, a little round toilet with an orange rust halo in the bowl, and a mildewed shower curtain that always stuck to you when the water was turned on.

Pulling out several drawers one at a time, he eventually found a man's fancy silver hairbrush filled with wavy black and gray hairs. He drew a ziplock out of a pocket and used Alverez's toothbrush to dig out a number of hairs, letting them drop into the bag without him touching them. He took a moment to swirl the toothbrush in the toilet. A brief smile came and went. Then, he returned to the lit-up room, the source of the harsh laugh track that disturbed the peace of the house but beneficially covered up his sneaking about.

Carefully peering in, he saw a woman and two boys cuddled up on the couch, covered in throw blankets, with eyes glued to the TV. Harm backed away from the room and sneaked upstairs, finding bedrooms, an office, and an immense play area filled with toys. OK, good to go—Alverez wasn't lurking around the house. He tiptoed down the stairs, keeping quiet, not that it mattered, as the noise from the TV was loud enough that the wife had no clue what was coming.

Harm stepped into the room and fired the shotgun at the TV. The center of the screen cratered with cracks radiating to the edge of the large panel, smoke and sparks roiling out of the hole. An ear-piercing scream emanated from the woman's mouth, her arms wrapped around her sons who looked like they were screaming, too, but Harm couldn't hear them over the woman and his ringing ears. What with all the noise, he wondered whether the neighborhood was going to get stirred up, but then he immediately discounted the thought—it was the Ninth Ward after all.

"Stop screaming, or I'll shoot your boys," Harm yelled at her. She didn't stop until Harm pointed the muzzle at the youngest. Then she tried to clamp her lips shut, but her sobs and moans were still escaping her mouth in spurts. "Where's your phone?" he asked but then saw it on the end table next to her. He grabbed it and saw it was locked. "Where's your husband?"

"The...The...Loco," she stuttered between gasps and cries.

Good, Harm thought, *that'll buy me some time.* He handed the phone to the wife. "Call him!"

Harm could hear the pickup on the other end and waited till the wife said, "Help! There's a man—" then grabbed it out of her hands and placed it to his ear.

"Qué? Qué? What's happening? Tell me—"

Harm interrupted Alverez's frantic questions. "Hola, Señor Alverez—"

"Listen, you pendejo, I will kill you and all your fam—"

"Oh, I know what you think you can do," said Harm overriding Alverez.

"What do you want—don't hurt my sons! I've got money, I can pay you—"

"Stop!" yelled Harm. "Money? I'll take your money whenever I want. No—this is what happens when you hurt my friends and family—I hurt your family. Y'all come on now. You'll get here in time to see three warm heads in a pool of blood on the couch." He paused a beat, then disconnected the phone, thinking, *We'll see how Alverez's head works after this.*

Harm zip-tied the wife and sons, all of them frozen in place with fear. He set the phone on the end table, reached down, and pulled his knife out. He raised it over his head and swung it down, the wife screaming, and rammed it through the phone, then walked out of the room with his knife at his side, the phone speared on the tip.

Tank and André weren't home. Isabelle herself answered the door before he knocked. "Harmon, I've been waiting for you."

The house was unlit, and it was dark outside. The skin on her face was tight to her cheek bones so in the vague moonlight it seemed like he was looking at a skull, not a human face. "I've got some hair from Alverez—he's the head of the gang that hurt Callie."

"Give it to me." The look on her face sent a chill up Harm's back.

The night sounds and the murmur of the Gulf breeze dropped away as if he had clamped his hands over his ears—he felt disoriented, his eyes a fraction behind were he wanted to look.

Harm quickly pulled the bag from his pocket, and she snatched it from his hand. He started to say, "What—"

but she slammed the door in his face. He stood there for a moment, then returned to his truck. He sat behind the wheel, watching her place; an occasional faint flickering light could be seen in one of the windows. The wind in the treetops picked up, rushing through the leaves like the warning of an approaching storm.

TWENTY-NINE

A lverez stared at Garcia across the desk in the back room of The Loco. Garcia had never seen that particular expression on his face—a mixture of anger and sickness. He waited for Alverez to speak, but there was silence. He waited, not sure what was behind Alverez's demeanor. Had he found out about him working with Gomez behind his back?

Alverez broke the silence. "They entered my house. They attacked my family. They killed the guards." Alverez's eyes bored into Garcia's. "Why did they do this, Hector?"

"Maybe they—"

"DO NOT!" screamed Alverez, his eyes bulging. "I have already spoken to Gomez. I said we were dealing with the AB first. You directly disobeyed me, and as a result, you put my family in danger. It is like YOU held a gun to their heads yourself. I should kill you right now."

But he will not, thought Garcia. *He has lost his cojones.* "Did he hurt them?" Garcia asked.

"He frightened them. They will never be the same! I thought they were dead, and I was going to find their heads cut off when I got there. He killed two of our soldiers—

practically sawed off one of their heads. And it was just one guy."

"So everything is OK, your wife and kids are OK. You will be OK—you are just upset."

Alverez almost had an aneurysm. "How dare—"

Garcia held up his hand. "Wait." Alverez paused long enough for Garcia to speak. "Why didn't this pendejo kill them? Is he sending a message? Was he just trying to make you loco? Does he think this is a game, and he can set the rules?"

Somewhat calmer, Alverez asked, "This girl you assholes hurt, who is she to them?"

"I do not know yet, but she is important—family, I think. But listen, I have seen all their faces. I know where this Abel Kane lives. They have our money, but we have them."

Alverez examined Garcia, silent for a bit. Finally, he said, "What the fuck is wrong with you? You look like shit."

"Nothing—I am fine," he insisted, but he thought of this morning with Ramón. He was not able to perform for the first time in his life, and Ramón had teased him, which had pissed him off and made him want to kill the puta. Ramón had said he smelled like death. When he'd looked at himself in the mirror, his eyes were bloodshot and had dark smudges around them.

"Go see a doctor—you are no good to me dead. Anyway, I think you misunderstand these gringos. I think he was sending us a warning."

"Oh, I don't think so. They were mewling like kittens. I will show them AND their families how the Maras play. They will curse the day they learned of us."

"Because you lack the bonds of family, you underestimate what a man with loved ones might do. You've struck a hornet's nest; you better prepare yourself. You and Lúcido must find out about each of them—their families, their homes, their cars, their banks, their girlfriends, their bars, their cars, their properties. You must find them all and end them your way."

Diego Gomez was surprised to see Alverez walk into the whorehouse, the puto wrinkling his nose at the smell or the girls lolling on the beds or some fucking thing. Fuck him— el jefe didn't turn up his nose at the money that Gomez delivered every week. Alverez motioned for him to follow him out to the parking lot and reversed course back out the door. *Maybe he does not like my smell,* Diego thought.

They stopped a short way outside the building, Alverez keeping his distance from Gomez. Seeing Gomez in the bright light, he said, "What happened to your tattoos? They are faded!"

"I am just pale—I think I am sick. Maybe I have the flu."

"First Garcia is all fucked up and looks like shit and now you. You catch something from him? You sucking his dick now?"

"Fuck you, pendejo! I am no marico!" said Gomez, crowding in on Alverez.

Alverez didn't back up. "Move back, puto. I want to make sure you understand I am the boss, not Garcia. From now on, you do not do shit with Hector without talking to me. You tell me everything you see him doing. Comprende?"

Gomez stood there, keeping his inked face impassive, and thinking, *Fuck you both! Your day will come...* But he finally answered, "Sí."

CHAPTER
―――――
THIRTY

T he guys in the crew, minus René, were gearing up in Harm's garage in preparation to take down the sex trafficking building when René pulled up the driveway in his Jag and slammed on the brakes. The car's door was thrown open, and René tried to launch himself out of the driver's seat, but his entrance was somewhat diminished due to the still tender burns on his belly. "You didn't tell me we were going now!" he angrily said to Abel.

Yeah, because you're a problem, Abel thought. René's story was bullshit. There was something wrong with it, and Abel was going to find out what. Till then, René was out. He knew that somehow it was part René's fault that Callie got hurt. He could see it in René's face. Abel felt pissed off every time he looked at him. "I'm sorry, I thought André had told you—we're doing this one without you. Your burns have to heal."

"I'm fine! I can do my part," insisted René.

"No, man, you can hardly move. You could barely get out of the car. We can't afford to watch your back for this job. There are a lot of moving parts. Look, Cuz, just sit this one out. Can you go sit with Callie at the hospital? Isabelle has been there all morning, and she needs a break."

René was fuming. "Fuck all y'all!" he shouted at them and got back in the Jag and tore back down the driveway, raising a cloud of dust off the dirt and gravel. The tires chirped, and he shot down the road.

"I don't think he's going to go sit with Callie," Rabbit said. Tank and André laughed.

Abel snorted and asked him, "Where did you get the bus?" referring to the shiny white van on the curb.

"Boosted it from the Baptist church over'n Slidell. Being the middle of the week, probably no one will notice for a few days. I swapped plates though, just in case," answered Rabbit.

"Shit, stealing from a church—don't you feel guilty?" joked André.

"Well, I figured we're doing a good turn with it; them Baptists won't mind. I'll leave the original plates in it, and after we're done, the po-po will get it back to 'em. Maybe I'll leave a note, you know—'please return to the First Baptist Church of Slidell.'"

"What's the plan, Abel?" asked Tank. "It's almost lunchtime. How we doin' this?"

"I gotta figure that late morning is a slow time for a whorehouse. Everyone is still at work, the cops are gearing up to get lunch, and we know that the Maras don't get going at The Loco till later. Alverez is probably sleeping in or getting ready to eat with his wife. Garcia is out making collections or banging his boyfriend. And if he's at the house, or shows up, then we deal with him. Hell, I hope he shows up," said Abel.

"OK, that all makes sense, but what's the step by step?" Tank prodded.

"Alright, we gear up like we're taking down a semi. Vests, pistols, shotguns—the ammo is your choice. It's going to be close work, so I'm going with deer slugs. Do you two pig hunters have any Hevi-shot left?"

André answered, "Yeah, my gun is still choked for that, so that's what I'm using."

"Me, too," chimed in Tank. "Well, I mean I'm still set up for hogs anyway—the Triball. Shit, it practically blew that banger's arm off. It'll work."

While everyone else was chattering, Harm had quietly put on his armor, then shrugged on a black tactical vest. He zipped it up and started filling the front pockets with magazines. "You all set, Harm?" Abel asked.

He slapped his pockets, tugged at his knife strapped to his leg, drew his pistol to make sure it wouldn't hang up, and slid it back in the holster. He looked at Abel, started to say something, paused and then reached into his back pocket to make sure he had a handful of zip cuffs. Harm grunted an assent.

Abel looked around at the rest of his buddies. "Are you all geared up tight?"

The guys nodded, and Rabbit said, "Yes, Sarge!"

"Alright, wiseass—here's how it's going to go. Rabbit, you drive the church van to the whorehouse, and park it in the lot. Y'all are going to stay in the neighborhood, close but discrete. I'm going to walk in the front door acting like a regular john, looking for some pussy. I'll find out if the front door is locked and see whether the side door is locked or whether I can open it when the shit goes down.

"I'll scout the situation as I'm getting to my girl, but before I get into it with her, I'll ask to go to the bathroom. I'll text you the details and give you the go countdown." Like the rest of the guys, Abel was using a cloned iPhone. They were more expensive than a burner but offered better functionality. At the end of the job, they would be trashed.

"Wait, you're walking in there without a disguise and without armor?" Tank asked incredulously.

"The plan depends on having an inside guy. I'll put on those fake glasses and mess with my hair. That'll be good enough. We didn't have time to do a recon, and anyway, which one of you guys would have wanted to go in and bang one of those little girls? Putting aside how wrong that is, I don't think two condoms woulda made it safe."

Harm looked at Abel with concern on his face. "You can't go in without a weapon."

"I'll carry my switchblade. If they search me, I'll lose it, but a knife's not that big of a red flag. They'll just take it. I'll leave my phone on, so y'all can hear if I get in trouble. Then, when it's go-time, I rocket out the side door, and the two guys coming in hand me my shotty as they go in. Oh, and the point guy is coming in behind the SWAT shield— so make sure that's in the church van."

"That's shaky as fuck," argued Tank.

"Look, it's a whorehouse. We've been down here before. There's never been more than one guard. If it looks wrong when I get inside, I'll abort."

"If we hear anything on that phone, we're coming in blasting," said Harm.

"What do you think, André?" asked Abel.

"It's risky. I don't want to be coming in blasting with you in there. So, if anything, and I mean anything, looks south when you get in there—get the fuck out."

"We good?" Abel looked at each of them in turn. "Rabbit, you're driving the van. I'll go with Harm in his truck. André ride with Tank. Keep a tight convoy on the way down."

The area was as dead as every other time they had checked it out. No active businesses. No people about. They continued past the building, and Abel noticed a banger leaning next to the side door, smoking but paying attention to the surroundings. "Rabbit, hold off for a minute, we've got to do something about that guy by the side door."

Abel flipped down the visor mirror and watched Rabbit drive the church van past the whorehouse lot behind him. Harm found an inconspicuous parking spot just down the street and pulled in. Tank drove past and slid in between two buildings. Rabbit kept going.

They weren't that concerned about being seen in broad daylight since they were driving Ford F-150s, the most common truck in America. While they were staging at Tank's, Rabbit had swapped their plates with cold ones from his stash, so they weren't worried about anybody getting their numbers either.

Harm jumped out and said, "Wait for me . . ."

"Don't kill the asshole," Abel cautioned.

The four guys waited quietly in the vehicles—even Rabbit had his mouth shut for once. A long few minutes later, Harm popped open the truck door and slid in. "OK, I didn't kill him, but he's gonna have a headache."

Abel picked up the phone and announced they were good to go.

The last thing they did before taking off from Lacombe was to throw large mechanic's coveralls over their tactical outfits so when André and Tank grabbed tool duffels from the back of their trucks, they just looked like workies on the way to the job as they walked down the street toward the building.

Abel, in jeans and a flannel shirt over a tee, had already walked ahead of them, separating himself, getting into the role of a john, hesitant, but like he needed some relief. He made one last check of the phone to make sure everyone was still on conference, then dropped it into his shirt pocket.

He dithered in front of the whorehouse, trying to look through the blacked-out windows, and appeared to be gathering his courage, while Tank and André posted up at the edge of the building, quickly removing their coveralls behind a shrub and getting their weapons ready.

Harm casually ambled down the sidewalk, walking past Abel and the whorehouse door, carrying a duffle, still in the guise of a workman. Once past the whorehouse windows, he jogged left into the parking lot and made his way over to the church van and Rabbit. He dropped the duffle, and he and Rabbit stripped off the coveralls, then rifled through the bag, grabbing their weapons, keeping their backs to the street, and the van between themselves and the building. The last thing Harm did was pull the SWAT shield out of the rear of the van.

Back at the front door, Abel figured he'd allowed the crew enough time to get ready and not so much time that the people inside would be getting suspicious if they had noticed him through the blacked-out windows—counting on them to think he was just a chickenshit first timer. He pulled on the door, expecting it to be locked, but it swung open invitingly.

The room reminded Abel of a waiting room for some cheesy insurance office with a couple of flimsy vinyl chairs, a stack of ancient magazines, and a wooden desk covered with cigarette burns and an ashtray filled with butts. The room stank of smoke with an underlying wild odor that he couldn't quite pin down. Behind the desk was a hard-looking gang chica who was busily rubbing out her cigarette on the desk. "Took you long enough to get ahold of your balls and come in," she jeered.

"I wasn't sure I was at the right place. You can't tell from the outside."

"Whatever—first time here?"

"Yeah."

"I got to ask you. Are you a policeman?"

"Nope, I work over at the rail yard."

"Let me see your driver's license."

"I don't want to show it to you." Abel had prepared himself with a wallet and fake ID, figuring they would try to vet him but continued the charade of an embarrassed and nervous newcomer.

"Not going in unless I see it."

He pulled out his wallet and flipped it open to the window that held his counterfeit license, hoping she wouldn't insist on handling it—it wasn't that great of a fake.

"You sure look like a douche in that picture, puto," she said, demonstrating superb customer service skills. "Hope you got plenty of cash. It's fifty for a BJ, two hundred for the whole ride, and if you want to go bareback, it's another hundred."

"I heard you got some young ones?"

"Yeah, we got a couple. You can hit one of them for a thou."

Abel's head started to throb, and he pushed back the anger. *Be cool, asshole, be cool.* He fiddled with his wallet and fished out ten crumpled hundies, handing them over to the girl.

"Bueno—I'll buzz you through. There's a guy on the other side. He's going to search you and then hook you up." She reached under the desk, and the door into the back unlocked with an urgent buzz.

Abel walked through and began narrating jokily for the crew's benefit. "Man, is this what you do all day? Sitting with your ear to the door buzzer going deaf and feeling up guys' balls? Muchacho, how can you stand the smell in here?"

"Shut up, puto." The Mara guard roughly started patting him down and found his knife. "You can't have a knife in here, shithead." He noticed Abel's phone, and Abel could see the wheels turning in his head. It could go south right here . . . "I'm keeping your knife, pendejo. Follow me." Abel breathed a sigh of relief.

The guard's phone buzzed, and he looked down at the screen. "It's your lucky day, puto. You get one of the special ones." Abel thought to himself, *I'm not sure I'm letting this one out alive.*

They walked down a loose corridor in the middle of a large room. On the right and left of the pathway were makeshift rooms made out of sheets and shower curtains hung from the ceiling. Abel looked into each room as he passed, counting the men, and seeing if he could catch sight of Tattoo Face. He didn't want his guys to be surprised by him. He counted three men going at it in the front part of the place and no one who looked like that inked motherfucker.

"You got a lot of girls in here. What, you got like twelve or fourteen girls to pick from? Wait, you can see into every room? You'll be watching me fuck her? No privacy?" Abel babbled like he was nervous.

"Listen, asshole, I'm one guy watching all this shit. There're five or six johns here now, and it's not bothering them. No one will be watching you doing some kid."

They were standing in the center in an open area. Abel could see the side door to the place, and he knew Harm and Rabbit were standing right behind it. The door had a standard push bar, so it wasn't going to be a problem. "When I'm done, can I go out that door, so I don't have to put up with that bitch in the front?"

"Sure," the guard replied. "C'mon." He led Abel to the last partition, which was conveniently located next to the bathroom and drew back the sheet. A disturbingly young girl, maybe twelve, tangled in the yellowed bed linens, was lying on the bed. Matted clumps of hair surrounded her face, and tear tracks made lines through the grime. The guard prodded her shoulder. "Wake up, chica, you have a customer." The girl looked blearily at the guard.

Abel had no intention of even touching the child, but just being there as a representative of humanity made him feel guilty and sad. He gazed at her, trying to send her telepathic messages that this would soon be over. She rolled onto her back, her eyes blank and unfocused, staring into the distance. Abel watched one tear roll out of the corner of her eye.

He said to the guard, "I'll take it from here."

The man backed out through the sheet that barely covered the opening to the girl's cubicle and could be heard walking back to his station by the entrance to the front office. Abel waited a minute and then stepped out of her little room, casually opening the door to the bathroom and watching the guard out of his peripheral vision, making sure he wasn't paying attention to him.

He stepped in and closed the door and started texting the details and instructions to Tank and the crew. His phone was still open on conference to the guys, so his last text was "Listen for my GO in 10."

Abel shook his body, relaxing his arms and shoulders, then popped his neck left and right, then took a deep breath. He opened the door carefully and started walking down the aisle toward the side door and the guard up front. The guard looked at him quizzically and said, "What the fuck, you've shot your load already?" Abel waved goodbye to the guard, then made a left turn, yelled "GO" and hit the push bar, driving the side door open.

He stepped all the way out, holding the door with his foot while Harm rushed in holding up the SWAT shield. Rabbit was directly behind him, ducking down, holding his weapon and Abel's shotty. Abel grabbed his shotgun. Harm and Rabbit headed for the guard, and Abel reentered, holding station where he could see both up and down the aisle, watching for some dumb john trying to be a hero.

Seeing the SWAT shield, the guard mistook the boys for actual police and threw up his hands. Rabbit and Harm hustled down the aisle between the hung-up sheets and forced the Mara soldier against the door to the front office. Harm placed his pistol on the guy's neck, while Rabbit zipped his wrists behind him.

Meanwhile on the "Go" from Abel, Tank yanked open the front door and went in left, while André went right, both shotguns on the girl. She emitted an abrupt shriek. Tank kept his gun on the banger while André grabbed her shirt behind her neck and roughly forced her face into the desk, banging her nose, which caused her to let out a groan.

He handed his gun to Tank and wrestled the chica around and cuffed her hands, then zipped her ankles, pulling the strand tight. André shoved her down and placed himself next to the inside door. Tank felt around under the desk, finally hitting the unlock switch.

After the buzz, André pulled open the door and was confronted by the guard standing right in the opening, too close to get the shotgun barrels pointed at him, so André drove the steel barrels smack into his face and kept pushing, until he realized Harm was yelling, "Stand down! Stand down! We've already got this motherfucker!"

André stepped back and lowered the shotty, the gun pointed at the banger's belly. Harm forced the soldier to his knees, then encouraged him to go face down and flat on the floor with a boot in the butt. Rabbit zipped his ankles, then adjusted his feet next to the chica's feet and zipped them both together. "Let's see how good y'all are at the three-legged race!" He laughed.

André reminded Rabbit to get the phones, and he pulled out his blade and efficiently cut the guard's phone out of his pocket. The chica's phone wasn't in her pocket, and they couldn't find it.

While the other four were dealing with the Maras, Abel was ensuring that none of the other men were causing trouble by yelling, "All you fuckers behind the curtains, if I see anything—even a twitch—I'm unloading on you!" They were either smart or frightened because no one moved, the divider sheets hanging still.

"Hey, guys! Start working your way down to me. Leave the girls, but bring the men. Look out for Tattoo Face, and make sure no dipshit is playin' hide-and-seek under a bed."

André yanked the sheet down from in front of each cubicle while Harm trained his pistol on the room. Rabbit stayed back, keeping an eye on the gang girl and the guard, while the other three worked their way down toward Abel, collecting three men that Tank partially immobilized with zip cuffs.

André snapped photo after photo, documenting the men with the girls, the girls lying in bed, and the overall nature of the place. The girls in each room stared at them, not knowing what was in their future.

Rabbit tried to allay their fears. "Don't worry, girls, we're not going to hurt you; we're taking you to get help." His words didn't seem to sink in. Most seemed dazed, and one pulled the covers over her and scrabbled to the wall, hunched into a ball at the top of the bed.

Just as Tank cuffed the third john, two men burst out of the curtained rooms on Abel's right. The closest man rushed Abel who raised his shotty and snapped his hips, putting force behind the gun's stock as he struck the man on the side of his head. The attempted escapee dropped to the floor. The other loose man instantly changed course and ran back into the bathroom, slamming the door. *A lot of good that's going to do,* Abel thought, remembering that there was no lock on the flimsy door.

Rabbit tied up the man on the floor; the unfortunate john was conscious, but his eyes were unfocused and moving strangely back and forth like the little ball in the old Pong game. "You really rang this guys' bell—not dead though," he said to Abel.

Before dealing with the guy in the bathroom, Harm and André cleared the room next to it—finding a cramped office with a desk, a seedy couch, and a TV—probably the place where Tattoo Face hung out.

Harm came out and stood next to the bathroom door. Abel could hear Harm convincing the last john to come out of the bathroom.

"I'm coming out—don't shoot," the man screamed. He tentatively stuck his head out the door and saw Harm's pistol and ducked back in like a turtle. "Don't shoot!"

"Jesus Christ, get out here, I'm not shooting you," Harm said, frustrated.

Once they had the last man tied up, Rabbit managed all the prisoners while the other four started moving the damaged girls out to the church van. Most looked to some degree sick and strung out and weren't able to really understand what was happening. André wrapped one of the girls in the sheet and picked her up; she had scabby arms and had vomit in her hair. Looking into his eyes she asked, "Am I dead?"

"No, honey, we're taking you to the hospital."

"You're an angel then," she said drowsily.

They had the church van filled with thirteen sick and disheveled girls. The interior smelled like puke or worse. Rabbit removed all his battle gear and jumped up behind the wheel. André had already jogged down the street and retrieved Tank's truck and had it idling next to the van. He yelled over to Rabbit, "I'll follow you to the hospital. Just drive the van into the emergency entrance. I'll call you in a minute." Rabbit slowly pulled out of the lot with André tight behind him.

Abel watched the van drive off, knowing the girls were in good hands and were going to be taken care of. He turned to Tank and Harm. "Alright, let's finish up in there. I'm kinda bummed that piece of shit, Tattoo Face, wasn't there—I wanted to deal with him."

Harm angrily added, "That fucker has a lot to pay for."

They had intended to drag everybody out and burn the place down, but Abel decided to call 911 after they left, hoping that the police would have more luck dealing with the assholes if he left the place intact.

They reentered the whorehouse prison and collected all the cuffed people who had wormed their way apart from each other and were feebly trying to escape. Harm got some rope from his bag of gear and threaded it through all the zip ties and then tied the group of prisoners to one of the bed frames while Abel and André quickly searched the place for loose cash, finding a couple thousand in the desk and a small roll of hundreds in the gang chica's pocket.

They took off in Harm's truck, and Abel dialed 911, reporting shots fired and the location, then tossed the burner out the window. When they got back, André was going to create a package of the photos with a description of the situation and send it anonymously to the po-po as well as the *Times-Picayune* to make sure it got the attention that it deserved.

The van of damaged girls pulled into the emergency room entrance. Rabbit opened the door and casually walked back to André's vehicle, a ball cap pulled down over his eyes and a hand obscuring the remainder of his face. André pulled slowly through, passed the van, and called the hospital. "There's a van load of hurt girls parked in the ER entrance. They've been repeatedly raped, they're malnourished, dehydrated, and kept high on smack for I don't know how long."

"Who is this?" the hospital operator asked.

"It doesn't matter. There are thirteen girls in a van in front of the ER door, and they need help. Are you going to help them?"

"Yes, sir, I'll make sure the ER staff is notified."

"Thank you." André hung up and tossed the phone to the street before continuing down the road.

THIRTY-ONE

René looked at Tank's house in his rearview mirror. Abel was standing there with his hands on his hips, watching him leave. *Fuck him! Fuck all of them!* he thought angrily. They were always making him out as a joke. Even his own father thought he was a fuckup. After all he'd done for his dad, the asshole still thought Abel was God's gift. He'd picked his nephew over his own son.

The thoughts kept going round and round . . . Deacon taught Abel everything he knew about the business. *He could have spent all that time teaching me and bringing me along. No wonder I don't get any cred. He treated me like I was stupid and chickenshit, so all his crews and buddies in the Life think the same.*

René continued down the road, hitting the accelerator too hard, taking corners fast, his tires keening. He'd had enough. He'd show them—"I'll kill that bitch, Lúcido!" he shouted out loud. He'd force her to tell him all their plans, tell him where Garcia was, then kill them both, maybe even get the rest of the money out of Garcia's walls. Come home with a bag of money and both of them dead? Yeah, they'd change their tune, and his daddy would reconsider about the business.

René was quiet for a while, just driving in big circles all around Lacombe. There was another way to go, too. Lúcido probably set him up with the gang, but she was hot for him, that was obvious, and maybe she didn't know he suspected her, so he totally had the upper hand. He could feel her out . . . make something else happen and fuck 'em all.

He slowed down and pulled out his phone and sifted through the contacts, hearing the lane rumblers throb as he accidently drifted over the line. He found Lúcido's number and held it to his ear.

"Hola, muchacho! How are you?"

"I'm doing great. How's The Loco?"

"Ha, the same. It uses about one percent of my brain, and it's never going to be anything but what it is—a dive."

"Well, that's what I wanted to talk about. Why don't we put that brain of yours to work making money for the both of us?"

"Sounds like you are just making another play to get in my pants," she teased.

"No really, I've got a business proposition," he said in earnest. "I've got some money to invest."

"De verdad?" asked Lúcido, sounding incredulous.

"How about I come down there to The Loco and we talk about it?"

"Now?"

"Sure."

Lúcido hesitated and said, "I don't think that is a good idea. How about someplace else?"

"What about the Starbucks in Slidell off of Town Center?" offered René. "Do you know where that is?"

"No, but I can find it. I'll see you there at two pm. I have to take care of some things here first."

"OK, I'll be there—looking forward to it," said René, signing off. He drove home to get his pistol.

"Hello?" answered Abel.

"Abel, what's going on? Why're you ghosting me? You dropped off the face of the earth!" said Olivia angrily.

"Olivia, I'm sorry."

"What did I do wrong? Did I get too serious and desperate?"

"No...No!"

"I thought we really had something. Is it because of Owen—because I have a kid and a history?"

Abel interrupted her questions. "Wait, no—my sister got really hurt, and it's been chaos here." Well, it was that and the fact that he'd helped Deacon kill her father, but he didn't know how to tell her or what to do about that.

"What? What happened?" she exclaimed, interrupting his train of thought.

"There was a home invasion at our house. Some gangbangers were looking for money, and they hurt my sister and my cousin. They hit her, and she has a skull fracture. It's been touch and go since then. Callie is still in the hospital."

"Is she going to be OK?"

"She's still messed up, but she's improving."

"You should have told me; I could have helped you."

"Yeah, you're right," said Abel. "I was pretty out of it though—I still am . . ."

"What happened to your cousin?"

"René has some burns. He's home—a little sore but up and around."

"That's a blessing," she said in a comforting tone. "When is Callie getting out of the hospital?"

"I still don't know; she's confused and doesn't have any memory of what happened. We don't know the extent of the damage."

"What are the police doing?"

"Well, they took descriptions and are investigating." Another lie. Abel had told the hospital that Callie fell in the kitchen accidently, and René had made up a story about the burns.

As far as the hospital knew, they were two separate events, just two random accidents. More and more, Abel was realizing that there was no way to bridge his existing life with the everyday normalcy that regular people experienced. He was building a wider chasm between Olivia and himself.

"You must be so worried. Now I feel like a complete self-centered shit. I guess I'm just insecure. It's been a while since I've been in a solid relationship. I'm sorry. What can I do to help?"

"Just know that I might be checked out for a while. Please don't give up on me. I'll call you and keep you in the loop as much as I can, I promise." He really did need space to figure things out. Who wouldn't? How do you tell someone you care about that you're actually a criminal and that you helped murder their father?

"OK, just please don't block me out," begged Olivia.

"I won't. I'll call you and let you know what's going on. I promise."

CHAPTER

THIRTY-TWO

When René got to his house, he walked around to the back porch. It wrapped around the house on the far side, and his bedroom opened onto the deck. As a teenager it was the perfect setup, allowing him to sneak out without his mama catching on, and now it suited his needs again, enabling him to get into his bedroom and get his pistol without her being aware. He wasn't up for her shrill questions.

Ever since he had gotten hurt, she had been in a state. If she had known exactly what had happened to him, that he had been tortured, she would still be hysterical. She had stopped talking to his daddy after René had gotten hurt—she alternately blamed Deacon and Abel for getting him wrapped up in the Life, like he didn't have a mind of his own, like he just did whatever they said. She was as bad as the rest of them. She thought of him as a little boy who couldn't take care of himself—not a grown man, a decision-maker—a guy who coulda led Deacon's business if he'd only been given the chance.

He carefully opened the door and tiptoed in, heading straight to his night table. The Glock was in the drawer on top of a *Maxim* magazine. The magazine had probably been in there five years, and he still hadn't finished it. He took the gun out of the drawer and popped the gun's mag, making sure it was full, then snapped it back in and tucked it into his pants at the small of his back.

Before leaving the room, he stopped to check himself out in the mirror. He picked up a hairbrush and spent five minutes working his hair to perfection. Not happy with his shirt, he unbuttoned it quickly and went back to his closet and found his favorite cornflower blue broadcloth shirt, the one that set off his bleached hair. He tore it out of the dry cleaning plastic and put it on, leaving it untucked. Turning left and right, he eyeballed himself in the mirror, making sure the gun didn't telegraph through the shirt.

Moving over to the inside door to the rest of the house, he placed his ear against it, listening to see if his mama was moving around. All he heard was stillness and the quiet rushing of the blood in his veins, so he tiptoed back out of his bedroom, then retraced his steps around the house to his Jag. Starting up, he gradually hit the gas, gliding smoothly away from his home, relieved that he hadn't had to deal with his mother.

It was still before noon, so he had some time to kill before the 2 o'clock meet. He intended to get to the Starbucks early so he could watch Lúcido drive up, but he wanted to stop at the bank and pull some cash out of his box first, then maybe grab a bite. His stack was getting thin, and he wanted to be able to pull out a hefty bankroll that was all hundies to flash around Lúcido. His hand went unconsciously to his throat, fishing around to make sure his chain was there. He ran his hand down his shirt front, feeling the cross and the lockbox key hanging off the gold chain. He headed to the bank.

After lunch and the bank, he headed to the Starbucks and parked across the street. René watched the lot, waiting for Lúcido to drive up. He couldn't quite remember what her car looked like, but the lot was small, so it wasn't like he was going to miss her. He passed the time running through the things he was going to say. Twenty minutes after that started getting boring, she drove into the lot. She was at least fifteen minutes late, probably trying to mess with his head.

Lúcido got out of the car and took a few minutes getting herself together using her reflection on the driver's side window. She was wearing jeans and a pale lime-colored sweater with tiny jade buttons up the front. Her dark hair cascaded down her back, contrasting with the green. Pulling her large purse off the hood of the vehicle, she drew the strap over her shoulder and headed into the café.

René gave it another few minutes, then crossed the street and entered the coffee shop. Lúcido was sitting at a spare wooden table. When she saw him and caught his eye, she wondered again what motivated him to call her. If he had an ounce of brains, he had to have figured out that she had something to do with Garcia and Gomez showing up at the house. He couldn't be that stupid that he had no idea. Maybe he meant to do her harm; she was ready for that. Could he possibly be trying to get her to broker some kind of deal with the gang—his safety for his money? But what if he was sincere, oblivious to everything else and was actually trying to go into business with her? She figured the odds of that were about seven percent. Still, this was going to be interesting.

René leaned on the table with both arms and moved in and gave her a short kiss next to the corner of her mouth. "You look great, nice to see you. What can I get you?"

"Hola, muchacho," she responded. "A tall mochaccino would be great."

After a few minutes, René set down two drinks, then sat across from her, wrapping a leg around one of hers under the table. "Thanks for coming. I'm very glad to see you."

"So what's this all about?" she asked impatiently.

"First, I need to get something off my chest. My name really isn't Abel—it's René. I just gave you a fake name to make things simpler if things didn't work out. You know, make things less complicated down the road." Lúcido gave him a look. "Yeah, it's chickenshit. I know. I'm sorry. Can we start over from here?"

Lúcido nodded, thinking, *What a piece of work . . .*

"Alright, let's get straight to it. I've got some cash. Actually, a lot of cash. In order to use it, I've got to work it through a legitimate business. A restaurant is a perfect operation to launder cash. All sorts of ways to cover cash infusions and super easy to cook the books, so to speak. But I don't know anything about the food business, plus I couldn't be less interested in it. That's your area of expertise. I'm thinking we could start something up. I'll supply the money; you supply the brains—you run the place. We split the proceeds fifty-fifty. What do you think?"

This pendejo is serious, she marveled. "Wow, when you mentioned this the last time I saw you, I thought you were just talking out of your ass—and you're right, I can run a restaurant. I've been managing The Loco for a few years already. I even own a piece of it." She held up her hand palm out, as if to stop René from commenting. "Yeah, I know it's a shithole, but it makes money and I run the kitchen, do the ordering, make sure we aren't getting ripped off at the bar, and direct the staff. Another restaurant would just be more of the same."

"So you want to do this?" René asked.

"How serious are you?" she asked. "You know a decent place would take a few hundred thousand to get set up."

"I've got that easy, and I've even scouted out some places we could take over and make our own. But will there be a problem getting loose from El Luz Loco?" he asked.

"No, don't worry about that. I've got people that can handle it. Do you want to drive around and look at possible locations?"

"Sure," René answered. "I've got some ideas." He went up to the barista and got another set of drinks to-go. He held the door for Lúcido as they left, then asked her, "How about we take your car? I can navigate while you drive us around."

"OK, that works," she replied as she walked him to her car in the lot. René reached in and grabbed the oh-shit handle and swung his ass into the seat. Adjusting himself till he was comfortable, he reached into his pocket, pulled out his phone and manipulated the screen with his thumb.

"We're going to want to hang a right when we leave the lot," René instructed Lúcido. She buckled herself in, then started the car. They sat there for a second and René nudged her. "Just go out of the lot up there, then hang a right."

Suddenly, the rear passenger door behind René opened, and a man slid into the seat behind him. René launched himself up onto one knee and looked over the headrest. Garcia had a pistol aimed squarely at his face. A wild animal odor boiled off him, tainted with the stench of rotten fruit. René had his own weapon on Lúcido, growling, "I've got my gun on this bitch, asshole!"

Garcia called him on it. "Kill her, I don't care. I'll just shoot you the second you get the shot off." They stared at each other for a brief moment. "Or toss your gun onto the back seat, and maybe you'll survive this." René paused, then folded and slowly brought his hand up, the pistol hanging down, and carefully tossed it onto the back seat.

"Muy bien," said Garcia. "Now you are taking me to your money, and then you are going to do everything I ask, and tell me everything I need to know. If you want to live, you are not going to make me work for it. This is the second time I've tried to get you to cooperate, and this is your last chance."

"Please don't hurt me again," René begged. "That's why I'm down here. I was going to get Lúcido to make a deal with you. I've got the key to my safety deposit box.

See, it's right here around my neck." He pulled the chain up and dangled it outside his shirt. Lúcido gave a quiet snort and took her hand out of her purse.

Garcia instructed Lúcido. "Head to the bank. You get to pretend this piece of shit is your husband. He's nothing like my brother, but you're a good actress, so you better come out of the bank with my money."

Lúcido looked over at René questioningly. "Go out of the lot and turn left," he said.

CHAPTER

THIRTY-THREE

T he doctor came in to Callie's room just as Abel
had moved over a chair to be nearer to his sleeping
sister, so he stood and slid the chair back to give
Callie's army doctor friend room to examine her. The
doctor woke Callie and asked her questions, trying to
gauge how confused she was and to see how much she
remembered. At first, she seemed out of it, but as she
became more awake, she grew less disoriented, and she
could remember long-term things like where she lived, her
name, and Abel's name. Closer to the injury time frame
though, her thoughts became less clear, and she couldn't
remember the week of the injury at all.

To some degree, Abel was relieved. If Callie had started
talking about a home invasion in front of the doctor it
was going to cause problems; still, he wanted her to heal
completely, so if those memories came back, he would
deal with the fallout. The doctor kept talking to Callie and
patiently listening to her answers. Occasionally, she would
ask him a question, too.

The doctor was less worried about the amnesia as he
was about Callie's immediate mental state. She kept asking

him questions that he had already answered just a minute before, immediately forgetting what he'd just said. Abel was getting more and more concerned, and eventually the doctor noticed. "Don't worry, Abel, this is to be expected. Brain injuries take a while to heal, but she's actually doing pretty well. She's getting better. Her reflexes are improving, and she has sensation in all the places that she is supposed to feel things.

"Callie, let's try to sit up a bit," he said. The doctor pulled back the sheets and helped Callie swing her legs over the side of the bed, then he put his arm under her shoulders and lifted while she pushed off with her hand. The doctor kept one hand on her shoulder to steady her, then removed it a few inches. Abel got a good look at the side of her head; a section of her beautiful hair had been shaved off, and he could see where the pressure sensor was implanted. He watched her try to stay upright, but she was swaying some, and her eyes were unfocused. The doc gently lowered her to the bed and brought the covers back up.

"Well, we'll keep trying that, and maybe tomorrow we'll have you stand up for a few minutes. Pretty soon you'll be walking down the hall. Get some rest, and don't worry," he said.

"How long is she going to be like this?" Abel asked as the doctor was leaving.

He stopped on his way out the door and turned. "Every case is different, but she's doing better than I expected, so she could have a full recovery." Abel realized the doctor hadn't really promised anything. He steeled himself to have hope and made a silent promise to Callie to be there for her, whatever it took.

Abel moved the chair back and did his best to have a conversation with her, figuring the more he worked her brain the better it would be for her in the long run. "I heard you had some visitors—who came to visit?"

"Yeah, that girl came, that little girl that was in trouble. When is the doctor going to come?"

"Callie, the doctor just came a few minutes ago. He said you were doing great and that you are going to get up and walk some tomorrow."

"Oh."

"Isabelle was here, wasn't she?" Abel prompted.

"I don't remember," she answered and was quiet for a moment, her face working in concentration. "An old Black woman was here. I think it was night. She was thin and old—her face was bony, and I had trouble seeing her eyes."

"That was probably Isabelle, you remember? Tank and André's mama? You've known her all your life."

"I don't think I could see right. It didn't feel like Tank's mama." Callie had a confused expression. "She talked and talked."

"What did she say?" Abel asked, curious.

"I didn't understand the words. It was kind of singsong—like a chant. It went on and on, then it stopped, and she was gone." Two vertical lines appeared between her eyebrows as she struggled to recall.

Abel realized that all his questioning was making Callie tired. He wished he could talk over the Olivia situation with her, but she wasn't with it enough to handle that. Her eyelids were creeping down, sometimes closing but then opening halfway. Abel thought she was going back under, but then she asked, "Has the doctor come yet?"

"Yes, he's been and gone. You're tired—I'm going to go so you can rest." Abel stood and pushed the chair back into the corner with his foot, then leaned over Callie and adjusted her sheet and blanket up to her chin. The IV lines were tangled in the bedclothes, so he smoothed them out and made sure they were unkinked and out of the way, then bent down to kiss her on the forehead.

Her eyes snapped open. "Harm visited me. He said he went to Alverez's house to teach him a lesson."

"Wait, what? Callie—what?"

But before she could respond, Callie's eyes drifted closed.

"What the fuck?" Abel asked Harm who was leaning on his truck, cleaning his fingernails with his switchblade. Instead of inviting him in, Harm had come out and walked over to his truck that was parked in the front yard. There had been rain off and on, and they were in a lull.

"Dude, Callie said that you went rogue over at Alverez's house?"

"Abel, it wasn't exactly a rogue operation. It was the other day, just before we rescued the girls. Your head still wasn't on straight."

"You should have told me."

"If I did, we probably woulda disagreed, and I needed to do it. Isabelle wanted me to get some of Alverez's personal things, you know, hair and shit."

"Are you kidding me? Shit?"

"No, I just mean like some hair from his brush."

"Don't tell me you're buying into her hoodoo-voodoo bullshit? Look, you aren't helping her. She's losing her mind; you're just making things worse."

Harm raised his eyebrows. "Abel, I'm not so sure. Belle is tapping into some weird stuff. What if she could hoodoo them and fuck 'em up? I say we need all the help we can get."

"Jeez, whatever," Abel said in frustration. "Did you kill Alverez or hurt his family?"

"Nope, he wasn't there—I just tied up his wife and kids. Got the hair, then split."

"Is that all?" asked Abel, sure he wasn't getting the whole story.

"Well, I might have spun up Alverez a little, gave him something to think about." Harm shrugged his shoulders. "I called him on his wife's cell and said he was going to show up and find the heads of his wife and kids cut off and bleeding out on the couch."

Abel threw his hands up. "FUCK!"

"Oh, and I had to kill a few guards."

CHAPTER

THIRTY-FOUR

Abel had gone back to the Chevals' house after talking with Harm and had complained about him going off on his own, but Tank wasn't having it. His viewpoint was Harm's brain wasn't normal, and they all knew it. In fact, they all depended on it. What did Abel expect? A cat isn't going to act like a dog.

Abel had calmed down after knocking back a couple of beers, then headed home to get some clean clothes. The short-lived storm had just passed through Lacombe, making the roads slippery. The night seemed darker than usual, so Abel had his off-road light rack lit, illuminating ahead of him, as well as off to the side of the country road that led to his house.

The driveway to his home came into view, and he eased off the gas to make the turn, then continued through the trees until the clearing came into view, his floodlight bar blanketing the yard on both sides of the drive. About halfway to the house, something white showed up in his peripheral vision, and he turned toward the spot to see it better.

It appeared to be a hog or maybe a large dog, definitely not something that belonged in his yard. Jockeying the truck around, he aimed his truck at the animal, bathing it in light. He slipped the truck into park and jumped out and sloshed through the grass.

When he got about thirty feet away from the animal, the shape of the creature resolved. With a sick feeling, Abel realized it was a naked man facing away from him—his skin pale and translucent, reminding him of a fish that had been left on the shore for a few days. The body was capped by blond hair with vivid black roots. He took the last few steps to reach the corpse—no living person could look like that.

In shock, he held René's head up in the palm of his hand and examined his cousin's face, the eyes open, the irises milky and faded, the mouth set in a rictus. A big gash opened up his neck, but the rain had washed away any trace of blood. Multiple bloodless stab wounds could be seen all over his torso. He let out a wail. First Callie—then this.

His mind immediately went to the morning, when he had blown off René, blocking him from going with them to rescue the girls. His heart knew that René had gone and done something stupid because of him. He screamed and pounded the dirt over and over, beating the grass into the ground until the mud splashed up and began dripping down his face.

He slowly wound down, leaning on both of his hands in the mud, then sank back onto his haunches. A pinging noise came from his pocket. He fished out his phone and saw a text from René. Thumbing it open, he read, "I got part of my money back from this son of a bitch and Im getting the rest from you putos, whatever he looks like now you going to look worse! he was lucky he did not suffer to much but the rest of you fucker you are dead your frends are dead, you family is dead". A spear of anger pierced his brain. He waited till it subsided, then dialed his phone.

"911," said the dispatcher.

"I came home and found my cousin's dead body in my front yard."

"What's the address?" asked the dispatcher. Abel gave her his name, address, and condition of the body. "OK, stay on the line. We'll have a car over there in a few minutes."

"No, I can't stay here. I've got to go tell my uncle and aunt. They can't be hearing this from anybody else."

"Sir, this is a possible murder scene. You have to stay."

"Ma'am, I'll come right back, I promise, but I've got to go tell them." He disconnected, then stood up and jogged over to his truck. Once he was back on the road, he dialed Tank.

"René is dead," he said before Tank could even say hello.

"Shit! What happened?"

"Those MS bastards killed him and dumped him on my front yard—they fucked him up bad. I'm heading to Deacon's to tell them right now, and the police are headed to my house as we speak."

"What are you going to tell them?"

"Who? Deacon? Or the police?"

"The police."

"Nothing. I'm going to say he wasn't with us. They're going to be looking closely at all of us. We've got to get everybody on the same page. Listen, we were at your house from before lunch till after lunch for like three hours. We left all our phones there anyway while we were hitting the whorehouse, so they'll back that story up. They'll be pinging the towers around your place. Our story is that we were throwing around ideas to start a business over lunch."

"OK, I'll call everybody right now or go find 'em if I have to."

"Yeah, flesh out the story a little bit and let me know. I need to know the details before they talk to me. Do you think your mama will go along with it?"

"She's in some kind of state—I don't even know how to describe it. It's like she's got a fever. She's talking church stuff all mixed up with some spooky horror shit. I'll get her to go along with this. I'll convince her it's part of the whole thing."

"OK, I got to go. I'm almost at Deacon's house, and I have to figure out what I'm going to say."

"Wait—don't hang up. Are you OK? Brother, I'm sorry, man. You know I love you; we all love you. I'm there for you—for anything. I'll get Mama and André and come over there. We'll be there in about a half hour."

"No, man, I'm not OK. You know René, he was René. But he was my family. I didn't love him like a cousin—I loved him like he was my brother, and I fucked up again."

"Yeah, bro, I know. We all did."

Abel climbed the porch steps. It took a supreme act of will to lift one foot and place it, then force the other to take the next step. He rang the bell instead of using his key. There were no sounds from inside. Maybe they weren't home. A cowardly feeling of relief flooded through him momentarily, but he made himself ring it again. He heard a door slam inside. The porch light came on, and he saw the outline of Aunt Hennie in the sidelight. The door pulled open.

She looked at him, reading his face, then her lips started to quiver. A scream rose from her throat as she collapsed to the floor, writhing around, and slapping herself in the face over and over.

Deacon came running down the stairs to the foyer. "What—what happened?" He knelt and put his hands on Henriette and looked up at Abel and said plaintively, "René?"

Abel nodded, and Deacon released a gasping sob and curled around Hennie on the floor, crying and saying, "My boy, oh my boy," over and over.

Abel stepped a little way back on the porch and phoned Deke's lieutenant and friend Gerard, telling him what happened and asking him to come over and bring his wife.

Deacon stood up, tears leaking down his face, then bent over and picked up his wife. She had stopped screaming, and her head was drooped over Deacon's arm, her face hanging slack. He plodded up the steps to their bedroom. When he came down the stairs again, he roughly grabbed Abel's arm. "What happened? Tell me!"

"I don't know exactly what he did, but the Maras got him. They dumped him on my front yard. He was pretty fucked up."

"Let's go. I want to see my son."

"No, the police are there. I gotta go back, but you need to stay here. They're going to send a patrol car for me or put out a **BOLO** if I don't go back. You've got to stay here . . . I don't want you to see him like this."

Deacon stepped into the living room and sat on the couch, his head in his hands, and cried some more. Between bouts of tears he asked, "Are you sure it was the MS?"

"I got a text from René's phone, basically saying it was retaliation for the robbery, they wanted their money back, and the rest of us were going to get worse than he got."

Deacon started getting angry, choking back his tears. He exclaimed, "Alverez is dead!"

"Yeah, we're going to kill that motherfucker," Abel agreed.

"You're going to help me, right?" said Deacon, grabbing Abel's hand desperately. "Where is this fucker? Let's go now!"

"No, wait. I got to figure some things out, and I have to get clear from the police before I can do anything." Abel sat next to Deacon and put his arm around him, noticing how bony his shoulders had gotten, wondering when that had happened. "Listen, Uncle Deacon, now is the time for René and Hennie. We have to put René in the ground first." He pulled Deacon in, squeezed tight, and growled, "Then, we kill that motherfucker!"

CHAPTER
_____

THIRTY-FIVE

T he police didn't finish with Abel till the early hours of the morning. They came at him from multiple directions, and while Abel tried to be helpful, or at least act helpful, he essentially didn't tell them anything. He'd had an alibi for the hours before René got dumped, and he told the detectives that he was in the company of his friends for the time before that. The questioning eventually petered out, and they finally let him go home. They hadn't seemed satisfied though; Abel figured they knew he was bullshitting them somehow. They understood that René might have gotten himself mixed up in something and gotten killed, but why was he dumped in Abel's front yard unless Abel was involved somehow?

He crashed in bed without taking off his clothes—mud and all. He was dead tired, but he couldn't drop off. There were too many thoughts in his head and an excess of adrenaline that hadn't dissipated yet. At some point, he fell asleep but woke up as soon as the first morning light beamed through his window.

Sometimes he'd wake up from a horrific dream, and it took him a minute to realize that it was just a dream. This time, when his head cleared, it wasn't a dream. It was real. A wave of grief engulfed him. It washed over him, and he lay there paralyzed. After a while, when enough of it passed and he could function, he ran down the list of tasks he had to do that day. He forced himself out of bed and got ready to face things.

Abel drove himself to the hospital and made his way to Callie's room, hoping to see some progress and not more bad news. When he entered her room, he was surprised to see her sitting up, sipping juice from a straw. A feeling of relief passed through him, almost blocking out the memories of the previous night. "Hi, Abel," Callie chirped. Abel was amazed. She had made a leap from the last time he'd seen her. It felt like a miracle; she was like the old Callie.

"How are you feeling?" he asked.

"Pretty good. They got me out of bed this morning, and I walked a little bit. I'm still kinda dizzy, but I did it."

"That's great! You don't know how happy that makes me feel!" Abel beamed at her. "Are your memories coming back?"

"Things seem clearer, but I still don't remember what happened."

Abel asked, "Do you want to know?"

"Yeah, what's gone on since I've been out?"

"I'm not going to tire you out and drag you through everything, but basically the MS bangers showed up at our house and somehow hurt you and tortured René. They were looking for the money we stole from them."

"You robbed them?" she exclaimed. "What were you thinking? Is René OK?"

"Tank and André showed up and stopped them, and the MS assholes escaped, but we got you to the hospital. René just had some burns, and he was alright. But yesterday, he did something else and got mixed up with them—we don't know what—and they killed him. I found him last night."

Callie started crying. René could be annoying, but they'd grown up with him, and René had always treated Callie like she was special to him. Deacon had been tough on all of them, so the three of them had an us-versus-Deacon alliance; it was like losing a brother.

"Do you want me to keep going?"

"Leave me alone for a while, but come back. I feel like I've been away for a long time, and the whole world changed while I was gone."

When he got back to Callie's room, she was asleep. Her face was peaceful, and he was looking at the side of her head that hadn't been shaved, so she looked like nothing had happened to her. Lost in thought, he just sat there. He may have dozed off, he wasn't sure, but he heard someone call his name. "Abel... Abel..."

Callie's head was on the pillow, but she was gazing at him and quietly calling him. Abel rubbed his face with both hands, pressing his palms against his eyes and running his hands over his mouth. "Did he suffer?" she asked.

"I don't think so," Abel lied.

"What happened?"

"Well, when the Maras hit our house, they messed it up. The guys fixed up our house. But before that, we were all at the hospital with you. We told the hospital people that you fell in the kitchen; we didn't tell them it was a home invasion. René went to the ER and said his burns were from a welding accident.

"We couldn't figure out how the MS knew it was us that robbed them. René somehow led them to us. We don't know how, but it had something to do with a gang chica that he got involved with. He didn't tell us what happened, and everybody was pissed at him. He wasn't telling us the whole story.

"Anyway, we decided to hit the sex trafficking building because we figured that was what you would have wanted us to do—to fix that."

"Not if one of you was going to get hurt," she cried.

"Well, none of us were thinking straight. We were just going to take those assholes down. Harm went out on his own and attacked Alverez's house and family. You know, the MS head guy? Then, the next day we took apart the building, got all the girls to the hospital, got the police involved, and closed the place down. Tattoo Face wasn't there, so he's still running around on the loose."

"Good for you. What those people were doing with those girls was pure evil." Callie shifted gears. "When Harm went to Alverez's house, did he hurt his family?"

"Well, he killed a few guards, but he didn't hurt Alverez's wife and kids. He was pretty crazy and upset that they had hurt you, so I'm amazed that he didn't. He told me he was just messing with Alverez's head."

"I'm concerned about Harm. He doesn't feel things the same way we do."

"Yeah, I worry, too, but he's got our back. I know he loves us, and I love him. I don't know what to think. It's like he doesn't care about people," said Abel. "Still, I've never seen him hurt someone who didn't in some way deserve it. I know right from wrong, yet people around me get hurt all the time, and it feels like it's my fault."

"Abel, it wasn't your fault I got hurt. It's not your fault that René got killed."

"I didn't let René go with us to the whorehouse. I was still pissed at him for the thing with you. I felt like it was partly his fault that you got hurt. His story was full of holes, and I decided not to trust him and blew him off. He left angry and then went and did something stupid with the MS and got killed for it. He really wanted to come, and I pushed him away. Now he's dead, and I'll never be able to tell him I'm sorry for being a dick to him."

"Abel, don't you think it's time to get out of this before someone else gets killed? Just give them back all their money and walk away from all this. It's escalating. They kidnapped Katie, we robbed them, they hurt me, you destroyed their sex trafficking operation, and then they killed René.

"Don't you see? It's going to be you or Tank who gets killed next, and I couldn't handle that. And as far as it being someone's fault for René? It wasn't you; it was me. I told you about the MS-13. I encouraged you all to go after them. It's on me, and now I want you to stop. Isabelle said it was a storm, and she was right; it's a tornado. Give 'em back their money and then disappear—all of you."

"I don't think we can. They left me a message about René. They said that René told them everything about all of us. The last thing they said was they were going to take everything we have and kill our families, our friends, and everyone connected to us that they could find.

"Isabelle told me all this was going to happen and that I didn't have a choice—that I had to step up. She said something like our futures were a river, and they flowed in one direction and that we had to ride them out. She said God was preparing me for this, preparing all of us, and that it was going to get bad before it got better. I feel like she was right. We've encountered filth, and we have to clean it out because we're the people who can."

Abel could tell Callie had reached her limit. Her eyes were drooping, and one side of her face was slack, almost sagging. "Callie, I'm sorry I dropped all this on you. You need to rest and get better. I'm going to go."

Abel watched Callie try to gather her strength, then she whispered, "Wait . . ." Then a little bit louder she said, "Isabelle was right. You're right. They're pure evil, and they aren't going to stop. They don't even really care about the money. They just want an excuse to hurt people. You can't let them hurt anymore of us. Kill them. Kill them all. Do it to them before they do it to us."

THIRTY-SIX

I t was cold in the morgue, and there was an odor of pine disinfectant that didn't fully hide the smell of death and corruption. Someone had painted the place with bright colors, attempting to offset the nature of the place; instead, the effect was jarring. Abel took shallow breaths like a panting dog—it didn't help much. He had volunteered to officially identify René, wishing to spare Deacon and Henriette the trauma, but he hoped the formality wouldn't take very long. He'd already identified René to the police at the murder scene but the medical examiner preferred to have it explicitly done at the morgue.

An assistant to the coroner guided him to a panel of cabinets and slid out the long drawer. A whole new level of smell assaulted his nose, and he quickly swallowed several times. The gowned and masked assistant noticed his discomfort and hurriedly pulled down the sheet covering René's lifeless face, trying to get it over with as soon as possible.

"Yes, that's my cousin, René Baptiste Kane."

"OK, that's all we need," the staff member said. She drew the sheet back over René and pushed the drawer back in. It slowly glided in with the sound of a bowling ball rolling down the lane. "Thank you, sir. I know this is hard, and I'm sorry for your loss."

Abel signed his name and then directed his attention at the girl. "When can we get René's body? His parents want to have his funeral this weekend."

"Oh, I thought you knew. This is a murder investigation. They won't be releasing his body for a few weeks at the earliest. There is going to be an autopsy, lab tests, and the medical examiner's office is very backed up. It takes a while."

Abel's face fell. He knew that Deacon had already started moving on the funeral. "What am I going to tell his parents?"

"Many people have a commemorative memorial service as soon as they can. Sometimes they put up a picture of the deceased and have the ceremony, and everybody speaks, just as if it was the funeral," she said. "Then, when the body is available, they have a small service for the close family at the grave."

That made sense to Abel, and he figured he could help make that work for his aunt and uncle.

Lacombe was too small to have a selection of funeral homes. Deacon found a nice facility in Slidell, and they were able to accommodate his wishes to have the service immediately. It was scheduled for Saturday afternoon.

Henriette was not able to function and was mostly sitting in one spot, either quietly weeping or staring off into space. Gerard and his wife helped Deacon put together a memory board with prom and baby pictures, along with a selection of group photos. Tank and André found some photos as well, and Abel downloaded some pictures of René from Callie's computer that she had accumulated over the years. There was a funny picture of René playing soccer in his little shorts that showed his skinny white legs when he was about six.

On Saturday, Abel got to the funeral home early and helped Deacon set up the memory board and a big framed picture of René from his high school graduation. It was the dark-haired version that resembled his daddy before he had decided that blonds had more fun.

After that, he and his uncle milled around, at loose ends, not sure what to do other than wait for the service to start. The funeral director eventually guided them to stand in the foyer where they could welcome attendees. There was no way Henriette was going to be able to stand there and greet people, so Abel found a small upholstered chair and dragged it into place.

Deacon went into the large chapel and found Henriette in the same spot where he had sat her an hour before, and he coaxed her to come out into the foyer. Abel helped Deacon situate her in the soft chair, and then they stood there uncomfortably waiting for people to arrive. The foyer was packed with flowers, every available surface had a bouquet, and big freestanding arrangements took up space along the walls, flanking the doors to the chapel. The accumulated perfume of all the flowers was overpowering.

Eventually, people started filtering in—an unending line, all of them saying kind things to Abel and Deacon, most bending down to hug Henriette or grasp her hands that were lying lifeless in her lap. Tears were silently running down her haggard face, forming tracks and tributaries in the makeup that Gerard's wife had plastered on her.

Tank, André, and their mother approached Abel. Isabelle wrapped him up in her arms. "I'm so sorry, mon cher." Abel was too choked up to respond. She moved on to Deacon, making room for Tank who shook Abel's hand, then wrapped him up with a one-armed hug.

"I'm sorry we're late. We had to walk about a half mile. There isn't any parking close. The streets are packed with cars. You should see it outside—there are hundreds of people."

"I've set aside seats for you in the chapel. You're with the family in the first row," said Abel.

André hugged Abel and said, "Everywhere René went he was the life of the party. It's no wonder all of Lacombe is here and half of Slidell."

"Yeah, I know. I just didn't imagine all these people would show up," Abel said, following Tank into the chapel.

Deacon put his arm around Henriette and helped her up, and the three of them walked into the chapel and took their seats at the front with Isabelle and her sons. The funeral director made some generic remarks about René and the Kanes. When he finished, he consulted a list of people who had signed up to talk about René and called up the first one. A woman about René's age, standing in the back, slowly made it through the throng of mourners to the dais. The director removed the microphone from the stand at the lectern and handed it to her.

"Everybody liked René," she began and proceeded to recount how she'd known him since elementary school and how they had even dated for a while. "The thing about René was that he listened to you," she said. "Yeah, he dated a lot of girls, and nobody could pin him down, but when he was with you, he was with you. I'm going to miss him so much." She set the microphone down and walked with her head down, sniffling, to the back of the chapel.

The director called up another mourner. Rabbit's little sister took the microphone, very poised for a sixteen-year-old, and gave her condolences to René's family. Then she said, "I'm sure we're going to hear from a lot of girls who were in love with René. But I loved him in a different way. He was like another brother to me. He was always watching out for me and never treated me like I was a little kid. He was maybe ten or twelve years older than me, but he treated me like a friend. Sometimes he even asked me for advice. He did things for me. One time, some boys were being mean to me, saying nasty things, and when René heard about it, he figured out where they all lived, drove to each of their houses, and spoke to them individually—like five different kids. To this day, I don't know what he said, but those kids stopped what they were doing. My life will be less without him."

And on it went, person after person telling little anecdotes about René, some that Abel had heard before, others that were new to him. He had always thought of René through the lens of his family and their shared relationship with Deacon and Henriette, but René had a whole life that was apart from that. He was sorry that he was hearing all of this too late to change how he had treated René. Maybe he could have been a better person to him, no—he should have been a better person to his cousin.

Then it was his time to speak. Deacon had asked him to perform the eulogy. Deacon was a charismatic man of action, making him a persuasive speaker, but Abel understood that Deke, in his own way, was as shattered as Henriette and would not be able to do his son justice.

Abel stood in front of the gathered grief-stricken people and scanned the crowd. He hadn't prepared anything; he figured he'd talk from the heart. He let out a long, drawn-out breath. "My parents died when I was six, then Callie and I went to live with Uncle Deacon and Aunt Hennie. I had lost my parents but gained another family. It had been just me and Callie, and then there was René, my cousin, but really more like a slightly younger brother. We did everything together; we were even in the same classes in elementary school."

He talked about the fun things he'd done with René and the trouble they'd gotten in together, the big fight with Henrí and how they'd met Tank, and then André, Harmon, and Rabbit. "The thing about René was that he could tell when you were sad, and then he would do his darndest to try to make you feel happier. He literally couldn't take it if you were sad—and I was sad a lot after my parents died for a long time—and René helped me get through that..." Abel stopped, too choked up, so much so that he couldn't continue and began crying, his shoulders jerking up and down.

Deacon and Hennie were crying, too. Hennie's sobs were clearly heard by everyone in the front of the chapel, while tears streamed silently down Deacon's face. Tank went up and collected Abel, putting his arm around him and guiding him back to his seat. Abel lost track of the rest of the service after that but managed to get himself together enough to stand out in the lobby and thank people for coming.

Still in a daze, he responded automatically to the people as they walked by him, shook his hand, and gave their condolences. Suddenly, an elegant woman in a demure black dress, squeezed his hand and said sharply, "Abel!" He snapped out of his locked-in state and realized it was Olivia. He hadn't recognized her in the current context, and he'd never seen her in a dress. She'd obviously spent time on herself, and even in his grief, he noticed how striking she was. He was embarrassed for not immediately recognizing her and hoped she hadn't noticed.

"Abel, I'm so sorry for your loss. I really liked René—everybody did. He was so much fun to be around. But I wish you had called me. I heard about René from one of my friends, and I feel bad that I couldn't be there for you."

"I'm sorry. I've been in shock since it happened. I can't seem to get my mind straight. It feels like I'm drowning, and I can't make my way to the surface to get a breath of air."

"That was what it was like when my father died," she said, causing a sharp pain in Abel's heart and pushing him deeper underwater.

"I'm sorry," he told her.

"I can't stick around; I've got to get ready for work, and I know you have to be here for your family, but we need to talk. First Callie, then your cousin? You're involved in something, I know it. If you can't be real with me and let me into your life, we're never going to have anything together. I can't bring some unknown into Owen's life. I have to think of him."

"Olivia, I promise we'll talk. As soon as I get through this, I'll tell you everything." She looked at him, gave a slight nod, and kissed his cheek.

The service had ended, but Abel hung around till the bitter end before ushering Deacon out the door with Aunt Hennie and then cleaning up all the items that Deacon had put together to tell the story of René's life. Tank and André had offered to stick around with him and help, but he told them he wanted to be alone and that they needed to get Isabelle home. Abel was concerned about her.

He picked two of the best flower arrangements and put them in his truck to take over to the Kanes' house and then talked to the funeral director about donating the rest. The last item left was the big picture board of René's life. He stopped to look at it one more time, but this time he noticed how few of the family photographs had him and Callie in them. He wondered whether Deacon had ever considered them family or whether it was always only the three of them: René, Deacon, and Hennie, with his brother's kids just vaguely floating around the periphery. He shoved that thought out of his mind, grabbed the poster board, and headed back out to his truck. The back seat still had enough room to slide the memory board behind the front seats. Placing it, he stepped back and slammed the door on René's things.

Out of the corner of his eye he saw movement in the cemetery. The vast expanse of green lawn started at the edge of the parking lot and extended away in all directions. Headstones and vaults covered the undulating terrain with brick pathways interspersed between sets of graves. A man was watching him from the path, half his face obscured by a limestone vault, the stone yellowed from age and covered with black mold.

Abel started slowly walking toward the man, and as he got closer, it dawned on Abel that it was Garcia—that Mara fuck. He picked up his pace, and Garcia turned and began quickly walking away. Abel started to run, and Garcia followed suit, loping down the path, the older man confoundingly increasing the distance between them.

Abel sprinted full tilt, chasing after him, trying to close the distance, but Garcia stayed frustratingly out of reach. He fixed his eye on Garcia, occasionally checking the path to make sure he wouldn't trip. He continued after him, eventually his steps slowing, his breath coming in great gasps. The air was heavy—closing around him—and his feet started to feel like he was dragging them through mud. He couldn't catch up. Garcia was getting farther and farther away, and his image started flickering and fading away as if mists were blowing around it.

The path ran behind a vault, and Abel pounded up to the crypt, thinking the MS-13 bastard would be waiting for him, but when he rounded the path, he was gone. He couldn't see him ahead on the path, and he wasn't crouched hiding behind the tomb. He had simply vanished. Abel bent over with his hands at his hips, sucking great lungsful of air.

The sun beat down on him, but he felt a chill. *What the fuck?* he thought. *I must be losing it.*

THIRTY-SEVEN

"Rabbit, I need one, maybe two cars. They have to be totally generic, and they just need to run. I don't need performance, but they have to be rock solid—no starting problems—and quiet."

The phone was silent for a beat, and then Rabbit asked, "When?"

"When can you get 'em?" replied Abel.

"I'll have them by tomorrow morning. You can pick them up before lunch at my dad's shop. I'm helping him tomorrow, so I'll be there—find me." Rabbit dropped the connection.

Abel mulled over the timing, thinking about the surveillance they had done on the MS a few weeks ago. Then he thought of all the things he needed to put in place. Wednesday morning would work.

The next morning, Abel showed up at Rabbit's father's auto repair shop. He went into the office and spent a few minutes with Rabbit's daddy, who kindly asked him how he was doing. He still was getting emotional when people asked him, and their sympathy made it worse. The kinder they were, the more it hurt. Right now, he needed to keep those thoughts at a distance, so he cut the conversation short and asked where Rabbit was.

"He's out in the back lot, pulling some parts from one of the wrecks I brought in last week from the auction," answered Rabbit's dad.

Abel made his goodbye to Mr. Walker and went through the shop, enjoying the smells of gas and tires and saying "hey" to the mechanics that he'd known since he was little. They all stopped him, wanting to give their condolences. *I should have walked around the building,* he thought. It took twice as long, and their words were gutting him.

Eventually, Abel had run the gauntlet and found Rabbit bent over the radiator of a Chevy Cavalier, in the process of removing a starter. The car was already up on cinder blocks, the tires piled in a jumble, and all the seats had been pulled out. Their junkyard dog, a sweet old Rottweiler bitch, was curled up on one of the seats, snoring in the sun. "Dude!" Abel said. Rabbit jerked up, startled.

"Fuck! Don't sneak up on me like that!" Rabbit grabbed his hand and pulled him into a chest bump, putting his other arm around him and squeezing him tight. He let go, and Abel noticed that his hand was covered in greasy dirt.

He wiped his hand on his jeans. "Where are the cars?"

"Over here—c'mon." He motioned, then walked toward the back of the lot. "What's going on? Do you need my help?" he inquired over his shoulder.

"You don't want to know," Abel answered. "I'm good. You stick around and help your dad. I'm just doing some surveillance. I'll let you know what we're doing when I figure some things out—OK?"

"Sure." They had reached two similar Toyotas—Camrys, the most ubiquitous cars in America. One was dark blue or even black, Abel couldn't tell. The other was metallic beige. "Take your pick. They both run like clocks; you won't have any problems."

"'K, I'm going to leave my truck here. I'll go with the blue. If I need the second one, I'll be back. Give me the keys for both because I may have to get the brown one after hours. Do I need a key for the lock on the chain?" asked Abel, pointing to the chain piled next to the opening in the fence surrounding the junkyard.

"Naw, it's a combo, and we never set it. It's hanging there for show. Nobody is going to steal any of these pieces of shit back here."

"Thanks, man, I owe you." Abel jumped into the Camry and started it. He leaned out the window. "Later."

The next stop was a convenience store where he picked up a couple of six-packs of Gatorade, sweet-hot jerky, and some greasy Slim Jim's. He laughed to himself because the sausage made him flash back to when Deacon showed him how to steal his first car, how he had used a "slim jim" door lock popper.

While he was at the gas station, he was going to top off the tank, but when he checked, Rabbit had already taken care of that. Of course he had. He motored away from the pumps and headed home.

Checking his fridge, he grabbed a sandwich left over from the funeral. Deacon's house had been overrun with sandwiches, casseroles, and snacks. Deke had forced some of it on him the previous evening when he had dropped off René's things. Licking his fingers, he went into his bedroom, reaching under his bed to drag out his black nylon gun case.

He laid it on his bed and unzipped it, exposing a Remington Model 7, all black and stainless steel. It was made out of some synthetic material and was shorter and lighter than a typical rifle, good for navigating the dense bayou brush. The gun was scoped and fired a .300 short Magnum cartridge, a round capable of taking down a large buck. The .300 WSM was overkill for the smaller deer in Louisiana but was well suited for taking down a 250-pound wild hog. He opened a pouch and took out a full box of Winchester cartridges, and rooting around in the other pocket, he found another half full. It was enough for what he needed and enough to use some to zero the scope.

He packed the rifle and ammo backup, then got his pistol out of his bedside table and put it on the bed as well. He found two mags and spent some time emptying them, then thumbed the bullets back in, making sure there wouldn't be any hang-ups. The last thing was to find his binoculars. Anything could happen on a stakeout—he'd learned his lessons over the years and wasn't going to be caught short.

He loaded the Toyota and headed over to his uncle's junk shop, thankful that it was a Tuesday and Deacon was at the store instead of home. He couldn't face Henriette and her grief. He'd been reminded all day of his own. He pulled right up to the shop door, parked, and went in. The place was even more disheveled than the last time he'd been in, and Deacon wasn't behind the counter. Abel gave a yell: "Hey, Deke!"

A muffled reply of "Back here . . ." came through the half-open door between the front of the shop and the warehouse area. Abel followed the sound, finding Deacon sitting in the rear office staring into space.

"Get your guns, Deacon," Abel said. "Your rifle and maybe one of your pistols. We've got work to do tomorrow early."

"What are we hunting?"

"Pigs," snorted Abel.

"Why do I need my rifle? I'm going to be looking him in the eye when I take the shot."

Abel said, "I hear you. But if that chickenshit asshole Alverez is surrounded by guards, we might have to take the long shot. I'm bringing mine. Get your Whelan. I want to go to the range and dial it in. We need to make sure your scope is zeroed, too."

Deacon got up and went deeper into the warehouse. Abel sat down and listened to the sounds of his uncle puttering around, getting his gear together. He came back into the office and set down his rifle still in its soft carrying case.

"You got ammo?" asked Abel.

Deacon patted a pocket on the gun tote. "Yep." Then he pulled out a drawer of his desk, retrieving a .357 Magnum, his Smith & Wesson 27. He popped it open, held it up to the light, and checked the cylinder, spinning it, then flicked it closed with a snap.

"Let's go," he said. He'd been down at the mouth at first when Abel had come in, morosely staring at the wall, but now he was animated and champing at the bit. Deacon came out of the shop and saw the Toyota. "Rabbit?"

"Yeah, he got me two in case we need another."

They spent an hour at the range making sure their rifles were sending the rounds where the scope was aimed. Deacon's gun fired accurately, but Abel had to adjust the elevation on his scope because the gun was shooting high. They got squared away. All business. Then Abel drove Deacon back to the warehouse.

He drove in a circle in the graveled lot, raising a cloud of dust, and let Deke out in front of the door. Deacon bent down and looked through the passenger window. Abel buzzed it down and said, "Be ready. Give me your phone. I'm going to give it and my phone to Tank and André. I'll pick up a couple of prepays tonight for us to use instead. I'll pick you up at six am sharp, at the house."

At 7 am they were parked down the street from Alverez's house watching a flurry of activity. There were two cars, Garcia's Lexus and a beat-up beige Chrysler minivan with fake woody sides. Several soldiers had spilled out of the van and taken positions around the property. Two of the MS bangers had joined up with Garcia and another soldado, then gone around the back of the house.

"Pretty big show of force. We're not going to get in close to use the pistols," said Abel.

"Yeah, let's just watch how this rolls out and get a feel for how these dipshits are handling security," advised Deacon.

A tight group of people came around the side of the house from the back. They briefly showed up between the house and the Lexus, and Abel saw that Alverez's two boys were in the group. The bodyguards blocked off easy visibility to the Mara leader and his family, and they shuttled them immediately behind the Lexus and into the back seat. "Taking the kids to school," Abel said. Both of the MS vehicles moved off at the same time, the Lexus leading.

Abel and Deacon followed at a substantial distance, and when the black sedan turned off the main drag to a side street, Abel sped up to close the distance. They got close enough to see the whole Mara entourage form a scrum around Alverez and the sons. Abel watched Alverez kneel and hug his sons, reminding him of the moments before Deacon shot Benny Marks, when Abel had seen him drop Olivia off at school.

"We can catch him when he comes back out of the school—drive up and blast away with our pistols. They won't have their guard up after they drop off the boys," said Uncle Deke.

"OK," said Abel, but Alverez didn't go up to the school with his sons. Instead, he dipped back into the Lexus, and two bangers stood in front of the sedan, shielding him. "Wow, that chickenshit is letting the bangers protect his kids, and he's hiding in the car," Abel said derisively, then watched the group of guards scuttle up to the building, keeping the Alverez boys surrounded.

They dogged the two Mara vehicles and tracked them back to Alverez's home. The guards reversed the previous procedure, keeping the MS leader protected the whole time and that was that. "We're going to have another opportunity tonight when they go do their regular appearance at El Luz Loco—it won't work here, but at the bar, they have a long walk from the parking lot." *All that surveillance they had done before was paying off,* Abel thought.

Abel dropped Deke off at his house, reminding him to be ready by 6 pm, then went to the hospital to visit with Callie.

Abel and Deacon were posted up on Abel's favorite cul-de-sac by The Loco—the one that had a good sight line into the bar's parking lot and sidewalk leading to The Loco's entrance. Deacon was in the back seat and had the passenger window down. He could clearly see through it to the walkway in front of The Crazy Light. He had his back against the opposite door with his left leg bent over the armrest in the middle of the back seat and was locked in with his rifle, head cocked behind the scope, the barrel resting on his knee. Abel had covered him with a blanket.

"What time does he normally show up?" Deacon asked impatiently. "I'm getting a cramp."

"Anytime now."

"Turn on the AC, I'm fucking sweating under here."

"Wait! There they are!" Abel had the binoculars up, acting as the sniper's spotter.

"About time!" Deacon grumped. "Any longer and I wouldn't be able to make out his features."

Once again, the guards performed their choreography and formed up around Alverez and Garcia. The group moved down the sidewalk. Deacon tracked the group with his rifle, waiting for a shot if a gap showed up between the soldiers. They weren't as tight around him as they had been earlier. They probably felt secure on home ground.

Suddenly, there was a loud bang followed by a crash.

"Shit—don't shoot! There's a guy out in the street messing with his trash can," exclaimed Abel.

"Aw fuck! This is a bust." Deacon groaned. He lowered his rifle and sat up and stretched his neck. Abel put the Camry in gear and drove down the street, the Maras already piling through the door of the bar. They drove back to Lacombe.

Pulling in to Deke's driveway, Abel said, "We've got to rethink this. I've got an idea, but I'm going to have to do some scouting and check it out to see if it'll work. I'll come by the junk shop in a day or two."

They'd been on the roof since before the sun came up. The problem was that at ground level, they couldn't get a good look at Alverez when he was surrounded by his guards. Abel solved that by finding some higher ground. He and Deacon were lying flat on the roof of a building about seventy-five yards down the street from Alverez's church. They couldn't be seen from the street as the roof edge of the building gave them cover, and a giant billboard and its support installed on the roof shaded them from any eyes looking down from other higher buildings. It felt exactly like a hunter's blind—the kind of arrangement that they spent hours in every deer season.

Abel had staged a ladder at the back of the building the night before, planting it in place and climbing up to the roof and scouting the location. He proved to himself that it would work, that it would give them a good sight line right to the front door of the Catholic church—the same church that Alverez and his family had attended a few weeks earlier.

They weren't sure which service the gang leader would attend. There were three Sunday services before noon, and then a Mass in Spanish at 1:30. Abel had Rabbit watching Alverez's house, and now he and Deacon were waiting on a heads up from Tank that the Mara banger was on the way.

They had been killing time talking, unusual for Deacon; he was usually taciturn, every word seeming to cost him some emotional currency. Abel took advantage of Deke's mood and asked him a question that had been bothering him for a long time. "Uncle Deacon, why didn't you want René to run the business?"

Deacon sighed. "It's like that story about that man that finds out he has an appointment with death, so he runs to a different town to get away. But then at the new city, he runs into death, and death says that this was where fate had set him up to die or some shit like that. You know, basically, you can't escape your fate.

"Your aunt didn't want René involved with the Life. She begged me every day to keep him out of it. I tried my best, but René didn't want that. And every time I made a move to block his involvement, it made him try harder to get in."

"I guess she didn't care whether I was involved . . ." Abel said.

"No, René was her baby. There was no getting around that—I'm sorry. Henriette never thought of herself as your mother. And no matter what, René wanted to be in the business. It was his fate, but he just wasn't suited for it. Somehow that was my fault—I failed my own son."

Abel thought about that for a minute and decided to be forthcoming about what was on his mind. "All this shit happened before I could tell you—Tank and I are getting out of the Life."

Abel's phone buzzed before he could finish. "What's up?"

"Alverez is on the move," Rabbit said. "The whole family is out, dressed up for church. Two cars, Garcia and Alverez, the kids, and his wife in the Lexus and another van filled with soldiers."

"OK, thanks," Abel said and disconnected. "They're coming. Get set. We'll talk about all this other stuff later."

Deacon rested his rifle on the lip of the roof and sighted down the barrel, his finger, covered with a blue nitrile glove, on the trigger. They had a good look at the front of the church. They would be able to watch the group walk right up to the double doors. Alverez would be walking almost directly toward their position, so it would be a cake shot—like he was almost standing still.

Abel tucked in next to Deacon, his gun parallel to Deke's. They waited. Not fifteen minutes had passed before Abel saw the Lexus and the minivan pull into the church lot. The guards assembled around the Lexus and created a living shell around Alverez and his family.

The snipers stared down their scopes. Abel could see the top of Alverez's head. Abel noticed that the gangbanger was all curled in on himself, like he was sick or afraid. He projected weakness, trying to hide himself behind the bodyguard. Abel said, "Take a bead on Alverez. See that guard in front of him? I'm hitting that guy on three. When he drops? Pull the trigger on Alverez."

"One—two—three!" Abel's gun bucked. The front guard started to crumple, his head dropping and leaving Alverez fully exposed.

Deacon's rifle fired. Blood and brains splattered out of the back of Alverez's head. In the scope, Abel saw Alverez's wife, covered in blood and tissue, turn away, covering her face and head with her arms. He swiveled, looking for Garcia, trying to get Garcia in his scope—gone! Like a fly sensing a swat.

"We're good! C'mon." Abel was up and grabbing at Deacon's shirt. "Let's go . . . c'mon." Deke got up on his knees, Abel helping him the rest of the way. They ran to the ladder, Deacon clambering down first, Abel looking around wildly. When Deacon hit the ground, Abel slid down the ladder, his feet barely slowing him down. They ran through the lot behind the building, got to the Toyota, and pulled open the front doors, throwing their rifles into the back seat, and dove in. Abel turned the key and hit the gas. Pulling away from the curb, they both slammed their doors.

Sitting at the head of Isabelle's kitchen table, Abel took stock of his crew, looking at each of them in turn. René's absence was a punch in the gut. He cleared his throat, then said, "Alverez is dead."

"Wait, what?" asked Tank incredulously. He looked at Abel. "Oh." Everyone went quiet for a spell. "You should have let us help," he said.

"Naw, it was something that Deacon and I had to do." Abel let that sink in. "But after the whorehouse and now this, there is going to be serious blowback. We need to get everybody out: Isabelle, Harm's mother, and Rabbit—your whole family."

"We can take turns watching Callie," said André.

THIRTY-EIGHT

G arcia and Gomez looked at each other across the desk in the office of The Loco. "What the fuck is wrong with us? I feel like shit, and you look like shit," Garcia said.

"I have news for you, jefe. You look muy enfermos, too. You stink. You must have shit yourself," retorted Gomez.

They glowered back and forth for a while, and finally Garcia broke the silence. "Alverez is dead. That makes me número uno."

"Sí," agreed Gomez, grudgingly. "And I am number two."

"Of course," said Garcia. "Maybe those gringos did us a favor taking out Alverez. He was getting weak. But they have taken our money. Ruined the whorehouse. And all we've done is killed one weak, unimportant puto."

"Sí, we have to do something," said Gomez. "But how do you know it was the boys from Lacombe who killed Alverez and not the Aryans?"

"Because we just killed their amigo, estúpido!"

Garcia's treatment rankled; Gomez wished he was dead instead of Alverez. At least Alverez had treated him better than a dog.

Garcia continued, oblivious. "This time we start at the top and systematically kill everybody. By the time we get to this Abel Kane and his men, they will fall all over us to cooperate, and we will take back all that is ours, all that is theirs, and cut off their cojones."

"What are we going to do?" asked Gomez.

THIRTY-NINE

Several cars showed up on the parking lot feed to his security monitor, oddly generating a feeling of relief in Deacon; it was the shoe finally dropping. He knew there would be consequences for killing Alverez. He watched a group of men pile out of the vehicles. He recognized Garcia. Quickly, he shot off a text to Gerard and to Abel, then reached under his desk and unsnapped an AR15 with a bump stock that he had squirreled away. Deacon moved back into the bowels of the warehouse.

Out in the lot, Garcia issued a string of commands, one car peeled off, and he and the remaining men advanced on the junk shop. Garcia took up the rear. Gomez and another man flanked the door and gingerly tried the knob—locked. The next guy stepped up with a sledge and swung it, striking to the right of the lock and smashing the door open. Expecting gunfire, he immediately stepped out of the door opening. Gomez and the other guy went in the door, brandishing their AK-47s, clearing the room as they had been trained back in the day when they were real soldiers with the Salvadoran army. The other men came in behind them. The entry to the building was anticlimactic. They all milled around in the front of the shop, seeing a hodgepodge of junk and pawned items but no people.

Garcia had seen Deacon's car in the parking lot, so he directed them. "He's here, he's in the back."

One soldier yelled, "Over here—here's the door," and the men lined up behind him. Gomez and the experienced soldier put another gangbanger in front of them, and all three pushed through the door at once, Gomez firing auto at man height, and the second man firing down lower. The cannon fodder soldier was shooting wildly with his pistol. Deacon poked the muzzle of his AR over the lip of a large wooden crate and fired a burst of rounds, catching the lead man in the face and the throat. He dropped, but by then, Gomez and his partner had gotten all the way into the warehouse and taken cover behind some metal shelves.

"COVERING," yelled Gomez, and both Salvadoran soldiers fired long bursts at the crate, forcing Deacon down. The four other gangbangers ran into the back of the warehouse, and two took up positions behind an old metal desk sitting out in the space, and the remainder went behind another set of shelves holding what looked to be auto parts.

Garcia had stayed in the front of the building but poked his head around the warehouse door and yelled, "Stop shooting and stand up. Just give us back our money, and we'll let you live."

Deacon answered with a snap shot, catching the doorframe right next to Garcia's face, blowing splinters into his cheek. Garcia jerked his head back with a curse. The warehouse erupted with a barrage of shots, the soldiers firing their AK-47s and the other men firing their pistols, running them dry and popping in new magazines. Chunks of wood from the crate in front of Deacon launched into the air as the soldiers chewed it up with their bullets.

During the melee, Deacon scuttled back behind his next line of defense—a stack of tires.

Gerard had been only a few minutes out from the warehouse when he got Deke's text, and he hammered the pedal to the floor, showing up amid all the shooting. He heard the shots through his window, the sound feeling like it was physically pounding on his chest as he slammed on his brakes. Reaching under the seat, he grabbed his pistol, then stretched out and opened the glove box and pulled out a handful of magazines for his Glock. He jumped out of the vehicle and ran straight into the building without regard, thinking that the action was all in the back. But Gerard didn't notice Garcia crouched behind the shop counter and ran full tilt toward the door to the warehouse.

Garcia popped up and started firing at Gerard point-blank. Gerard managed to get three shots off as he wheeled around, two bullets missing Garcia and pinging inconsequentially off a light fixture, the last catching the counter and shattering the glass front, as he fell to the floor, his gun arm resting across his body.

The MS-13 leader calmly walked over to Gerard and stared down at his face. Not recognizing him, he fired two shots into Gerard's head. He returned to the doorway and yelled, "I just killed your amigo, Kane!" There was no answer. "There is no chance for you!" Still no answer.

One of the bangers stepped out into the opening, intending to creep over to the crate. Deacon fired three shots, hitting the man in the torso, the man's arms flailing awkwardly. Gomez conferred with the other experienced soldado. He started firing at Deacon's new position, and the other soldier ran out the warehouse door, back into the front of the store.

"We're going to burn him out," he told Garcia, then ran out to the parking lot. In a minute, he came running back in with an armful of flares, reached the inner doorway, and yelled, "COVER!" The MS-13 men all started firing at once, driving Deacon down, and the soldier with the load of flares ran back into the warehouse.

He lit the flares one by one and tossed them deeper into the warehouse, the purple actinic flames lighting up the gloomy corners of the place. The Maras waited till the accumulated debris and junk caught, and when the front portion of the warehouse was involved, the MS-13 bangers backed down the hall and out of the warehouse, firing the whole time.

"Fuck!" screamed one of the men as he got hit in the leg by a blind shot from Kane. Another man grabbed him by the shirt and helped him the rest of the way.

The men ran out the front door and around the side of the building, the one hurt soldier limping—not able to keep up. Garcia grabbed the wounded soldier. "Watch the front door. If he comes out, shoot him in the legs." Then, he followed the other Maras around the building.

The rear door of the building was closed, blocked by the car that Garcia had sent around back when they first arrived. Deacon was still trapped in the warehouse, which was making a roaring sound that could be heard even outside—some window high on the side wall blew out with a thump followed by a tinkling crash.

The Maras stood in a rough circle, their weapons trained on the rear door, and Garcia motioned to the man in the car to back up. As soon as the car moved off the door, it burst open. Deacon stood in the doorway, firing his gun and spraying them with shots. His hair was smoking and his shirt sleeve was in flames. Two MS men were hit, one in the eye, the other stitched across the body.

The soldiers reflexively fired back, round after round knocking into Kane, forcing him back into the inferno. The shooting gradually died out, the men lowering their weapons. Suddenly, Deacon staggered back into the doorway, his whole body engulfed in flames. He tried to raise his gun, but the Maras let loose another barrage. He collapsed. Garcia walked up to the door and kicked it shut. The door slammed against Deacon's arm that was protruding out of the entrance and bounced open. Garcia raised a boot and kicked the door again. Once again, it refused to close. Garcia got ready for another kick.

"Mierda!" exclaimed Gomez, and he reached over and roughly grabbed Garcia by the collar and pulled him away from the heat spilling out of the building. He gestured to his men to throw the dead MS soldiers into the fire, then yelled, "VÁMANOS!"

Harm pulled into the junk shop's lot and could feel the heat through his windshield. He had to pull back out and park on the road. Abel's truck was down the road a way, so he stopped behind it and then ran back to the burning building, seeing Abel jogging toward him along the side of the road.

"What happened?" Harm asked.

"The MS," Abel gasped. "I think Deke and Gerard are in the building —dead. Their cars are in the lot. On my way here, I could hear gunfire, so they were fighting the motherfuckers. I don't think they got snatched. I think they're dead and burned up in there," Abel said and turned his head toward the pall of smoke rising above the trees. "We have to tell the rest of the guys to be on alert and button up their shit. Deacon knew these guys were going to be coming after him, and see what happened?"

"Got it, but we've got to get out of here," said Harm. "Before the police and fire department get here—let's go!" he insisted.

Abel sprinted to his truck and headed to Deacon and Hennie's house, a sinking feeling in the pit of his stomach.

CHAPTER

FORTY

W hen Abel had talked to Hennie, he couldn't definitively say that Deacon had died, but he prepared her for the worst. There wasn't any reaction. She looked at him blankly, then turned around and sat on the couch, staring off into the distance. He had to tell Gerard's wife the bad news, but he didn't think he could leave Henriette alone; he was worried that she might do something to herself. Tapping Isabelle for help didn't seem to be an option, given her mental state, and eventually Rabbit's mother agreed to come, so Abel had waited till she showed, then he left for Gerard's house.

The response of Gerard's wife, Elizabeth, was the opposite of Aunt Hennie's. She immediately burst into tears and hugged Abel, squeezing him spasmodically in time with her sobs. Between the cries she said, "I knew this was going to happen... I knew..."

Abel found her phone and called Elizabeth's sister and kids. He stuck around for an hour, tending to her, getting her a drink, and putting her in a comfortable chair. When the sister arrived, Abel slipped out, Elizabeth's words stuck in his mind: "Oh, what am I going to do?"

Deacon and Gerard's deaths were confirmed after the junk shop had cooled down and the arson investigator and the forensic team had gone through the ashes. Deacon's remains were found just inside the rear warehouse door, a sad little pile of teeth, a splotch of melted gold, powdered bone, and ash. Gerard's body was located in the front of the junk shop. Through some fluke of the fire, his body was mostly intact, although it was not a pretty sight, curled up in a frightening posture, his head thrown back in a silent scream—an effect of the heat, hopefully postmortem.

Abel was in a quandary about a memorial service for Deacon. Once again, as with René, the remains weren't going to be available for quite some time. The main question in his mind was what was the best for his aunt. In the end, he decided on a small service the next weekend at the same funeral home that they had used for René.

There was no obituary, no scheduled hours for a service, and he minimized the publicity the best he could. Given Hennie's condition, he felt he couldn't put her through another funeral like René's; she hadn't come back from it yet, if she ever would.

After the funeral, Abel stood with Tank and the guys, no one saying anything. Abel couldn't generate much grief. He was numb inside. His feelings were complicated—he wanted to be sad and remember Deacon like a father, but he had been gone a good part of his life and had treated René like a son, but him—something less. Was this all there was? Forty years in the Life, and Deacon's whole life boiled down to a handful of family, a couple of business associates? Even Aunt Hen hadn't shed a tear, although that hardly counted. She was practically in a coma. It was hard for him to comprehend that Deacon, larger than life, was gone.

FORTY-ONE

"Abel! You said you'd talk to me," said Olivia on the other end of the phone. "I tried to give you some space and left it up to you to call me. You didn't! Do you even have room in your life for another person? It feels like you're just playing me."

"I know. I'm sorry—my uncle Deacon was killed last week. His warehouse burned down, and he was trapped inside," Abel said, purposely leaving out key information.

"What the fuck? What are you mixed up in?"

"It's complicated—we need to talk," he said.

"No shit!"

"Can you come over to my house?" he asked.

"When?"

"Now."

"I can come later, after my mom gets home. Around nine?"

"That works."

"You better come clean," she demanded, "or I'm done."

"Yeah, I understand."

Olivia hung up abruptly, making Abel feel depressed, like she was already done in her mind. Now she just wanted an explanation. Well, he owed her that, regardless.

Abel paced around the house, ruminating over what he was going to tell her. Deacon was gone, so that weight was off his back. He and Tank had decided to get out of the Life, but the business with Olivia's father? Nobody could get past that. But fuck it—he had to take his lumps if he was going to move forward. Seeing how Deke ended up, he didn't want that for him or Callie.

That reminded him to go check on her. Abel had brought her home from the hospital that morning. He looked in on her, and she was still napping under the covers. A wheelchair was parked next to the bed. She needed it because she was dizzy, her eyesight was still off, and she couldn't quite focus. He was so relieved—if she had been hurt worse, he wouldn't have been able to live with it. She was going to be OK.

Olivia knocked on the door early. *Fuck! He wasn't ready...* Abel walked to the door and opened it. They stood there looking at each other awkwardly. Olivia finally moved up to Abel and gave him a tentative hug. Abel gave her a gentle kiss at the corner of her lips, pressing his face against hers for a moment.

"You're trembling," she said softly. "You're scaring me. It can't be that bad." She tried to smile, but it didn't hold.

Abel pulled back. "Callie's sleeping—let's go outside and talk on the back porch." They went through the living room and then the kitchen—the rooms that had been scrubbed clean of blood. Liv sat in a chair on the porch and put both hands on the arms of the chair, as if she was bracing herself. Abel dragged a chair over and set it close, facing her. When he sat down, he was so close that his feet were touching hers.

He took a deep breath and let it out through his nose. "I'm a criminal."

She started to respond. "Like I didn't figure that—"

"No, let me talk. Let me get it out. Deacon was head of the Dixie Mafia or whatever was left of that bunch of crooks. And when we came here—me and Callie—we didn't know that. He got caught holding some stolen property—one of the guys in one of his crews ratted him out. He went to prison in 2001. Our world changed. I think I was about eleven, and I found out I wasn't a normal kid. I was part of a family of criminals."

"You were a kid. You weren't—"

Abel plowed on, running over her words. "Well, things were OK for a while. Hennie held everything together, but Deacon hadn't had a chance to set her up because he was caught in the middle of some deal, and all his money was locked up. Hennie couldn't get at it, so eventually we ran out of money.

"From prison, Deacon reached out and set me up with some work. I got involved with drugs, moving them here and there around the city and as far away as Lake Charles. René and some of my friends helped, and we made some money—enough to hold it all together. I brought in enough money to support Callie, René, and Hennie till Deacon got out of prison.

"When he came home, he fixed all the money problems, but by then I was already wrapped up in the Life. I built my own crew. We did warehouse jobs, hijacked trucks, and burglary. And that is what I've been doing since then." He paused and looked at Olivia.

"Is that what you're going to do now—I mean are you going to be a criminal the rest of your life?" she asked, her expression neutral.

"Well, just about the same time I met you, I had been doing a lot of soul-searching and trying to figure out how to break away from Deke and maybe get out of the Life. And some of the stuff that has been happening recently—

Callie getting hurt and René being killed—has convinced me that I've got to get on a path that feels right to me."

"That's good. So you're going to walk away?"

"I can't just now. We're in trouble."

"Who's we?"

"My family, my friends, and their families and friends."

"What are you mixed up in? People are getting killed! Is this why you've been keeping me at a distance?"

"Yes. The MS-13 are after us—and everybody close to us."

"Who?" she asked, a confused expression on her face. "Just call the police on them."

"It's gotten way beyond what the police can do, and we're in deep—too deep. And this gang is bad. They stabbed René twenty times and burned up Deacon."

"How did you get crosswise with these people?"

Abel told Olivia the full story, something he hoped to never have to speak of again.

"So they could be watching us now? They're going to know about me?" Olivia started to get out of the chair in a panic.

"Wait, wait!" Abel grabbed her arm. "I've got people watching our street—on both ends. Nobody is coming down the street. Nobody is going to see you." He tugged on her arm gently, pulling her back down into the chair.

Olivia sat back into the chair and stared at Abel. "I've got to think about Owen. We've got to stay away from you. Maybe if you get clear from all this..."

"There's more," Abel said quietly.

"I don't want any more!" she said, starting to get out of the chair again.

"No, wait. You have to hear this."

Olivia paused, then put her weight back in the seat. "What?" she asked hesitantly.

"I didn't bring you here to tell you about all this stuff. I'm sorry. It's something else... Remember me telling you about someone ratting out Deacon, which sent him to prison for six years?" Abel locked eyes with Olivia. "It was you father, Benny Marks, who turned on Deacon and informed to the police."

Her face was confused and frightened. "What are you telling me?"

"Your daddy put Deke in jail, and when he got out, he was pissed."

"NO!"

"He told me he just wanted to talk to your father. He asked me to drive him to see Benny. I thought Deacon was just going to yell at your daddy. I didn't know what he was going to do. But when we found your father down in the city, Deacon pulled out a gun and shot him."

Olivia was gripping the arms of the chair, her knuckles white. "Murderer!" she hissed. "YOU! YOU MURDERED MY FATHER!" she screamed, saliva spraying from her mouth. She stood abruptly, knocking the chair over backward with a crash. "I can't believe I let you be with Owen—for even a second!" She started moving toward the door.

"Don't leave! Let me explain! What are you going to do?"

"What you deserve," she said as she turned and left.

FORTY-TWO

"André, get everybody over here. We've got to talk."

"Abel, it's almost midnight. Tank's asleep for Christ's sake," protested André.

"Wake him up. Meet here in half an hour. Track down Rabbit. I'm going to find Harm—he's not answering."

Abel disconnected and sped over to Harm's house. Ringing the doorbell didn't bring Harm or his mother to the door, so he traipsed around the house and hammered on Harm's bedroom window. The curtain was ripped apart on the inside. "What the fuck?" yelled Harm through the window. "I about shot you!"

"C'mon. Get out here. We're all meeting at my house. We have stuff to talk about—emergency shit. I'm going back home. Are you coming?"

"Yeah, I'll be there in a few minutes."

Abel drove back to his house, ran back inside, and threw on the porch lights, then went into the kitchen and turned on the halogen floodlights, blasting the yard and dock with their bluish glare.

Tank and André came in the front door. "Rabbit's on the way—be here in five," said Tank.

"Yeah, I woke up Harm. He's on the way."

"What's happening?" asked André.

"Look, grab some beers and sit. I don't want to go into all this twice 'cuz we have to move fast. Rabbit and Harm will be here in a minute." There was a ruckus at the door. Rabbit pushed his way in first followed by Harm. "Guys, get a beer. We're meeting in the kitchen."

They all sat around the table staring at Abel expectantly. He got right to it. "This morning some banger from the Maras called me. It was the bartender from The Loco, said his name was Luis, and he told me he had some information to sell—twenty-five thousand bucks. I called bullshit, of course. Figured it was just another one of their moves. Maybe that's what they did to René.

"But the guy said I could set the meet, and he would tell me the info before I gave him the money. I could decide whether what he told me was worth it. His exact words were that he guaranteed that I would fork over the cash. The information was that good and further that I would owe him.

"So I bit. I decided that I'd just be careful, and if it looked like a trap, I might be able to outmaneuver them and kill them myself—get 'em back for René and Deacon. I agreed to meet."

"What the fuck?" exclaimed Tank. "That is the exact kind of shit that you don't do by yourself. How do you think René got killed?"

"I'm here. I'm not dead. The fucker insisted it was just me, by myself, and he would take off if I brought more people. He told me that I would be sorry if I didn't hear what he had to say. So I went. But look, I did all the right James Bond shit. I got to the meet first and got an eye on him. Then, I called him and moved it. Did that a couple more times. By the end, I knew he was alone."

Tank let out a frustrated groan.

"Tank, I know, I'm sorry. But it was legit. The MS are having some internal battle, and the bangers are choosing sides. He said the leaders were acting crazy, and they were sick or something. One faction wants to walk away from this. But the bigger group, the one with the fucked-up leaders, are coming here tomorrow night to kill all of us."

"You believe him?" asked Harm.

"Yes, I can't figure out what their play would be to warn us before they are going to kill us, unless it's exactly like this Luis said. And anyway, what do we have to lose by taking this seriously?"

"That's it? They're coming tomorrow to kill us?" asked André. "Did he say anything else?"

"Yes, they're coming in boats, on the bayou, maybe twelve men. Gonna hit Tank's house and my house at the same time, after dark. Maybe I wouldn't have believed him, but he knew where we all lived. Knew what we drove. He named Rabbit's sister and Isabelle. Said that Garcia was the head honcho now, and he was bringing it to us. I asked him about Tattoo Face, and he said that fucker's name is Gomez, and he's coming, too. I gave him the twenty-five grand."

"He knew about my sister?" blurted out Rabbit, the expression on his face dark.

"Yeah," said Abel. "It's good we got everyone out."

"No one's gonna find Callie or my mama," said André.

Tank said, "A'ight, we got some planning to do."

FORTY-THREE

A full spring moon had come up over the bayou, frosting the ripples in the black water with silver. Abel and the remainder of his crew, except for Tank, were on the north side of the water, watching and waiting for the Maras to show up. They'd been in their hide since 6 pm and were getting impatient, slapping at mosquitos.

There had been a lengthy discussion about where they should post up, hinging on where they figured the MS-13 would put in their boats. The major question was—which direction would the bangers arrive from?

Tank was sitting in Harm's boat in the middle of the bayou, northwest of their hide but before the edge of Abel's property. Rabbit had spent part of the morning armoring the back end of the boat with steel plate. Tank was hunkered down behind this shield, waiting for the heads up from the guys that the Maras had shown up.

There had been some desultory conversation in the hide, which eventually petered out as it got darker. They concentrated on watching the water and listening for the first sounds of the MS arriving.

Rabbit broke the silence. "I know we got kinda sidetracked with these assholes, but have we decided what we're going to do after this? My dad is talking about retiring. He wants me to take over. I'm thinking about it. Hell, we could all work there."

"Fuck that!" said Harm brutally. "No offense, but I'd go crazy stuck in one place. Anyways, let's talk about it later, after all this—we got to listen for these bastards."

Rabbit held his tongue for a while, then—SLAP! "Another mosquito bites the dust . . . I don't think these guys are coming. Maybe you got it wrong, Abel," he said.

"I hope these fuckers come," said Harm. "I'm sitting here all night if I have to, so quit your bitching. This is no different from sitting in your deer stand, anyway. And if they don't show? We come tomorrow night . . . and the next night. Abel's info is good."

"Yeah," chimed in André. "They're coming. Since Deke killed Alverez, we knew they'd come at us, for sure. And if are our families are gone, and we're out here—they aren't going to be able to find us. We're going to be directing the action."

That shut up Rabbit for a while except for the occasional slap, followed by a whispered, "Fuck!" The boys sat for a while, the moon climbing the sky, lighting up the slot in the trees where the water cut through. "Listen!" he hissed.

A faint buzz could be heard, and after a minute it turned into a chord of humming motors. "OK, showtime," Abel whispered.

"Let's just shoot them here!" Rabbit said.

Abel rolled his eyes in the dark. "Follow the plan! We're too close to the road and civilization. We gotta get deeper in the woods so nobody pays attention to the gunfire. If we start something here, we won't have time to clean up our mess. André, text Tank, and tell him they're here."

Harm said, "Let's roll!" and filtered back through the trees and brush, away from the bank, the rest of the guys following until they reached a game trail that ran along the bayou. They started quietly loping up the path toward Tank's position.

As soon as Tank saw the three boats come around a bend in the bayou, he started his boat and moved away from the Maras. Raising his head above the armor at the back of the boat, he yelled, "Hey, Garcia—tú traga leche mamaverga!" André had armed him with some choice phrases. That one was something like "you cum-swallowing cocksucker." He waited for a response . . . nothing. "Hey, pendejos, tú jefe es joto!"

The water next to him splashed, and he heard two pistol shots followed by Garcia saying, "Alto, estúpido!" *Ahhh, that hit a nerve,* Tank thought, laughing to himself. He looked over his shoulder and checked his course, then turned back to the MS.

"Garcia, we're going to shove your own cock into your mouth instead of tú verga de maricón. We're going to take your huevos, little bitches . . ." He fired three shots in their general direction and sped up his boat. Taking the bait, they followed suit.

Tank motored through the bayou, dodging shallow water and snags. He passed Abel's house first, then a few minutes later, his. He kept checking over his shoulder — yep, still there—and sped toward the wild hog wallow, he and his brother's favorite hunting spot.

Yeah, they were going to bag some pigs tonight. He came up to the wallow, a rough muddy circle, thirty yards at its widest. He beached his boat on the nearest side of the open expanse, about the 6 o'clock position, leaving room for the banger's boats to his left. Jumping out of the boat, Tank ran to his hide that he had set up earlier at the 5 o'clock position on the wallow. It gave him a good position on the incoming boats and most of the open area.

While Tank was ensuring that the MS boats followed him up the bayou, Abel was getting the guys in position around the wallow. Harm was positioned on the banks of the bayou, just short of Tank's hide. Rabbit was in the trees at the top of the wallow at the 12 o'clock spot next to a trail that went deeper into the woods. Abel went up the trail further into the woods, and André passed him and kept going.

At about the same time that Abel and André were getting into their spots, the Maras arrived at the edge of the wallow. Seeing Tank's boat beached, they stopped and seemed unsure of their next move. Harm, now downstream from them, started firing on them from his position, urging them to beach their boats to the left of Tank's and jump out and dash for cover.

To Harm, it felt a bit like herding cats. The MS soldiers ran out of the boats, looking for protection. Abel's crew had previously set up "convenient" cover for the bangers, and the frightened soldiers headed to these obvious areas.

They tried to move fast, but the mud of the wallow sucked at their feet, and some of the MS comically lost their shoes, the glutinous mess transforming their frantic efforts into slow motion. The fake shelters appeared to be a safe haven, but the path to the shelters left the MS exposed to Harm. He let loose a spurt of shots.

The rear most soldiers turned around and fired toward Harm. But Harm had already left his shooting spot, heading through the trees to hook up with Abel.

Realizing that no one was shooting back at them, the Maras stopped shooting and concentrated on reaching the protection that Abel's crew had staged. The fastest moving banger had made it to the first barricade at 9 o'clock on the wallow and tucked in behind it. Suddenly, he started screaming, "Help, help—quicksand." He continued screaming for help over and over. Warned, the whole group of soldiers shifted away from him and headed to the other shelter barricade.

It was at this point that Tank stood up and started shooting at the backs of the group who had passed him and thought they were safe. He didn't hear any screams—dammit! How could he miss? But this forced the MS, at a panic, to slog toward the opening of the game trail at 12 o'clock where Rabbit was hiding. Rabbit got ready. A few soldiers turned around and sent another barrage at Tank—he ducked behind his cover.

The lead soldier was lifting his knees high, like he was running in shallow water, trying to make it to the opening in the forest at the top of the wallow as fast as he could. He lost his balance and jammed his shotgun, muzzle first, into the mud to keep upright. He was almost at his imagined escape route when Rabbit stepped out of the trees, showed himself, then slipped back behind a tree.

The banger raised his gun and fired, but the mud had been driven all the way up the muzzle, and the gun blew all the hot gases back into his face. He dropped the gun and brought his hands to his face. Rabbit stepped around the tree, fired, and hit him in the face with a load of buckshot, practically amputating the banger's hands at the same time.

Rabbit turned and ran up the game trail, leaving the banger with his face blown in behind. Garcia yelled, "This way—get him!" ordering his whole gang up the trail after Rabbit. Garcia grabbed the shoulder of one of the MS-13 and screamed, "Stay here—guard the boats!" Then, he ran up the trail.

The soldier gazed at the boats all the way down the wallow dubiously and paused just long enough for Tank to get a bead on him, his outline clearly visible in the moonlight. Tank squeezed off a shot. The banger dropped like a heart-shot buck. Tank looked around—the wallow was clear. He thought about checking on the banger in the quicksand who had been quiet for a while. Fucker probably drowned—all he had to do was relax, and he woulda floated...

Instead, he hustled over to the MS boats, and seeing that they had inflatable rubber hulls, drew his knife and gashed each just above the waterline. Then, he ran to the outside of the wallow, running along the hard dirt just inside the tree line toward the game trail at the top of the wallow. *If only those dipshits knew all they had to do was stick to the sides,* he thought, laughing to himself.

While Tank was dealing with the soldier in the hog wallow, Rabbit was playing mouse to the MS-13 cats. He stayed just out of reach in the distance, bobbing and weaving in the path, moving fast enough that the bangers had to pound after him, unable to slow down and take a good shot.

Abel heard the commotion coming down the path in front of his spot and watched Rabbit stream by, knowing that the MS were hot on his heels. Harm had made it up to his position earlier and was backing him up, hiding in the trees, motionless and ready.

Abel held a rope in his hands, and when the first soldiers came into view, he gave it a hard yank. The deadfall trap that they had set came tumbling down on top of the group. Five fat logs had been leaned over the trail, held up by a figure-four trigger, and when Abel pulled the rope, the trigger collapsed, dropping the logs onto the Maras.

The pile of logs caught one of the soldiers, crushing him flat, and knocked another down. The rest of the bangers clambered over the pile as Harm popped out of the woods behind them and started firing. As the last soldier cleared the logs, Harm shot him in the middle of his back. The man landed face first in the trail. Harm skirted the logs, and Abel came out of the woods. The two of them joined up and began unloading their magazines at the fleeing soldiers, then gave chase. One banger turned around and took a wild shot at the two of them.

"Fuck!" yelled Harm.

"What?" shouted Abel, slowing.

"I took one in the hip—not deep. I'm good, keep going." They continued down the path, popping their mags and reloading. When they reached a tree next to the path that Abel had tied a white rag around, the two veered right, returning to the woods.

Meanwhile, Rabbit was still ahead of the pack of slavering bangers. He could go fast as hell, but he was egging them on, teasing them, periodically slowing down, then squirting ahead with a burst of speed. The MS were taking occasional shots, and Rabbit could hear them zing by.

Up ahead, Rabbit knew the path was going to appear to end. He hit the spot and kept going, disappearing from view. What the gangbangers didn't know was that right at the end of the path the ground dropped about six feet. You couldn't tell because a giant bush of vines and brambles had grown up, disguising the drop.

André had plopped two long, wide boards on top of the thorny growth, giving Rabbit a safe passage through the vicious spikes. As soon as Rabbit hit the bottom of the ramp, André moved in and pulled the planks down and dragged them back out of the way. They hustled to a barricade of logs and jumped behind it.

The Maras saw Rabbit run straight off the path. Two soldiers slightly ahead of the rest crashed after him through the brush and instantly vanished, yelling, "Ahhh . . ." then, "Mierda!" Jabbed by the thorns from every direction, the soldados thought they were under attack by a thousand knives and started randomly firing their guns.

The second the bangers in the briar patch started shooting, André and Rabbit returned fire with their shotguns.

In the meantime, Harm and Abel had navigated the woods to their last hide. They saw the bunch of soldiers slam on the brakes and watch two of their own go over the edge. They piled up like a cresting wave, and Harm and Abel started shooting into the group. The desperate men scrambled off the path into the woods like a bunch of cockroaches caught in a bright light, leaving one of their own lying wounded or dead on the trail.

Harm ran into the woods, chasing after the bangers just as Tank ran up the path from the wallow and bent over, gasping for breath. "Fuck! I need more cardio," he wheezed to Abel, who slapped him on the back and yelled, "Go—go, they're in the woods." He pointed and pushed him. I'll be right behind you!" Tank launched into the trees following the yelling and snapping of branches.

Abel turned back to the briar trap and yelled down to Rabbit and André. "Go back to the boats and post up. We're going to flush them out of the woods right into you. Make sure you don't shoot us when we come out for Christ's sake!" Then, he pulled a flashlight out of a pocket and dashed into the woods.

Harm could hear the Maras up ahead, crashing through the trees in panic, feeling déjà vu—just like the night in the woods with the Aryan Brotherhood, only this time, instead of being chased, he was the pursuer. He took a deep breath and howled, "We're coming for you, putos!" The crashing furor ahead increased. Harm followed as fast as he could. He had lied to Abel earlier—his hip hurt like a bitch and was slowing him down.

Most of the MS had stupidly left home without flashlights, and under the tree canopy the moonlight was dim and sporadic. They couldn't see and were tripping over each other. Garcia, the oldest of the men, and the only one smart enough to bring a flashlight, said,

"Fuck this" and peeled away from the pack of stumbling, cursing men.

Harm saw the light veer off and decided to hang with the men making the biggest racket, while Tank, who was some distance behind, caught sight of the bobbing light and readjusted his direction. Meanwhile, Abel, who had entered the woods after Tank, was even further back.

He could hear the action up ahead but couldn't catch up. He was using his light, scanning it back and forth to make sure he didn't come up on a banger playing opossum. Abel could tell the Maras were circling the wallow back toward the bayou but taking the hard route through the trees.

He followed them till he popped out of the woods just below the quicksand part of the wallow, having run the whole way, never catching sight of a single person. He quickly scanned for the Maras but didn't see a one of them; instead, he noticed Harm, Rabbit, and André standing on the bank of the bayou next to the boats, staring out over the water. He jogged up to them, skirting the muddiest part of the wallow.

Rabbit was laughing and pointing.

"What's up?" asked Abel.

"When we got back here, three MS guys had already come out of the trees and gotten into a boat. By the time we got down here, they were already out in the middle."

"Why didn't you shoot them?" asked Harm, getting ready to shoot them himself.

"Wait!" said Rabbit. "We didn't shoot 'cuz this is funnier. Their boat is sinking, and those dipshits are going swimming in just a minute. As soon as they go in, I'm going to start doing my alligator mating call."

"We'll see how fast they can swim!" joked André. "Anyways, I didn't want to shoot out over the water and send some wild shot into the road or pop some guy walking his dog."

Abel asked, "Could you see who got on the boat?"

"No, but we took care of nine or ten of them. With the other's we've killed, we've done a number on them. Odds are we got Garcia and that tattooed motherfucker, Gomez," crowed André.

"Yeah, I say we've just about put 'em down. Those fuckers didn't know what they were getting into," gloated Harm.

The bangers out in the water started yelling, and Abel clearly heard one guy say, "Help me, I can't swim!"

Rabbit started making loud noises—first short grunts, then longer grunting noises that almost turned into a bellow.

"Hey, pendejos," André yelled, "you hear that? You've stirred up the alligators. They're going to take you down and roll you, then stuff you under a log and eat you later after you've rotted some."

This time high screams could be heard. Rabbit jeered, "You sound like little girls!"

Suddenly, Abel grabbed Rabbit's shoulder. "Hey! Where's Tank?"

André looked around. "I thought he was with you!" He climbed up higher on the bank and shone his light across the wallow and toward the top, where the game trail intersected.

Rabbit said, "Aw, he's probably just lost in the woods. I'll get him." He called Tank on the burner and held it up to his ear. It rang out. "He's not picking up."

"Fuck!" said Abel. "You said there was only three guys on the boat, right? I saw four Maras go into the woods at the briar trap. Tank's out there alone with one of them! Rabbit, run up to the briar trap and come into the woods from the top. Keep yelling his name. Call me if you find him. The rest of you come with me."

Abel took off down the trail that led along the bayou. About twenty yards west of the clearing around the pig wallow, Abel sent André into the trees. After another twenty, Abel gave Harm a push, and he slipped into the scrub. Abel ran another twenty, then crashed into the trees, slashing his flashlight left and right in fast, broad strokes.

The thorny vines that hung from the trees tore at him. He barely noticed. "TANK!" he yelled, then stopped and listened. He could hear a faint "Tank" being called north of him. *Must be Rabbit.* He heard crashing off to the right—that would be André and Harm. He started running again. A vine caught his foot, and he went down but was back up and running instantly. "TANK! TANK!"

He scanned his light from left to right. Out of the corner of his eye, he saw another light to the left, in the dark spot just vacated by his own light. He killed his flashlight and ran toward the speck of light, oblivious of the branches slapping him in the face. He burst into an irregular open area.

Two men were on the ground in a sitting position, a flashlight leaned against a rock, its beam lighting up a skeletal tree. Abel turned his light on and aimed it at the men. It lit up Tank's face, his eyes open and rolled up into his head. Garcia was choking Tank from behind, his arm tight around Tank's neck. Abel lunged across the space between them, drawing his combat knife out of its sheath.

Garcia let go of Tank and scuttled backward, but Abel was over Tank and on Garcia, grabbing him by the hair with his left hand and stabbing down with his right. He caught the banger in the neck, a gargled cry bursting from his lips, and then Abel was stabbing down again and again. He finally let go of Garcia's head, pushed off him, and stood up.

Tank was on his hands and knees, his head hung down like a sad dog. Abel knelt next to him. "How bad are you hurt?"

"I'm OK," he said in a raspy voice. "My arms are all cut up, but they still work. Man, you came just in time. I was about done for. It was going black..."

Abel sat back on his haunches and fished out his phone and called André. "I got him. He's alive! He was tangling with Garcia. Yeah—yeah, he's OK. Yes. Dead. Go find all the others. I'm going to drag your brother's sorry ass back to the boats."

Abel looked at Tank. "Can you help me get this piece of shit up onto my back? We can't leave him here." With Tank's assistance, Abel got Garcia up on his shoulders in a fireman's carry and started plodding back to the wallow, Tank moving the bigger branches out of the way and lighting the path. The trip seemed to take forever compared to his mad dash previously, but finally the muddy expanse showed up, peacefully bathed in the moonlight.

Abel shrugged Garcia off his shoulders. He landed with a wet splat. Abel straightened up, groaning and pressing his fists into his lower back.

The guys clustered around Abel and Tank. "What happened, Tank?" asked Rabbit.

"I chased him for a while. I think he was out of ammo because he came at me with a knife and caught me by surprise. Gashed up my arms some, but I got in close, and it turned into a wrestling match, and he lost the knife. That little fucker was strong though, I'll give him that. I was getting my ass handed to me. He got around me, got a lock on my neck, and was choking me. I was about gone when Abel showed up and went psycho on him."

"Yeah, he looks pretty dead," said Rabbit.

"Deader than dead," said Harm. "Good job. That's payback for René, but you're covered in blood. You need to go swimming." He motioned with his head toward the bayou. "I'll get the cleanup started."

The crew found all the bodies where they had dropped and dragged them to the top of the wallow where the game trail opened out. They stripped the dead men and arranged them with space between them so the wild pigs could get at each of them.

"The hogs will pick these bastards down to the bone and then eat the bones," said Rabbit.

They dumped all the weapons, including their own, into Harm's boat and stuffed the Maras' clothes into a garbage bag that had been brought along in the boat for that exact purpose. Harm climbed into boat, saying, "I'll take care of this shit," and Abel and the rest started down the east leg of the game trail, heading for their dirt bikes cached at the first hide.

FORTY-FOUR

O n the hike back to where they started the night the guys debriefed the action. Overall, they felt they'd done some serious damage to the Maras. Between Alverez's death, and Garcia's, they had pretty much decimated the obvious leadership of the MS. But it was a sore point that Gomez—Tattoo Face—had escaped. Rabbit ventured that he might have drowned, what with all the screaming, when their boat sank. Still, it was a loose end and a worrisome one at that.

The four guys finally made it to their original hide where they had stashed their dirt bikes. Abel looked at Tank. "How you doing? Can you ride outta here?" Tank hadn't complained about anything since Abel had stopped Garcia from choking him to death, but Abel could see the pain in his face.

"These cuts aren't deep, and my hands still work, but I don't think I'm going to be able to hold onto my bike if we hit any bumps."

"Alright, we'll drag your bike deeper in the woods, and you can ride home with André. Rabbit and I'll come back later and get your bike."

They took off down the game trail toward Highway 190 but veered north so they could hit some back roads instead of a major thoroughfare. Instead of Tank riding bitch, he was in the front, in André's lap, captured in his brother's big arms, like a little kid going for a ride with his daddy. But even Rabbit didn't seem to have it in his heart to tease him.

When they got back to Abel's house, Rabbit dumped his bike and mounted the back of Abel's. His ass was barely hanging on, so he put his arms around Abel's waist, but first he goosed Abel in the crotch to lighten the mood. Abel elbowed him. Rabbit laughed like he was twelve and locked his hands, then they went to get Tank's motorcycle.

Meanwhile, Tank and André had gotten home and shifted to the Bronco. They cruised over to Harm's house; he had just pulled in with his boat on the trailer behind his truck. Tank rolled down his window. "Get in, we're going to get my mom. She has a friend in the neighborhood who can get us fixed up."

Abel woke, not even remembering going to sleep the night before, after they had retrieved Tank's bike. He cleaned himself up, taking a half hour shower, even Q-tipping deep in his ears, then doused the walls and drain with bleach. After getting a cup of coffee, he cracked the front door and peeked out—nothing. It would probably be a while till the paranoia wore off. There was a package lying on the welcome mat. He gingerly picked it up and tore it open.

It was from some lawyer. All official, it named him as Deacon's executor—he wasn't even sure what that meant. It went on to say that Deacon had left Henriette some actual stocks and bonds, surprising Abel, because it was a real-world thing, like normal people did. But deeper in the envelope was another smaller envelope holding some safe–deposit box keys. *Ahhh, that was more like it,* he thought, laughing to himself. *His real stash.* The envelope also contained a list of banks and box numbers. It looked like Deacon had set things up for Hennie.

He set that all aside and went to get Callie from Isabelle's friend's house. The woman was a widow, like Isabelle, but where Belle had turned bony and somber lately, her friend was plump and happy. *Good for both Callie and Isabelle,* Abel mused, and it was visible in his sister. She was on the mend, surer on her feet, and there weren't as many pauses in her speech.

Navigating her own way to the truck, she managed to get herself situated without his help, even though he tried—too hard. She finally had to tell him, "I've got this!"

On the way home, he gave her an abbreviated account of the night before. "Is it over?" she asked.

"I think so," he said earnestly. "I hope so," he added with just a touch of lingering doubt.

They were quiet for a bit, then Abel said, "I'm getting out—for good. Tank and André, too. Rabbit's daddy wants to retire. Rabbit's going to take over the shop. He offered jobs to all of us."

"Harm working for Rabbit?" she asked skeptically.

"I don't know for sure, but his exact words to Rabbit were that he'd go crazy working in the shop."

Callie laughed. "Yeah—no shit." Abel laughed, too; the old Callie was back.

Abel dropped her off, and then went on to André and Tank's place, making a quick call along the way.

At the Chevals' house, Abel entered through the back and found Isabelle in the kitchen staring into a coffee cup. She started to get up to pour him a mug, and he motioned her to sit, since he knew where everything was in her kitchen. He sat next to her with his black coffee and took her hand, noticing how light and fragile it felt, like a dried leaf.

"You look tired, cher. But it feels like you let go your load of rocks..." she said.

"Yeah, Callie's doing so much better. You helped her, didn't you?"

"We all did, cher."

"Harm told me you did some root work on the MS guys. That true?"

"Some."

"I saw Garcia—he looked sick. Something about him wasn't right. He wasn't thinking straight. It helped us last night."

Isabelle usually didn't share much about her conjuring, but she said, "His soul was being separated from his body. I don't know much of the dark spells. It took something out of me that I don't think I'll get back."

She had definitely been affected by the whole experience—she had aged. He still didn't know what to believe. If he hadn't seen how that motherfucker looked . . .

"Storms come and go, Abel," she said, interrupting his thoughts. "Come and go." He gazed into her eyes. They were distant, not focused on him. "Come and go," she whispered.

She shook her head and looked at him with a tender smile. "You go find my sons now, and leave me be. They're waiting on you."

Abel bent down and kissed her on the forehead, and she reached up and squeezed his hand. As he left the room, he turned back. She was as he'd found her, hands around her cup, her head bowed.

Harm had stayed the night, so he found all three guys out by the bayou, basking in the sun in the mismatched chairs. "Don't you all look fat, dumb, and happy?" he said.

Tank looked at him, loopy. "Mama's veterinarian man, he fixed us up."

André laughed. "Don't expect anything out of these two idiots right now."

"Yeah, what did he give 'em?"

"After stitching them up, he gave them each a big glass of bitter tea he made with this green powder. They've been stoned ever since."

André got serious. "Is this thing over?"

"On the way over here, I called that Luis guy. The one that gave us the heads up. He said it was done. They're letting it go. We fucked them up pretty bad. Who's left? That Gomez fucker? Do you think he'll come after us?"

"We need to look out, for a while I guess," André said. Then he paused, and his mood changed. He gave Abel a once-over. "What? What about you? Did you change your mind? Did you decide to take over Deke's business now that we kicked those assholes' butts?" He smiled over his wordplay.

"No, it just convinced me more. Seeing Tank getting choked like that? I could see it in his face. I caught them just in time. No, I'm out. Out for good. I'm getting my GED, first thing. Then, we'll see—we'll figure something out. How about you, André?"

"Me, too. We can make it legit. Be like regular people." He laughed.

Tank laughed in his chair, a goofy smile on his face. "I'm with you, too."

Harm just sat benevolently, a dreamy look on his face. "Yeah... regular people..."

Abel hung out a while more, four brothers in the sun. Tank's eyes were closed, a soft rasp coming from his nose. Harm's head was tipped forward. Abel got up quietly and smiled at André. André grinned back, a giant bear in a chair.

Driving down his road, Abel saw Olivia's car parked in front of his house. His heart missed a beat. He could see her sitting on his front steps as he pulled up the drive, and he wondered what it meant. Abel walked up to the porch, examining her face intently, but couldn't read a thing. She motioned for him to sit next to her.

"I was pretty shocked about what you told me. Part of me didn't want to believe my daddy was a part of all that. After he died, nothing was ever the same with my mother. Something was off, and she would never explain. There was just something unsaid, something wrong. I don't know. I can't describe it."

"I'm sorry, Olivia. I know that's not enough, but I am. I am sorry. I wish I could make it up to you. I wish I could bring him back. My heart feels sick."

"I don't hate you, Abel. I thought about what happened. You were a kid, too. You didn't know Deacon was going to do that. You were a victim almost as much as me. Your uncle stole your innocence. But I can't be with you now. Maybe never. I didn't tell my mama what happened. It wouldn't help her. Hell, maybe she even knows exactly what happened. Maybe she convinced my daddy to rat out your uncle. Anyway, I didn't tell the police. Deacon already got his."

"Yeah, he did. It wasn't a good ending."

"I hope you were sincere when you said you were getting out of the Life," she said, looking into his eyes, holding him to it. "I still have something in my heart for you, Abel Kane—who knows?"

Abel watched her get up and walk across the grass, get in her car, drive off, and never look back. "Yeah—who knows?" he whispered. That was good enough for him. It felt right. He stood up and went in to check on Callie.

EPILOGUE

L uis, busy drying glasses with a bar towel, watched Lúcido come in the door. As she moved by him, he held a glass up, looking for smudges. The glass caught her face, the curves acting like a lens, distorting her beauty and drawing her features out, briefly transforming her into a grotesque creature. The malevolent face slipped off the edge of the glass, a trick of light, and she slowed her step and gazed at him, a slight smile turning up one corner of her mouth, her features restored. She continued on and pushed the door to the rear of the building with just the force necessary to open it all the way and kiss the stop.

She streamed down the hall and turned into the office. Gomez was already there, sitting behind the desk. Disguising a gasp at his appearance, she sat across from him and placed her large purse on her lap.

The bold tattoos on his face were washed out, and his complexion was a shade of gray reminiscent of dried soap scum. The ink normally so stark sank into the background and became part of the whole. *He is a zombie,* she thought. A smell roiled off him, filling the cramped office, like bait shrimp left too long in the sun. Despite his condition, he sat at the desk with erect posture, his chin up.

Look at this pendejo! A day after Garcia is killed, and he has promoted himself! El jefe! The king, sitting at the head of the table. She stifled a derisive laugh. She could see his legs spread out under the desk, like he needed to make room for his giant testicles and four-inch verga.

Gomez fixed her with a glare, staring down his nose. "They knew we were coming."

"Why do you think that?"

"Because they were prepared. We didn't take them by surprise. They surprised us. They were waiting and killed us off, one by one. Garcia led us straight to our slaughter. It was only a miracle that I escaped." He leaned forward. "Someone tipped them off," he said angrily.

"Who?" she exclaimed.

"The only other person who knew the details of the plan—you!"

She snorted. "Why would I do that? Hector was my brother-in-law. He was the only family I have left. It could have been anyone. It could have been his boyfriend. Maybe a lover's quarrel? Who knows?"

Gomez's expression softened, though doubt still lingered in his eyes.

"What are you going to do, now that you are in charge?" she asked. Manipulating her face into an open expression, she willed sweetness into her voice.

"I'm going to finish the job that Alverez and Garcia started but didn't have the cojones to complete—those stupid putos. I'm going to do it my way. That joto Garcia and his little torch! Mierda. I will cut apart Kane's sister in front of him, finger by finger, then peel off her face." Gomez's face contorted in a grimace of perverse bliss. "He will beg me to put her out of her misery and then kill him. And I will—after I spend an hour on him."

"Don't you think it's best to put this all behind us? Move forward and recover our bank?" she asked gently. Gomez snorted. She reached into her purse and pulled out a lighter and cigarette, carefully placing it between her lips, trying to avoid smearing her lipstick. She flicked the lighter and brought it close. The cigarette quivered, passing in and out of the flame. She took two quick puffs, drew deeply, and then put the lighter into her bag. Breathing out, she looked up at him through the swirling cloud of smoke.

BANG, BANG! Tendrils of smoke drifted up out of her purse. Gomez dropped his hands to his lap, a quizzical look on his face—the eyebrows arched and squeezed together, like he was trying to figure out a difficult math problem. She could see his hands under the desk, cupped around his crotch.

Her hand relaxed, and the gun dropped back into the recesses of her purse. She fished around a bit and came up with a long, thin knife, stood up, and walked around the desk. Gomez leaned back to look up at her, raising his bloody palms in front of his face. Lúcido's arm darted forward, driving the blade through Gomez's hand and into his eye behind. It met with resistance, and she grabbed his hair, grunted, and pushed harder. The knife went in all the way to the hilt. She let go and stepped back. Gomez fell forward, his head propped up by the knife for a moment, then slumped to the side, his cheek resting on the desk.

She shook her head and ran her hands through her hair, then straightened her blouse. She grabbed her purse and walked out to the barroom. Luis was staring at her, his mouth slightly open. Lúcido reached into her purse and took out her car keys, then looked back up at Luis. "Get in there and get rid of Diego's body before he bleeds all over my office."

Acknowledgments

I couldn't have written this book without the help of so many generous people. **Sarah Fraps** gave me the editorial clarity I needed, and **Vinnie Corbo at Volossal Publishing** brought the story to life with his cover and interior design. To my wonderful beta readers—**Margaret Dickson, Doug Wilson, Cynthia Gabriel, Sue Ellen Larkin, Kevin Wilson, and Joseph Wilson**—thank you for the time, care, and honesty you poured into reading draft after draft. And to my friends at the writers' club—**Eliah, Cody, Sherman, Emma, and Chris**—your encouragement, honest comments, and camaraderie carried me through the hard days and kept me going.

About the Author

John Wilson is a former engineer and inventor with over a hundred patents. After a career developing computer systems, a life-altering accident led him to pursue writing. He is the author of the crime novels *A Shadow of Black Water* and *The Devil's Breath*. John lives on the Gulf Coast with his wife and their exceptionally furry dog, Blaze.

Website and further developments

www.johnwilsonbooks.com

Disclaimer

www.ingramcontent.com/pod-product-compliance
Lightning Source LLC
Chambersburg PA
CBHW030357030726
47497CB00002B/383